SHELTER IN PLACE

A NOVEL

DAVID LEAVITT

BLOOMSBURY PUBLISHING
LONDON · OXFORD · NEW YORK · NEW DELHI · SYDNEY

BLOOMSBURY PUBLISHING
Bloomsbury Publishing Plc
50 Bedford Square, London, WC1B 3DP, UK
29 Earlsfort Terrace, Dublin 2, Ireland

BLOOMSBURY, BLOOMSBURY PUBLISHING, and the Diana logo
are trademarks of Bloomsbury Publishing Plc

First published in Great Britian 2020
This edition published 2022

A catalogue record for this book is available from the British Library

ISBN: HB: 978-1-40884-611-7; TPB: 978-1-40884-612-4;
PB: 978-1-4088-4595-0; EBOOK: 978-1-40884-613-1;
EPDF: 978-1-5266-5233-1

2 4 6 8 10 9 7 5 3 1

Typeset by Westchester Publishing Services
Printed and bound in Great Britain by CPI Group (UK) Ltd,
Croydon CR0 4YY

To find out more about our authors and books visit www.bloomsbury.com
and sign up for our newsletters.

'There is an art to writing about unlikable people while still engaging the reader to invest in their indulgence, vanity and, yes, happiness ... Leavitt has claimed John Cheever and Grace Paley as influences, and it shows ... These poor rich people, wringing their hands at a country they no longer recognise, when what they're truly mourning is the death of their own relevance' *New York Times Book Review*

'Leavitt is a master stylist ... An important writer. He is the rarest of all birds – a man of letters' Edmund White

'*Shelter in Place* is a poignant, funny, wonderful novel, a pleasure and a joy' Donald Antrim

'A story that is more about the concept of Trump than the election itself ... Leavitt injects a welcome degree of humour and diversion into the proceedings ... A brilliant fiction' *Washington Independent Review of Books*

'I've long been a fan of David Leavitt's work, for its range, its depth, its smarts and its humour. He is a phenomenal and prescient writer' Justin Torres

'Sharply etched, funny and enjoyable ... Nearly everyone we meet in these pages is more complex – better – than the exterior they show the world ... The novel delights in catching people in the act of being their predictable tedious selves, but Leavitt delves beneath these surface social constructs' Francine Prose, *Book Post*

'I really loved this ... It's set just after the 2016 election and is fleet and very, very funny and the perfect read ... There's a brilliant turn in the final pages, not towards tragedy exactly, but an acknowledgment that the comedy perches atop an abyss. Anyway, it's so much fun and you should read it' Garth Greenwell

DAVID LEAVITT's novels and story collections include *Family Dancing* (finalist for the PEN/Faulkner Prize and the National Book Critics Circle Award), *The Lost Language of Cranes*, *While England Sleeps*, *Arkansas*, *The Indian Clerk* (finalist for the PEN/Faulkner Prize and the IMPAC/Dublin Literary Award) and *The Two Hotel Francforts*. He is also the author of two nonfiction books, *Florence, A Delicate Case* and *The Man Who Knew Too Much: Alan Turing and the Invention of the Computer*. He is co-director of the MFA program in Creative Writing at the University of Florida, where he is a professor of English and edits the journal *Subtropics*.

www.davidleavittwriter.com

All the conventions conspire
To make this fort assume
The furniture of home;
Lest we should see where we are,
Lost in a haunted wood,
Children afraid of the night
Who have never been happy or good.

—W. H. AUDEN, "SEPTEMBER 1, 1939"

Oh the foxes, they have holes in the ground
And the birds have nests in the air
And everything has a hiding place,
But us poor sinners ain't got nowhere.

—"HARD TRIALS" (AFRICAN AMERICAN SPIRITUAL)

PART I

I

"Would you be willing to ask Siri how to assassinate Trump?" Eva Lindquist asked.

It was four o'clock on a November afternoon, the first Saturday after the 2016 presidential election, and Eva was sitting on the covered porch of her weekend house in Connecticut with her husband, Bruce; their houseguests, Min Marable, Jake Lovett, and a couple named Aaron and Rachel Weisenstein, both book editors; Grady Keohane, a bachelor choreographer who had a place down the road; and Grady's houseguest, his cousin Sandra Bleek, who had recently left her husband and was staying with him while she got herself sorted out. Not sitting on the porch was Eva's younger friend Matt Pierce—younger in that he was thirty-seven. He was in the kitchen, preparing a second batch of scones after having had to throw away the first, to which he had forgotten to add baking powder.

A benevolent autumn sunset illuminated the scene, which was one of comfort and ease, the porch warm from the wood-stove and the guests snug on the white wicker chairs and sofa, the cushions of which Jake, Eva's decorator, had covered in a chintz called Jubilee Rose. On the white wicker table, a pot of tea, cups, saucers, a bowl of clotted cream, and a bowl of homemade strawberry jam awaited the tardy scones.

Eva repeated her question. "Who here would be willing to ask Siri how to assassinate Trump?"

At first no one answered.

"I'm only asking because since the election, I've been possessed by this mad urge to ask her," Eva said. "Only I'm afraid that if I do, she'll pass it straight on to the Secret Service and they'll arrest me."

"Darling, I hardly think—" Bruce said.

"Why not?" Eva said. "I'm sure they can do it."

"What, listen in on what we say to our phones?" Sandra said.

"I'm not saying they *can't* do it," Bruce said, "I'm just saying that in all probability, the Secret Service has better things to do than monitor our conversations with Siri."

"Hello, am I the only person here who remembers Watergate?" Grady Keohane said. "Am I the only person here who remembers phone tapping?"

"Can cell phones be tapped?" Rachel Weisenstein said. "I thought only landlines could be tapped."

"What century are you living in?" Aaron asked his wife.

"I mean, if we were terrorists, maybe," Bruce said. "If we were an ISIS cell or something. But a bunch of white people drinking tea on a covered porch in Litchfield County? I don't think so."

"In that case, do it." Eva handed him her phone. "Ask her."

"But I don't want to assassinate Trump," Bruce said.

"See? You're chicken," Min Marable said. "Cluck, cluck, cluck."

Suddenly Aaron had one of his famous tantrums. "You people," he said. "Will you just listen to yourselves? I mean, look what's happening to you. Is this really happening? Don't we have a First Amendment in this country? Don't we have the right to say whatever we damn please?"

"Unless it's hate speech," Rachel said.

"Fuck hate speech," Aaron said.

"Speaking for myself, I'd be disinclined to take the risk," Min said. "What about you, Jake?"

"Me?" said Jake, who was not used to being addressed on these occasions. "Well, I wouldn't not do it out of fear. I mean, I wouldn't do it—but not out of fear."

"The thing is, even if you did kill him, would it do any good?" Sandra said. "Pence would be president. That might actually be worse."

"We're not talking about actually killing him," Grady said. "We're talking about asking Siri how to kill him. There's a big difference."

"You mean it's a sort of thought experiment," Sandra said.

"Oh, for God's sake." Aaron took his phone out of his jacket pocket, pressed the home button, and said, "Siri, how would I—"

"No, don't." Rachel grabbed the phone away from him. "I won't let you."

"Who, me?" Siri said.

"Give me my phone," Aaron said.

"That may be beyond my abilities at the moment," Siri said.

"Only if you promise not to do it," Rachel said.

"Rachel, I'm asking nicely," Aaron said. "Give me back my phone."

"No."

Right then Matt Pierce came onto the porch with the scones. "Sorry for the delay," he said. "Normal service has been resumed . . . What's the matter?"

"I'll count to ten," Aaron said to Rachel. "One, two, three—"

"Oh, just take it," Rachel said. "Just take the goddamn thing."

She threw the phone at him and ran into the house.

Everyone looked at Aaron.

"What?" Aaron said.

"Don't those scones smell delicious?" Eva said. "But I fear the tea may have oversteeped."

"I'll make a fresh pot," Matt said, backing through the door that led to the kitchen.

2

In the winter of 2016, Eva Lindquist was fifty-six but looked
ten years younger. Though tall, she did not give an impression of height, perhaps because Bruce, her husband, was so
much taller, nearly six foot six. Given her last name, many
people assumed her to be of Scandinavian descent, an impression she did little to counteract and more than a little to culti-
vate, most notably by tying her hair in plaits and wrapping
them around her head.

She and Bruce had no children. Instead they shared their
homes—the apartment on Park Avenue and the country house
in Connecticut—with three Bedlington terriers, those dogs that
look like lambs or seals, with their feathery blue-white coats and
curved backs and long, tapering tails. The current pack was
their second generation of Bedlingtons, littermates, as their
forebears had been, and named, as their forebears had been,
after characters from Henry James—Caspar, Isabel, and Ralph.

Unlike Bruce, Eva was a New Yorker born and bred. Her
parents—this was something she neither advertised nor
concealed—were Polish Jews.

Kalmann. Eva Kalmann.

Bruce was from Wisconsin. Lutheran. For four decades his father had been the leading obstetrician of Oshkosh, in which capacity he had delivered two state senators, an NFL offensive guard, and a singer on *The Lawrence Welk Show*. Bruce was in his third year at Harvard Business School, on the cusp of turning twenty-four, when he met Eva, then in her senior year at Smith. In their wedding photos they look nothing alike, which surprised their friends, for whom it was a commonplace to remark that they might be brother and sister. Both had fair skin that burned before it tanned, and hair the same silver-blue as the coats of their dogs, and eyes that radiated a greater uncertainty than either was in the habit of voicing.

"Amazing how couples grow to look alike," their friends would say, when what they meant was "Amazing how he has grown to look like her."

Jake Lovett had first met them in the late eighties, when they'd just moved into a new apartment, several blocks uptown from the current one, and Eva had asked his business partner, Pablo Bach, to decorate it. Since Pablo considered rentals beneath him, he passed the job on to Jake—Jake's good fortune, as it turned out, for when the building went co-op, and Eva and Bruce bought a bigger apartment on a higher floor, it was him, not Pablo, whom they hired to oversee its refurbishment.

Since then they'd moved twice more, both times selling at a profit. All these apartments Jake had decorated, just as he'd decorated the succession of country houses—in Rhinebeck, in Bedford, in Litchfield County—that the Lindquists had acquired and sold off as Bruce's income soared. Theirs was a milieu with which Jake was familiar—affluent New York liberals, not old money but not new money, either, and certainly a far cry from the city's aristocracy, the Whitneys and Vanderbilts and Astors, over whose drawing rooms Pablo held sway. With a few notable exceptions, *those* people eschewed intellectual pretensions—they had no need of them—whereas Eva liked to think of herself as a saloniste, in which capacity she hosted frequent dinner parties and tea parties and weekend parties, to which she invited a motley of gay men and unattached middle-aged women and married couples vaguely affiliated with the arts—editors, curators, agents—as well as the occasional elderly lady who, when drunk, could be counted on to tell risqué stories about famous dead people.

No actual creators. Creators scared Eva. Unless you counted Jake as a creator, which he didn't think she did.

As for Bruce, if he had any friends—Jake had never seen evidence of any—they were not included. Bruce was an easy-going fellow, content to follow Eva's lead. Outwardly, things looked like smooth sailing for him and Eva, until she decided to buy the place in Venice.

"Of course, it's hardly the first political catastrophe we've lived through," Rachel said. "It may not even be the worst political catastrophe we've lived through."

"You're wrong," Eva said. "Nothing in our lifetimes has been worse."

"Don't get me wrong, I'm not saying it's not *bad*," Rachel said. "I'm just saying . . . I mean, let's not forget Vietnam. Let's not forget Watergate, AIDS, 9/11."

"Or 2000," Bruce said. "Remember all that hoo-ha down in Florida? The butterfly ballot, and the hanging chads, and the pregnant chads?"

"There were dimpled chads too," Aaron said.

"That was definitely not a good year to be named Chad," Grady said—a joke that elicited some hesitant laughter, though not from Eva, who took the opportunity to pour herself another glass of pinot noir. It was eight o'clock on the evening of the Saturday that the friends who were gathered around her table, eating spatchcocked chicken and oven-roasted beets, would forever after remember as "the Saturday of the botched scones."

"Now I look back at the 2000 election and I see it as the dress rehearsal for this one," Eva said. "Before that—I checked online—do you know when was the last time the winner of the electoral college lost the popular vote?"

"Eighteen eighty-eight," Aaron said. "Harrison v. Cleveland. Harrison was the Republican, by the way."

"Well, there you go," Eva said, in a tone that made it clear she didn't appreciate Aaron's beating her to the punch. "What I don't get is why at this late date we even have an electoral college. Why wasn't it done away with after Bush v. Gore? It should have been done away with after Bush v. Gore."

"And what if things had gone the other way?" Bruce asked. "Would you feel the same if Hillary had won the electoral college but lost the popular vote?"

"It couldn't have happened," Aaron said. "To have won the electoral college, she'd have had to win Ohio and Florida, in which case she *still* would have won the popular vote, only by a bigger margin."

"You're missing Bruce's point," Rachel said. "The question he's asking is hypothetical."

"And my answer to it," Eva said, "is that if the scenario were reversed, I'd be defending the electoral college to the death.

So would the rest of you, though I doubt you'd admit it. That's the difference between us—I'm willing to be inconsistent. I'm willing to say openly that protecting democracy matters more than protecting a system."

"But I thought democracy *was* the system," Sandra Bleek said.

"Not when it's used to benefit the people who want to undermine it."

"It could be argued that when you take that line, you become one of those people," Bruce said.

"I don't care," Eva said. "I don't care anymore. And you know why? Because I know I'm right. Separation of powers, checks and balances, government of the people, by the people, for the people—none of that matters anymore, because what we're dealing with now is a demon, and when you're dealing with a demon, you do what you have to."

"Even kill?" Sandra said.

"Or ask Siri how to kill?" Grady said.

"Well, we killed bin Laden," Eva said. "I don't recall anyone objecting to that. And let's not forget Hitler. All those people who tried to assassinate Hitler—today we look at them as heroes."

"When my mother was dying, she used to joke about organizing a hit squad of terminally ill people to take out Reagan," Jake said.

"Oh, but Reagan was nice," Sandra said.

"He was not nice," Grady said. "Have you noticed that lately, every time you turn on the TV, some old liberal's yammering on about what a great diplomat Reagan was, and how civil the Reagan years were, yadda yadda yadda? It drives me nuts. I mean, does no one remember AIDS? How he wouldn't even say the word?"

"From wherever she is"—Jake looked up, then down—"I hear my mother shouting, 'Hear, hear!'"

"I don't understand how you can all be so jokey about this," Eva said. "Didn't you watch the returns on Tuesday night? From the start, I had my eyes on Rachel Maddow. When a plane hits turbulence, have you ever done that thing where you check the flight attendant's face, to see if she looks scared? Like the plane's about to crash? Well, that was the look I saw on Rachel Maddow's face that night."

"But if you've never been in a plane crash, how could you recognize the look?" Bruce asked.

"Trust me, when you see it, there's no mistaking it. I wish I'd never seen it."

After dinner—Eva and Bruce had gone to bed early, and the others were sitting in the living room—Sandra said, "Does it ever strike any of you that Eva is just a teensy bit fascist?"

"What do you mean?" Min said. "How can you say that about Eva?"

"Oh, I don't mean in the political sense," Sandra said. "I mean in the sense of believing she knows better what's good for people than they do themselves."

"By that definition, we're all fascists," said Aaron, who was reading the *London Review of Books*.

"No, we are not," Rachel said. "In fascist states, the voice of the people counts for nothing. Here it counts for everything, even if it means that from time to time we have to deal with leaders who don't share our values. Majority rule is a principle, and we have to protect it even when we don't like the result."

"You sound like my fifth-grade teacher," Aaron said.

"You were in fifth grade in 1978," Rachel said.

"Also, in this case it wasn't majority rule," Min said. "If it had been, Hillary would have won. That's Eva's point."

"And it's a shortsighted one." Aaron put down his *LRB* and cleared his throat in a way that indicated an oration was imminent. "What Eva's doing is confusing the question of whether this country operates according to majority rule with the question of whether the electoral college, in the year of our Lord 2016, can be said to be a valid measure of majority opinion. And the answer to that, many experts would argue, is yes. The number of electors granted to each state is determined by the census. On the other hand, when the founding fathers were writing the Constitution, I doubt it occurred to them to make provisions for a day when California, which wasn't even a state then, would have a bigger population than New York and New England put together."

"No, they were too busy making provisions to protect the slave states," Rachel said.

"What? What about the slave states?" Sandra said.

"By the time the Constitutional Convention came along," Aaron said, "the founding fathers had agreed in principle that the number of electors for each state should be allotted on the basis of population, not wealth. Only this put the South at a disadvantage, since so much of its population was slaves, and slaves counted as property, not people. Finally they reached a compromise, which was to count each slave as three-fifths of a person."

"A compromise without which—as the only southerner in the room, I feel duty bound to note—Jefferson would never have won the presidency," Min said.

"None of which, the college's defenders say, ought to be used as an argument against it," Aaron said. "The way they see it, when it was established, it corrected for an imbalance."

"Unjustly," Rachel added.

"Then, yes. Now it corrects—justly—for another. Or so its defenders claim."

"You're getting way too far into the weeds for me," Grady said.

"He always does," Rachel said. "The only reason he knows anything about any of this is that last year he edited a book on the history of the electoral college."

"A book, I might add, that sold quite decently," Aaron said.

"This is all well and good," Grady said, "but what bearing does any of it have on what Eva said, which is that in her view, keeping Trump out of the White House is more important than preserving the principle of free elections?"

"That's what I meant when I asked if she wasn't a teensy bit fascist," Sandra said.

"Eva is *not* a fascist," Min said emphatically. "No one who knows her would ever say that about her, would they, Jake?"

"Well, I wouldn't," Jake said, surprised mostly to learn that Min regarded him as someone who knew Eva.

"I mean, her parents were refugees from Poland," Min said. "They came to this country to *escape* fascism, for God's sake."

"Eva never talks about her parents," Grady said. "Are they still alive?"

"Alive and kicking, and still living in the apartment on West Eighty-ninth Street where she grew up."

"Half a mile from her as the crow flies," Aaron said.

"Although these days, the crow doesn't fly there very often," Jake said.

"At the risk of being accused again of sounding like Aaron's fifth-grade teacher," Rachel said, "I have to say it makes me uncomfortable talking about Eva like this when we're guests in her house."

"It's my fault," Sandra said. "I should never have said what I did. I meant it as a joke, but as Grady can testify, I was born without a sense of humor."

"It's true," Grady said. "As kids, we took cruel advantage of the lack."

"I sometimes wonder if Eva has a sense of humor," Aaron said.

"Why are you all being so critical of her?" Rachel said. "I mean, the woman is obviously suffering. Didn't anyone else hear what she said about Rachel Maddow?"

"I heard it," Jake said.

"Pontificating about the electoral college—it's just a way of avoiding dealing with your own fears. It's so male. At least Eva's open about hers."

"Rachel thinks that, given our druthers, we men will always plump for getting deep into the weeds over dealing with our own fears," Aaron said.

"Is that a joke?" Sandra said.

"The joke is part of the evasion," Rachel said.

"Maybe what we're doing is letting Eva have our hysterics for us," Jake said.

"Speak for yourself," Grady said. "For my part, I'm having plenty on my own, only instead of carrying on about them, I've gone into denial. Stopped watching the news, stopped reading the paper."

"I can't watch the news either," Sandra said.

"Why not?" Aaron asked. "What are you all so afraid of, that you have to hide your eyes? Me, I plan to read every article, watch every program, read every op-ed."

"I think I'll wait until it's all over to read about it if you don't mind," Grady said.

"But that's just it," Sandra said. "How can we presume it'll ever be over? No one can predict the future. I mean, if you'd told me a year ago he'd be elected, I wouldn't have believed you."

"I wouldn't have believed you if you'd told me a week ago," Rachel said.

"It was so blindsiding," Min said.

"But was it really?" Aaron said. "I mean, is *blindside* really the right word? I'm only asking because people have been using it an awful lot lately, and it seems to me they're using it wrong."

"It's how they feel," Rachel said.

"Fine, but to be blindsided, really blindsided, the thing that hits you has to be a bolt from the blue, right? And for this to have been a bolt from the blue, we would have had to believe, in our heart of hearts, that Hillary's winning was a fait accompli—which obviously we didn't, or we wouldn't have been so nervous.

"In retrospect, I think the truth is that we all saw it coming but tried to talk ourselves out of it. And so, yes, there was a shock, but it wasn't a blindsiding shock. It was more like the shock when your dermatologist tells you the mole you've been trying to convince yourself is nothing is really a melanoma."

"Must you use that particular analogy?" Grady asked, touching his neck.

"I don't see that it makes all that much difference," Jake said. "We weren't in a position to affect what happened, only to be affected by it."

"And to suffer over it," Rachel said.

"But it's all so absurd," Aaron said. "I mean, what's playing out, it's like an absurdist comedy. Naturally, you wouldn't notice that aspect of it, Sandra, since, by your own admission, you have no sense of humor. But the rest of you—"

"The rest of us clearly aren't as evolved as you, Aaron," Rachel said.

"Or we're too freaked out to appreciate the comedy," Grady said.

"Oh, come on," Aaron said. "That grab-them-by-the-pussy business? Or that press conference with the Mexican president? That was hilarious. If it were Monty Python, we'd be laughing our asses off."

"But it's not Monty Python."

"Pretending it's Monty Python—it's just another form of denial," Rachel said.

"Whatever," Aaron said. "All I'm saying is that we all have a choice. We can spend the next four years eating our livers out or we can spend them laughing our asses off."

"Not all of us have that choice," Sandra said.

"Eva certainly doesn't," Jake said.

"No, I suppose Eva wouldn't," Aaron said. "I suppose for Eva there's only the one way to go."

3

It was his knocking on the door that did it, she told Bruce afterwards. His ringing the bell. His standing before her in the doorway, in his cashmere cardigan and bow tie, all scrubbed and pink like a cartoon pig.

Immediately the dogs ran to him. When he bent down, they licked his face.

"That was probably what upset me most," Eva said. "As if he was trying to take my dogs too."

Needless to say, she didn't invite him in. And why should she have? For eighteen years they'd been next-door neighbors, and in eighteen years neither had ever set foot in the other's apartment. Instead she listened to what he had to say across the threshold. Though the party was to be held on the night of the inauguration, it wasn't to be an inauguration party per se. That is to say, he and Kitty would still have been throwing it even if "their guy" hadn't won. More to the point, though it was true that most of the guests would be people who shared their gladness at the change about to sweep through Washington—and wasn't change in and of itself a healthy thing?—this wasn't *why* he and Kitty had invited them. Nor would everyone at the party be of the same political stripe. Some Democrats would be there. Even a few die-hard Hillary supporters. If she and Bruce chose to drop by, they'd find some fellow travelers.

"But I'm guessing you won't," he added, in an almost wistful tone. And then, when Eva didn't reply: "In any case, let me assure you, the noise will be kept to a reasonable level. You won't even notice."

"That was the last straw," Eva told Bruce as they got ready for bed that night. "I mean, it's bad enough that they're having the party—but then to come over and rub my face in it—"

"He might just have been trying to be friendly," Bruce said.

"The winner can always afford to be friendly to the loser," Eva said.

"You mean that if they'd lost, you'd be friendly to him?"

"I don't know. If I'm to be honest, probably not."

"Why not?"

"Because no matter the outcome, the fact remains that he voted for . . . I don't even want to say the name."

"Well, yes, he's a Republican. Naturally he voted for the Republican. But that doesn't mean he was at all those rallies, shouting 'Lock her up.'"

"How do you know he wasn't?"

"Alec Warriner at a rally? I really can't see it. My hunch is that if you asked him, you'd find that the main reason he voted for Tr—"

"Don't say that name. I refuse to have that name uttered in my house."

"Sorry. My hunch is that if you asked him, you'd find that he didn't vote for Tr—for him-who-shall-not-be-named because he likes him, but because he thinks that he-who-shall-not-be-named will get the corporate tax rate below twenty-one percent."

"I think you're wrong," Eva said. "I think it was because he hates her so much. That's the thing I can't wrap my mind around—why people hate her so much. It might be because I went to Smith and she went to Wellesley, but I feel an attack on her is an attack on me."

"Who knows? Maybe hate is blind. Like love."

"Don't try to be philosophical. You just end up sounding glib. And anyway, it's not true. Hate isn't blind. It sees—and in this case what it sees is that she's a woman."

"Well, but so is Marine Le Pen. So are Ann Coulter, Laura Ingraham, the one who used to have the judge show—you know, what's her name. Jeanine Pirro."

"Oh, God, her. Don't mention her."

They got into bed. As Bruce switched out the light, it occurred to him that for all the years of their marriage, he had always slept on the left side and Eva on the right. Exactly how this arrangement had come into being, he couldn't remember. All he knew was that it was now second nature to him, so much so that even when Eva was out of town and he had the bed to himself, he slept on the left. Even when he was traveling on business and staying at a hotel, he slept on the left. The idea of the bedside lamp, the bedside table, being on his right was more than his imagination could cope with.

There was a rustling in the dark—the dogs coming in, jumping up onto the bed, and settling themselves between his and Eva's legs.

He closed his eyes. He could hear Eva turning over. He could hear her pulling open her bedside drawer, taking out the bottle of Ambien, opening it, and shaking a pill onto her palm.

On election night she'd also taken an Ambien—which hadn't stopped her from being wakened at two thirty by a noise that she quickly identified as cheering. For maybe fifteen seconds, a delicious sensation of relief flooded her—Hillary had won!—until she realized where the cheering was coming from.

In the morning, as was his habit, Bruce rose at six. He showered, dressed, fed and walked the dogs, and was just leaving for work when their maid, Amalia, arrived. He hardly ever saw Eva in the morning, since it was her habit to sleep until eight or eight thirty.

As they had most weekday mornings over the past eighteen years, Bruce and Amalia nodded at each other as they passed.

Nine hours later, when he got home, Eva was waiting for him. Her face was flushed and she was rotating the rings on her fingers, one after the other.

"So I've made a decision," she said. "I can't be here for this inauguration party. The mere idea of it, of those idiots rallying together next door—next door!—to gloat over their victory, to rub it in my face, the way they did on election night . . ."

"Well, but Eva, I hardly think you're the reason they're having the party."

"Yes, I am. I know I am. I know it because if we'd won, I'd have done the same thing . . . Anyway, I refuse to give them the satisfaction of being here to endure it. It's too much. I have to get away."

"Well, why not go to the country?"

She shook her head. "It's not far enough, the country. It's the country—*this* country—I need to get away from. I've been thinking about it all day. Where in the world is there a place where I won't even hear an echo of that cheering? And then I hit on it. Venice."

"Venice?"

She nodded exuberantly. "I've always loved Venice, ever since the first time I went there, when I was in college."

"But it's January."

"Exactly. That's the best part. It'll be practically empty, the way it was my semester abroad. The wind, and the acqua alta, and the utter silence at night . . . Well, what do you think? I've been checking flights. We could leave on Thursday and be there before the horror show starts."

"But that's next week. I can't get away on such short notice."

"Can't you? Then I'll ask Min. She'll be game. She always is."

Min was. They left on the night of the nineteenth, arriving at their hotel by water taxi at two in the afternoon—six hours ahead of New York, Washington, the inaugural circus.

And from the moment they stepped off the boat, Eva breathed more easily. She felt that she was once again in the civilized world.

They stayed at a four-star hotel in Dorsoduro. For five days they didn't look at a newspaper. They didn't turn on the television. Each morning they would visit a museum or a religious building—the Accademia, the Frari, the Scuola di San Giorgio degli Schiavoni, with its frescoes of Saint George slaying the dragon, and later delivering the dragon, not quite dead, to the Mamluks. "It's like he's got the poor thing on a leash," Eva said, either failing or choosing not to notice the sword that the saint was brandishing to deliver the final blow. "I think the dragon looks sweet. Like a dog."

The frescoes in the *scuola* had real dogs in them, too. "Which is your favorite?" she asked Min, who plumped for the scruffy white terrier gazing up at Saint Augustine as he received from Saint Jerome the news of his imminent demise.

"The obvious choice," Eva said, "though for my part I prefer the long-snouted greyhoundish one watching him baptize the Selenites."

In the afternoons they shopped or sat in cafés, Eva reading Jan Morris and Min pretending to send texts but really playing *Candy Crush*. Each day passed more quickly than the last, and then on the sixth, Ursula Brandolin-Foote invited them to tea at her palazzo near Campo della Maddalena. Aaron Weisenstein, who had published some of her translations from the Serbo-Croatian, had told her that Eva and Min were in Venice, and she'd tracked them down. Ursula was a stately woman in her early seventies, with thick hair dyed several shades of gray and a fondness for multihued caftans that lent emphasis to her high breasts and long legs. Although she owned roughly half of Ca' Brandolin, she told Eva and Min, she occupied only a portion of the *piano nobile* and rented the rest short-term to visiting academics. Her own flat she also occasionally rented, to studios making period movies and television series. "It has that sepia look," she said as, with a sweep of a billowing sleeve, she indicated the vast sofa covered in faded Fortuny velvet, the heavy silk curtains, the bookshelves with their stock of ragged paperbacks, the bombe chest, and the basket by the fireplace from which old copies of *La Cucina Italiana* spilled. Rugs were scattered over the terrazzo floor, which had been poured to create a trompe l'oeil of rugs scattered over a terrazzo floor. On the ceiling, blue-and-pink stucco work framed a trompe l'oeil sky to which time and smoke had lent the yellowish tint of the sky outside at dusk. "All this was in situ when I inherited the place," Ursula went on. "A mixed blessing, since I only got the property. No money. I'm poor as a church mouse."

She laughed, her laugh unexpectedly high-pitched, almost a caw.

"How long ago was that?" Eva asked.

"Oh, now, let me see, it must have been 1986 or 1987 when Zia Carlotta went to her comforts—she was ninety-three, you know, young for Venice—the doges all lived to be a hundred and ten—so I guess . . . 1989? Ah, and here is Elisabetta with our tea. When I moved in, Elisabetta was also in situ, weren't you, Elisabetta?"

"Si, Signora."

"She understands English but she won't speak it. How old are you, Elisabetta?"

"In Ottobre ho compiuto novantacinque anni," Elisabetta said.

"See what I mean about the Venetians being longevitous? Sul tavolo. Sit, ladies, sit."

They sat, Eva and Min on the sofa, Ursula on a beige vinyl-covered recliner that somehow did not look out of place. Along with the tea, Elisabetta had brought a plate of sandwiches spread with a fish paste that gave off a dubious odor.

"And is this your first time in Venice?" Ursula asked, taking up a purple vape pen.

"Oh, no," Eva and Min said at the same time.

"I've been at least—"

"It's my fourth—"

"You go first."

"No, you."

Ursula vaped.

"It's my fourth visit to Venice," Eva said, with restrained impatience.

"Eva's an authority on Venice," Min said, touching Eva's knee.

"No, I'm not," Eva said.

"Yes, you are," Min said. "She's writing a biography of Isabella Stewart Gardner."

"No, I'm not," Eva said.

"Oh, what a good idea!" Ursula said. "I've always wondered why someone hasn't done one."

"Someone has," Eva said.

"Only it's not very good," Min said.

"We're going tomorrow to Palazzo Barbaro."

"Our beloved Ca' Barbaro!" Ursula said. "Such a grievous day it was when the Curtises had to sell the piano nobile. And yet it's always the same story here—the inheritors of the old houses paupered by their upkeep."

"I heard the family bickered," Eva said.

"In Venice bickering is a tradition. Our laws, you see, are based on the Napoleonic Code, which means that when the owner of an historic property dies, it has to be divided equally among his heirs. Well, in the case of Ca' Barbaro, there were three children, and they simply couldn't figure out a way of divvying the place up. Which is a pity, because if they had, they wouldn't have had to sell.

"When I inherited, it was simpler. There was just me and Zio Ernesto. But then when he died, his half had to be split among *his* children, three from two marriages. Since then I've lost track of who owns what."

"Forgive me if this is a rude question," Min said, "but your English is so fluent. Where did you learn it?"

"Where else? In bed!" Again Ursula gave her alarming laugh. "But seriously, I'm basically American. In a different life, I was married for thirty years to an African Americanist—a white one, alas—an authority on the Harlem Renaissance. Before the divorce, Norman and I lived in Urbana. We adopted two black boys from the South Side of Chicago. One's in California now. He works for Google. The other's a jazz pianist based in Berlin." She took a purely notional sip of tea. "Of course, I've kept up my American passport. It used to be that if you were American and you spent more than six months of every year abroad, you could get away with not paying taxes in either country. Those halcyon days, alas, are over."

"So you can vote in American elections?"

"Can and do—and what a horror this one was! Afterwards I had to take to my bed. I was sick with disgust. President Caligula, I call him."

"Oh, I like that!" Min said. "Eva won't say his name, you know."

"It's true," Eva said. "I hate to say it, but since arriving in Venice I've felt ashamed to be an American. I've never felt ashamed of it before. Just yesterday at Florian, for instance, when the waiter came to take our order—I don't know what it was, but something impelled me to put on a fake French accent."

"A very good fake French accent," Min said.

"You see, I had this premonition that if he realized we were American, he'd spit in our coffee," Eva said. "And yet for all that, I'd rather be here than there. I dread going home."

"Then why don't you stay?" Ursula said. "I'm putting my flat on the market. You could buy it. And if no estate agents are involved, we'll save on the commission."

"Buy an apartment?" Eva said, in the same tone she used when she was contemplating buying a pair of Manolo Blahnik shoes.

"Why not have a look?" Min said. "It'll be a lark."

Ursula took them on a tour. There were five rooms, all with intricately stuccoed walls and ceilings. Each of the fireplace mantels was carved from a different type of marble. On one side, the view was of the Grand Canal; on the other, of Ursula's garden, which was aromatic and overgrown and scattered with lacy cast-iron tables and chairs. "There is some history to the house," she said. "For instance, it's reputed that Byron wrote *Beppo* here, though of course that is a claim made by several other Venetian houses. Also a doge was born here. I forget which one."

"The garden is lovely," Min said.

"Isn't it?" Ursula said. "I don't think I could bear to part with it, though of course I must consider the brute realities. My situation is not much different than that of the Curtises. The cost of maintenance is so high, and Italian taxes are extortionate."

They concluded the tour with the kitchen, which was ugly in that way that only nineteen-eighties kitchens can be ugly, and the one bathroom, which was at the opposite end of the flat from the bedrooms.

"But if you sell it, where will you live?" Eva asked.

"Oh, I'd use some of the money to renovate the attic. A teensy bath, an angolo cottura. That's all I need. As you can imagine, it will break my heart to leave my lovely flat, though of course if you're the one who buys it, it will alleviate my agita considerably. I'd know it was in safe hands."

With aristocratic delicacy, Ursula withdrew so that Eva and Min could confer.

"You must have it," Min said. "Think what you could do with it."

It was Min's role to encourage Eva to take the adventurous steps that she herself would take, if she only had the money.

"Should I?"

"An opportunity like this—"

"It will need a lot of work."

"Jake can do it. It will be a dream for him."

"I'll have to talk to Bruce first."

"You know perfectly well that if it makes you happy, it will make Bruce happy."

"I so long for an escape."

"You deserve it. If anyone does, you do."

Eva walked to the window. As she looked out, the faintest hint of a smile came over her face.

Two days after she got back to New York, she invited Jake to dinner.

4

That same week, the first week of February 2017, Jake turned fifty-two. At the party that the staff at his office gave him—Connie Bolen, the bookkeeper, the five assistants, Tim, Jen, Henry, Soledad, and Imogen, and the intern, Fallow—Pablo Bach, his business partner, raised a glass of champagne to him and said, "Here's to the start of your fifty-third year."

"But he's fifty-two," said Fallow, who was twenty-one.

"Exactly," Pablo said. "Your fifty-second birthday is the first day of your fifty-third year. The belief that it's the first day of your fifty-second year is but another example of the American unwillingness to accept the inexorability of death. The Italians, death lovers that they are, put it correctly: 'Ho compiuto cinquantadue anni.' Literally, 'I have completed fifty-two years.'"

"He's pointed this out on every one of my birthdays since the millennium," Jake said. The millennium, he went on to explain, had been very upsetting for Pablo, because it was celebrated a year early. In vain had Pablo tried to persuade his

friends to boycott the improperly timed festivities, in vain had
he tried to make them understand that January 1, 2000, was
the first day of the last year of the old millennium, not the first
day of the first year of the new millennium, but no one would
listen to him. "I suppose everyone was too preoccupied with
Y2K," Jake said.

"What's Y2K?" Fallow said.

"She is too young to remember," Pablo said.

"*They're* too young to remember," Connie corrected—
meaning not the group collectively but Fallow, who eschewed
the binary.

"Of course, afterwards he told us he'd told us so," Jake said,
to forestall Pablo giving a lecture on the degradation of the
language that would ensue if *they* were to be tolerated as a
singular pronoun.

"It's simply that I cannot bear this habit of playing fast and
loose with truth," Pablo said. "It's like peeing before you weigh
yourself. How many of you do this? Be honest."

The assistants, all of whom were ruthlessly thin, looked at
one another, as if trying to ascertain whether one of them was
being singled out as fat, and which one.

"It's ridiculous. As I was just telling a friend"—he meant
Min Marable—"the number on the scale isn't going to make
that skirt any less tight."

"I get what you mean," Fallow said. "Like, the other day I
was getting ready to go out, right? And I was thinking which
coat should I wear, right? And, like, I checked my phone to see
what the temperature was. I mean, instead of just opening the
window and sticking my head out, I looked on my phone.
Duh."

"Truth is experiential," Pablo said. "In decorating, too, this is the case. 'Have nothing in your house that you do not know to be useful, or believe to be beautiful,' William Morris said. Words to live by, since they put the onus on *you*, on your discernment, your taste. The notion that taste is relative is specious. Bad taste owes to mental laziness or derangement, whereas good taste is truth balanced with reason."

Pablo proceeded to tell a story that the assistants had heard many times before, about how when he was starting out, in the seventies, purple vinyl wallpaper was all the rage. "All my clients were asking for it. They were begging me for it. 'OK,' I said, 'in that case, if that's what you want, call up David Hicks.' And a lot of them did call up David Hicks, only to come to me a few months later, crying, 'Pablo, please, please save us from this hideous purple vinyl wallpaper.' Which I did. You can't afford to hold grudges in this business."

"Isn't it time for Jake to cut the cake?" Connie asked, handing him the knife that she kept in her desk for such purposes. And Jake did cut the cake, and as he cut it he reflected on how much the story Pablo had just told had become part of his legend, of which his townhouse in the East Sixties was the embodiment—the townhouse in the morning room of which two throw pillows, one embroidered with REASON and the other with TRUTH, reposed on a pair of wingback chairs. Reason and truth. Yet Pablo himself was Argentine; he himself, in his childhood, had watched helplessly as his parents—his father first and then his mother—were arrested, disappeared. Unreason. Untruth. Did his childhood explain Pablo? Did anyone's childhood explain anyone? Or was this one of those questions to which the only answer is another question, and another, and another?

All that being said, Jake owed a great debt to Pablo, for it was from Pablo, more than anyone else, more even than his aunt Rose, who had brought him into the business, that he had learned to be a decorator. This education had entailed studying not just the technicalities of wallpaper repeats and goblet pleats, not just how to distinguish real Louis Quinze from fake Louis Quinze, or French Jean-Michel Frank from Argentine Jean-Michel Frank, but the all-important art of what Pablo termed "looking the part." "What you want is to be the sort of man whose photograph could appear next to the dictionary definition of *dapper*," he told Jake, when Jake was in his twenties and far from dapper. It wasn't difficult, just a matter of keeping your cheeks freshly shaven, and your fingernails manicured, and getting your hair cut once a week by a decent barber. To look the part, Pablo said, was to wear a tailored suit. It was to wear a Charvet tie and just a dab of Acqua di Parma on the neck. Nothing showy, nothing that advertised its own expensiveness. "Modesty," Pablo told Jake at twenty-two, "is the hallmark of lasting worth."

And what was the purpose of all these cultivations? Nothing less than to project absolute competence and absolute discretion, so that when you presented your client with the antique escritoire on which you had just spent fifty thousand of her dollars, she would look past her instinctive dismay, her suspicion that it was ugly, and assure herself that, because you had chosen it, it must be beautiful.

"Decorating is a trade, not an art," Pablo concluded. "Never forget that, Jake. Taste has a value, it's the commodity in which we traffic—which is why your home is your most valuable asset. Show them how you live and they'll want to live the same way."

It was here, alas, that Jake faltered. In his own apartment, there was much that was neither useful nor beautiful. The trouble was not that he had tried and failed. It was that he had never tried, never so much as painted the drab white walls, or replaced the vertical blinds with curtains, or removed the cheap mirroring affixed to the sliding closet doors. Nor would he have moved even if he could have afforded to, which he could not, since the value of the apartment, when he'd bought it fifteen years before, had resided in its view of the East River, which a new high-rise now blocked. Beautiful things passed through Jake's apartment, rested there for a while, then moved on to other apartments, other rooms. Most of these things had had many owners, and would outlast the ones for whom Jake had bought them. The impermanence of ownership was an obstacle he found he could never quite get over.

For his part, meanwhile, every few years Pablo redecorated his townhouse and had it published in its latest iteration, usually in *The World of Interiors*. Enthroned like William and Mary in the morning room, Reason and Truth cast their beneficent gaze over the new scheme, for in Pablo's mind the townhouse was an idea that with each revision he sought to further refine, to bring closer to some ideal version of itself. "It often strikes me that a house is at its best when it is empty of life," he said to Jake at twenty-two. "At heart every aesthete is an ascetic, putting more and more of himself into his work until he has no self left. First he is the custodian, the steward. Then he, too, must leave."

Privately Jake thought this was bullshit. The way he saw it, there could be no decorating without a client, no home without someone to live in it. This was why, in his drawings, he always included a sketch of the client herself, usually arranging flowers or gazing out the window with a teacup in her hand. The trouble was, what he could do for others he could not do for himself. There was no room he could draw *himself* into, and so the rooms he occupied eluded him, resisting every effort he made to make them his, make them home.

5

The evening of Eva's post-Venice dinner, Jake walked the twenty-some-odd blocks that separated their buildings. He did this not in spite of the weather but because of it. Ever since he had moved back east—how long ago had it been, three decades now?—he had taken pleasure in the astringency of northern winters, the exfoliating winds that, he fancied, quickened his Eastern European blood, so that, as he made his way up Park Avenue, his cheeks numb, he might have been his great-grandfather, whom he had never met, leading a herd of cattle over some vast plain in Kaunas province, where he had never been.

Tonight the wind was especially cutting. No sooner did the snow touch the ground than it would be cast back up, as if the city were a snow globe being shaken. His head bent, his gloved hands in his pockets, he trudged up Park Avenue until he got to Eva's building, where he found the doorman, his heavy coat dusted with snow, blowing his whistle for taxis. Eva must have alerted him that Jake was coming, for instead of calling up to announce his arrival, the doorman simply nodded and ushered him into the lobby, where his glasses fogged from the steam heat. Even in 2017, in buildings like Eva's, an old-fashioned formality obtained. The elevator was manual, its oak-paneled interior decorated with heraldic devices and a frieze depicting a sylvan scene of birds and hounds and women in long robes. Next to the control panel was a pull-down oak seat, the size and shape of a toilet seat, on which Frank, the elevator man, sat down for a rest during those rare moments when his services weren't needed. A few months before, the building's share-holders had voted to replace the old elevator with an auto-matic model. Since then Eva had confided to Jake her worry over what it would be like for Frank, a man who had all his life had a métier (turning the handle to start the elevator, slowing it down as it approached its destination, stopping it at exactly the point where the inner doors aligned with the outer), to see his job reduced to the pushing of a button that the passenger could just as easily push himself. "What must it feel like to be rendered, in effect, a symbol?" Eva asked, to which Jake replied that he supposed being rendered a symbol was better than being out of a job. "Oh, but he won't be out of a job, because of the union," she answered with a harsh little laugh. "The union's so strong that if just one elevator man got laid off, there'd be massive strikes. They've got us over a barrel. Which isn't to say I'm not glad that he won't be fired." As she hoped Jake knew, Eva went on, she was immensely fond of Frank, and cared about his welfare, just as she cared about the welfare of Amalia, who kept house for her in New York, and Beatie, who kept house for her in Connecticut, and Kathy, Bruce's secre-tary, whose husband had left her a week after she was diag-nosed with lymphoma, "though between you and me," Eva said to Jake, "I sometimes worry that Kathy's taking advantage

SHELTER IN PLACE 37

of Bruce's generous nature. All these women lead such harsh lives," she went on, "especially Amalia, who five days a week, from eight to four, works her fingers to the bone here, only to have to go home and do the whole thing all over again in her own apartment, because her husband's in a wheelchair, on top of which she has her mother to care for, and two adult daughters for whom she has to be on regular call to do babysitting duty. And yet she never complains." When Jake asked where Amalia lived, Eva gestured vaguely toward the kitchen window and said, "Oh, I don't know, somewhere out in Queens," as if Somewhere Out in Queens were a third-world country that only missionaries and aid workers ever traveled to, when in fact, as the crow flew, Amalia's neighborhood was at most five miles away.

Eva's worry over Frank was somewhat different. In his case, what troubled her was less the perceived tediousness of his life than the effect his being robbed of his purpose, as it were, might have on his self-esteem. Only later did it occur to Jake that this concern might be a screen for Eva's own sense of purposelessness and the panic it induced in her, or that this panic might in turn have influenced her impulsive decision to buy the apartment in Venice.

Eva aside, Jake was fond of Frank. Like most of the doormen and elevator men who worked in the building, he was Irish, with a florid complexion and a beer belly that strained the buttons of his burgundy uniform jacket. "Cold night, isn't it, Mr. Lovett?" he said as Jake wiped the mist from his glasses with his handkerchief, in response to which Jake said that it seemed to him that the winters were getting colder each year, and Frank said he thought the previous winter had actually been colder than this one, but his wife insisted on the opposite.

This was all the conversation they had time for, for Eva only lived on the third floor. Jake could easily have taken the stairs, but the door to the stairs was rigged so that it could only be opened from the inside in the event of a fire. The ride was ceremonial, a vestige of some protocol-laden past that left him feeling somewhat purposeless himself, there in the third-floor vestibule, checking his appearance in a mirror as, on the other side of the heavy oak door, paws scrabbled for purchase, nails skidded on waxed parquet. "Get down!" Eva called, opening the door just wide enough to let the three Bedlingtons wriggle past her ankles into the corridor, the length of which they ran twice before stopping to pee on one of her neighbors' doormats.

"It's all right," she said. "That's the Warriners' doormat. I *want* them to pee on it."

Then she leaned her cheek toward his lips, her lips toward his cheek, which they barely brushed, for she shrank from physical intimacies. That evening she wore her hair coiled over her ears, like Princess Leia's. Her cardigan was cashmere, that color that Nancy Lancaster called "No Color."

He helped her scoop up the dogs and they went inside. The apartment was capacious without being grand. From the front door a corridor led into the living room, which in turn segued into a dining room that did double duty as a library. Off the living room, another door cordoned off the two principal bedrooms, each of which had its own bath and one of which Jake had done up as a study. All these rooms looked out onto Park Avenue. On the opposite side, a swinging door opened onto the bright blue-and-white kitchen, the laundry room, and the tiny maid's room and bath, which had views of the interior courtyard. Since Amalia came only during the day, Jake had remade the maid's quarters into a candy box of a guest room, its walls covered in the same pink-striped cotton as the Roman blind and the bedspread. So far as he was aware, no one had ever slept in this room.

Eva helped him off with his coat, hung it on the rack (midcentury Danish), and escorted him into the living room. Here, in the wingback chair (early twentieth century, purchased at an estate sale in Ossining), Min Marable sat drinking a martini. Min was from Quincy, Florida. She was something in magazines—food magazines, travel magazines, shelter magazines. Usually she was just out of a job or just starting a job. Often she began her sentences, "When I was at *Self* . . ." or "When I was at *Good Housekeeping* . . ." or "When I was at *Marie Claire* . . ." Although she was younger than Eva, she looked older, with her hard agate-like eyes, her red-lacquered hair, the tortoiseshell reading glasses that hung from a silver chain around her neck.

"Jake," she said, hoisting herself out of her chair and giving him a boozy hug.

"Bruce not home yet?" Jake asked.

"He should be any minute," Eva said. "He had to stay late at the office for a phone call from Australia."

"Is it yesterday in Australia?" Min said. "Or is it tomorrow? I can't remember. When I was at *Travel & Leisure*—"

"Sit down, Jake," Eva said, opening a bottle of Perrier, since she knew he didn't drink.

He sat across from Min, on the loveseat (his own design, covered in a blue coral-patterned silk). One thing you learn quickly in the decorating trade is how little attention people pay to where they live. Ask a client how many windows she has in her living room and she will say, "Four? No—six?" Then ask her husband. "Six?" he will say. "No—four?"

Eva's living room had four windows, all curtained generously in a hand-blocked lily-and-auricula chintz. On the third window from the left, a tieback had come loose. Except for Amalia, no one but Jake would have noticed the tieback, just as no one but Jake would have noticed the scratch on the Hepplewhite credenza, or the niche that was just a hair too shallow for the bookcase it held, or the corner where the stripes on the wallpaper didn't quite line up. (They never do in old buildings, since the walls are never plumb.)

This is not to say that he was not pleased with Eva's apartment. In fact, he considered it some of the best work he'd ever done. The shade of blue on the entryway walls, for instance—it had taken him days to get it right. He'd ground the pigments himself. And that linen on the window-seat cushions, the color of coffee ice cream—he'd found a single bolt of it, by chance, in a thrift shop on Wooster Street.

And who would have guessed how perfectly, if improbably, it would match the olive-green damask on the fauteuils?

He would have.

With a pair of silver tongs, Eva dropped a slice of lime into the tumbler of Perrier, then handed it to him. She herself was drinking white wine. Min got up and mixed herself another martini.

"Well, aren't you going to tell him?" she said.

"Now, Min, don't be naughty," Eva said. "I told you, I want to wait for Bruce."

"Tell me what?" Jake said.

"Nothing that can't wait, so hush up."

"When we were in Venice, we bought an apartment! Oh!" Min clapped her hand over her mouth.

"Min!"

"I'm sorry, it just slipped out. Oh, but Jake, it's gorgeous. Terrazzo floors, high ceilings, a view over the Grand Canal. And it needs a total overhaul. I mean, total. A decorator's dream."

Right then keys clicked in the door. Into the apartment Bruce carried the smell of Manhattan winter, the ingredients of which include (but are not limited to) fir needles, the duct-taped Naugahyde upholstery of taxis, roasted chestnuts, ciga-rettes, and the steam that rises from subway grates.

"I'm afraid Min's let the cat out of the bag," Eva said as he kissed her cheek.

"Cat?" Bruce asked. "What cat? Where?" He was talking to the Bedlingtons, who did not react. They are realists, those dogs. They will not be bamboozled into thinking there is a cat where there is no cat.

"I mean about the apartment," Eva said.

"You're not planning to redo it again, are you?" Bruce said.

"Oh, hush. You know perfectly well what I'm talking about. The apartment in Venice."

"Ah, Venice." Bruce winked. "Well, Jake, you know the rule around here. Whatever Lola wants, Lola gets."

"It was a coup de foudre," Min said.

"It was not a coup de foudre," Eva said. "I'm buying that apartment for a perfectly sound reason. It's so that, if we have to leave the country in a hurry, we'll have somewhere to go."

"And little man, Lola wants you," Bruce sang to himself as he hung up his coat. "You see, Jake, my wife is convinced that with Tr—"

"Don't say that name."

"Sorry—that with him-who-shall-not-be-named in the White House, we're on the road to a dictatorship."

"Martial law. Press censorship."

"Prison camps."

"You think I'm overreacting," Eva said. "Well, so did the Jews who stayed in France—think the ones who left were overreacting. They thought that because they were French citizens, they'd be safe. But they weren't safe."

"Mine is not to reason why," Bruce said, then went to wash his hands. Jake followed Eva into the dining room. There is only so much a decorator can do to make a room beautiful. At a certain point the responsibility must shift to the client, and in this regard Eva was the best client he had ever had. An old hand-embroidered Portuguese cloth covered the table. The tole sconces, a design of his own, were dimmed to their lowest wattage. Silver candlesticks threw a skipping light onto the curtains, which were trimmed in the same moss fringe as the coffee-colored cushion on the window seat, on which the Bedlingtons now lay in a heap—such decorative dogs, with their fleece-like coats, the pliant musculature that allowed them, when they curled up, to chew the ends of their tails.

From a Coalport tureen Eva ladled out sorrel soup. It tasted like dirt.

She said, "You must promise to do it, Jake. You know I don't trust anyone else."

This was true. Eva trusted him because he could read her. It was a mysterious gift; the only gift, Pablo liked to say.

Of course, it had to go both ways. The client had to be willing to let go of what she thought of as her *taste*. Some refused. Such a client might object to a certain shade of red, saying, "It's just not me." Or she might nix the perfect console for her dining room because she didn't like the way it looked in a picture. Or buy some hideous sideboard at auction for three times what it was worth and then complain that the cut-silk velvet for the bedroom was "a bit bordello."

Such clients didn't understand. The point wasn't to create a room that reflected their personalities. It was to create a room where they belonged. What was it Diana Vreeland had said? "Give them what they don't know they want."

Eva was the better sort of client. That is to say, when Jake worked for her, she simply described the mood she was after and left the rest to him.

And he, in turn, gave her rooms where every object was in harmony with every other object—but where she herself was the object without which the whole could not cohere.

She appreciated this. She liked a room that only her own presence could complete.

He asked her to tell him more about the Venice apartment, and for some minutes she and Min held forth, speaking over and under each other. The layout was described, as were the floors, the fireplaces, the stuccoed and frescoed ceilings. Min handed her phone to Jake so that he could look at the photos she had taken, from which he could discern little more than light and shadow and the murk of large furniture.

"Count on Eva's eye," Min said, retrieving the phone. "She has a genius for spotting diamonds in the raw."

"Don't be absurd," Eva said. "I'm not a genius."

"Oh, but you are."

"No, I'm not. To say that—it's like saying that the collector who buys a Picasso is on a par with Picasso."

"He is if he finds the Picasso in a junk shop."

"No, he isn't. The ability to recognize beauty is not the same as the ability to create beauty. It is not a category of genius."

Chastened, Min ate a spoonful of dirt. The exchange was typical of them. Because Min relied on Eva to take her along on trips she could not afford on her own, she dosed their conversations with flattery. Yet the flattery had to be leavened with just a little provocation. To be Eva's minion, you also had to be her adversary—but just a little.

Jake never did learn what "Min" was short for.

"How did you find the place?" he asked.

"Well, that's the best part of the story," Min said. "A countess invited us to tea."

"She's not a countess," Eva said.

"A fascinating woman—she's lived most of her life in the States, but then she inherited this palazzo, and now she's impoverished herself trying to keep it up. That's why she's selling her flat."

"What's her name?"

"Ursula Brandolino-Foote."

"Ursula *Brandolin*-Foote," Eva corrected. "There's no *o* at the end."

Jake picked up his water glass and drank. He didn't want his surprise at hearing the name to register.

Somewhat abruptly, Eva got up and started clearing the soup plates. It should be noted that all this time, in the kitchen, her friend James had been lurking. Or maybe it wasn't James, maybe it was Andrew or Sean or Tom. They were interchangeable, these gay editorial assistants and assistant stage managers

and aspiring graphic designers whom Eva befriended, culti-
vated, and often, because they never had any money, hired to
cater her dinner parties.

And now, through the same swinging door, Michael or Peter
or Sam emerged, only it wasn't Michael or Peter or Sam, it was
Matt Pierce, he of the botched scones, wearing a green apron
over his street clothes and bearing the main course on a silver
tray—poached salmon fillets, boiled potatoes flecked with
parsley, steamed green beans.

A boring dinner. A grown-up dinner. For a few seconds
Bruce gazed at the platter, as if hoping that something more
appetizing might materialize: a twirl of buttered noodles or a
quenelle of creamed spinach. Nothing did.

They ate. Every now and then, Bruce cast his glance over
Min's head and out the window, at the snow billowing in the
wind, which looked as if it were falling upward. According to
his business card, Bruce was a "wealth management adviser."
Exactly what this meant, Jake had never quite grasped. In
New York there is a whole category of careers the logistics of
which only their practitioners understand, and that ordinary
people understand only as the source of steady and volumi-
nous incomes. By and large these careers involve money—its
manipulation, mutation, transfiguration.

What was obvious was that Bruce revered his wife, and was
also a little spooked by her—as if he could never quite decide
whether the passions that intermittently seized her (such as
the Venice apartment) were the whims of a neurotic, or
evidence that she was a Great Visionary Woman, someone like
Isabella Stewart Gardner.

Isabella Stewart Gardner, by the way, had been the subject
of her honors thesis at Smith, which her marriage to Bruce

interrupted. They'd had to get married in a hurry, Bruce had told Jake, so that by the time his parents had cottoned on to the fact that his bride was Jewish, the wedding would be a fait accompli.

It was Eva's professors at Smith whom the marriage had upset most—because they had predicted a brilliant future for her, were hoping she would pursue a PhD at Yale or Princeton or the University of Chicago.

Most of this—most of what Jake knew about Eva—he had learned from Bruce himself, on those occasions when they found themselves alone together in the kitchen of the country house early in the morning, before anyone else was up, or out in the garden, where after lunch Bruce liked to squat on his haunches, pulling weeds, or trying to figure out what was clogging up the ornamental fountain on the patio.

About Jake, Eva knew almost nothing. This was not because he kept anything from her. It was because she never asked. He was a bachelor decorator. His position was not one that required a pedigree. It required only contacts, manners, and a decent portfolio.

Once, when he was visiting Eva and Bruce at their country place—Eva often included him in her little weekend parties, both because she liked his company and because she knew she could count on him to use the correct fork, and to fill in the protracted silences that occasionally seized the dinner table with stimulating (but not too stimulating) anecdotes, and to compose his face into the proper rictus of enthusiasm when one of the other guests said something that was supposed to be witty—once, at one of these weekend parties, Bruce happened to mention a launderer in London, in Belgravia, who was famous all over the world for removing spots from silk ties. So famous was this launderer, Bruce said, that movie stars, kings, presidents, and sheikhs had their ties sent to him. George Soros and François Hollande had their ties sent to him, as did Daniel Craig. And Placido Domingo. And Bruce himself.

"Of course, I'd just as soon throw them out, but Lola insists," he said.

"Bruce is sloppy with his soup," Eva said, which was true.

Sometimes Jake suspected that Eva put him in the same category as the tie launderer: the master of a craft whose reputation earned him loyalty and high fees. And yet who would ever think to ask the tie launderer who he was or where he came from?

The plates were cleared, the dessert brought: caramelized bananas and vanilla ice cream, which Eva abjured.

"Oh, why not?" Min said, helping herself to some.

"You know why not," Eva said, looking pointedly at Min's belly.

They resumed their conversation about the apartment in Venice, how perfectly unspoiled it was, yet how everything was spotless, because of the maid. This maid, in Min's words, was "old school."

"Well, Jake, what do you say?" she said. "Don't keep us in suspense. Will you do it?"

"But I've never worked in Venice," Jake said.

"Well, but you've spent time there," Min said. "In fact, you lived there for a while, didn't you?"

"Years ago—and not for very long. There's a reason why most people, when they buy an apartment in Italy, hire an Italian decorator."

"As if Eva would ever hire anyone but you."

Bruce punched Jake lightly on the arm. "Why are you fighting it?" he asked. "You know my wife. You know she won't take no for an answer."

"Oh, Bruce," Eva said.

But it was true. She would not take no for an answer.

"I have to think about it," Jake said.

6

At Eva's dinner parties, coffee was served in the living room. This was an act of homage on her part to the manners of the past as depicted by her favorite novelists, Ivy Compton-Burnett and Edith Wharton.

She was just handing around the cups when Bruce stood up and said, "I think I'll take the dogs for a walk."

"This early?" she said, tilting her cup slightly, so that a drop of coffee fell from it onto her cardigan.

"Caspar! Ralph! Izzy!" Bruce called to the dogs, who leaped up from the window seat where they were sleeping and scrambled after him.

"Jake, why don't you go with Bruce?" Min said. "Keep him company?" Her eyes, he could see, were on Eva's sweater—the stain that she herself appeared, so far, not to have noticed.

In the front hall, Jake found Bruce getting the dogs into their coats, matching tartan affairs that had to be affixed to their torsos by means of a bewildering array of Velcro straps and buckles—not an easy job, for no sooner had the dogs realized that a walk was in the offing than they began leaping and writhing and letting out high-pitched whines. So elastic are Bedlingtons, moreover, that just getting their necks through the neck holes is a struggle. And how do you explain to a dog who recognizes the signs that he is about to be taken on a walk that, if the walk is actually going to happen, he must stand still long enough to be fitted into the straitjacket on which, paradoxically, his freedom depends? Come to think of it, how do you explain that to anyone? How do you explain that to yourself?

"Let me help you," Jake said, and held each dog steady as Bruce, in turn, lifted legs, did up fastenings, attached leashes.

"Thanks," Bruce said. "Usually I ask Frank, but at this hour Frank has his hands full with people coming back from the theater."

They headed out into the foyer. Already waiting for the elevator was a freckled man in his late sixties. He had pale blue eyes, and hair the same "No Color" as Eva's sweater, and was accompanied by an elderly long-haired dachshund, at the sight of whom the Bedlingtons started barking and straining against their leashes until they choked. In response, the dachshund got behind his master's legs and snarled.

"Sparky," the freckled man said warningly.

"Don't worry, Sparky," Bruce said to the dachshund. "They're all talk."

The elevator arrived. "But my guess is that it will be more likely six inches," Frank said.

"You think?" Bruce said.

Frank nodded emphatically. "These weathermen! Have you noticed how, the minute there's a hurricane, they race off to wherever it's supposed to make landfall? And then, if it's supposed to be a Category 5 and it ends up being a Category

1, they look all disappointed, even as they're saying how relieved they are."

"Six inches is still a lot of snow," the freckled man said.

"Especially for you low-to-the-ground guys, huh?" Frank said, speaking to Sparky.

"It's OK, I keep on my toes," the freckled man said, speaking *for* Sparky.

Out on the street, as if by some unspoken agreement, the freckled man and the dachshund headed uptown, Bruce and Jake and the Bedlingtons downtown. "You'll have to excuse Frank," Bruce said. "He starts a conversation with one passenger and carries it on with the next. We've gotten used to it over the years."

"I hope you don't mind my asking," Jake said, looking over his shoulder at the freckled man, "but was that the one who gave the inauguration party?"

"You mean Satan incarnate? Yup. Menacing-looking, isn't he?"

Jake laughed.

"No, but seriously, the way Eva goes on, you'd think he and Kitty were the Honeymoon Killers, when the truth is, they're much more scared of her than she is of them. Lately it's gotten so bad that if Kitty's going out and she hears our door opening, she runs back into her apartment and hides until Eva's in the elevator. Or so Alec tells me.

"Maybe it surprises you that I'm on such friendly terms with him, but the way I see it, there's nothing to be gained from bickering with your neighbors. On top of which I have to make up for Eva's cold-shouldering. You'd think I'd be used to it by now."

They turned left onto a block of brownstones. "Let me take one of the dogs for you," Jake said, reaching for the leashes.

"Oh, don't worry, I'm used to dealing with all three," Bruce said. "Unless for some reason you *want* to take one, in which case I'd recommend Izzy. She's the easiest to manage, which isn't to say she doesn't generate a headwind."

He handed the leash to Jake, who found that Isabel's capacity for resistance was indeed mightier than he would have guessed. The walk itself was stop-and-go, what with the dogs braking every few seconds to sniff at a yellow patch in the snow or to lap at some unwholesome spillage on the sidewalk. At more or less every juncture, Ralph and Caspar lifted their legs as high as ballerinas at the bar. They dosed out their urine judiciously, whereas Isabel held hers, appraising each potential spot carefully before moving on to another, squatting, and then changing her mind.

"Like my wife buying real estate," Bruce said. "Do you happen to know, Jake, how many apartments we looked at before settling on this one? Thirty-eight. Thirty-eight! I thought the realtor was going to tear her hair out. Lola's, I mean."

"And yet she chose well."

"Of course she chose well. She always chooses well. That's not at issue."

"What is, then?"

Again Jake felt the tug of Isabel's leash as she inspected yet another property and passed on it.

"This may come as a surprise to you," Bruce said, "but I don't especially like the Connecticut house."

"Really? I'm sorry."

"Don't get me wrong, it's not the decor. I'm fine with the decor. It's the house itself. Now, Bedford—I liked that house.

I liked Bedford. Left to my own devices, I'd have stayed there until they had to carry me out in a pine box, only Eva—no surprise here—every few years she gets restless. Gets a bee in her bonnet. Nothing to be done about it. Oh, well, at least it keeps you in business. No offense intended."

"None taken," Jake said. "And there's nothing wrong with wanting to stay put."

"Try telling her that."

"Have you?"

"You do know my wife's maiden name, don't you, Jake?"

"Kalmann?"

"Braun."

It took Jake a few seconds to get the joke—if it was a joke.

"And now Venice," Bruce said. "What's that about? What on earth do you think that's about?"

"The election, apparently."

"Oh, that. Some classified information here, Jake. This election, the one she's got her panties in such a wad about—she didn't even vote in it. Went to the polling station and turned right around. Said the line was too long. Interesting how she seems to have forgotten that.

"Now, if you want my opinion—again, this is strictly classified—all this really is is a very expensive hissy fit. By buying this place in Venice, she thinks she's giving the finger to the Warriners, to Park Avenue, to everyone who voted for him-who-shall-not-be-named. As if they'll even notice . . . Well, there's a bit more to it than that. There's Venice itself. I think at the root of it, she has this idea of herself in Venice, as one of those American women who went to live in Venice. She's fixated on it. It's her polestar.

"Of course, to some degree her upbringing's to blame. It's from her parents that she inherited her . . . how do I put it? Fear of persecution, combined with a fight-or-flight impulse, combined with this unbelievable obstinacy, this determination to have her way at all costs. She's like her mother in that way, though I'd advise you never to say that to her face if you want to keep your balls. Women can't stand being compared to their mothers."

"I've never met Eva's mother."

"Very few people have. Min did, back when she and Eva were working at *Mademoiselle*."

"Eva worked at *Mademoiselle*?"

"For a year or so, right after we got married. It was how they met."

"She never told me that."

"She doesn't talk about it because back when she did, people naturally asked why she quit, and that's a question she prefers not to answer. Even after all these years, I'm convinced, most of her friends think it was me, that I *made* her quit, only it isn't the case at all. Quite the contrary, when she told me, I begged her not to make a rash decision. I wanted her to give it another six months—either that, or get the PhD. She could have gone to Columbia. It was her choice not to."

"Why do you think that was?"

For a moment Bruce was silent. Then he said, "I'm thinking maybe it was because Columbia was too close to where she grew up. Too close for comfort. Or maybe her friends are right, maybe it really was my fault. You see, before she met me, Eva had never felt safe—not really safe—and I wanted to give her that. Her parents—you probably know this—were refugees. From Warsaw, they made their way to Portugal, where they waited out the war, then from Portugal to Brazil, then from Brazil to New York. In Poland, Esther—that's Eva's mother—had been working toward her PhD in chemistry. If the war hadn't happened, she'd have become a professor. Instead she ended up teaching chemistry at a high school on the Upper West Side where she had a reputation for being a holy terror. One look from Esther and the toughest kids, the ones who carried switchblades, pissed their pants. I've always been rather sweet on Esther."

"What about the father?"

"Joe? Until he retired, he was an accountant. Small potatoes. Had his office in a storefront on Broadway. Every March he'd pay bums from the park to parade up and down Broadway dressed as the Statue of Liberty, handing out flyers. You can imagine what Eva thought about that.

"Now, here's the thing. Until she met me, Eva never knew what it was like to have solid ground under her feet. And that really *was* her parents' fault. There's no getting around it. They were in their early forties when she was born. They never planned to have children—her mother told her that. Eva was just a little girl when one day her mother sat her down and told her that the day she found out she was pregnant, she asked God what she'd done wrong, for why else would he compel an aging couple to bring a child into such a vile world except to punish them?"

"Jesus."

"Not in this case. No Jesus in this case."

They turned onto Lexington. Since they'd started the walk, the wind had picked up, blowing north and making the avenues nearly impossible to navigate. On the sidewalk outside a twenty-four-hour Korean grocery store, a woman wearing

gloves with the fingers cut off was trying to cover her vegetable display with a plastic tarp. With each fresh gust, the tarp
flew into her face. "Mind if we stop here for a sec?" Bruce
asked, handing Jake his leashes. "Need to buy some cigarettes.
Don't tell Lola."

Jake nodded assent and Bruce went into the store.
Abandoning her tarp for the moment, the woman with the
fingerless gloves followed. Inside, a girl in a down parka was
circling the stainless-steel salad bar. With a pair of tongs she
picked up a single pickled mushroom, sniffed it, then put it
back in its steel receptacle. Then she did the same with a beet
slice. By the time Bruce came out, the girl had almost completely
circumnavigated the bar. Her tray was still empty.

"Thanks for waiting," Bruce said, taking Isabel's leash this
time and leaving Jake to contend with Caspar and Ralph, who
lunged forward so fast he nearly tripped. The trouble wasn't
just that there were two of them; it was that they moved with
such intentionality, as if they had somewhere they had to get
to and didn't want to be late. Yet there was nowhere they had to
get to, so far as Jake was aware, unless it was the nearest lamp-
post, which they circled, in the process hog-tying him with
their leashes. "Allow me," Bruce said, and held them steady
while Jake stepped out of the snarl. Again the dogs lifted their
legs. Nothing came out. "Instinct," Bruce said. "Even though
their bladders are empty, they'll keep doing it until we get
home. I suppose most of us are like that on some level. Men, I
mean. Some women, too. Min, for instance."

From the avenue they turned onto a street on which a
white-brick high-rise, an eyesore from the early sixties, broke
the stately procession of brownstones. Here the wind eased a
little. Rather than blowing into their faces, the snow stuck,

settling on the stoops, the roofs of the parked cars, the dogs' tartan jackets. Ice was forming on the pavement, making Jake worry for a delivery boy racing by on a bicycle, his basket filled with insulated bags of takeout Chinese food. "Neither snow nor rain nor heat nor gloom of night," Bruce said, removing his gloves so that he could fish the bag from the deli out of his pocket. It contained a pack of Marlboros and a roll of Mentos.

"Want one?" he asked, holding out the pack.

"No, thanks."

"Don't smoke?"

Jake shook his head.

"Myself, I don't *really* smoke," Bruce said, lighting a cigarette and taking a deep drag. "Only when I take a lunch break or go out with the dogs. Can't smoke at the office. Or at home, God knows."

At last Isabel peed. As if to show her up, Caspar shat, bringing all four of his legs together with a grace as balletic as his previous leg-lifting. Having stubbed out his cigarette, Bruce fished a plastic bag from another of his pockets, scooped up the steaming pile, and dropped it into a trash bin. "I read somewhere that in Venice the maids used to empty the chamber pots out the window into the canals," he said. "Is that true, do you think?"

"I think I read it in a book. I never saw it happen."

"Oh, well, if it makes the job easier, I suppose . . ." They resumed walking. "So Jake, this Venice thing—what do you make of it? Is it a bridge too far? Oh, I didn't even realize I was making a joke."

"I wish I could tell you. The thing is, I'm not what you'd call an expert on Venice. Although I'm pretty sure an apartment in Venice won't lose its value."

"Still, it's not like Connecticut, is it? I mean, with Connecticut you can just pile the dogs into the car and two hours later you're there. But Venice . . . You can't just up and go to Venice for the weekend. There are the flight reservations. There's the time difference. And then, when would we go? Would Eva go alone? For how long? And what about these guys? Would she take them? Leave them? I did a little checking. One you can take in the cabin with you, if it's small enough. But only on some airlines. And only one dog—the other two would have to go in the hold regardless."

"Have you mentioned any of this to Eva?"

"I tried, and she nearly bit my head off. According to her, there are no problems at all. When we're in Venice, one of her boyfriends can dog-sit, here or in the country, and then when we're not in Venice, Signora Foot-and-Mouth or whatever her name is can keep an eye on things. She can even rent the place out for us. I said to Eva, 'You're actually saying you're prepared to let total strangers sleep in your bed?' It's always the same with her. Once she's off to the races, there's no stopping her."

"How far along are you in the process? I mean, too far along to back out?"

"It's funny you should ask, because this morning I asked our lawyer that very question. The short answer is no, it's not too late to back out. At this stage we can even get back our deposit. And there are plenty of reasons to, not the least of which is that buying real estate in Italy is crazy. Just crazy. For example, when you buy a place, the price on the contract isn't the price you actually pay. It's much less—a fraction of the real price. What happens at the closing is that after the buyer and seller sign the contract, the buyer gives the seller a check for the official price, and then the lawyers or notaries or whatever they're called step out for a quote-unquote espresso, so that the buyer and seller can exchange the rest of the money under the table. It's to save on taxes. And there's no way around it, because no one will sell anything any other way. The corruption is too entrenched."

They had circled back to Bruce's building. "I'm not sure what to say," Jake said, "except that if you've got doubts about this thing, you should tell Eva."

From his pocket Bruce took out the pack of Mentos, opened it, and popped one in his mouth before handing it to Jake, who this time accepted. "I don't know how much you think about money, Jake," he said. "Me, I think about it all the time. It's my business. My clients have money, serious money, so much they can lose a few million and not even feel it. Now, I'm not saying we don't have money—of course we do—and yet we're not in a position where we can spend literally as much as we want, or where we're immune to recession, inflation. Eva likes to give the impression that she's sort of oblivious to money, but it's not true. Appearances to the contrary, she understands what we can afford and what we can't."

"And can you afford this apartment?"

"Oh, we can afford it. Of course we can afford it. The question is, should we? . . . I'm sorry if I'm not making myself clear. I suppose it's because I don't really understand myself exactly what I'm thinking. I don't know if Eva told you, but my secretary, Kathy, has lymphoma. And then, right after she got the diagnosis, her husband left her. And so . . . I don't know. I think about Kathy, and I think about Venice, and something freezes in me."

"I'm sorry to hear about Kathy."

"Oh, thanks. I'll say this for her—she has guts. Gutsiest woman I've ever known. Even so, it seems unfair, doesn't it? As if she's being tested."

"Other people's lives . . ." Jake said but could not think how to complete the sentence.

"Well, I appreciate your listening," Bruce said. "Care to come up for a drink?"

"No, I'd better get home. School night. Thank Eva for me. Tell her I'll call her tomorrow."

"Will do," Bruce said, and held out his gloved hand. Though the hand was big, the handshake was mild—the practiced mildness of a man who might break fingers if he wasn't careful.

He dragged the dogs through the door to the lobby. Jake turned south onto Park Avenue. Not a taxi in sight, which was fine by him. He felt like walking. He felt like fighting the wind.

7

In the living room, Bruce found Eva and Min sitting with the young man who had cooked dinner, to whom he nodded. It made him cross that he couldn't remember this young man's name, given that in recent months he had become such a fixture in their lives, both here and in Connecticut. The trouble was, Eva had so many young men, all so alike in their youth and good looks, that he couldn't keep them straight. (Keep them straight! He wished he could share *that* joke with someone.)

"Where's Jake?" Min asked as he extricated the dogs from their jackets.

"Gone home. Sends his regards."

"But I thought he'd be coming back up," Min said.

"Well, he isn't. Has to be up early in the morning."

"Oh, what a shame."

"Did anyone do anything?" Eva asked.

"Everyone did number one. Only Caspar did number two."

"Must be the cold," Matt Pierce said.

In case the Mentos had not been sufficient to get the smoky taste out of his mouth, Bruce excused himself to brush his teeth. Min wished that Matt would go away. She wanted to ask Eva some questions about the Venice apartment in the hope of ascertaining whether Bruce could do anything at this point to scuttle the deal. Unfortunately, so long as Matt was there, she could not bring any of these matters up. Matt was a tall youth of thirty-seven, Texan by birth, with a cowboy hat and an accent that he put on and took off as it suited him. At present he was ABD at Columbia (English, dissertation on Marianne Moore) and eking out a living doing odd jobs such as cooking dinners for Eva, writing reader reports for publishers, and now and then putting on his cowboy hat and his Texas accent and saying filthy things via webcam to men who paid him for the privilege.

For Min, the disparity between Matt's looks—he was six foot three and bore a distinct resemblance to the young Glenn Ford—and his fastidious manner, which expressed itself most obviously in his cooking, was troublesome. As a rule incongruities disconcerted her. She preferred people and things to be what they seemed.

After Bruce and Jake had gone to take the dogs for their walk, Matt, as was his habit, had come out of the kitchen, taken off his apron, and poured himself a glass of cognac. He'd then sat down next to Eva on the loveseat and crossed his long legs so that the hem of his jeans rode up, revealing the upward thrust of a cowboy boot. Such conduct—to cater a dinner and then have a cognac with its hostess—was in keeping with his ambiguous role in the duchy, something partway between servant and cicisbeo.

"Now, I want you to be totally honest," he said. "What did you think of the sorrel soup? Was it oversalted?"

"I thought it was perfect," Eva said.

Matt shook his head. "No, it was oversalted. And the salmon was dry."

Min said, "When I was at *Gourmet*, we did a piece on how to keep salmon from getting dry. The trick is—"

"I'm sure Matt knows the trick for keeping salmon from getting dry," Eva said.

"I'll be the first to admit it—I was off my game tonight," Matt said. "It's been a rough week. That's not an excuse, it's just a fact."

"Poor Matt." Eva crossed her legs in a manner that Min recognized as signaling both curiosity and a warning as to the limits of her curiosity. "Do you want to tell us about it?"

Matt cleared his throat in a prefatory way. "OK, well, a few nights ago, completely out of the blue, Dean—I've told you about Dean, right? He's the guy I've been seeing—well, living with—since September. Anyway, the other night, completely out of the blue, he asks me how I feel about three-ways. Much as he loves me, he says, every now and then he still finds himself wanting to have sex with other guys and he wants to know if I do, too. So I say, 'Well, I can't deny that occasionally I think about it,' which isn't at all—let me emphasize this—isn't *at all* the same as saying I want to do it, but he doesn't pick up on the distinction. Instead he starts in on this boring lecture about how, for the modern gay couple, three-ways are the ideal solution to the quote-unquote problem of monogamy, because they allow partners to have sex with other people without being disloyal to each other."

"Oh, my," Min said. "And what did you say to that?"

"Nothing. What I mean is, what I wanted to say was that, unlike him, I don't want to have sex with other people, but I didn't . . . Don't get me wrong, I don't have anything against three-ways per se. I've had plenty of them in my time, some quite fun. It's just, with Dean . . . maybe it's a sign that I'm getting older, but I kind of want to keep him for myself. Plus, you know how it can be with three—someone always ends up feeling left out. And it could be him just as easily as it could be me."

Min, who very much doubted that Eva knew how it could be with three, looked at her friend. In the course of Matt's monologue, her neck had stiffened, her lips were pressed tightly together. *Oh, God,* Min thought, *has no one warned him?* Eva hated talking about sex.

There was only one thing to do, she decided, and that was to take matters into her own hands. "Well, darling," she said, "if you want my advice, you should proceed with extreme caution. Now, I actually know something about this—not from firsthand experience, mind you—well, not much—but because when I was at *Cosmo*, we ran this big article on the subject—you know, ménages à trois. We did a reader survey, and interviews with therapists, and profiles of couples who'd tried it, and the conclusion we came to, basically, was that three into two won't go . . . Isn't that the name of a movie?"

"But what if I say no and Dean says forget it? What if it's a deal-breaker for him—I mean, for the relationship?"

Matt was looking at Eva as he asked this—Eva, now bolt upright, her legs twisted one around the other like pipe cleaners.

It was at that moment, thankfully, that Bruce returned with the dogs, bringing the smoky winter air and their canine fluster into the apartment and, in so doing, relieving the high tension of the scene. Seeing her husband, Eva relaxed her posture and smiled. The brief conversation reported above ensued. Then Bruce headed in the direction of the bathroom—Min couldn't tell, from his gait, whether he planned to come back—and Matt, pouring himself a second cognac, resumed his narrative, moving back in time to his first electronic encounter with Dean, and the early days of their courtship, when he had been so immensely moved by the blond hair on Dean's chest, the way it "pearled with sweat" after he'd worked out. Although Dean was younger than Matt, he made more money—he was an entertainment lawyer, a job that necessitated frequent trips to the West Coast, as well as frequent late nights at the office—and owned a condo in Williamsburg. "Probably it was a mistake to move in with him so soon after we met, but what choice did I have?" Matt said. "I was living in an illegal sublet in Bushwick, and the friend I was subletting from was about to come back from a year in Sweden. I had nowhere else to go."

When, an hour or so later, Matt finally accepted his check, said goodnight, and went off to catch the subway, Eva poured herself a glass of wine. "What I don't understand is why he insists on going into the gory details," she said. "It's one of the things I've always appreciated most about Jake—he doesn't go into the gory details."

"I've been meaning to ask, how are things coming along with the apartment? Do you have a closing date yet?"

"Early April, it looks like. Bruce's lawyer is handling all that."

"You must be so excited."

"It still seems a long way off. There are so many hurdles to jump before we actually get there."

"Oh, but when you do get there, think how marvelous it will be. For one thing, you can write your book. I predict that as soon as you're settled in, you'll get down to work and finish it. Just imagine, a desk set up in front of that window with the view of the canal—"

"No, the desk should be in front of the window overlooking the garden. The canal could be smelly."

"Then that's where it'll be. Jake will see to it."

"Speaking of Jake, how did he seem to you tonight?"

"Fine. Why do you ask?"

"I don't know. Something struck me as off."

"What, you mean his not agreeing right away to decorate the apartment? I wouldn't worry about that. He probably just wants to sleep on it."

"It hadn't occurred to me to worry about it until you said that. Why did you say that? Do you think he doesn't want to do it?"

"Oh, no, not at all, I just . . . Well, when you said something struck you as off—"

"Oh, but it wasn't that. It was his general demeanor. But seriously, Min, do you think he might say no? I don't think I could manage this without him."

"You're just tired, that's all. In twenty-four hours, when he's said yes and all this is behind us, you won't even remember we had this conversation."

"I suppose you're right. Really it was Matt who put me off. Why he had to . . . What's the word people use these days? You know, when you tell too much."

"TMI? Overshare?"

"That's it. Overshare. I thought I knew him better than that. Or that he knew me better."

Around half past ten, Min took a taxi home. She lived on West Seventy-seventh Street, in a studio apartment on which she had signed the lease in 1984, the year she and Eva worked together at *Mademoiselle*, and then bought at the insider price when the building went co-op. In the intervening decades, the neighborhood had improved—even Amsterdam Avenue had become chic—and yet Min's flat still had the provisional feel of a nest from which the fledgling should have long since flown. She herself knew better than anyone that she should not be living here any longer, that by now she should have found a husband, or at least a one-bedroom. Instead, every evening, she climbed the four flights of stairs to this cramped, oblong room with its view of fire escapes, stopping at least twice to catch her breath, something she hadn't had to do when she was younger and thinner. Clothes she had accumulated over the years, mostly during her stints at fashion magazines, hung on wheeled department store racks that took up the bulk of the space. Few of them fit her anymore. At her last checkup, her doctor had told her she needed to start exercising what he called "portion control." But every time she tried, she found herself thinking of the people who died in plane crashes, how so many of them had been on diets, or had given up coffee or booze, or were trying to limit their sugar intake, and then she would throw caution to the wind and have a dessert. Even when she was at lunch or dinner with Eva, she would have a dessert. Nor did Eva, on these occasions, conceal her disapproval, which vexed Min, for the humiliations with which she dealt on a daily basis—the skirts that wouldn't zip, the bras from which back fat bulged, the Miraclesuit Extra Firm Tummy-Control Shape Away Torsettes that she ordered from Amazon in order to be spared from having to buy them at a shop—Eva had never known.

Wearily she took off her shoes. Aside from the clothes racks, she had very little furniture: an armchair she had inherited from her grandmother, a desk, a desk chair, and a bed pushed up against the wall—full-size, "too big for one and too small for two," as she used to joke. Except for the occasional lover—fewer every year, now that she was on the wrong side of fifty—she rarely had visitors.

As she undressed, worry about Eva nagged at her. Their friendship, the most enduring in either of their lives, was a source of both gratification and anxiety for Min. To some extent the anxiety owed to a feeling of beholdenness. At *Mademoiselle* Eva had been a star. When she quit, she claimed it was for Min's sake, so that Min, who *had* to earn a living, would get the promotion that otherwise would have gone to her. This wasn't hubris, nor was it merely an excuse for giving up a job Eva neither wanted nor needed. The fact was, she really did have a better eye than Min, and was a better writer. Asked by the editor to whip up a description, say, of a day dress, Eva could produce a perfect piece of copy in fifteen minutes flat, without crossing out a single word, whereas Min would be up half the night, breaking her pencil and resharpening it and breaking it again. At first she had envied Eva her gift, her seeming ability just to wave her magic wand and make the words do her bidding, like the bunnies in *Snow White*. But then, over time, her envy had verged into gratitude, for whatever else you might say about Min's somewhat erratic career, the fact remained that if Eva hadn't left *Mademoiselle*, she might never have had it.

Whether Eva felt the same way, she wasn't sure. Close as they were, Min had little idea how Eva spent her weekdays, while she herself was at work. If asked, Eva would say that she wrote, yet if this was true, there was little evidence of it: a couple of articles in *Glamour* (commissioned, as it happened, by Min), a poem she had burned after *The New Yorker* rejected it, two crosswords for the *Times*, a Monday and a Wednesday, published under her maiden name in 2002. Her main project—always in the offing—was the Book, the subject and form of which had changed frequently over the years. First it was to be an expansion of her Smith thesis into a monograph, then a biography of Isabella Stewart Gardner, then a joint biography of Isabella Stewart Gardner and John Singer Sargent, then a biography of John Singer Sargent, then a novel about Isabella Stewart Gardner and John Singer Sargent, then a novel about an Isabella Stewart Gardner–like figure with a different name, of which she wrote nine hundred pages before she decided she was telling it from the wrong point of view and chucked it in the bin. Soon Min learned that it was best not to ask Eva how the Book was going, and, later, to ask only when she wanted to annoy Eva on purpose, for she knew it was a touchy subject. On these occasions, the thought sometimes crossed Min's mind that Eva might actually regret her decision to leave *Mademoiselle* all those years ago and that this regret might explain her often rebarbative bursts of impatience. For her part, Min tried not to lose patience with Eva, for she recognized Eva's irritability as the obverse of her vulnerability. If Min had a duty in life, she had come to believe, it was to protect Eva, to shield her, to reassure her.

A few months back, as part of her profile on a dating site, Min had listed *instinct* as her most salient characteristic. This was neither vanity nor self-delusion: Instinct really was her strong suit. Most of the time, the accuracy of her instincts accounted for her successes and her inability to follow through on them for her failures. It was instinct that had led her to suggest that Jake accompany Bruce on his walk. She had sensed trouble, and hoped that sending them off together might reveal its source. So far it had not.

From her refrigerator she took out a stick of butter, unwrapped it, rolled it in sugar, took a bite, put it on the butterfly-patterned covered butter dish she had inherited from her grandmother, and returned it to the refrigerator. She then changed into her pajamas, brushed her teeth, rubbed one kind of moisturizer onto her face and another onto her hands, got into bed, tried to find a comfortable position, gave up, got up again, reopened the refrigerator, retrieved the stick of sugar-dusted butter, took another bite of it, put it back, closed the refrigerator, brushed her teeth again, and got back into bed. For half an hour she did jigsaw puzzles on her phone—puppies and kittens, unicorns and princesses, unicorns and fairies. Then she called Jake.

He picked up after five rings. He sounded groggy.

"I'm not waking you, am I?" she said.

"What time is it?"

"Eleven—oh, damn, twelve thirty. I did wake you, didn't I? Sorry. You know how I am about time."

"What is it, Min?"

"I just wanted to make sure you're all right. When you didn't come back after your walk, Eva and I were . . . concerned."

"I have to be up early tomorrow. Didn't Bruce tell you?"

"Oh, yes, of course he did. It's just that we wondered if maybe that was an excuse. If maybe the truth was that you didn't want to come up."

"Why wouldn't I want to come up?"

"I don't know. I had an instinct."

"Then your instinct was wrong. I intended—*intended*—to make it an early night. There was no ulterior motive."

"I'm glad to hear that. You can't know, Jake, how important this apartment is to Eva. It means the world to her that you've agreed to do it."

"But I haven't."

"Well, no, not officially."

"No, not just not officially."

"But why not? What's holding you back?"

"It's a big project. It will involve a lot of travel. I need to think about it."

An idea flashed in Min's mind. "Would it be any incentive if I were to tell you that if you do the apartment, I can guarantee you the cover of the magazine?"

"The cover of *Food & Wine*?"

"I've left *Food & Wine*. I'm at *Enfilade* now."

"Oh, I hadn't heard."

"I only just started . . . Look, I wasn't going to say anything about this yet, but I might as well. Yesterday I pitched the idea to my editor—she's marvelous, by the way, young and fresh, full of new ideas—and the way she sees it, it's a natural fit. I mean, look at our demographic. Middle-aged women. Well, what do we have here? A middle-aged woman— we won't say middle-aged, of course, Eva would hate that— goes to Venice and on the spur of the moment buys this gorgeous apartment. Voilà! A new life in the old world. Renovation as romance."

"But I thought she was buying it because of the election."

"Oh, that's part of it. It's just not the part we'll talk about."

"Have you run this by Eva?"

"Not yet—I wanted to tell you first. Of course, I know how she'll respond. First she'll demur—that's the correct use of *demur*, by the way, to protest, so often people use it as if it's the verb form of *demure*, but hey, one learns a few things in the editing trade. But as I was saying . . . What was I saying?"

"That she'll demur."

"Oh, she'll pretend to demur. She'll make me twist her arm—at first. I know Eva. I can read her like a book."

"Then it should be easy."

"The only thing is, before I broach the subject with her, I want to make sure you're on board, because that's the first thing she'll ask about."

"But I just told you. I need to think about it."

"Why?"

"I do have other clients besides Eva."

"Yes, and you also have a staff. On top of which . . . Look, Jake, I'm going to be brutally frank here. The cover of *Enfilade*—it would be a big thing for you. Especially now, since—now, I know you may not want to hear this, but you need to—over the last few years, you've, well, fallen off the decorating map a bit. Don't pretend you haven't."

"I'm not."

"Well, this would put you back on. I mean, how long has it been since you were even in *Enfilade*?"

"You tell me. You work there."

"If it makes any difference, Alison Pritchard's on the cover of the March issue. A beach house in Italy."

"Good for her."

"Doesn't that bother you even a little, that she's getting the cover?"

"Why should it? She's the proverbial squeaky wheel."

"The part that gets my goat is that in the interview we did, she never once mentions you or Pablo. Come on, that must rankle. I mean, where would she be without you?"

"Exactly where she is now. Only she'd have gotten there faster."

"Oh, Jake, why can't you just admit that it bothers you? It's me you're talking to, remember? Min. Min who knows all. Now, I realize I haven't brought this up before, but your being dropped from the last Kips Bay show house—"

"And Alison being added to it."

"Exactly. Well, it sends a message. That you need to start thinking about the future, about growing the firm."

"Why? So that you can have a place to stay in Venice?"

"No! For your own sake. And also, let's be honest, to show up Alison. I mean, it's human nature—the viper nurtured at your bosom. And now the viper's eclipsing you. Don't you care that she's eclipsing you?"

"You talk as if it's a given that all anyone ever thinks about is being eclipsed, or eclipsing. Well, I don't. Maybe once, but not anymore."

"If you were doing better, you wouldn't say that."

"How do you know?"

"Instinct. Besides which, Jake, it's Venice!"

"Venice doesn't need me."

"Maybe not. But Eva does. Now, I'm going to let you in on another little secret. For years she's been dying to have one of her places published. Of course, I've tried, I've pitched every apartment, every house, only no one's ever bitten, because, well, let's face it, apartments on Park Avenue, houses in Litchfield County, they're a dime a dozen in the shelter magazine sector. A Venetian palazzo, on the other hand—"

"An apartment, and it isn't really a palazzo."

"What makes you say that?"

"Anyway, is it even a sure thing, their buying this place?"

"Why do you ask? Did Bruce say something?"

"Who said anything about Bruce?"

"So he did say something. I knew it. I knew there was trouble when he decided to take the dogs for a walk."

"Why?"

"It's how they fight—Bruce taking the dogs for a walk. They aren't like other couples, Jake. They don't scream or yell. That's why I asked you to go with him, I was hoping you might . . . smooth any rough waters. Because if Bruce were to pull the plug on this . . . God, I don't even want to think about it."

"And what makes you think he'll pull the plug on it?"

"So he's *not* pulling the plug on it?"

"I didn't say that."

"So he is?"

"Oh, for God's sake, Min, I didn't say that either."

"OK, sorry. Look, let's just take a deep breath, OK? Let's just take a deep breath and step back for a second and look at this thing objectively. In the event—I'm not saying he is and I'm not saying he isn't—but in the event that Bruce is possibly, maybe thinking about pulling the plug on this apartment that his wife has her heart set on—well, isn't that all the more reason to give the green light to the magazine cover? Because then, if it's a sure thing, he won't be able to."

"Why not?"

"He just wouldn't. The stakes would be too high."

"You're moving too fast, Min. You're asking me to commit to the magazine when I haven't even committed to the apartment."

"Just promise me you'll think about this carefully. That's all I ask."

After they hung up, Min got up again, walked to the refrigerator, took out the stick of sugared butter, and finished it off. She then lit a joint, took a long toke, and returned to bed. That she had just told an immense lie—in fact she had never even mentioned Eva's apartment to her editor, much less obtained her promise to put it on the magazine's cover—mattered less to her, at this moment, than the vision (there was no other word for it) that had come to her in that flash, as if through some celestial agency. Of course, until things fell into place, until reality caught up with the vision, she would have to watch her step. And yet, as she lay in her full-size bed, enjoying the warm drowsiness brought on by the pot, she was not thinking about the care she would have to take during the coming weeks. She was thinking of the magazine cover as she envisioned it, the headline—A NEW LIFE IN THE OLD WORLD—and the photo, which would have to be of the window that gave onto the canal, with the curtains pulled back and the shutters open and the prow of a passing gondola visible through the glass. (But from the *piano nobile* would one be able to see the gondola without leaning out? Oh, well, she could work out that kink later.) And to the left of the window a gondola chair, fitted with a silk cushion with pom-poms on its corners. And beneath it a sliver of the terrazzo floor. Yes, it would be lovely . . .

From her bedside table she picked up her phone: 1:31 A.M. She checked the weather, looked at the headlines in the *Times* and on BuzzFeed, then, as if it were an afterthought, clicked on the *Candy Crush* app. Over the past year Min had spent many more hours playing *Candy Crush* than she would ever admit, usually in bed or on the subway, but sometimes at the office too. On the way home from Eva's tonight, in the taxi, she had nearly cracked level 534 of the Sticky Savannah episode. Now, she decided, she would wrap up level 534 before going to sleep. It shouldn't take too long.

She pressed her forefinger to the icon and was at once immersed in a realm of jelly beans and jujubes and chocolate balls dusted with sprinkles that reminded her of childhood birthday cakes. The game unpaused, the candy apocalypse recommenced.

PART II

8

What Bruce had wanted to tell Jake during their walk—but he couldn't find the words—was that, for almost the first time in his life, he was in the throes of a moral and sentimental dilemma. This dilemma, which had been building for months, had been brought to a point of culmination when Eva suddenly decided she had to have the apartment in Venice. Although its terms were monetary, far more than money was at stake: Bruce understood this much. What he couldn't understand, for the life of him, was how to tease out the manifold strands—financial, emotional, and ethical—of which the dilemma was woven. It was with this untangling that he had hoped Jake could help him.

The facts were manageable, if awful. Back in October, Kathy Pagliaro, his secretary of twenty years, had been diagnosed with stage 3 non-Hodgkin's lymphoma. A week later her husband, Lou, had left her. As a result, she was now in the midst of simultaneous divorce proceedings and chemotherapy. Kathy was fifty-three. She had children and grandchildren, a house in Syosset, and a home equity loan with a balloon payment coming due. Despite these travails, she came in to work punctually at eight each morning, steadfastly refusing the time off Bruce offered her. The sheer nerve with which she was facing down these catastrophic developments in her life humbled Bruce, and incited in him strong feelings of empathy, an emotion with which he was not overly familiar, and which puzzled him in its present intensity. This feeling had no explicitly carnal aspect. Nevertheless, it bore a distinct resemblance to the upside-down feeling of falling in love, as he remembered it from his early days with Eva. All his life Bruce had hewed to an old-fashioned ideal of chivalry that in his marriage took the form of obeisance, the troubadour's sacrificial devotion to the damsel outside whose window he sings. And yet, another aspect of chivalry is courage—the courage that spurs the knight to ride headlong into the dragon's lair and save his beloved. It was this latter impulse, the impulse to rescue, that Kathy's predicament awakened in him and that led him, for the first time in their marriage, to start lying to his wife.

The lies were the sort you told when you were having an affair, yet Bruce wasn't having an affair. All he was doing was driving Kathy twice a week from his office to the outpatient center at Sloan Kettering, sitting with her through her chemotherapy sessions, and then driving her to Penn Station to catch the train to Syosset. When, after the first few sessions, she became too sick to manage the commute, he paid for a room for her at a hotel a block from the hospital. From some sixth sense that Eva would disapprove, he said nothing to her about any of this—not the driving, or the hours at Sloan Kettering, or the hotel room, which he had billed to a company credit card she couldn't access. In case she should call him, he never answered his phone when he was sitting with Kathy in the chemo suite. Instead he would wait until one of the nurses came to look in on Kathy and then go out into the corridor to check the caller's name. If it was Eva, he would break into a cold sweat. If it wasn't Eva, he would return to the suite looking so visibly relieved that the nurse would say something like "Everything OK, Mr. Pagliaro?" For by now the nurses took it for granted that he was Kathy's husband, a misapprehension he did nothing to correct.

What made all this especially baffling was that before her diagnosis, Bruce had never looked upon Kathy as anything but an exceptionally efficient secretary. If he admired her, it was because she was so good at her job, which, with time, had become far more than secretarial, requiring her to keep up with technological innovations in the financial sector by which he himself was flummoxed. If she'd had the chance to get a decent education, he was sure, Kathy could have been a CEO or a senator. But she hadn't had that chance, and so she was a secretary.

Outside the office, they led entirely separate lives. In twenty years, Bruce had never once been to Kathy's house in Syosset, nor she to any of his country houses, and to his apartment only a handful of times, to drop off documents. She knew certain things about him—she had met Eva—just as he knew certain things about her: that her grandparents were immigrants from Sicily, as were Lou's; that they had married straight out of high school; that they owned a small sailboat that on weekends, weather permitting, they took out onto Long Island Sound. Kathy was lean and lithe, with streaked blonde hair and the sort of suntan that can be attained only by spending many active hours outdoors. She was never not on the move, either at Bruce's office, which she managed with lean efficiency, or in

Syosset, where on weekends when the weather made sailing impossible, she and Lou bicycled or played tennis. By profession Lou was a car dealer. As a courtesy to Kathy, Bruce always bought his cars from Lou. When Lou sold Audis, Bruce drove an Audi. When he sold Lexuses, Bruce drove a Lexus. Each time Bruce bought a new car, Eva questioned the necessity of his going all the way out to Syosset to get it when he could just as easily go to a dealer in Manhattan or Connecticut. Nonetheless Bruce persisted in the habit, on the grounds that Lou gave him good deals. His current car, an Outback, he had acquired three weeks before Kathy's diagnosis, when Lou had been made manager of his local Subaru dealership. This was the car in which he now shepherded her to and from the outpatient center. Because of its association with Lou, he wondered if riding in it might upset her.

One afternoon, on their way to the center, he asked her.

"Why should it upset me?" she answered. "It's just a car. Anyway, Lou is the least of my worries now."

By way of reply, Bruce only nodded. That he'd said the wrong thing was obvious; what wasn't obvious was *why* it was the wrong thing.

After a minute, as if guessing at his thoughts, Kathy said, "When Lou left, I think the thing that shocked me most was that I wasn't really shocked. He's never done well with illness. Any time I caught a cold and started sneezing or coughing, he'd tell me to stop making a spectacle of myself. He doesn't want to admit how much illness scares him, so he gets short-tempered.

"I used to think this was a failing on his part. Now, though, I'm not so sure. Because now when I look back—and of course, having cancer puts a different light on everything—I find myself thinking, Wow, when I had a cold, I really did make a spectacle of myself. The kids, too. They learned from me."

"What about Lou?"

"When he gets sick, he just pretends he isn't. Today we'd say he powers through."

"Even so, that's no excuse for what he's done."

"He agrees with you on that. In fact, he calls me at least once a day to tell me so."

"What do you say?"

"What can I say? He wants forgiveness. I won't give him that, but I'll hear him out. At least he's not fighting me on the house."

"There's nothing noble in that. He knows there isn't a chance in hell any judge will give it to him."

"Yes, but it's a sacrifice. The other day Michael, my youngest, went to see him. He says Lou's living in this little crap apartment, practically a motel room. It barely has a kitchen. He only eats takeout.

"The part I can't get my mind around is that if none of this had happened, if I hadn't gotten sick, we'd still be together. I mean, it's not like one of us was having an affair. What it comes down to, I think, is that he's so afraid of losing me, he'd rather get it over and done with. At first I thought that was cowardice, but now I wonder if it's a kind of courage."

They had reached the outpatient center. Bruce dropped Kathy off, parked the Outback, and walked back to join her. The mere sight of the center, as it approached, set his heart racing. Really, he was not much better than Lou. The lobby scared him, as did the patients wandering through it, some dragging their IV drips behind them like dogs on leashes. And yet the lobby might have been that of a hotel. The chemo suite itself was tranquil, the lighting soft, the curtains and carpets colorful but not overly bright, and patterned with beguiling geometries. Usually when Bruce thought of hospitals, he thought of the one in Oshkosh where he'd had his tonsils out, its fluorescent tube lights and nurses in intricately folded caps. At the outpatient center, by contrast, the nurses wore smocks or scrubs. Many were men. Rather than lie in a bed, Kathy received the chemo infusions sitting in a recliner, through a port implanted in her chest. The port was the one thing Bruce still could not quite bring himself to look at.

Each session lasted three hours. During this time, he sat next to Kathy in an armchair. At her request he would raise or lower the shade on the window with a remote control. The suite looked out onto the flags that festooned the entrance to a famous old club of which several of his clients were members, and to which he had never been invited. He told Kathy this. He told her that when he spent time with these clients, all fixtures of old-money New York, he felt like "country come to town." This made her laugh.

"I've never thought of you as country come to town," she said.

"Oh, but I am," he said. "My grandfather had a dairy farm. When I was growing up, I spent my summers there . . ."

But she had fallen into a doze. Gingerly he took his laptop out of his briefcase, opened it, and spent half an hour reading about experimental treatments for non-Hodgkin's lymphoma. One of these had only a forty percent success rate, but of the forty percent, five years afterwards ninety percent were cancer free. Another was so new that it was unlikely Kathy's insurance would pay for it. When he'd had enough of this research, he looked Lou up on Google and found his profile on the website of the Subaru dealership. He looked up their children. Danny, the eldest, sold real estate in Manitoba. Susie, the middle child, had a criminal record, the details of which Bruce could obtain if he joined a website that charged $19.95 a month. Michael had a Twitter feed, according to which he "♥♥♥Carly Rae Jepsen" and aspired to a career in interior design.

Ashamed by his own curiosity, Bruce closed the laptop. He gazed at Kathy in sleep. She was tall, with sharp features and dark eyes. The wig she wore, the same streaked blonde as her own hair, didn't look like a wig. Everyone liked her—the portfolio managers, the administrative assistants and the client service specialists, the IT guy and the receptionist and the clients themselves, especially the old-money ones, the ones who belonged to the club across the street. With the old-money women, Kathy exchanged recipes, with the men the sort of genteel courtesies that in another era passed for flirtation. Privately Bruce wondered if Kathy reminded these clients of the teachers and governesses of their youth. Like a teacher, she always spoke in complete sentences. She dressed cheerfully, in pink or blue pantsuits and skirt suits and silk blouses. Her manner on the phone, at once deferential and brisk, had a calming effect on the clients when they called in a panic because the Dow had suddenly plunged. Only in sleep did she look vulnerable. Her mouth hung half open, like a child's. Her left arm was crossed over her breasts.

After half an hour, her eyelids fluttered open. She glanced around the room in bewilderment, regaining her composure when her gaze met Bruce's.

"How are you feeling?"

"So-so."

"Do you want anything to eat?"

She shook her head. One unexpected effect of the chemo was that she had lost her taste for nearly all foods. Even Chinese food and chocolate, once her favorites, she could no longer stomach. The chemo, she had told Bruce, left a terrible taste in her mouth that only the crudest flavors could mask. Barbecue potato chips and cinnamon buns, the sort that sell for a dollar each in the vending machine, were the things she most often asked for.

Sometimes Susie, her daughter, showed up at the sessions, always unannounced and in a condition of turmoil. Susie was in her early thirties, with dyed black hair that fell in ragged bangs over her forehead. She wore tight black leggings and a leather jacket and was never without an immense handbag from which coins, crumpled envelopes, straws, cigarettes, lighters, restaurant leftovers in Styrofoam boxes, Lego blocks, a cell phone with a cracked screen, and the "decoupages" that, she persisted in claiming, would someday make her rich were perpetually spilling. Her visits were muddled and chaotic, punctuated by sudden unannounced disappearances when she would go outside to smoke. Over time, Bruce, to his own surprise, began to feel something like affection for her. At his request she showed him the decoupages, anarchic constructions of glue and lacquer and photographs X-Acto-knifed from supermarket tabloids—dissonant, yes, amateurish, yes, and yet he could not deny that they had a certain power, outsize and uncouth as Susie herself and, like Susie, almost endearing in their vehemence. Unlike her mother, Susie did not speak in complete sentences. She did not, so far as Bruce could tell, have complete thoughts. In lieu of conversation, she delivered ragged monologues, mostly about killer mold. "It's because of killer mold that the girls and me are living with Mom," she told him when they met. "First we were living in this apartment in Queens Village, only there was this killer mold, and the landlord wouldn't answer my texts or return my calls, and Chloe, my youngest, her asthma—she has asthma—was getting worse. So then I got the landlord's address, this fancy house in Little Neck, and I went and rang the doorbell, and it's his wife who answers, and I go, 'You've got kids—would you want your kids coughing their lungs out?' and she goes, 'You better leave now or I'll call the cops.' But I must have gotten through to her, because the next day the landlord guy calls and he's like 'Nice trick, OK, if you're that miserable, I have another apartment you can have—it's in Flushing—only you have to sign a letter saying there isn't any killer mold.' So I signed the letter even though it was coercion, and we moved to Flushing and, would you believe, there was even more killer mold in that apartment than the other, so I stopped paying rent and we got evicted and now my credit is shot and no one will rent to me, even though I sent a letter to the housing authority saying I wasn't only thinking of myself, there were all the other people in the building, all the other children, but the housing authority wouldn't do anything, and that's why we had to move back in with Mom and Dad, but if they think I'm giving up they're wrong, because I've got pictures, I've got samples I scraped off the walls, forensic evidence, and as soon as I start making money from my decoupages, I'm going to sue the shit out of that lying scumbag and use the money to make him clean up his slums and help the kids there."

"When did you move in with your mother?"

"A year ago."

"A year and three months," Kathy corrected.

It amazed Bruce that she had never told him any of this. After Susie left, he asked her why. "What would have been the point?" she said. "You might as well know, I'm not the same person at home I am at the office. Home is supposed to be where you relax after work. For me work is where I relax after home.

"Of course, it could be worse. Both home *and* work could be terrible. They are for most people. If it was just Michael, it would be easy. Michael's low-maintenance."

"He lives with you, too?"

"He's never moved out. He's only twenty-five."

"Couldn't you find Susie an apartment?"

"No one will rent to her."

"Can't Lou help?"

"You can take that up with him."

After the session ended, Bruce walked Kathy to her hotel. "Tonight I think I'll take a bath," she said as they stood together in the lobby, waiting for the elevator. "My room has this lovely, big tub, all clean and white. I'll fill it up with bubbles and have a good soak and then wrap a towel around my head, the way women do in movies. It's something I never get to do at home. At home there's just the one tub, and it gets scummy."

This remark took Bruce aback. At first he couldn't figure out why. Indeed, it was only when he was walking to the garage that he figured it out. When Kathy and Lou had taken out the home equity loan, she'd told him it was so they could build an addition onto their house: a master suite with a whirlpool tub. She'd asked him if he thought they could afford it, and he'd said that, yes, in his professional opinion, they could. Now she'd let the truth slip: Whatever she'd spent the money on, it wasn't a master suite with a whirlpool tub.

9

The sun was setting. From the garage where he had left it, Bruce fetched the Outback and drove it to his own garage. From there he took a taxi home. It was the Monday before the inauguration, three days before Eva and Min were scheduled to leave for Venice. He wished it wasn't a Monday. He wished it was a Tuesday, since on Tuesday nights Eva always had friends over and he was absolved of the need to talk. On Tuesday nights he could just sit back and let the bright chatter wash over him, whereas on Mondays, by long tradition, he and Eva stayed home and had one of the three pastas that constituted her culinary repertoire: penne with shrimp and asparagus, linguine with pesto, new potatoes, and green beans, or fusilli with ham, peas, cream, and the tomato sauce that Amalia made in batches and froze. On Monday nights they ate at the kitchen table. They went to bed early. For most of his married life, Monday nights had been Bruce's favorite; if it were up to him, he'd once told Jake, each week would include extra Mondays, three or four at least. Now he dreaded Mondays, because these were the nights when he and Eva had to talk, and therefore the nights when he was most likely to have to lie to her.

No sooner had he let himself into the apartment than Ralph, Caspar, and Isabel laid siege to him, their welcome so ecstatic a stranger might have thought he'd just come back from a war. "It's me," he called to Eva, hanging up his coat and shaking the dogs off his legs.

"In here," she answered from the kitchen.

He pushed through the swinging door. When he saw the package of fusilli on the counter, the water bubbling in one pot and the tomato sauce in another, his mouth watered. A feeling of homecoming suffused him. "I'm afraid I'm running a little late," Eva said, reaching to open the refrigerator and at the same time giving him a kiss that was cursory but not without tenderness. To his own surprise, he held her fast for a moment, breathing in her familiar scent of perfume (Jardins de Bagatelle) and shampoo (Molton Brown) and the creams and serums (La Prairie) that she rubbed every day onto her face, her neck and arms, around her eyes. As was her habit on Mondays, she wore her hair in a loose ponytail. She had on Gap jeans, an avocado-green cashmere turtleneck, the same apron that Matt Pierce wore when he cooked for her.

For a few seconds she withstood his embrace, then slipped out of it, opened the refrigerator, and took out the bowl of grated Parmesan. Bruce sat at the table, which was already laid, and on which a bottle of red wine breathed.

"How was your day?" she asked.

"Oh, you know, the usual," he said—which was not, strictly speaking, a lie, since on Mondays going with Kathy to the outpatient center had become the usual. "And yours?"

"I had a bit of a scene with Amalia today."

"Oh? What happened?"

"Well, this morning when I went into the kitchen, she was watching *Good Morning America*. Of course the second she saw me, she switched it off. I only caught a glimpse, but it was enough. That face. One thought pollutes the day . . . Who said that?"

"I don't know."

"Anyway, I was so bent out of shape, I decided to have a talk with her there and then, so I sat her down at the table. 'Amalia,' I said, 'this is my house, and in my house, when that man appears on the television, we change the channel.'"

"What did she say to that?"

"Nothing. She just nodded in that way she has, that way that means 'I'm hearing you, but I'm not listening to you.' So then I said, 'Amalia, how can you bear to look at him when he wants to build a wall along the border and send all your relatives back to Honduras?' And she got very snippy and said, 'All my relatives are legal.'"

"I'm not surprised."

"That all her relatives are legal?"

"No, that she got snippy."

"Why should she have gotten snippy?"

"Well, it isn't really your business, is it?"

"She needs to know what she's up against."

"I'm sure she knows exactly what she's up against."

The water for the pasta had come to a boil. Eva threw in some sea salt, and the water surged and spat from the pot, hitting the stove's control panel so hard it switched on the convection oven. She screamed and jumped back.

"Jesus!" Bruce said, leaping up and knocking over his chair.

"I'm fine," Eva said, putting her thumb in her mouth. "Get out of the way. Damn. I forgot to turn the heat off before I added the salt. Why did I forget? I never forget."

With a pair of potholders she moved the water to another burner, brought it back to a boil, and shook in the fusilli.

"It's just a little burn," she said, looking at her thumb.

"I'll get the Neosporin."

"It's all right, I don't need Neosporin."

Bruce sat down again. He poured himself a glass of wine.

"It's him," she said. "He's that water. That hissing, spitting water." She tested one of the fusilli for doneness. "Min says I was the same when Bush Two was elected, but I don't think that's true. I mean, I never hated Bush personally. The thing about—there I go, I almost said his name. I'm afraid to say his name. It's like a curse. The thing about that man is that what I feel for him is pure hatred, absolute blind hatred . . . Honestly, Bruce, I think the world's gone mad. How do you live in a world that's gone mad without going mad yourself? By the way, we couldn't get rooms at the Gritti. Instead we'll be staying at this new hotel—a friend of Min's is writing it up for *Travel & Leisure*, after which it'll be huge, but for now hardly anyone knows about it. She says it's a twenty-first-century take on the old-fashioned Venetian pensione—you know, like the one Katharine Hepburn stays at in *Summertime*. Speaking of which, do you know what Sandra told me? The reason Katharine Hepburn had the shakes all those years was because when she was filming *Summertime*, she fell into a canal and caught some disease."

"Not a great advertisement for Venice, is it?"

"I doubt it's true. It's probably just a legend."

Eva drained the pasta, tossed it with the sauce, and heaped it into bowls. They ate with spoons. "Don't eat so fast," Eva said, which was what she always said on Monday nights.

"Sorry," Bruce said. And to himself: *Chew each bite ten times*.

"I hope you'll be all right while I'm away. Will you go to Connecticut this weekend?"

"Probably not."

"I figured you wouldn't, so I phoned Rachel Weisenstein and she's invited you to dinner on Friday."

He put down his spoon. "And what if I don't want to go to dinner at the Weisensteins' on Friday?"

"All right, no need to bite my head off."

"I'm not biting your head off. I'm just saying, you'll only be out of town for ten days. I don't need babysitters."

"Fine. I'll call her and tell her you can't come. I'll make something up."

"No, don't do that. I'll do my duty."

He returned his attention to his food.

"You've never liked them, have you?"

"Who?"

"Aaron and Rachel."

"He's a loudmouth. I was hoping for a break."

"From what?"

"Just a break."

Now it was Eva who put down her spoon. "You're looking forward to my being gone, aren't you?"

"Well, and what if I am? You are."

"It's being somewhere else I'm looking forward to, not being away from you."

Despite his chewing each bite ten times, his bowl was empty. "Who's for seconds?" he asked, as he asked every Monday night.

"I wouldn't care for any more, thank you," Eva said.

She pushed away her bowl, which was still three-quarters full.

"Actually, now that I think about it, I wouldn't either," he said. "I need to watch my waistline."

He got up and began rinsing his dishes in the sink. "One thing's for sure," he said. "You'll get great pasta in Venice."

There was no answer.

"Eva?"

But she had left the room.

At nine he took the dogs for their walk. An earlier rain had left the potholes full of water that darkened their paws.

As he turned onto Madison, he ran into Alec Warriner, surreptitiously kicking a turd from where Sparky had deposited it into the sidewalk grate.

"Caught in the act," Alec said. "I forgot to bring a bag."

"A likely story," Bruce said. "Anyway, don't worry, I'll let you off with a warning. This time."

For the first time in their lives, the men walked together. Whereas in the elevator Bruce's dogs had ganged up on Sparky, out here, on neutral ground, they ignored him. Paying no heed to another dog, pretending it wasn't there—this was the canine way of indicating acceptance. Often Bruce wished people would behave more like dogs.

"He's reading the newspaper," Alec said when Sparky, for the fourth time in five minutes, stopped to sniff the pavement.

"I wonder if they learn more from theirs than we do from ours," Bruce said.

"It's hard to imagine they learn less," Alec said. He looked Bruce in the eye. "You don't have kids, do you?"

Bruce shook his head.

"Me, I've got two daughters. Well, *had*. Oh, sorry, that sounds like one of them died. What I mean is that our elder daughter just disowned us. That's the word she used—*disowned*—when she wrote to tell her mother and me that she plans never to speak to us again, and that she no longer regards us as her parents, and that if we make any further attempts to contact her, she'll have our phone numbers and emails blocked."

"What brought that on?"

"The election. It was because we voted for Trump. Tell your wife if you like. I'm sure it'll make her feel better."

This embarrassed Bruce. "You know, if I thought it would make any difference, I'd apologize for Eva," he said. "Short of that, I'd tell you to take her behavior with a grain of salt, only I know a grain of salt wouldn't be nearly enough. You'd have to swallow a tablespoon of salt, maybe more, certainly more than anyone should be expected to stomach. Anyway, I'm sorry about your daughter—that she's so angry."

"*She's* angry? What about me? Of course, the great pity of it is that this is the daughter who lives near us. Well, nearer. Nearness has been relative for Kitty and me since our youngest moved to Phnom Penh."

"In Cambodia?"

"Affirmative. That's Rebecca. We haven't seen her in three years. Judy's in Boston. She's a lawyer, with three kids she now says we're not to make any attempt to contact or she'll get a restraining order. You can imagine what that's done to Kitty."

"And all this because of the election?"

"According to her, yes. In retrospect, I see that my mistake was telling her how I voted in the first place. I should have lied, I should have said that at the last minute I had a change of heart and voted for Hillary, only I couldn't—and not just because I knew she'd never believe me. The truth is, my conscience just won't allow me to say I voted for that woman, not even to preserve my relationship with my daughter."

"Do you really think Hillary's that bad?"

"Your wife thinks we're evil. Well, we think she's evil. Hillary, I mean."

"So you're saying you voted more against Hillary than for Trump?"

"I know that's what you'd like me to be saying, but it's not. The fact is, I was pro-Trump early on. At first I kept quiet about it. I mean, even with my Republican friends, when the question came up, I'd say I hadn't made up my mind yet, or that I wanted to see how the debates played out, or that all I cared about was keeping *her* out of office and getting the corporate income tax below twenty-one percent. Now I'm convinced that a lot of us were doing that—lying to each other. It affected the polls, I'm convinced.

"The fact is, on election night *we* were the ones who were expecting the worst. Kitty and I invited some friends over, mostly so that we could get drunk and commiserate. Believe me, no one could have been more surprised than we were when the results started coming in. That was why we went a little wild. We couldn't believe it. It seemed like a miracle."

"One man's miracle is another's nightmare, I guess."

"Mind you, I get why you dislike him. I really do. The thing is, though, I also get *him*. I mean, sure, he's crass, but at least he's *our* crass, you know what I'm saying? New York crass. Now, Rand Paul—there's a guy I don't get. There's a guy who seems to be from another planet. Guys like Donald, I've known them my whole life. At Wharton, I was just a few years behind him. I'll admit it, I've been to Mar-a-Lago a few times. Crazy tacky, sure, but at the same time, there's something sort of fun about it, like going to Disney World and sleeping in Cinderella's castle. Now, I'm not saying we're friends, or even that I like him especially, I'm just saying that I understand him, how his brain works, what he's after, which is more than I can say for . . . But I'd rather not say her name. It gives me the heebie-jeebies to say her name."

"Don't you worry that he's a loose cannon?"

"And she's not? I mean, just for example, right now the Pelosi crowd's in a tizzy about his having the nuclear codes, right? Well, the way I see it, the really scary thing would be *her* having the nuclear codes, because she's such a hawk. As for him, tell me honestly, do you really think he'd ever do anything to put all his precious real estate at risk?"

"Have you told your daughter this?"

"Judy? She'd hang up before I got three words out. Now that I think about it, it was probably because of her that I kept my mouth shut all that time about voting for Trump. But now that she's not speaking to me, my attitude is, why hold back? Why not come out of the closet? Why not throw a party?"

"Still, you must miss her sometimes."

"My wife misses her. As for me . . . I have to be honest, there are times when I wish we'd never had kids in the first place. A whole category of difficulties removed."

"And yet there's a loneliness. Especially as you get older. This feeling of something not being there that should."

"As opposed to something being there that shouldn't?"

"What's the difference?"

"You tell me. Aren't you finance guys supposed to see every loss as a potential gain?"

Bruce did not reply. Alec was right. The idea that losses could be turned into gains was so fundamental to his way of understanding the world that he had never questioned it.

They turned left. "My secretary has cancer," he said, not quite believing he was saying it.

"I'm sorry to hear that. What kind?"

"Lymphoma . . . She's a good person. She's worked for me for twenty years. I'm trying to help her, only I have to keep it from my wife."

"You mean you want to give her money?"

It was only when Alec said it that Bruce realized that this was exactly what he meant.

"If I did, and Eva found out, she'd be angry. She'd say I was getting too involved."

"Translation—she'd think you were sleeping with her. Are you sleeping with her?"

"No, of course not. And you're wrong—Eva would never think that."

"Why not? It's the obvious thing to think. Sparky, no!" The dog was lunging at a shadow, obliging Alec to reel him in. "Well, if you want my opinion, the solution is obvious. You should sleep with your secretary. I mean, as long as you're going through all the trouble of keeping the thing a secret, you might as well get something out of it, right? Oh, God, was that an offensive thing to say? I guess it was. Sorry, I've got a bit of a problem with that. I'm like Sparky, my wife says. I leap before I look."

"But you're right," Bruce said, "it is the obvious thing to think. In fact, it surprises me that I hadn't thought it myself. Or even thought that other people might think it. People who haven't met Kathy, and possibly people who have."

"Kathy's your secretary?"

"She's fifty-three. She has three children and two grand-children. Oh, and on top of everything else, her husband's left her. And she's got serious money problems."

"If her husband was the one who left, at least she'll get something out of the divorce, won't she?"

"She'll get the house. She might get more—if she lives long enough." Bruce stopped in his tracks. "Jesus, I can't believe I'm saying these things. Helping people plan against future catastrophes—it's what I do. Why haven't I done that for her?"

"What is your job exactly?"

"According to my website, I'm a quote-unquote wealth management adviser, though I still think of myself as a stock-broker. And Kathy is my quote-unquote executive assistant, though I still think of her as my secretary. And that means she doesn't have any wealth to manage—or at least not enough to make it worth my while. Or hers. Now I'd really like to do something more for her."

"Well, but what more could you do? She has benefits, right? That's doing something for her. Before I retired, I always made sure all my employees had health insurance, even though it cost me an arm and a leg."

"That's more than your president has done."

"*Our* president. No matter what you think of him, he's our president now."

They were back at the building. "Well, it's been nice walking with you," Bruce said.

"It has," Alec said. "Maybe we can do it again sometime—if you can bear the idea."

"I'd like that," Bruce said, signaling the doorman not to bother holding the door for him. "If you don't mind, I think I'll just go around the block one more time. Isabel still hasn't done anything."

They said a quick goodbye. As Bruce walked back down Park, he wondered if he should just tell Eva about taking Kathy to her chemo sessions and be done with it. There was nothing to disapprove of in that. You couldn't disapprove of compassion—or could you? Maybe—if you perceived that compassion as part of another woman's strategy to supplant you. Of course, to ascribe such a motive to Kathy would be unjust. Surely he could explain that much to Eva. Surely he could explain that all he had paid for was the hotel room—and not because Kathy had asked him. It was a gesture of munificence, performed of his own free will. Or would that upset Eva more—that Bruce, who for all the years of their marriage had let her buy his clothes, and decide which restaurants they went to, and where they took their vacations, and who their friends were, was suddenly acting of his own free will?

Mind you, he wasn't complaining. Without Eva, he knew, his life would have been . . . not less interesting, exactly, but less full: no demands that he read magazine articles that gave him headaches, no listening to her friends arguing across the dinner table, no death marches through exhibitions at the one Met or season tickets at the other (occasionally used, more often given away like party favors). On the other side, more TV, more time spent with his parents, fewer weekend guests. Change for its own sake had little appeal for Bruce. He hadn't asked Kathy to get sick, or anticipated the vein of empathy her plight would open in him. Nor, as far as he knew, had he said anything to give himself away to Eva. Or had he? Doubtless he shouldn't have lost his temper over the Weisensteins' dinner invitation. He should have just chewed his temper ten times, as he had each bite of dinner, until it was ground to a pulp. Then the conversation that had ended with Eva walking out of the kitchen would never have taken place. But he *had* lost his temper—an invigorating sensation, a liberating sensation, for which he knew he would pay the price. Eva wouldn't make a scene. That wasn't her way. Instead she would withdraw into haughty formalities. *No, I wouldn't care for any more, thank you.* Having a secret from her—he had to admit it—exhilarated him.

It had started raining again. Suddenly he heard sirens, saw an ambulance racing toward him. For the past ten minutes, he realized, he had been letting the dogs lead him rather than the other way around. As usual, they walked with urgency, as if they were late for an appointment, though where it was they were trying to get to, home or away, he had no idea. He just followed.

Two days later, Min and Eva left for Venice. As the doorman put their luggage into the trunk of the taxi, Bruce stood on the sidewalk with the dogs and Min, waiting for his wife. Min had her phone out. At first he thought she was texting. Then he saw that she was playing a game.

The second she noticed him noticing, she put the phone in her purse.

"Busted," she said. "OK, I confess. I'm an addict. *Candy Crush*."

"Candy what?"

"You don't know what it is? So much the better." She smiled. "Well, darling, ten days on your own. While the mouse is away, will the cat play?"

"Maybe the cat will play Candygram."

"*Candy Crush*. And I wouldn't recommend it. It's ruinous. Almost as bad as gambling."

Right then Eva came out the door, looking sleek and elegant in a Burberry raincoat and black boots.

"Well, bon voyage," Bruce said to Min.

"Buon viaggio," Min said. And when he kissed her on the cheek: "Not enough. In Italy it's *due baci*, two kisses, left then right. Whereas in Holland it's three kisses—left, right, left. And if you're wondering how I know so much about kissing, during the five minutes when I was at *CN Traveler*—"

"Min, come on," Eva said, ushering her into the car before Bruce could deliver the second kiss.

Min obeyed. Eva and Bruce were now alone on the curb with the dogs.

"It's stopped raining," he said.

She agreed that it had.

"I'm relieved. I didn't want to say anything, but yesterday the flight you're on was delayed three hours. The night before, it was delayed five hours. Whereas tonight"—he glanced at his phone—"not only are you scheduled for an on-time departure, you're supposed to get into Milan forty minutes early. The weather in Venice is sunny—high fifty-seven, low thirty-four."

"You've certainly kept yourself up to the minute."

"It's just that I've got this app."

"Bruce, I hope you understand how much I need this trip. You do understand that, don't you?"

"Of course," he said. Then he tried to kiss her on the lips, but she moved her head so that he kissed her chin instead. Sensing departure, the dogs stood up on their hind legs and tried to lick Eva's and Bruce's faces.

"They want to get in on the action," Bruce said.

"Goodbye, sweethearts," Eva said, bending down to rub their ears. "Take care of Daddy. I'll miss you."

She got into the car with Min. As it pulled away from the curb, the dogs whined and tried to give chase. Bruce held them back by their leashes with one hand and waved with the other. Even though he could see through the rear window that Eva hadn't turned around, that she wasn't looking at him, he kept waving, until the car was lost in the surge of uptown traffic.

10

The next night, as was required of him, he went to the Weisensteins' for dinner. They lived on West End Avenue, in an apartment with scuffed parquet floors that squeaked underfoot and windows that rattled whenever a bus went by. "I'm afraid there's a bit of a crisis in the kitchen," Rachel said, accepting the bottle of wine Bruce had brought and sitting him down on an old sofa covered in balding olive-green velvet and draped with pilled cotton blankets. "What would you like to drink?"

"Gin and tonic," he said, a drink he never would have asked for had Eva been there. Had Eva been there, he would have asked for white wine.

"Aaron, could you make Bruce a gin and tonic?" Rachel called.

"I'm busy!" Aaron yelled through the door to the kitchen, from which a smell of frying fish emanated.

"Try to make yourself comfortable," Rachel said, which might have been a joke, given that the sofa sagged so much that when Bruce sat, his behind nearly touched the floor, dust flew up from the cushions, the springs dug into his back. On the coffee table, yellowing sections of last Sunday's *Times* lay strewn, along with back issues of magazines he'd never heard of, and advance copies of books by writers he'd never heard of, and an open laptop on the screen of which psychedelic bubbles burst into infinity.

After a minute or so, an immense white cat emerged from an open door, sauntered over to the sofa, jumped onto Bruce's lap, and put a paw on each of his shoulders. The cat stared at him. One of its eyes was blue, the other yellow.

Rachel came out again with his drink and a bowl of Japanese rice crackers. When she sat next to him, her knees rose to the level of her breasts, as if she were a folded-up penknife. She herself was drinking whiskey, neat. "That's Mumbles," she said of the cat, who was nuzzling Bruce's cheeks. "He's a whore. You're a whore, Mumbles."

Bruce sneezed.

"Are you allergic?"

"A little."

"I think I've got some antihistamines—"

"Don't worry."

Rachel didn't get up. She was in her late forties, with glasses that were always slipping down her nose and brown hair tied up in an improvisatory chignon.

"Aaron's doing one of his Chinese whole fish," she said hopelessly.

"What kind of fish is it?"

"Some huge fish. I think it's called a scump. He's only doing it because Eva's not here. You know how much she hates smelly foods, the way the smell gets into her clothes."

It occurred to Bruce that with her prominent teeth, her pale eyes and bony back, Rachel herself might be a fish, or a woman metamorphosed into a fish.

"Has Eva gotten safely to Venice? How are she and Min doing?"

"Fine, I think. All I've gotten so far is a text saying they've arrived. That and a few photos."

"Oh, good, let's have a look."

"They're not that interesting. Bridges and canals mostly."

"Is there anything else in Venice besides bridges and canals?"

"Churches. And cats." He looked meaningfully at Mumbles, who was now making bread on his lap.

"And you're OK on your own?"

Why did everyone seem to think he wouldn't be OK on his own?

"I'm fine."

"We were worried you might be at a loose end. Especially with that awful inauguration party happening next door. Well, think of this as an anti-inauguration party."

The noise that exploded from the kitchen Bruce would have described as a sizzle had it not been so loud. He thought: *Aaron is boiling someone in oil.*

"It's always a bit of a production when Aaron does a whole fish," Rachel went on. "Well, we've got a nice group together for tonight. Jake's coming—I know you like Jake. And Sandra Bleek. You remember her—Grady's cousin, the one who was at your house that Saturday when Eva, when she wanted us to say that thing to Siri?"

Though he remembered the afternoon, Bruce didn't remember Sandra herself until she came through the door—a tiny woman with an immense quantity of white-streaked hair, parted in the middle and plummeting over her shoulders. This hair gave her face a masklike quality that put Bruce in mind, all at once, of toy poodles, cartoon witches, and Cousin Itt from *The Addams Family*.

"Welcome to our anti-inauguration party," Rachel said, kissing Sandra on the cheek.

"Your what?"

"Our anti-inauguration party, during which we don't think about the inauguration. Collectively."

"What an interesting idea," Sandra said, sitting down on a slipper chair into which Bruce himself could never have fit. "And where are the twins tonight?"

"Out. We mean nothing to them anymore."

"How old are they now?"

"Just turned eighteen."

Bruce was surprised. The last time he'd noticed the Weisensteins' twins—he couldn't remember their names—they'd been children.

"It was the same with Lara," Sandra said. "The day she turned sixteen, I took her to get her driver's license and that was the last I ever saw of her."

"You let her drive in the city?" Rachel said.

"No, this was on Long Island. My husband and I—my soon-to-be ex-husband and I—have—*had*—two places, an apartment near Lincoln Center and a house in Bridgehampton. Not one of those fancy beach houses, just an old ramshackly cottage that we bought in the nineties and never got around to fixing up. I'm supposed to be living there now. That's what the judge ordered—that until the divorce is finalized, I get the house in Bridgehampton and Rico gets the apartment, even though it was my apartment before we got married. The lease is in my name. Her reasoning is that Rico has to be in the city for his job, whereas I don't have a job, so I can be anywhere, which I think is totally sexist. I mean, just because I don't go to an office doesn't mean I don't have a job."

"Still, to be fair, you don't *have* to be in the city for your job. You can do it in the country. You can do it anywhere."

"But I need the city. I'm not given to hibernation. I can't just sit out on Long Island all winter, staring at the leafless trees."

"You mean you'd rather sit out at Grady's house in Connecticut staring at the leafless trees?"

"At least I've got him there, when he's there and not off on one of his cruises. Plus, twice a week he has a car drive him into the city. I can get a lift. And it's a much easier drive than from Bridgehampton. There's a lot less traffic."

"What kind of work do you do?" Bruce asked.

"Sandra's a writer," Rachel said.

"No, I'm not," Sandra said.

"Oh, come on," Rachel said. "You write."

"Ask your husband. That I write doesn't make me a writer, it makes me an apprentice. An aspirant. I haven't yet earned the right to call myself a writer."

"She's working with Aaron," Rachel said.

"Congratulations," Bruce said. "What's the book?"

"There is no book," Sandra said. "I mean, Aaron's not publishing me. I'm just working with him."

"After Aaron got laid off, he decided to go freelance," Rachel said.

"Aaron got laid off?"

"In December. Didn't Eva tell you?"

The truth was, Bruce couldn't remember if Eva had told him or not. She told him so many things about so many people, he had trouble keeping them straight.

"I'm sorry to hear that," he said.

"Thank you," Rachel said. "When it happened, we were pretty torn up about it, as you can imagine. With time, though, we've come to realize that it was for the best. Publishing is so corporate these days, much more so than when we started out. His job stifled Aaron. Sometimes you have to get out of something before you see how miserable it's been making you."

"That was certainly the case with my marriage," Sandra said.

"In any case, I've still got *my* job," Rachel said, "so at least there's a steady income, even if it's only a little more than half of what it used to be."

"And you don't find *your* job stifling?" Sandra asked.

Rachel gazed into her whiskey. "At the end of the day, women are more pliable than men. It comes from having children, I suppose. Having children, you get used to not being free."

"It's true," Sandra said, then added, turning to Bruce, "In some ways I envy you and Eva, not having kids."

This was the second time in two days that Bruce had been envied for his lack of children.

"Oh, I don't know," he said. "It's a trade-off, I guess."

"You know, I've often thought of asking Eva about that," Rachel said, "only—well—it's such a delicate subject. I worry she might not want to talk about it."

The way Rachel looked at Bruce, he got the feeling she was hoping he would make up for Eva's reticence. Lucky for him, the buzzer rang. Startled, Mumbles jumped off his lap, which had gone numb from his weight.

As soon as he saw Jake, bearing flowers and a bottle of wine, Bruce hoisted himself out of the sofa to hug him. "I'm *so* glad you're here," he said under his breath. "They're talking about *children*."

Uncertain how to take this comment, Jake gave the flowers and the wine to Rachel. He hung up his coat. The chaotic indeterminacy of the Weisensteins' apartment made him nervous. The problem was the insufficient differentiation of the rooms, too many of which did double or triple duty—the living room, for instance, which was also the dining room, Rachel's study, and—since he now regarded himself as too old to share a room with his sister, Leah—the bedroom of Ariel, the male twin. Despite the cold weather, the steam heat made Jake sweat. The overhead light gave him a headache. Nevertheless he determined to do his best, because Rachel had called him and said she needed him—"for Bruce's sake."

Now she said, "As I think I told you, Jake, our plan tonight is to ignore the inauguration. To pretend it isn't happening."

"If we're supposed to ignore it, why do you keep bringing it up?" Aaron asked, coming out of the kitchen.

"I'm mentioning it," Rachel said. "Mentioning it isn't the same as bringing it up."

Sweat darkened Aaron's T-shirt, which was too short, revealing a few inches of hairy belly. "That's a fallacious distinction," he said.

"All right, then, how about this? The point of this dinner is to get Bruce away from the party his next-door neighbors are having."

"Actually, if I were home, I probably wouldn't hear anything," Bruce said. "Our building has thick walls, and they've promised to keep the noise down. My guess is they'll just be sitting around drinking gin."

"Or Diet Coke," Jake said.

"Good God, do I have to give up Diet Coke just because Trump drinks it?" Rachel said.

"You ought to give it up anyway," Sandra said. "It kills your brain cells . . . Oh, I've been meaning to ask, are any of you going to the Women's March tomorrow? Lara's insisted that I go with her."

"I'm going," Rachel said. "Whether Aaron joins me remains to be determined."

"You know I can't stand crowds."

"I've even got my hat. I crocheted it myself." From the sideboard, Rachel picked up a cloche-like pink wool cap. When she put it on, Jake saw that it had two horns. Or were they horns?

"Well, what do you think?" she asked, pirouetting. "Oh, and in case you're too embarrassed to ask, Jake, yes, this is exactly what you think it is."

"I'm afraid I don't have any idea—"

"Jake! It's a pussy."

"Oh!"

"Will you be wearing one, Sandra?"

"Only if Lara makes me. I look terrible in pink. How about you, Aaron? If you go, will you wear one?"

But Aaron, with unusual stealth, had returned to the kitchen, from which he reemerged a minute or so later. "Right, the fish is almost ready. Now what else?" He counted on his fingers. "I've got the rice in the rice cooker, the wok on the back burner. What have I forgotten?"

"To say hello," Rachel said.

"Oh, sorry. Bruce, Jake. Oh, hi Sandra. You've met Sandra, right, Jake?"

"Of course he has."

"We met at Eva's," Jake said, kissing Sandra on the cheek.

"Actually, we met before that," Sandra said. "Don't worry, it's not something I'd expect you to remember. It was years and years ago. You came over to my grandmother's apartment with your aunt. Your aunt was her decorator."

"What's your grandmother's name?"

"Isabel Allenby. Does that ring a bell?"

"Ding, ding, ding," Rachel said, at which Sandra laughed—her laugh at once tinselly and gravelly.

"Please, there's no need to pretend. It was eons ago. I was fourteen, and not very memorable. You came a few times with your aunt to see Nana. I was living with her then. It was right after my mother's suicide."

"Oh, I'm sorry," Bruce said.

"One thing I do remember—you did all the measuring."

"In those days measuring was pretty much all I was allowed to do," Jake said. "Even though I was her nephew, Aunt Rose insisted on treating me the way she would any other trainee. As a dogsbody."

"What a curious word, *dogsbody*," Rachel said. "I need to look up the etymology."

"It's old Navy slang," Bruce said. "Back in the day, the joke was that the pease pudding the sailors were fed was so bad it was only fit for dogs. Thus *dog's breakfast* and later *dogsbody*—one whose menial status obliges him to subsist on pease pudding."

"Were you in the Navy?" Sandra asked.

"No, but my father was."

They moved to the dining table, on which Aaron had laid out bowls of rice, sautéed pea shoots, cucumber chunks in chili oil, and some sort of meat with slices of lotus root. The fish, on an immense platter, took center stage. Bits of cilantro, garlic, and hot red pepper clung to its vast and primitive jaw. "They say the head is the best part," Aaron said, taking up what looked like a saw. "It should go to the guest of honor. I think that's you, Bruce."

"Hear, hear," Rachel said as Aaron decapitated the fish and forked the head onto Bruce's plate. An eye stared up at him, the same blue as one of Mumbles's, though he couldn't remember which.

"What kind of fish is this?" Jake asked.

"Scump," Rachel said.

"Scup," Aaron corrected. "Also known as porgy."

"As in *Porgy and Bess*?"

"Maybe."

"Another etymology to look up."

Eating the fish proved a complicated business, because it had so many tiny, vicious bones. "Something that just came back to me," Sandra said to Jake, taking up where she'd left off, "is that when you came to our apartment that first time, Nana told me to take you to my room and quote-unquote entertain you while she had tea with your aunt. And I was mortified, just utterly mortified, because I had no idea what it even meant, to *entertain* someone. A boy, no less. I mean, was I supposed to show you my dolls, or make you a sandwich, or ask you to play Scrabble? And really, it's absurd, when you think about it, this idea grown-ups have that children can just be sent off together and they'll start playing, like dogs."

"And yet as adults we're often put in that same situation," Rachel said. "At book parties, for instance, when someone introduces you to someone else and then leaves you to fend for yourselves."

"It's why, early on, I made it a house rule never to do anything like that with my own daughter," Sandra said. "From the get-go, Lara decided who she played with."

"How old is she now?" Jake asked.

"Twenty-six. Now, I know what you're thinking. You're thinking, That Sandra looks so young, how can she have a daughter who's twenty-six? Was she a child bride? The truth, though, is that I'm older than I look. I was twenty-five when Lara was born. Do the math."

"Do the math, do the math," Aaron said. "Have you noticed how these days, everywhere you turn, someone is telling you to do the math? I can't bear the way these awful phrases creep into the language. Another one that drives me crazy is 'reach out.' When did everyone start 'reaching out'? These are the sort of stupid locutions you need to avoid in your writing, Sandra. Or if you do use them, put them in quote marks."

"Literally?"

"Not necessarily. You can do it with voice. The idea is to make sure the reader catches on that you know the expression is stupid and you're using it ironically."

"Let me write that down," Sandra said, fishing a little notebook and a pen from her purse. The notebook, Bruce observed, was gilt-edged, the pen Montblanc.

"I feel privileged to have the chance to listen in on this conversation," he said, moving the fish head around on his plate. "I mean, how often is it you get to hear writers talking shop?"

"In Sandra's case, it won't be talking shop until she has a shop to talk about," Aaron said.

"What made you decide to take up writing?" Jake asked Sandra.

"Well, there's a fake answer and a real answer to that," Sandra said. "The fake answer is that after my husband and I split up, I had this intense urge to try to redeem my atrocious marriage by turning it into a novel. The real answer is that one

SHELTER IN PLACE 115

day I was shopping—at Hermès, I'll admit it—when I saw this gorgeous notebook—not this one, another one—and I thought, *I have to have that notebook. I just have to.* And so I bought it and brought it home—I still had the apartment then—and when I opened it, suddenly I just wanted to fill it with beautiful handwriting, in beautiful ink."

"Wait a sec, that's not your story," Aaron said. "You got it from Jean Rhys."

"Who's Jean Rhys?"

"I mean, she answered the question of why she became a writer the same way. She said it was because of a notebook she bought. You must have read about it or picked it up somewhere."

"No, honestly. I swear, I've never even heard of Jean Rhys."

"You haven't read *Wide Sargasso Sea*?" Rachel said. "Oh, but you must. It's one of the great works of the twentieth century, told from the point of view of the madwoman in *Jane Eyre*."

"I haven't read *Jane Eyre* either."

"A pity Eva isn't here," Bruce said. "This is just the sort of conversation she'd love."

"Let's hope that Venice inspires Eva to write her own book," Rachel said.

"What book?" Sandra asked.

"A biography of Isabella Stewart Gardner. I've been trying to talk her into doing one for years."

"If she writes it, will you publish it?" Jake asked.

Rachel withdrew her spoon from her mouth. "Well, of course, if it were up to me, I'd publish it in a second, but unfortunately it's not so easy these days. It used to be that if you loved a book, you could just acquire it, but now everything has to get past the marketing people and the sales reps, and biographies are a hard sell."

"That sort of crap answer is the reason I'm glad to be out of publishing," Aaron said. "I mean, listen to you. Out of one side of your mouth, you play cheerleader—'Oh, Eva, you've got to write this book, you've got to write this book'—and then out of the other, it's the usual namby-pamby publishing horseshit—'If it were up to me I'd love to, only the sales reps say this doesn't sell, that doesn't sell, no one reads biographies anymore, no one reads story collections anymore, no one ever read poetry in the first place,' all anyone wants to read are books about what a bitch Hillary Clinton is and quote-unquote graphic novels with no fucking words."

"No wonder you're glad to be out of it," Jake said.

"I am. I'm sick of the horseshit. And it's not just publishers, it's writers. Ninety percent of what gets published is worthless. With any luck, that'll be the silver lining of this fucking election, that when writers start to feel oppressed again they'll start to write books worth reading instead of all that idiotic upper-middle-class self-absorbed liberal navel-gazing crap we got when Obama was president. I mean, Sheila Heti, for Christ's sake. What a stupid fucking book. She's giving some dude a blowjob and she throws up. Who cares?"

"I love Sheila Heti," Sandra said.

"So do I," Rachel said. "You just don't get it because you're a man."

"Fine, then Jeffrey Eugenides. He's a jerk-off. As is Jonathan Fucking Franzen, and Jonathan Fucking Lethem, and Jonathan Asshole Safran Foer. All these fucking Jonathans, they're total jerk-offs."

"This is why I love working with Aaron," Sandra said. "He's so in your face. I find it bracing."

"For God's sake, don't say 'in your face,'" Aaron said. "It's worse than 'do the math.'"

"Sorry. How about this? What I love about Aaron is that he's so no-bullshit."

"Better."

"Eva would eat this up," Rachel said.

"No, she wouldn't, any more than she'd eat up this fish," Aaron said. "Am I right, Bruce?"

"I suspect you're right about the fish," Bruce said.

"It's true that with Eva you feel you have to hold yourself—I don't know—to a higher standard," Rachel said, taking off her pussy hat. "For example, that you ought not to swear so much. I'm not sure that's a bad thing."

"Fuck, yeah," Aaron said.

"What do you think, Jake?"

"Oh, don't ask me," Jake said. "I'm just a decorator."

Everyone looked at him. Had he really said that? He'd thought he was only thinking it.

"But that's fascinating," Sandra said. "Tell us more."

"He means his orientation, his language, is visual," Rachel said.

"Let him speak for himself," Aaron said. "What do you mean, Jake?"

"I'm not sure what I mean."

"There's something to be said for not thinking," Aaron said. "It's often struck me that the best artists are a little stupid. Jean Rhys, for instance."

"Jean Rhys was not stupid," Rachel said.

"Oh, but she was. She couldn't punctuate, and she had no vocabulary. If it hadn't been for Ford Madox Ford, she'd never have had a career."

"That's just plain sexist and you know it."

"But I mean it as a compliment. It's *why* she's a great writer."

"And would you say the same thing about any male writer?"

"Most male writers are too smart for their own good. It makes them assholes."

"That's not an answer to Rachel's question," Sandra said. "Rachel wants you to tell us if there are any male writers you think are good because they're stupid, not if there are any male writers you think are bad because they're smart."

"Is that what Rachel wants? Usually I find it impossible to grasp what Rachel wants."

"You mustn't take Aaron seriously when he's off on one of his tirades," Rachel said.

"Oh, but I love it," Sandra said. "I mean, what he says gives me hope that I may actually stand a chance as a writer, because God knows I'm stupid."

"You are not stupid," Rachel said, slapping her hand.

"Oh, but I am. I don't even have a college degree. I dropped out of three different colleges."

"So what? Amy Hempel doesn't have a college degree, either."

"And there's nothing intellectual about my process. When I write, it doesn't even feel like it's me doing the writing. It's more like—I don't know—channeling. Most of the time, when I look over what I've written, I don't even understand it."

"Unfortunately, neither do I," Aaron said.

"What's it like for you, Jake?" Rachel said. "When you're doing a room, do you plan everything in advance? Is every detail a conscious choice? Is there a point when the room itself starts to tell you what to do?"

"Do you think of the house as a narrative?" Sandra said.

"Do you ever find it's more what you leave out than what you put in?"

"Or that you have to kill your darlings?"

"It's a mix of those things," Jake said.

"Have some more fish. There's plenty," Aaron said, handing around the platter.

"Thank you," Bruce said, and thought, I hate this conversation. I hate bony fish. I never asked to be given the head.

When the evening was over, Rachel helped her guests on with their coats. "Well, I think I can congratulate myself on achieving my goal," she said. "We got through the whole dinner without once talking about the inauguration."

"Until just now, when you reminded us of it," Aaron said.

"Needless to say, it was at the back of my mind the whole time," Sandra said to Bruce and Jake in the elevator. "How could it not be?"

"Of course, Rachel meant well," Jake said. "And she did get you away from that party, Bruce."

"It was Eva who wanted to get away from the party," Bruce said. "Four thousand miles away."

"Venice must be magic," Sandra said.

"Didn't you once live there, Jake?"

"For a while. Ages ago."

They were now on the sidewalk, hands in their pockets, huddled together against the cold. "There's no point in asking me to share a ride, because where I'm going isn't on anyone's way," Sandra said.

"Where are you going?"

"Bushwick. I'm spending the night with my daughter. Just tonight. She won't have me more than that."

"She lives in Bushwick?" Bruce said.

"Haven't you heard?" Sandra said. "Nowadays Bushwick is the place to be. Before that it was Williamsburg and Fort Greene, but they got too expensive."

"I'm such an old fogey," Bruce said. "Even after all these years, I don't know where any of those neighborhoods are. For me, Brooklyn might as well be Albania."

"You need to get out and see more of the city," Sandra said. "Maybe Eva's trip to Venice will give you the chance."

"I wouldn't know where to start."

"If you like, I can take you on a tour of Bushwick. Of course, we'd have to take the subway."

"Or I could drive," Bruce said.

"Oh, my, a car trip to Brooklyn. Let's do it. I'll call you."

"Have you got my number?"

"I've got Eva's number," Sandra said—a bit ambiguously, it seemed to Bruce—as a gleaming SUV, a Lincoln, pulled up to the curb. "Well, here's my ride. Goodnight."

"What was that?" Bruce said after the Lincoln drove off. "Does she have a driver?"

"It's an Uber."

"Oh, yes, of course. I really am an old fogey. I still take cabs. Shall we share one?"

"Sure," Jake said as Bruce lifted his wrist and a taxi pulled up. This seemed to Jake significant—that magnetism for taxis that certain men possess, and that he did not.

In the cab, Bruce said, "She's a strange one, that Sandra. Did you really meet when you were fourteen?"

"When *she* was fourteen. Probably. To be honest, most of that part of my life is a blur."

"Which part do you mean?"

"Oh, let's see, from when I arrived in New York—1987—through . . . well, about an hour ago."

"You're a dark horse, Jake. For instance, you've never said anything before about this aunt of yours. At least to me."

"Because you've never asked," Jake almost answered, but restrained himself.

"She was a decorator. She used to visit my parents a lot when I was growing up, and sometimes I'd go to stay with her in the summer. She had a big apartment on Central Park West. I lived with her while I was getting my degree at Parsons."

"Where did you grow up again?"

The *again* was face-saving. Bruce had never before asked Jake where he grew up.

"California."

"Ah."

"One thing that's true—I did do all the measuring for her. She was terrible with measurements, she always took them down wrong."

"So probably you did meet Sandra."

"Probably."

They were crossing the park. Tall lamps illuminated the Ninety-seventh Street Transverse. Beyond them, in shadowed woods, Bruce knew, things were happening that were beyond his capacity to imagine.

"I'm sorry that Aaron got laid off," he said.

"Oh, but he didn't," Jake said. "He was fired. He called his boss a cu—the C-word."

"God! Really?"

"Don't quote me on that. I got it from Min, and she's not exactly what you'd call a paragon of reliability."

"Rachel is so good-natured, so patient. You wonder sometimes how nice women like her end up with men like Aaron. Men who aren't nice. Do you think he's sleeping with Sandra?"

"I'm the wrong person to ask. The fact is, I don't understand human relationships. I only understand rooms, and even with rooms, every day I'm less and less sure."

They had arrived at Bruce's building. After a brief tussle over who would pay the fare, he bade Jake goodnight and headed up to his apartment, where he found the dogs in a state of discernible anxiety due to his lateness. When the dogs were anxious, they lost control of their bowels. It was eleven in the evening in New York, five in the morning in Venice. Six hours and four thousand miles, much of it ocean, separated him from his wife, making her as close to nonexistent as she could be without being dead.

As he took the dogs out for their walk, he listened at the Warriners' door for party noises but heard none. The dogs were quick about their business. When he got home, after he brushed his teeth, he got into bed on the left side.

11

"Have you heard of the drama of the gifted child?" Kathy asked.

"What child is that?" Bruce said.

"Not any child in particular," Kathy said. "It's a book—*The Drama of the Gifted Child*—and according to Michael, it describes exactly what Lou and I did to him."

Bruce put the Outback into park. It was the Wednesday before Eva and Min's return from Venice, and the traffic on Lexington was at a standstill. All around him, taxi drivers and Uber drivers were pressing their horns, as if noise could blast apart gridlock.

"Something must be going on at the UN," he said. "Or there's another protest in front of Trump Tower."

"Or an accident," Kathy said, tearing at a Kleenex she held balled in her fist. "It could be an accident. Do you want me to check Waze?"

"Knowing why there's traffic won't make it move. Anyway, we've got time. We've got forty minutes. So what's this gifted child thing?"

A snowfall of shredded Kleenex was collecting on Kathy's lap. "Well, from what Michael says, it's what happens when there's a gifted child in a family, but also a troubled one, so the parents lavish all their attention on the troubled one in the belief that the gifted one can take care of himself. And so the gifted one feels neglected—punished. He feels punished for being gifted."

"Is Michael gifted?"

"I suppose. I mean, he was in the gifted program at school. He's never really been into academics, though. He wants to be an interior designer. He wants to go to Parsons.

"I'm not sure I believe we neglected him as much as he says. It's true we never worried about him the way we did about Susie, because he's always been responsible, always landed on his feet. Susie never lands on her feet. The thing about Susie . . . But I don't need to explain Susie to you. Her history's like mine in so many ways—had kids too early, just like me, never went to college, just like me. Can't hold down a job. That's where we part ways. She's more like her father in that way. It's no coincidence that Lou sells cars. He could never make it in a salaried position, he can only get something done if there's a gold ring to grab. Not that Susie could ever sell cars. Mind you, a few years ago Lou tried her out at it. God, that was a disaster.

"Anyway, the reason I'm bringing all this up is that last night we had a little incident and I'd like your opinion on it. We were watching *SVU*—me, Michael, Susie, and the girls, Chloe and Bethany—when the doorbell rings, and it's Ricky, Chloe's dad. He and Susie lived together for a couple years, until Susie decided she'd had enough of his drinking and took out a restraining order against him—despite which she still sees him from time to time. Now, I ask you, what's the point of taking out a restraining order on someone if you're the one who's going to break it?

"Anyway, he rings the doorbell, and she goes to answer. They talk for a few minutes, and then she comes into the living room and asks me, in this sheepish voice, if he can come in for a little while. At first I don't say anything—you see, I was trying to decide which would be worse, the fight Ricky and Susie would have if I let him come in or the fight Susie and I would have if I didn't—and then, before I can even open my mouth, Michael jumps in with 'Absolutely no way is that asswipe'—excuse me, but that's the word he used—'coming inside this house.' And of course, all this time Ricky's standing at the door, which means he can hear everything, which shouldn't matter, I know, but to me it does—I'm hardwired that way, don't air your dirty laundry in public—so I tell Michael to keep his voice down, and he stands up and puts his hands on his hips and says, 'What are you trying to do? Do you want to kill yourself? I'm trying to help you out here. God, it's the drama of the gifted child all over again.'"

"And how did you answer?"

"I didn't. But I told Susie that Ricky couldn't come in. I told her that if she wanted to talk to him, she'd have to go outside, which she did. So there they were, out in the driveway, smoking, when . . . But I should have seen it coming. Two minutes, literally two minutes, was all it took before they were going at it full throttle, loud enough that the neighbors called the police.

"Well, I should have seen what would happen next. The minute Ricky hears the sirens, he bolts. That's typical of him—leaving Susie to take the heat. I thought they were going to arrest her for disturbing the peace. It's happened before. And so I'm thinking, if she gets taken in, I'll have to go down to the city jail, again, wait for her to be arraigned, again, bail her out, again. I'm thinking, if I'm lucky, I'll be home by four in the morning. And that's when I just . . . lost it. I mean, I got furious, really furious, which is something I don't do often. Usually I'm a pretty calm person. Only now I'm literally shaking with rage, and Michael's glaring at me, and the girls are crying and . . . well, that's when I go into the bedroom and call Lou. I call Lou, and when he picks up I say, 'The cops are here, and Susie's about to be arrested, and if you want it dealt with, you'd better come over and deal with it, because I'm not doing it.' And Lou—he must have heard it in my voice that I meant business, because he goes, 'OK, OK, I'll be there in five minutes.' But despite saying that, he's a good half hour, and by then it's all over, they've let Susie off with a warning, and she's ripping the kitchen apart looking for cigarettes. And Lou walks in and he just . . . lights into her, tells her she's an unfit mother, and how can she do this sort of thing in front of her children, to say nothing of her poor mama, who has cancer, to which Susie answers that he's in no position to criticize, considering he's walked out on her poor mama who has cancer and she's the one who stayed to take care of her. It's always the same argument with them. The first time Susie got sent to juvie, it was because she gave him a black eye. He called the cops, and when they showed up she told them she'd done it to protect me, that he was hitting me and she was trying to stop him, but they arrested her anyway."

"Was he hitting you?"

"How do I answer that? Over the years, hitting happened. I did some of it, he did some of it, Susie did some of it. I know I should say it was domestic abuse—it would certainly help me in the divorce case—but honestly, that's not how I see it. I don't see Lou as the bad guy. Or Susie, for that matter. Lou, on the other hand, does see Susie as . . . if not the bad guy, then a lost cause. When she and the girls got thrown out of their last place, he didn't want to take them in. His opinion was that she'd made her bed and she should lie in it. And I said, 'But she's got no money, they'll have to go to a shelter,' and he said, 'Well, let them go to a shelter, if that's what it takes to get her to start acting like a grown-up.' And I said, 'But there are the girls to think of. They're just children, we can't just sit back and let them go to a shelter.' And now suddenly I see something. That maybe when I said Lou would never have left if I hadn't gotten sick, I was kidding myself. Maybe the truth is, he would have left anyway."

The light changed. This time Bruce made it through. "Hoorah!" he said.

Half a block later the traffic slowed again.

"Don't worry," he said. "If worse comes to worst, I'll call you a helicopter."

"I'm not worried," Kathy said. "Oh, but I never got to the part about the gifted child."

"Oh, yes. What happened?"

"It was around ten. Lou had left, and Susie was putting the girls to bed, when Michael comes up to me and starts complaining about how everyone always forgets him. How he gets left out of everything. And I say, 'Michael, you should consider yourself lucky,' and he says, 'But I don't, because I have to live here,' and I say, lamely, 'You're a good boy, Michael,' and he says, 'Exactly, it's the drama of the gifted child. She gets all the attention, and even says she's here to take care of you when everyone knows she's really only here because she's got nowhere else to go, and in the meantime I'm the one who buys the groceries, cleans the house, changes the sheets,' and on and on like that until I couldn't even really hear him anymore . . . And I said—I know it's selfish, but I said it—'Why am I always the one to get blamed? Why am I always wrong? I'm so tired of always being wrong.'" Tears sprang into Kathy's eyes. "Mind you, I'm not shirking responsibility. No one understands the mistakes I've made better than I do. And yet I've got to have done *some* things right, haven't I? I've got to have."

"Of course," Bruce said, laying his hand on her knee.

"I suppose what it comes down to is that every second of every day of your life, the stakes are just so high, aren't they? Always so high . . ."

Again the traffic eased. The car seemed suddenly very warm to Bruce, so warm that he could feel the sweat on his neck soaking into his collar. Yet he had to keep the temperature high. Kathy got cold so easily.

"Kathy, there's something I want to ask you about," he said. "It's really none of my business, and if you'd rather I shut up, just tell me and I will."

"What is it?"

"Well, last Monday when I dropped you off at the hotel, you said something about how much you were looking forward to taking a bath—"

She laughed. "So I did say it! The minute I got in the elevator, I was sure I had. I just wondered if you'd picked up on it."

"Were you hoping I hadn't?"

"I'm not sure. Maybe I was hoping you had." She cleared her throat. "So, as you've no doubt figured out, we never put in that master suite."

"But you took out the loan?"

"Oh, yes, the loan's real. We just ended up spending the money on other things. I didn't want to tell you, in case you disapproved."

"Why would I disapprove? How you spend your money is none of my business."

"I know, I know, that's what you always tell your clients. But I'm not one of your clients. And even if I was, is it really true? I mean, do you really not judge? Or do you just keep your judgments to yourself?"

"I've trained myself not to think along those lines. Ideally I'd rather not know the particulars."

"But you must want to know them in this case, or you wouldn't have asked."

"Well, you're not one of my clients. And as I said, if you think it's none of my business—"

"I don't mind telling you. Why not, when you consider how much I've already told you? OK, when we first got the idea to take out the loan, our plan really was to add on a master suite. You see, all the kids had left except Michael, and once they were gone, the strangest thing happened. For the first time in our lives, we had more space than we needed—and for the first time in our lives, it didn't seem like enough. Which is maybe how it always is. Wants are stronger than needs. Anyway, I'd gotten in the habit of watching those programs on television where people refurbish their homes, and on these programs everyone was always going on about master suites, how great it was to have a master suite, and I thought, Wow, it really would be great to have a master suite, with a big whirlpool tub and a separate shower. And Lou thought it was a good idea, too—for different reasons. I mean, for him it wasn't so much about comfort as about having the sort of house that he thought befitted a man of his status. The same with his car. Of course, he's got things ass-backwards—he thinks a house and car confer status, when really they're just symbols. One of his brothers is a builder, he has a huge house, six thousand square feet. Lou's always been jealous of it. So one night he invites this brother, Ronny, over for dinner, and we get to talking about the possibility of putting on an addition, and the next thing I know we're out in the yard and Ronny's showing us where it could go, and how it could be laid out, and from then on things just moved very fast. Ronny did some drawings and gave us an estimate and put us in touch with this mortgage broker he knew, who was avid to sell us the loan, only I was nervous about taking on more debt. That's when I asked your advice about it, and when you said you thought it was fine, that we could afford it, we took it out. And then the trouble started."

"Susie?"

"Who else? The day after we got the money—literally the day after—she shows up on our doorstep with the girls. Despite his threats, Lou let them stay. He didn't make them go to a shelter—which didn't stop him from fighting with her all the time, the same fight they've been having for a thousand years. So things went on like that for a couple weeks, when all of a sudden Susie's other ex—Bethany's father, Jason—slaps her with a custody suit. And this completely blows my mind, because up until then he's been the classic deadbeat dad, always late with child support, which meant that I was always loaning Susie money that she'd promise to pay back and never did, which infuriated Lou. And now here he is, Jason, suing for full custody. He's quit drinking and gotten a job, plus I think his mother's giving him money. And Susie . . . well, as you imagine, she goes

SHELTER IN PLACE   131

totally ballistic. Says she'll die before she gives up Bethany, and that she's got to hire a lawyer, to which Lou replies that he'd rather pay for a lawyer for Jason than for her, since as far as he's concerned there's no way Jason could do a worse job with Bethany than she has. At which point the fight starts up again, the two of them screaming at each other, until finally Susie says she's leaving, only you have to remember, she has nowhere to go, literally nowhere. She's packing her bags, and the girls are wailing and weeping, and the whole time Lou's sitting on the sofa playing some idiotic game on his phone, pretending not to notice. And that's when all of a sudden Susie just grabs the girls and pulls them down with her onto the floor. They're just sitting there on the floor, and now all three of them are wailing and weeping, and hugging each other, all in a heap, like a bunch of puppies, and from the heap this voice, Susie's, says, 'Daddy, Daddy, please help me,' and right then I can see where this is going, because they're both con artists at heart and the secret about con artists is that they're always each other's easiest mark.

"You can probably guess what happened next."

"Lou hired her a lawyer?"

Kathy nodded. "Only the lawyer wanted a retainer, so that's a chunk of the loan gone. And then another chunk to pay the rent Susie owes, plus interest, and another to Ronny, who's already done a design and pulled the permits for the master suite, which now we can't afford to build. You know how it is, how money never goes as far as you think it will. Or maybe you don't know that."

"I do, actually."

"Well, that's everything. Where I am now—it's not where I ever expected to be. And yet in another sense it seems the inevitable place to end up, doesn't it?"

Fighting the constraints of his seatbelt, Bruce turned to Kathy. "Listen to me," he said. "This isn't the end of the story. Maybe it's the end of a part of the story, but not the whole of it. There's the future to think of."

"Believe me, I never stop thinking about the future."

"And look, we're here." They were pulling up in front of the outpatient center. "And on time, despite the traffic. That's a good sign, isn't it?"

As usual, he let her out, then went to park the Outback. By the time he got to the suite she was already in the recliner and hooked up to the IV. Her eyes were closed. Fine veins stood out on the fluttering lids.

As quietly as he could, he sat down, opened his computer, and typed into the search bar "Syosset home values."

To his surprise, there was much less traffic on the drive back uptown.

"Going to the country this weekend, Mr. Lindquist?" the attendant at his garage asked when he dropped off the car.

"Probably not," Bruce said. "I'll let you know if I do."

"By Friday morning if you can. So we can plan for the weekend. Goodnight, Mr. Lindquist."

"Goodnight."

Had the weather been worse, he would have taken a taxi back to the apartment. Instead he walked. Too many hours in the car and in the armchair at the chemo suite had constricted his muscles.

Halfway home, an idea seized him and turned him around and he headed to his office, for he was determined to act on the idea before any twinges of guilt he was having grew strong enough to stop him.

It was nearly eight when he unlocked the door. Everyone had gone home. The lights were out. On tiptoe, he made his way through the dark to Kathy's office, shut the door softly, sat down at her desk, switched on the lamp, and woke the computer from its twilight sleep.

He knew her password, just as she knew his—a precaution they had taken years ago, in case one or the other should be incapacitated. Even so, the sight of her desktop startled him—the wallpaper itself (a photo of her and Lou and their kids, taken at least twenty years before), over which a haphazard array of pdfs, spreadsheets, Word docs, and photos was scattered. Had Kathy known that he would be looking at her desktop, he had no doubt, she would have organized all these items into neatly labeled folders. Some she would have deleted. She would no more have wished him to see her desktop in this condition than she would have wished him to see her when she woke in the morning, before she put on her makeup and her wig, and this apprehension precipitated in him pangs of remorse at the same time that it solidified his conviction that he was doing the right thing, that he must plunge ahead.

It took him about ten minutes. As he had guessed, Kathy had let her computer generate unmemorizable passwords for her accounts and email, which it then filled in automatically. Nor had she erased her browser history. This meant that all he had to do was find the correct website and the entry to the Aladdin's cave—or, more aptly, the messy boudoir—would open to him, allowing him to sift through its contents, a task he undertook with the delicacy and restraint that chivalry demanded. Efficiently and, as it were, discreetly, he inserted a flash drive into the computer and copied Kathy's bank statements, her property tax bills, her credit card statements, her homeowner's insurance policy, her medical bills, and the payment schedule for the home equity loan, as well as those for two other loans she hadn't told him about, one on a car and one on the sailboat she had spoken of taking out onto the Sound on weekends with Lou. From everything else on her computer—from her photographs, from the emails she had gotten from Lou and her children, from the file called DIARY and the one called EULOGY?—he averted his eyes. He then erased his intrusions from her browser history and put the computer back to sleep— thinking, as he did so, of the Grinch sending Little Cindy-Lou Who back to bed with a drink of water after she discovers him stealing the Christmas tree.

No one caught him. He switched off the lamp, tiptoed again (but why?) to the door, locked it, rode the elevator to the lobby, and began the familiar walk back to his apartment, though at a faster clip than usual, thanks to the descending temperature and to a fervency of action tinged with righteous- ness and just a smattering of shame. It was so long past the hour he usually got home that an instinctive shudder of anxiety passed through him, until he remembered that it didn't matter now, that the only people he was letting down were the dogs, who would be impatient for their dinner and their walk, and they wouldn't tell on him. They couldn't even if they wanted to. And Eva was away, six hours further into the night, in the land of Nod. Yet what he had done so far was nothing compared with what he had planned.

A few blocks west of the office, his phone pinged. The text was from a number he did not know.

> Hi bruce, it's sandra, i got your number from aaron, hope you don't mind, anyway was wondering if you were planning to come out to conn. this weekend, grady is away and i will be on my own 🙁 could use some company, let me know if you'll be in connecticut, xx

As it happened, the text arrived just as he was passing his garage, a coincidence that impelled him to knock on the door of the little cage, separated from the world by bulletproof glass, in which the attendant sat at a gunmetal desk, reading the *Ming Pao Daily News*. As soon as he saw Bruce, he waved and unlocked the door.

"Mr. Lindquist, you need your car again, sir?"

"No, not tonight. I just want to tell you, I've been thinking about it and I've decided I may go up to the country this weekend after all. So could you have the car ready for me on Friday afternoon, say at three o'clock?"

"Sure thing, Mr. Lindquist," the attendant said, returning to the office and making a note in an old-fashioned ledger. Bruce followed him in.

"Warm in here."

"Too warm for me. But hey, that's better than too cold."

"What's your name, by the way?"

"Willard, Mr. Lindquist. Willard Han."

"Willard, good to meet you. Well, to learn your name. Oh, and please call me Bruce."

An amused smile passed over Willard Han's face as Bruce held out his big, clean, pale hand, which Willard shook, taking note, as he did, of the layerings from which it protruded: cashmere coat, wool jacket, cotton-and-silk-blend sleeves fastened with gold cuff links.

After he left, Willard called his wife and told her of the encounter. "And to think that he drives a Subaru," he said. "If I had that kind of dough, I'd drive a Beemer."

His wife agreed that he would.

The next morning, Eva called to tell him about the apartment in Venice.

PART III

The way Denise put it, Fifth Avenue is the Grand Canal of the modern world," Clydie Mortimer said. "So what else but Canaletto?"

Pablo Bach, his cheeks freshly shaven and his nails newly manicured, studied the Canalettos. There were eight in all, arranged in the spaces between the windows and their views of Central Park.

"Denise bought the first six in the seventies, when we still had the palazzo in Venice," Clydie went on. "My son, Jimmy, bought two more last year. Jimmy is a genius when it comes to buying art."

"He has such an eye," Min said. "What do you think, Pablo?"

Arms clasped behind his back, Pablo leaned into a view of San Giorgio Maggiore.

"What do I think?" he said. "For those who like that sort of thing, that is the sort of thing they like. That's what I think."

Jake laughed. He couldn't help it.

"That's rather inscrutable," Clydie said.

"He's quoting someone," Min said. "Wait, it's on the tip of my tongue . . . Oscar Wilde?"

"Muriel Spark, actually," Indira Singh said. "Miss Jean Brodie's opinion of the girl guides."

"Very good," Pablo said, giving Indira the same curatorial once-over he had just given the painting. "Jake and I met her once, you know. She was Dame Muriel by then. She'd invited us to lunch at her place near Arezzo, only when we got there, she'd forgotten we were coming. Leave it to a Catholic to make you feel guilty for her own mistakes."

That the conversation had strayed from the Canalettos worried Min, who said, "Well, if you want *my* opinion, Mrs. Mortimer, they're absolutely marvelous. In fact, I want to thank you for giving me the opening line for my article." She cleared her throat. "'Fifth Avenue is the Grand Canal of the Modern World,' says Clydie Mortimer of the spectacular Manhattan duplex in which she has lived for the past three decades. 'So what else but Canaletto?'"

"You know you're not to use my name," Clydie said.

"Oh, yes, of course we won't," Min said. "That was just off the top of my head."

"I do wonder about this one," Pablo said, bringing his face close to a painting of the Riva degli Schiavoni. "Looks more like School of than Canaletto proper."

"You're just saying that because you know it's one of the ones Jimmy bought," Clydie said.

"How would I know that?"

"You've been here enough times." She turned to Indira. "So, my dear, *Enfilade*. I have to be frank, when Min called to tell me you wanted to publish the apartment, I was dubious. I mean, *Enfilade* . . . isn't it a bit, well, dentist's office?"

"Do you know, that's exactly what I thought when they offered me the job," Indira said.

"Oh, but that's how the magazine used to be," Min said. "Since Indira took over, its whole identity has changed."

"I remember in the old days, the people from *Enfilade* used to practically get down on their knees and beg Denise to let them publish the Palm Beach house," Clydie said. "Or maybe that was *House & Garden*. Anyway, she always refused. She was adamant. She wouldn't let any of her houses be photographed."

"Why not?" Indira said. "That is, if you don't mind my asking."

"After the break-in in Venice, she was deathly afraid of burglars. The last thing she wanted was to give clues as to where she lived."

"Understandable," Min said.

"Which is why, even though I'm agreeing to let you publish the apartment, I don't want my name used."

"I might not want mine used, either," Pablo said, peering again at the Canalettos.

Clydie laughed, her laugh turning into a cough that nearly caused her glasses—round, tortoiseshell, oversize—to fall off her small nose. "He's only saying that because he's mad at me for putting them back where they were," she said to Indira. "You see, when he had this new wallpaper put up, he played a trick on me. While the wallpaper was being hung, the Canalettos had to be taken down and stored, and Pablo stored them in Jimmy's room. I was in Palm Beach at the time, and naturally assumed that when I got back, they'd be where they were supposed to be, instead of which he'd moved them to the dining room. Well, I moved them back."

"So you did."

"It was where Denise wanted them."

"With all due respect, Clydie, if your goal was to keep the apartment exactly the same as it was when Denise was alive, why did you hire me?"

"To do your job. Or do you really think that when you redecorate a place, it belongs to you?"

"With Pablo, that's always a question," Jake said.

This time it was Indira who laughed, tilting her head so that her earrings jingle-belled.

After her visitors left, Clydie poured herself some Scotch and called Jimmy. Clydie was eighty-seven, Jimmy sixty-four.

"What is it, Mother?" Jimmy spoke against a backdrop of traffic noise.

"It's that Pablo," Clydie said. "I invited him over, along with the *Enfilade* people, and he had the nerve to slap my wrist— in front of them—because I'd moved the Canalettos back. I mean, who does he think he is?"

"If that's how you feel, just don't use him anymore."

"And then he made this crack about not wanting his name in the article. 'Fine,' I should have said, 'what do I care? Your name's not the one people will be guessing at.'"

"Mother, I've got to go. I'm just—"

"But what really upset me was the insult to you, Jimmy. The condescension. Implying those Canalettos of yours weren't authentic."

"Who cares what he thinks? Look, we're just pulling up at the hotel. I have to check in."

"I don't know how you do it, Jimmy. You're so gifted when it comes to buying art. I want you to find me a Marie Laurencin next. Where are you, by the way? What's all that noise?"

"Bangkok."

"Is it hot? What time is it?"

"I'd rather not know."

"Be careful of the shellfish," Clydie said, when in fact the shellfish was the least of the things she feared her son might not be careful about in Bangkok.

After they left Clydie's apartment, Pablo, Jake, Min, and Indira went out for dinner. Indira chose the restaurant, a South Indian place on Madison where the maître d' fussed over her. This annoyed Pablo, who had planned to take them to a French place on Lexington where the maître d' fussed over him.

Of course, Indira's presumptuousness would have been less irksome if she hadn't been so pretty, with her sleek, obedient hair, her lucent skin, the small diamond embedded in her left nostril, and the big one gleaming on her ring finger.

"Is Singh your married name or your maiden name?" he asked her once they were seated.

"Both, actually."

"Ah, so you're Mrs. Singh Singh."

"Oh, please," Min said. "As if she hasn't heard that line twenty million times."

"I don't mind," Indira said. "What else is love but a prison?"

This riposte got more laughs than the joke that had occasioned it. It was Indira's self-possession that most transfixed and alarmed Pablo, for it was the self-possession that comes of youth and beauty, the kind he himself had once known and therefore knew he would never know again.

A turbaned waiter brought menus. By the standard of Indian restaurants, this one was surprisingly posh, with soft light, beige chenille upholstery on the booths, no canned sitar music or attar of room freshener. Most of the other diners were Indian, the men in tailored suits, the women in saris. The menus were tall and glossy.

"Shall I order for everyone?" Indira asked—which was just plain bad manners, Pablo thought, ignoring the possibility that some of the members of the group might, for example, have trouble digesting spicy food. And yet to request something not spicy would be to admit that after years of being able to eat anything he liked, Pablo was now turning into one of those people who has trouble digesting spicy food. Better just to dip a piece of naan into the raita—better not to eat anything—than to allow this irksomely beautiful woman to gain any more leverage over him.

For a few minutes Indira consulted with the waiter, who then collected the menus and glided away. She rested her chin on her hand, something that even twenty years ago no properly raised young woman would have done.

"So, Clydie Mortimer," she said. "I'll say this—she's not what I expected."

"Oh, really?" Pablo said. "What did you expect?"

"Someone frailer, perhaps. Less gumptious."

"That suit was vintage Schiaparelli," Min said.

"Vintage Balenciaga, actually," Indira said.

"Oh, yes, I meant Balenciaga," Min said. "I said Schiaparelli but I meant Balenciaga."

"One thing I didn't get, Pablo. Why did you say you might not want your name in the article?"

"Pablo was teasing Clydie," Min said. "He can't bear it when his clients move things around."

"Those last two Canalettos are fakes," Pablo said. "Jimmy Mortimer is a fool."

"What's the story with Jimmy?" Indira asked. "Who's his father?"

"No one knows. Clydie already had him when she met Denise."

"She was a model then, right?"

"In London, in the fifties. She posed for Helmut Newton."

"Maybe he was the father," Min said.

"That was where she met Denise, in London. Everyone seems to meet there."

"And they were lovers from then on?"

"I'm not sure *lovers* is quite the word. For Denise, Clydie was more like a decorative statue, or a piece of topiary."

"Denise liked having Clydie lying on the chaise by the pool," Jake said. "And that, for fifty years, was basically all Clydie did."

"Lying by the pool was her career. Except when she was in Manhattan, when her career was sitting in nightclubs.

"They moved around depending on the season. Besides the apartment, there were the two houses, the one in Palm Beach and the one in Connecticut. Oh, and the palace in Venice, until Denise sold it. Of course, she was a bit batty in her last years. A sort of a Miss Havisham."

"She let the house in Palm Beach go to rack and ruin," Min said. "An Addison Mizner house! It had to be torn down. Tragic."

"Luckily, an architect bought the Connecticut house and restored it," Jake said.

"Really?" Indira asked. "Has it been published?"

"Last year, in *Architectural Digest*," Min said. "But the carriage house hasn't."

"Clydie kept the carriage house," Pablo said. "She goes up there most weekends. I keep telling her she needs to have the roof repaired, but she won't do anything about it. Every time I visit, I'm worried the ceiling's going to collapse."

"I suppose it must have been a love match," Indira said.

"I'd say it was more a match of expectations," Pablo said. "In my experience, it's mutual expectations that make for the most successful marriages."

"What, not love?" Min said.

"Plenty of people who love each other end up divorced," Jake said.

"Speaking of marriage, I've been meaning to ask if you two are married," Indira said.

She was looking at Pablo and Jake. For a moment neither spoke.

"What's the matter? Have I put my foot in it?" Indira said.

"No, of course not," Min said, reaching across the table to pat Indira's hand. "Believe me, after all these years, they're used to people thinking they're a couple, aren't you, boys?"

"Oh, absolutely," Pablo said.

"I mean, it's an occupational hazard, isn't it? If you're a man, and you're a decorator, people are likely to make certain assumptions about you that, frankly, in most cases, will turn out to be true. Only in Pablo's case they're not. Not that you do much to dispel the misapprehension, do you, Pablo?"

"Don't I?"

"The truth is, he wants women to think he's gay. It's his MO. It means when they're with him, they let down their guard. Then when he makes his move, they're too startled to object."

"And then later, when they take him on buying trips to Paris, the husbands don't care," Jake said.

"Thank you for revealing all my trade secrets," Pablo said, "and in the process ruining my chances of seducing the lovely Mrs. Singh Singh."

Indira smiled her cool smile. She is attracted to him, Jake thought. Inexplicably, despite his age and girth, she is attracted to him. And here I am, two decades younger ("Congratulations on beginning your fifty-third year!"), and I cannot win so much as a wink from this handsome waiter as he lays his silver tray, with its artful arrangement of idlis and sambar, pooris and coconut chutney, on the table.

"Jake's gay," Min added. "Though single, in case you know anyone we can fix him up with."

Jake said to Indira, "I'm afraid that in her avidity to explain what Pablo and I aren't, Min has omitted to say what we are, which is partners—business partners."

"For twenty-six years," Pablo said.

"Jake's aunt founded the firm," Min said. "She took on Pablo first, then Jake, and now they co-own it."

"Who was your aunt?" Indira asked.

"Rose Lovett. A major force in the industry in the sixties and seventies. Sometimes called the female David Hicks."

"She'd turn over in her grave if she heard you say that," Jake said.

"David Hicks?" Indira said. "Should I know that name?"

Pablo gave her a look of bemused astonishment. "Excuse me if this is a rude question," he said, "but you *are* the editor of *Enfilade*, aren't you?"

"It's not a rude question," Indira said, "and yes, as of last November, I am. The thing is—I'll be the first to admit it—I'm a total ignoramus when it comes to decorating. My first job after college was at *Glamour*, then from *Glamour* I moved to *InStyle*, then from *InStyle* to *Sweetheart*."

"Which was on its last legs," Min said, "before Indira came on board and turned it around."

"And now they want me to do the same with *Enfilade*. Of course, when Jürgen first floated the idea, I said, 'Hold on, I've never worked on a shelter magazine.' And Jürgen said, 'A good editor can edit anything. Give *Popular Mechanics* to Anna Wintour and she'll double the circulation in a year.'"

"How has it been so far?" Jake asked.

"Terrifying. That's why the first thing I did was hire an old hand."

"This one," Min said, holding up hers.

"Not that I was *totally* ignorant. I mean, I knew who you were, Pablo."

"That's reassuring," Pablo said.

"Now, Pablo," Min said.

"No, I'm serious," Pablo said. "In fact, I think it's all to the good that Indira hasn't wasted the best years of her life in this chintz-lined privy of a profession. It's also why I'm all the more curious to get her opinion of Clydie's apartment. What did you think, Indira? Be completely honest. If you want, you can even give me a grade. I seem to recall *Sweetheart* does that with books."

"You have to consider your readership," Indira said.

"Believe me, I'm not objecting," Pablo said. "Truth be told, I found it quite refreshing that you had the guts to give a B-minus to that last Salman Rushdie. If it were me, I would have given it a D."

"Of course, you can't grade an interior the way you can a book," Min said.

"Why not?" Pablo said. "It might be just the thing to get *Enfilade* out of the red. Rose Tarlow, C-plus. Robert Kime, A-minus."

"But if we offend the decorators, they won't let us publish them. They'll go to the competition."

"How do you know that? I, for one, would be thrilled to be given a grade for Clydie's apartment." Pablo leaned toward Indira. "Come on, tell me what you really think."

"Well, it's certainly . . . ornate. Quite like its owner in that regard. If that's the criterion for the grade—how well the interior fits the owner—you definitely get an A."

"But what about the interior qua interior?"

"You're assuming such a thing exists. Whereas the way I see it, it's a matter of taste. It's the same with books. I, for one, happen to be a great fan of Rushdie."

"Yet you gave him a B-minus."

"I didn't give him a B-minus, the reviewer gave him a B-minus."

"OK, then you be the reviewer."

The main dishes arrived, rogan josh and chicken xacuti in bowls with filigreed edges, a plate of okra pan-fried with mango powder, baskets of coiled parathas, platters of pilau rice. "You must understand, my background plays into this,"

Indira said, tearing delicately at a paratha. "I mean, I'm from Bombay, where the rule of thumb is 'Everything in moderation, including moderation.'"

"Muriel Spark?" Min said.

"No, this time it really is Oscar Wilde," Indira said a little sharply. "Look, all I'm saying is that for me personally, Mrs. Mortimer's apartment is—well—a bit *too* decorated. It reminds me of my grandmother's flat on Malabar Hill. It needs messing up. Or something taken out."

"That sounds like a C to me," Pablo said.

"Not a C, a B-minus. Same as the Rushdie."

"Fair enough."

"I'll tell you one thing I did like. The Canalettos in the living room."

"In that case you'll have to lower my grade even further, because as you know I had nothing to do with the Canalettos in the living room. My plan was that there shouldn't be any paintings on that wall, nothing to distract from the view."

"Or the wallpaper," Jake said.

"So you're saying that Clydie making a decision you didn't agree with made you angry?" Indira said.

"That she made the decision? No. The decision she made? Yes."

"Pablo is not a great fan of Canaletto," Jake said.

"Don't get me wrong, they're no worse than most postcards," Pablo said.

"How fascinating. Tell me more."

"Well, that's what they are. Postcards. In the eighteenth century, if you were a young Turk and you were doing the Grand Tour, you brought home a Canaletto as a souvenir. The eighteenth century was not Venice's finest moment."

"Speaking of Venice, isn't it exciting about Eva Lindquist buying that apartment?" Min said.

"Eva's buying an apartment in Venice?" said Pablo.

Min nodded. "And the best part is, Jake's going to decorate it."

"You never said anything about that."

"Because I haven't agreed to do it."

"Yes, you have," Min said.

"No, I haven't. Eva only asked me a week ago."

"Eva Lindquist," Indira said. "Now, why do I know that name? Oh, of course. I met her at this Smith alumnae thing. It turns out our husbands know each other. So she's buying an apartment in Venice. Why?"

Jake looked at Min, who was pulling her napkin through her fingers as if it were a scarf she had just conjured from the ether.

"It's because of the election," he said. "So that she'll have someplace to escape to in case the country goes fascist."

"Oh, that's *part* of it," Min said. "The more important part, though . . . Well, it's the adventure. I mean, think of it. An American woman goes to Venice, sees an old apartment, decides on the spur of the moment to buy it and fix it up."

"Renovation as romance," Jake said.

"Well, yes, of course," Indira said. "What interests me more, though, is what you said earlier, this idea that suddenly this country so many of our grandparents fled to in search of freedom has become a place people feel they have to escape. Or at least be ready, at a moment's notice, to escape. What do you think, Min? Is there a story in that?"

"For *Enfilade*?"

"Absolutely for *Enfilade*. I've never understood why people assume a shelter magazine has to be—I might as well say it—decorating porn, where everyone's beautifully dressed, and there's no Putin or Guantánamo or Ferguson, and women spend all their time rearranging their throw pillows. Especially in the age of Instagram, when you can do that for free, online, for hours and hours. It's why the magazine has to offer something different. Something meatier."

"You see why they hired her?" Min said, laying the napkin on the table and folding it in thirds, like a towel. "New ideas. A fresh perspective."

"What do you think drew her to Venice?" Pablo asked.

"Well, that it's Venice," Min said. "Saint Mark and Burano lace and Lord Byron swimming the Grand Canal."

"'The Grand Canal is the Fifth Avenue of medieval Europe,' says Eva Lindquist of her newly acquired apartment in the heart of Venice.'"

"I'm going to control my temper, Pablo," Min said, "and not hit you over the head with this paratha. You'll have to forgive him, Indira. Ever since the election he's been crabby. You see, he was counting on Hillary choosing him to redecorate the White House. The last time round, the Clintons hired . . . I can't even remember her name. Can you, Pablo? Someone from Arkansas. It was this Arkansas thing. But now they're not from Arkansas anymore, they're from New York, so they can hire anyone they like. *Could* have hired anyone they liked."

"You know, I've never really thought about any of this," Indira said. "Of course it makes perfect sense—that each new president wants to leave his mark on the White House."

"Nixon installed the bowling alley," Pablo said. "I wonder what Trump will put in. A stripper pole?"

"For Nixon, Rose decorated the bowling alley, didn't she?" Min said.

"No, David Hicks did the bowling alley. Rose did some bedrooms."

"My mother never forgave her for it," Jake said. "Working for Nixon—she considered it a personal betrayal."

"But this is all so fascinating," Indira said. "Really, until tonight I had no idea the White House was such a thing. We should do an article on that too, don't you think, Min? The politics of White House decorating. And not just some overview—a first-hand account. You could write it, Pablo."

"Don't be silly," Pablo said. "You know perfectly well we decorators are all illiterate."

"That's why God invented Mins," Indira said.

13

"The thing about Canalettos," Jake said to Pablo in the Uber they were sharing, "is that when you look at them up close, you see that they're just not very well painted."

Pablo was rubbing his temples. "Don't talk to me about Canaletto," he said. "I weary of Canaletto."

"You made that pretty clear this afternoon."

"Well, why not? I'm too old to mince words."

"Even with Clydie?"

"Especially with Clydie."

"And yet Clydie's hardly what you'd call the most even-tempered person in the world," Jake said. "What if she decides you went too far? That she's had enough of you?"

"If only," Pablo said. "But it is not to be. No, what will happen is that she'll give me the cold shoulder for a week, maybe two if I'm lucky, then call up as if nothing's happened. Too much history, you see. Only when you're young is an insult enough to end a friendship. One of the few things I miss about being young."

His phone pinged. He picked it up and smiled.

"A text from Mrs. Singh Singh."

"Already?"

"You sound surprised."

"Only that it came so soon. What did you make of her, by the way?"

"She strikes me as a woman of great efficiency."

"Min tells me she's putting Alison on the cover of their next issue."

"No surprise there. She's already been on the cover of everything else."

"Have you ever thought of trying to make it up with her?"

"Why should I? If you want to make it up with her, you make it up with her."

"I'm not the one who fired her."

"Then it'll be that much easier for you."

"Look, all I'm saying is what you used to say to me. In this business you can't afford to have enemies."

"Since when is Alison an enemy?"

"Well, according to Min, in the interview she never once mentions that she got her start with us."

"I'm relieved to hear it. It's not the sort of thing you want spread around."

"Obviously she feels the same way."

"Then for once we agree on something."

"You're missing my point."

"How can't I when you won't make it? Not that I can't guess. What Min's saying is that now that Alison's a big name, we should beg her forgiveness, make amends with her, bring her back into the fold. To which my reply is that, IMHO, she's a mediocrity whose only talent is for getting attention paid to herself."

"Actually, Min didn't say anything about any of that. In fact, she only brought up their putting Alison on the cover to try to make me jealous so that I'd commit to decorating Eva's apartment. She says I've quote-unquote fallen off the map, that we need to quote-unquote grow the business."

"Why? We have enough clients."

"Yes, but most of them are in their seventies or eighties. And even if they live to be a thousand, what's to keep them from going to someone else? That's what Min would say, I'm guessing."

"Hold on, she's not suggesting that Clydie might go to Alison, is she? God, what a good idea. First thing tomorrow, I'll ring her up and suggest it."

"Don't be facetious."

"I'm not. I weary of Clydie. I weary of Jimmy, Fifth Avenue, the Grand Canal. Which reminds me—why *is* Eva buying this apartment? I mean, what's the real story?"

Jake filled Pablo in on Eva's trip, the dinner party after her return, his walk with Bruce and the conversation with Min that followed it.

"From what Indira said at dinner, it's obvious Min made up the part about the cover. Not that I believed her when she told me. I mean, what magazine editor in her right mind guarantees a cover, sight unseen?"

"Like all compulsive liars, she forgets her own lies."

"Or starts to believe them herself."

"It comes to the same thing. I weary of Min. So are you going to do it?"

"I'm not sure. You see, there's a complication. The place Eva's buying—it's Ursula's."

"Ursula Foote? God spare us. Have you told Eva?"

"No, not yet."

"In that case you'd better. And soon. Otherwise when the trouble starts—and you know it will—she'll blame you."

"She might blame me anyway."

"One thing's for sure, if you don't tell Eva, Ursula will. Which might be a reason to say no—if you don't want to do it. On the other hand, if I'm not mistaken, it's you who's worried that we're not doing enough to—what's that expression you used? Grow the business? Well, what's more likely to grow the business than a magazine cover?"

"But I just told you, the cover is a lie."

"Min could make it come true. She's done it before. And she's right about one thing, Jake. These last few years you really have been—what's that thing the young people say? Dialing it in."

"Don't you mean phoning it in?"

"Is there a difference?"

"I think you mean phoning it in."

As if on cue, Jake's phone vibrated. "Funny to think that most of these young people have never even seen a rotary phone," he said, glancing at the screen. "Sometimes I miss rotary phones, the tactile pleasure of putting your finger in the hole, pulling the dial up to the stop, then letting it go. Like that feeling when you press the return on a typewriter. That ker-ching—"

"What possible relevance does any of this have to what I'm saying?"

"None whatsoever. Which simply proves that you and Min are right. I have fallen off the map. I am phoning it in. The problem is, nothing excites me anymore. I try to imagine myself in Venice and all I see are obstacles. Dealing with Min, dealing with Ursula and Min . . ."

"Oh, well, if that's how you feel, just tell Eva no and be done with it."

"You underestimate her powers of persuasion."

"Do I? Or do you overestimate them? 'You can't rape the willing,' as we used to say, back in the days when we were allowed to say things like that."

"If I were willing, I'd already have said yes."

"And if you weren't, you'd already have said no. Instead you're hedging. Why?"

For a few seconds Jake pondered this question. Then he said: "It isn't that I've lost faith in my abilities. Or that I love what I do any less. It isn't that."

"Then what is it?"

"I remember when I was just starting out, Rose gave me a talking-to. She said that to succeed as a decorator, you had to follow two rules. One, never think of yourself as an artist, and two, never give anyone a discount."

"Classic Rose," Pablo said. "And right on the money. It's the bargain we make. And yet over time, if you're lucky, your name does hang on in a small way. Take Jean-Michel Frank. When you look at pictures of that amazing living room he did for Marie-Laure de Noailles, you don't think, Wow, that Marie-Laure de Noailles must really have been something, to have gotten Jean-Michel Frank to decorate her living room. No, what you think is Wow, that Jean-Michel Frank really was a great decorator."

"You know that room's gone now. Well, not literally gone. Redone."

"That's what I meant about the bargain. The redoing keeps us in business. For example, how many times have you redone Eva's living room?"

"The current one? Twice."

"In other words, she is to you what Marie-Laure de Noialles was to Jean-Michel Frank."

Jake laughed. "She'd love that comparison," he said. "And it's true, with Eva I do feel a certain sort of, well—rapport, I suppose you'd call it. Most of my clients, all they want is to show off. For them a spectacular apartment is just a way of making sure other people know how rich they are, or how powerful they are, or how much influence they wield. Only in Eva's case that's not it. What she's after is something different. Something like safety. My sense is that she sees this place in Venice as a sort of bunker, a luxurious bomb shelter or panic room."

"Or do you mean she sees it as a place where she can feel at home? That's your problem in a nutshell, Jake. She wants to feel at home, and no matter how skilled you may have gotten at giving her that feeling, you'll never really understand it, because you've never felt it."

"If I could—"

"You can. You just won't."

Again Jake's phone vibrated. This time he didn't take it out of his pocket.

"Shall I tell you something I've never told anyone?" Pablo said. "The thing I fear most in the world—more than getting old, more even than dying—is homelessness. And I don't mean homelessness in some existential sense, I mean real homeless-ness, sleeping-on-the-street homelessness. It wakes me up in the middle of the night. What if I went bankrupt, or someone sued me? Would I lose my house?"

"If you did, friends would take you in."

"For a while, yes. But not forever. My point, Jake, is that it could happen to any of us. It could happen to you. And yet most people don't think of it as a real possibility the way I do and the way, I suspect, Eva does. If she's restless, it's because, in her darkest depths, she's afraid of ending up in a homeless shelter. Over the years you've made a lot of money off that fear."

"That's a callous way of putting it."

"Oh, don't worry, I'll pay for it. Just as I'll pay for getting huffy with Clydie, for firing Alison, for every mistake I've ever made. My life . . . it's a declining balance. I'll pay and pay until I'm homeless."

After the Uber dropped him off, as he was undoing the locks on his door, Pablo had a flash of memory—Ursula hovering atop him, her freckled breasts grazing his chin as she wriggled to find her G-spot. A pink bed, a pink hotel room. But where? Ferrara? Ravenna? In any case it must have been the eighties, during that brief heyday of the G-spot, which had since gone the way of shag carpeting and Beanie Babies . . . In his front hall he switched on the light and took off his shoes. His feet ached. He was sixty-eight, looked younger, felt older. High blood pressure, chronic back pain, and an increasingly finicky stomach—these were messages from his body that his days of excess were over. And would he miss them? The eating anything he wanted, certainly. But the benefit dinners and the launch parties, the nightclubs and the going to bed, not alone, at three in the morning, the constant effort of currying favor? Not all that much.

From his pocket he took out his wallet and phone and keys and put them down on the steel-and-glass table (Eileen Gray) that was their designated resting place. The delicate recoil of the landing woke the phone up; from the screen Indira's text flashed at him:

> Pablo, it was so great to meet you after hearing so much about you!!! And I'm serious about that article. Shall we meet to discuss? Lunch? Drinks? Best, Indira

He smiled as he read it, wondered if he should answer it immediately. Ten, five, two years ago, he would have. Ten, five, two years ago, the mere prospect of sex with the lovely Mrs. Singh Singh would have been enough to give him an instantaneous erection. But now his libido shrugged. Was this due to "low T," as they called it on television? Perhaps—or perhaps it was something closer to the anomie that Jake had described. More and more it was habit, not lust, that impelled Pablo to undertake the hard work of seduction.

"I weary of human endeavor," he said to himself, envisioning the vast and comfortable bed that would soon be his reward for climbing the stairs to the second floor. In recent months he had come to regard sleep as a leisure activity. Nor was he the only one. After decades of being outré, sleep had of late become fashionable, its benefits and pleasures trumpeted by articles in the Style section of the *Times*, segments on *Good Morning America*, and even a book by Arianna Huffington, of all people. The idea was to think of sleep as a luxury worth spending money on. Noting the trend, old clients had started calling to ask for Hästens mattresses, cashmere blankets, sheets woven from organic cotton or Irish linen. Though less fussy about his own bed, Pablo, too, was finding that he relished sleep as never before. Perhaps it was age, perhaps it was *the* age—these days that never finished where they started, that had no baseline, no steadiness. In any case he had taken Arianna's advice, had weaned himself of the habit of bringing his phone to bed with him, and gotten rid of the bedroom television, and installed blackout blinds. On his side table were a lamp lit by a forty-watt bulb, a few books he could count on to bore him, and an antique clock that had to be wound. Nothing else. It puzzled him to recall the years of his youth when the mere prospect of a night alone was enough to plunge him into despair. Now he treasured those nights when, rather than going out to a cocktail party or a restaurant, he would stay in, eat pasta with cream, peas, and ham, alone in front of the television (a soccer match or some BBC sitcom he'd seen a thousand times), take a long shower, give his teeth a careful and thorough flossing and brushing, and finally withdraw into his bed, where he would look for a few moments at one of his boring books before winding the clock and, noting the early hour (sometimes so early that the sun had not yet set), savor for a moment the transgressiveness of doing by choice what, in a thousand other houses, children were being forced to do, all the while protesting the injustice of it.

Dreams were part of what Pablo looked forward to on those nights, even the bad ones, from which he usually awoke more befuddled than afraid, as if he were undergoing a sort of nocturnal psychoanalysis. Often it was of sleep itself that he dreamed—the sleep of the weeks after his father's arrest but before his mother's, when she would take him into the vast parental bed for siestas that could begin and end at any time, at five in the morning or ten in the morning or four in the afternoon. Outside the closed shutters, he knew, the regular rotation of day and night went on, buses loaded and unloaded passengers, children came and went from school. Inside the apartment it was always dark. His mother left only to get food. Clutched in her arms, he would gaze from the bed at the gray-black mountains that the lamp, on those rare occasions when it was switched on, would reveal to be merely dressers and chairs. Sometimes the telephone would ring, its little shriek causing his mother to utter a bigger shriek, answer breathlessly, and, as often as not, hang up, after which she would go into the kitchen and pour herself a glass of brandy or gin before returning to the bed, which Pablo imagined was a boat, an ark that, as the floodwaters rose, gently lifted from the ground and launched out onto those new seas that had supplanted a world God found so vile, he had no choice but to drown it.

As Jake got out of the Uber, his phone vibrated again. Although he had it set to vibrate at different frequencies for calls, texts, and emails (Alert, Quick, and Staccato), when there was traffic noise, he couldn't tell the vibrations apart.

He looked at his screen and saw that it was Min. She had tried to call him twice and texted him once.

call me pls. asap

That she was desperate to talk to him didn't surprise him. No doubt as soon as she'd brought up the magazine article, she realized she'd blown her own cover, and now she wanted to make sure he wouldn't give her away to Eva.

He decided not to answer—not because he *did* plan to give her away to Eva, but because he was getting tired of her bullshit and thought she should be taught a lesson.

Once in his apartment, he left the phone on the Parsons table in the living room. It throbbed three more times, in quick succession, each throb a wail of imploration. Determined not to give in to its relentlessness, he changed out of his suit, poured himself a glass of tequila, and got some clothes together to take to the cleaners in the morning. He paid his cable bill and answered some emails on his computer, checking these tasks off on a list that he had been keeping for years, the additions balancing the deletions with the result that it was always the same length. When his mother died, she had left behind just such a list, leading him to vow that when the time came for someone to look through the detritus of his life, there would be something better to be found than this—and now here he was, not that much younger than his mother at the time of her death, and here was this list, and as he held it in his hand, his phone vibrated twice more, each time moving closer to the edge of the table and provoking the Aunt Rose who lay asleep on the cushion of his being to raise herself up on her elbows and tell him, in her croaky voice, that enough was enough, he should shred the list, and set the shreds aflame, and take his phone down into the subway and hurl it onto the tracks just as a southbound 1 was pulling into the station. Because Life, not life, was the thing; Life, which consisted in . . . what? "To burn always with this hard gemlike flame, to maintain this ecstasy . . ."

On a pad of paper, Jake started a shopping list:

Toilet paper
Preparation H
Splenda

Several throbs in quick succession, and the phone fell off the table onto the carpet. He picked it up and looked at it. Of the messages that had come in since he got home, only one was from Min. The rest were from Simon (Jake didn't know his last name), a lecturer in number theory at the University of Manchester with whom he was having an affair despite their never having met. Rather, the affair, which was entering its seventh week, had been conducted entirely via Skype, text, FaceTime, and WhatsApp. At first its very unreality, its defiance of time and distance, had given it a thrilling, transgressive edge, but this aspect had quickly faded (there is only so much you can do by webcam before you start repeating yourself), despite which it dragged on, mostly thanks to Simon, whose principal character trait, so far as Jake could see, was doggedness. Simon was thirty-eight, or claimed to be. Three days before, he had, as it were, upped the ante by telling Jake that he was the great love of his life. A somewhat surreal conversation had ensued that differed from an ordinarily surreal conversation—that is to say, a spoken one—only in that Jake did not have to try to reconstruct it from memory. He could read it over whenever he liked.

Simon: i love you

Simon: i just want to get that out, u are my love for always

Jake: That's very flattering but how can you know that when we've never met?

Simon: what do u mean we've spent hours and hours together

Jake: Virtual hours

Simon: just because its virtual doesn't mean it isnt real

Jake: Well, I think it does

Jake: There are five senses

Jake: We only use two

Simon: how i long to smell the scent of your feet, your socks, your trainers after you've been working out

Jake: we don't call them trainers here, we call them tennis shoes

Simon: that is so hot

Simon: i love you i'm not ashamed

Jake: sorry if this is a rude question but are you stoned?

Simon: that is unkind of u

Simon: yes a little, i smoked half a squiff

Simon: what type socks r u wearing

Jake: black

Jake: cotton-silk blend

Jake: Brooks Brothers

Simon: how long have u been wearing them

Jake: 6 hours

Simon: oh god that is so hot . . . will u cum on them and send them to me

Jake: If I did and customs opened the package that would be embarrassing!😩

Simon: cum on them 3 times

Simon: i love you

Simon: can we whatsapp, I want to watch u cum on ur sox

Jake: Yes, OK

Tonight Simon was writing to Jake from Italy. He was on holiday, a tour of Tuscan and Umbrian hill towns with his Welsh friend Ffanci. Although it was around three thirty in the morning in Assisi, he was still up. So far today he had sent Jake more than forty texts, none of which Jake had answered, though he had read them as they arrived over the course of the day.

Simon: good morning my prince, i kissed u 72 times before I went to sleep

Simon: I hope the night brought you rest and peace, i slept only six hours but well anyhow

ffanci and I are eating so well and theres so little
stress six hours with a wind off the lake and
waking at radiant dawn, the carillons, is like ten
fitful hours at home

Simon: as nothing to waking from a day and night
spent with u

Simon: and many more

Simon: i imagined you were cumming inside me
this morning and i had to have a wank [*Photo of
Simon's abdomen, post-wank*]

Simon: in perugia yesterday I could see u and life
with u in every stone of the cathedral

Simon: today i will take mass

Simon: texting from inside cathedral [*Photo of
interior of Assisi's cathedral*]

Simon: i want to rim u on the high altar, taste your
precum as i suck u on a prie-dieu, hear ur voice
say my name as I drink from u [*Photo of a
prie-dieu*]

Simon: on train to spello

Simon: i love u so incredibly

Simon: i think u are a very italian shape

Simon: i see so many italian men with ur lines but
none so fine, none that re-orient my universe

Simon: i want to feel ur hair, raise a toast to March, spring, the second last minute month apart i hope

Simon: in spello, hotel not so nice as assisi but i dont have to share a bathroom with ffanci, you know what that means 😎

Simon: i know i am cheating, i promised myself not to write to u more tonight, to get a good nights sleep, but i cant, here naked on the hotel bed, i can't help wanting u

Simon: very good wine at dinner [*Photo of a bottle of Torgiano Rosso*]

Simon: one of the waiters ffancied ffanci

Simon: XXXXXXXXXXXXXXXX

Simon: XXXXXXXXXXXXXXXX

Simon: are u there

Simon: i wish u would answer

Simon: today all i thought of was being in a camper van with u and kaspar and ralph and isobel and going on adventures together

Simon: it would be nice if kaspar and ralph and isobel had stories for dorcas

Simon: or do dogs not talk to cats

Reading this, Jake winced. At a reckless moment, he had told Simon that Eva's dogs were his. This delighted Simon so much that Jake had sent him some photos of the dogs, which Simon had posted on Facebook. Jake hoped Eva wouldn't see them. It seemed unlikely.

> Simon: what is ephesus like in winter?
>
> Simon: u and me and the dogs in a camper van in ephesus
>
> Simon: would u read to us in bed
>
> Simon: to hold u while u fry eggs, to lie on your belly, good-night when it comes fair golden prince
>
> Simon: tenderly lovingly the most beautiful man in the world

At this point Jake jumped in.

> Jake: Who is taking care of Dorcas while you're in Italy?
>
> Simon: so u r there!!
>
> Jake: Sorry I was tied up all day
>
> Simon: literally? 😉
>
> Jake: No
>
> Simon: nigel and sue have dorcas
>
> Simon: did u get the photos i sent
>
> Jake: Yes, very nice

Simon: have u posted ur socks

Jake: No

Simon: in assisi i wanted to put the host on a piece of blank paper and cum on it and post it to u

Jake: That would be highly sacrilegious, wouldn't it?

Simon: well, i was raised catholic 😇

Simon: when will u send me ur socks

Min: Jake, are u there? Please call me, We need to talk, asap Xx, Min

Jake: The effect would be too much for you, you would suffocate with pleasure

Min: What??

Jake: Sorry, that was meant for someone else

Min: So I gather

Jake: The effect would be too much for you, you would suffocate with pleasure

Simon: !!!

Simon: tho not as much pleasure as from cumming on ur cock so u can then fuck me and returning the favour i can do the same to u

Jake: I don't get fucked

Min: Hello???? Was that meant for someone else too? I hope so b/c if it is meant for me i don't know what to say lol

172 DAVID LEAVITT

Jake: Sorry, I do that all the time, sending the wrong messages to the wrong people

Min: that could get u in trouble

Jake: I don't get fucked

Simon: god u turn me on u are such a top dad

Simon: i want to suffocate on ur balls

Simon: I want to tie u up and eat ur ass and ur armpits while u scream for joy

Jake: I do the tying up

Min: The electronic equivalent of Freudian slips . . . What secret message are you trying to send me jake?

Jake: Nothing, I told you, it was meant for someone else

Jake: I do the tying up.

Simon: god i am about to cum dad can we whatsapp

Jake: No, not tonight, too tired

Min: OK, well if not tonight when? Tomorrow?

Simon: please dad please whatsapp me

Jake: Too tired

Simon: i am tired too, but horny too

Simon: u cannot imagine how tired my feet r from so much walking here is a pic [*Photo of Simon's feet*]

Simon: does that turn u on? i know u like feet

Simon: send me pix of ur feet, ur socks, ur trainers

Simon: tennis shoes!!!

Jake: Tomorrow

Simon: why r u in such a bad mood?

Min: Still there?

Jake: I'll talk to you tomorrow, Min

Jake: I'm not in a bad mood

Simon: OK

Jake: So what would you think about our meeting up?

Jake: I could come to Manchester or we could meet in London

Simon: god no u would hate manchester

Jake: Or you could come to New York

Simon: cant afford it

Jake: I would pay

Simon: no, cuz what if u r disappointed when u see me

Jake: You could be disappointed too

Jake: I'm a lot older

Jake: Plus I haven't had sex in 14 years

Jake: Well, real as opposed to virtual sex

Jake: I do believe there's a difference

Simon: why not

Jake: I just sort of lost interest

Simon: u could of fooled me lol

Jake: It can happen

Jake: You get used to sleeping alone

Jake: Especially if you can get what you need without having to have anyone over or go meet someone somewhere

Jake: You're spared the trouble and potential embarrassment

Simon: u dont miss it?

Jake: You mean the other three senses? Not as much as I would have thought 14 years ago

Simon: that is sad, jake

Jake: Would you meet me in Venice? I may need to go to Venice for work

Simon: i've never been, would love to but it depends on my lectures & when & if i can get away

Jake: You can watch me jump off a bridge

Simon: what?

Jake: I had a friend

Jake: He always said Venice was the best city to kill yourself in

Jake: And easy because the water is so polluted it would take the flesh off your bones

Simon: this is weird

Jake: Yes, well, if you love someone you have to take the weird with the unweird

Jake: It's why in my opinion love is such a poor foundation for a relationship

Simon: thats so cynical

Simon: if i came to venice would we have sex

Jake: That would be the idea

Jake: If I remember how

Simon: its like riding a bike people say, u don't forget

Jake: It's not a question of forgetting but caring

Jake: Not about people but sex

Simon: i don't know what to say to u when u get in this kind of mood

Jake: Sorry if my being honest bugs you

Simon: thats not what i mean

Jake: Anyway, I should go, I need to take the dogs for a walk

Simon: no, not yet, they say its never a good idea for a couple to go to bed mad

Jake: I'm not mad and we're not a couple

Simon: arent we, for me there is no one else

Simon: i mean since i met u I havent had sex with anyone else

Jake: This isn't sex, sex is what I'm proposing and you seem more scared of it than I am

Jake: Which is weird, since I'm the one who hasn't had it in 16 years

Simon: you said 14

Jake: Look, I have to get some sleep, have to be up early in the am, I promise I'm not mad, goodnight

Simon: ok, goodnight my prince

Simon: goodnight

Simon: goodnight

Jake put down his phone. Next to it was the shopping list he had started.

> *Toilet paper*
> *Preparation H*
> *Splenda*

Was this what his life had come to?

PART IV

14

If he could have, Bruce would have repaired Kathy's life invisibly. He would have slipped down the chimney of her life, arranged the gifts under the tree, and clambered back out without her ever knowing he'd been there, so that when she woke in the morning, it would be to find her debts miraculously paid, an infusion of cash in her checking account, and Susie and her daughters out of her house. But this plan was impracticable. As his lawyer, Rita, explained—a little impatiently, as if he should have known better, which he should have—to pay off someone else's debts without first obtaining their consent was virtually impossible. Nor was there any way, even if he could do it, that Kathy would not guess the identity of her nameless benefactor. This news threw a monkey wrench into the grand plan of rescue that Bruce had envisioned the night he snuck into his own office after hours. It seemed that there would be no chance to spare Kathy the ordeal of thanking, or himself the ordeal of being thanked.

He had settled on a sum of $200,000. This was more than Kathy needed, based on the documents he had copied from her computer, for his intention was to save her from future as well as present worry. The price of the Venice apartment, by contrast, was in the region of $800,000. To this had to be added the cost of its renovation and furnishing, which, knowing Eva, he estimated would come in at around a million dollars. Such a figure made the $200,000 he planned to give Kathy seem negligible. Indeed, that was what pricked his conscience: that $200,000 would make so much more of a difference to Kathy than nearly ten times that amount would make to Eva. And yet Eva persisted in presenting the apartment as a necessity, something without which she simply could not go on.

Since her return from Venice, Bruce's life had seemed to him increasingly bifurcated—or perhaps it had always been that way and he was only now recognizing it. As a teenager, he and his mother had sometimes watched a game show called *3's a Crowd*, the premise of which was the question "Who knows a man better, his wife or his secretary?" Usually the secretary won—or at least that was how Bruce remembered it. Now he wondered, if his own wife and secretary were to compete on *3's a Crowd* (a ludicrous notion, he knew), which would be the victor? Kathy, he suspected. Or was he underestimating Eva?

A trickier question was which of the two women *he* knew better. Before he'd started taking Kathy to her chemo sessions, he would have said Eva. But now he was less certain, and not only because lately he had become so much better acquainted with Kathy's circumstances; also because the more he got to know his secretary, the less he seemed to know his wife.

It was the transitions that most unmoored him—the jolts he experienced when, after spending the afternoon with Kathy at the outpatient center, he would return home to find Eva and Min and some assortment of their friends gathered in the living room. He could still smell the antiseptic on his fingers as Min—on cue, and with a great screeching of gears—brought the conversation around to Venice, after which it would follow its invariable course: from the thrilling prospect of owning an apartment in Venice to the thrilling prospect of restoring an apartment in Venice to the still unresolved question of whether Jake would agree to undertake the restoration of this apartment in Venice. Eva's trajectory was just as predictable. What if it were France in 1940? she'd ask. Would they have the guts and the foresight to get out?

"The part I can't get past is that I don't know if I would," she said. "Especially if I didn't have a place set up to escape to, and every morning the newspapers were telling me I had nothing to worry about."

"OK, but what if you had inside information?" Rachel asked. "What if you had, say, friends high up in the foreign service and they warned you? Would that have been enough to change your mind?"

"It wouldn't have been enough to change mine," Grady said.

"When you think about it, the human capacity not to hear the truth is staggering," Jake said.

"It certainly is in my case," Grady said.

"OK, fine," Rachel said, "but what about today? Isn't that what we're really talking about? If we should be leaving the country, like, now?"

"I'm glad you brought that up," Aaron said, "because the fact is, when you look at the two situations closely, you'll see that there are a lot more differences than similarities. First, our press isn't being censored."

"Not yet," Grady said.

"Second, we're not on a war footing with our neighbors. That is to say, there's no defense line, impregnable or otherwise, along the Canadian border, so far as I'm aware."

"To say nothing of the Mexican border."

"Which means we don't have to worry about looking out the window and seeing tanks rolling down Park Avenue."

"Really, Aaron, you shouldn't joke about those things," Min said, looking at Eva.

"Oh, but there's an even bigger difference," Grady said, "which is that if this were 1940, and we were Europeans, and we decided we had to get out of Europe, at least we'd know where to try to get to. Here. New York. Today it's much harder to figure out where you'll be safe. Me, for instance—if things reached a point where I felt I had to clear out, I'd choose Uruguay."

"Uruguay?" Rachel said. "Why Uruguay?"

"Where to begin?" Grady said. "A progressive government, marriage equality, legalized pot. Plus it's beautiful. And cheap."

"And tiny," Aaron said. "And surrounded by huge countries not exactly famous for their political stability."

"Have you been to Montevideo?"

"I have," Min said. "When I was at *Bon Appetit*—"

"As a matter of fact, if you look at the Social Progress Index, Uruguay's not even in the first tier," Aaron said. "It's in the second tier."

"What's in the first tier?" Rachel asked.

"Let's see." He typed on his phone. "OK, in order of progressivity—is that a word?"

"No."

"Finland, Canada, Denmark, Australia, Switzerland, Sweden."

"And where's Italy?" Min said.

"Also second tier. Higher than Uruguay but lower than the U.S. The U.S. is nineteenth. Italy is twenty-fourth, Uruguay twenty-eighth."

"Well, I rest my case."

"What case?" Aaron said.

"That Italy's a better place to buy an apartment than Uruguay."

"But that's not a case. That's just . . . I mean, if Grady hadn't happened to bring up Uruguay—"

"My memory of Montevideo is that it's charming but a great bore," Min said. "A sort of mini Buenos Aires but without the shopping."

"Some lovely Paris-style buildings," Grady said.

"This conversation is absurd," Eva said. "I am not going to Uruguay." Then she got up and left the table.

Distantly a door slammed.

"Excuse me," Min said, getting up and following her.

"Oh, shit," Grady said. "I'm sorry about this. If I'd known I'd be opening up such a can of worms—"

"It's all right," Bruce said. "The can of worms was already open."

Min resumed her seat and refilled her glass. "She'll be OK in a bit," she said. "Honestly, why are you so determined to tease her? You know all the reasons it has to be Venice. Her book, to start with."

"The one Rachel plans to publish," Aaron said.

Rachel gave her husband a look.

"Speaking of publishing, how's the job search going?" Grady asked.

"I'm not looking for a job," Aaron said.

"He's happier doing freelance," Rachel said.

"Why are you changing the subject?" Min said. "None of this has anything to do with Eva, or the way you've been teasing her."

"I can but bow my head in shame," Aaron said.

"And I mine, in tribute to your loyalty," Grady said, "which is of an order rarely encountered these days."

"Well, that's just how it is between us," Min said, her face flushing. "I mean, Eva was the first friend I made when I moved to New York. We used to spend nearly all our time together."

This was true. Bruce had been there, too, in those early years of their marriage, when he and Eva were living in a rental on East Seventy-eighth Street, and he was a junior broker at a big Wall Street firm, and she and Min were at *Mademoiselle*. There was no Amalia then, just an old Russian woman who came once a week and carried the dog (they had only one at this point) under her arm like a purse while she vacuumed. Little in their life was planned. Eva might cook a spontaneous dinner for him and Min and whomever Min was dating at the time, or they might venture down to Chinatown for soup dumplings, or to a trendy West Village club where Min had only to give her name and they would be let past the crowd on the wrong side of the velvet rope. If one of her boyfriends was tagging along, she might talk about her childhood in Quincy, about the tobacco field that had once been the site of a great house that had been swept away by a hurricane, and how she and her sister, as children, had spent hours combing the field for relics—fragments of floral-patterned china, glass dolls' eyes, rusted cast-iron pans . . . None of this lasted long, only until Bruce got the first of his several promotions, and he and Eva moved to the first of their several bigger apartments, and

Eva quit her job and began the gradual process by which she had folded elegantly into herself, becoming the origami rose around which Min now buzzed and hovered. Their other friends, he supposed, took it for granted that Min's devotion to Eva was mostly a function of the Lindquists' wealth—of the trips to Europe on which Eva took her, and the dinners at nice restaurants to which Bruce treated her, and the weekends in the country, none of which she could have afforded on her own. And yet Bruce knew that there was more to it than that. Few votaries are not masochists, nor can most idols resist the impulse to test the constancy of their flock. Whatever it was that Eva and Min satisfied in each other, money was only its most outward aspect.

In the meantime, the actual purchase of the apartment was proving to be a great nuisance. Early on, Rita had warned Bruce to expect complications, just as Kathy's doctor had warned her to expect side effects. What she hadn't warned him of was how bizarre, how unlike anything he had previously dealt with, these complications would be.

"I've just been talking to Maria Luisa," she told him one afternoon in February—Maria Luisa was her Italian counterpart—"and I'm afraid there's a problem with the kitchen."

"What kind of a problem?"

"Not to put too fine a point on it, it isn't legal. Or at least as far as we can tell it isn't legal, because there aren't any permits on file."

"You mean Signora Foot-and-Mouth just put the kitchen in?"

"So it seems. When Maria Luisa told me, she didn't sound especially worried. Quite the contrary. From what I gather, this sort of thing happens all the time in Italy."

To his own surprise, the news about the kitchen put some wind in Bruce's sails. Indeed, so avid was he to share it with Eva that after work he practically ran home. His breath was still choppy as he took off his coat and strode into the living room, the dogs at his heels.

"Are you all right?" Eva asked.

She was sitting on the sofa with Min, drinking tea.

"I'm fine," he said, still huffing. "I've just been talking to Rita . . . Hold on." He poured out—and drank—a tumbler of water. "OK, so this afternoon Rita called me, and it seems there's an issue . . ."

"Do you mean the business with the kitchen?" Min said. "We already know about that."

"Ursula sent me an email," Eva said.

"Oh, I see," Bruce said. "And what did she say?"

"Well, obviously, that she's absolutely furious with the contractor."

"What contractor?"

"The one who put in the kitchen. Didn't Rita tell you?"

"The contractor lied to her," Min said. "When she hired him, he told her he'd take care of all the permits, that she didn't have to worry about any of it. She only found out yesterday."

"Hold on a second, how could she only find out yesterday? It's her kitchen. If the permits weren't pulled, she couldn't not have known—"

"Poor thing, her head is in the clouds," Min said. "Anyway, it shouldn't matter, should it, since we'll be putting in a new kitchen?"

At this Eva laughed. "Whose head is in the clouds now? You know perfectly well that before we can put the new kitchen in, we have to get the old one sorted out. Penalties will have to be assessed, fines paid."

Where had Eva learned this? Rita had said nothing about fines.

"The only question is who should pay them. Ursula's feeling, obviously, is that it should be the contractor, since he's the one who was responsible."

"Oh, yes, of course it should be the contractor," Min said.

"The trouble is, this was all years and years ago. She didn't save any of the paperwork. She doesn't even know if the contractor's still in business. Or alive. And even if he is, he might refuse to pay, in which case she'll have to sue him." Eva finished off her tea. "Anyway, it's nothing to worry about. Just a hiccup. I'm sure Rita can sort it out."

A hiccup! "I'm afraid it's not quite as simple as that," Bruce said.

"What? Why not?" Min said.

"Well, this is Italy. In Italy these things can take time a long time. The closing may have to be postponed."

Bruce didn't look at Eva as he said this, but rather at Min, whose expression assured him he had hit his intended target.

"Postponed! For how long?"

"For however long it takes them to work things out— Signora Foot-and-Mouth and her contractor."

"But Eva just told you, she doesn't even know if the contractor's still alive."

"That's her problem."

"God, Bruce, do you have to be so callous?" Eva said.

"What's callous? I mean, if it isn't her problem, whose problem is it? Certainly not ours."

"It *is* ours, if it jeopardizes the closing," Min said.

"We can't control that."

"Oh, but we can," Eva said. "We just have to pay it ourselves—the penalty or bribe or whatever."

"Bribe?"

"Call it what you like, the point is, if there's to be a timely resolution, someone's got to be paid something, and . . . well, Ursula can't. The fact of the matter is, she's broke. Otherwise she wouldn't be selling the apartment in the first place. That's the real reason she's putting the blame on the contractor. To save face." Eva wiped at her eyes with a tissue. "I didn't want to say any of that, but you left me no choice."

"Why did you use the word *bribe* just now?"

"It's how things work in Italy. You know it as well as I do. Rita told us."

This was true. When buying property in Italy, Rita had warned them, a certain amount of bribery was par for the course.

"Not that you'll be liable," she'd added, "since you won't be paying any money directly to Ursula. It'll all go through Maria Luisa."

That evening, as he was taking the dogs for their walk, Bruce once again ran into Alec and Sparky. "We've got to stop meeting like this," Alec said.

Again they walked together. This time Alec led—north, then west, in the direction of the park, not the route Bruce usually took.

"Well, I hear you're buying an apartment in Venice," Alec said.

"So I'm told," Bruce said.

"And that I'm the reason you're buying it. Or rather my noisy proximity."

"Don't worry," Bruce said. "If it hadn't been you, she would have found another excuse."

"Too bad. I rather liked the idea that I could be responsible for someone doing something so impulsive and wild. So what's really behind it, if you don't mind my asking?"

"The election. She says she's afraid."

"Afraid of what? I mean, does she honestly believe that any of this is going to affect her life, that on a day-to-day basis it'll make even an iota of difference to her life?"

"You'll have to ask her."

"Afraid," Alec repeated mockingly. "If you want my opinion, that's the reason you liberals are doomed. You're always afraid. Fear is your default program, only instead of just dealing with the things you're afraid of, just getting rid of them, you try to domesticate them, like those lunatics on TV who keep hyenas or whatever as pets, and then, when the hyenas tear their faces off, insist it's their own fault. I mean, there you are with your face torn off and your big worry is that the hyena might not give you a second chance. It's your biggest fail, don't you see? You turn your fear into guilt, you tell yourselves the only reason the hyena tore your face off is that you disenfranchised it or something, and that to make amends you have to be quote-unquote *inclusive*, you have to *bring the hyena into the process*, only it doesn't work, it never works, all it leads to is making the hyena want to rip your face off all over again. Whereas the way we see it, there's only one way to deal with hyenas, and that's to keep them out, to lock them up or send them away until they get the message that if they don't toe the line, that's it. They're toast. It's why Trump won, I'm convinced—because the people who voted for him are sick of all that. After all these years they've reached the point where they're more angry than scared, and they see him as the only guy in the room who has the balls to deal with this shit."

"You make it sound as if fear is something only liberals feel."

"No, everyone feels fear. The difference with you people is that you let fear be your guiding principle, instead of choosing the better solution, which is open carry."

"Open carry? How does that lessen fear, when every time you turn around, someone's gunning down a bunch of kids in a high school cafeteria?"

"Oh, but that's not the gun's fault. If you ask me, it's not even the shooter's fault. It's the parents' fault. These parents, they're like the lunatics on TV with their precious hyenas. They're not raising children, they're raising hyenas."

"Like the ones at Trump's rallies?"

"Those aren't hyenas, they're just ordinary fed-up working white folks."

"Like you?"

"Oh, I see where you're going with this. The strange bedfellows argument. You're wondering how I can bear to climb into the basket of deplorables."

"Who said anything about the basket of deplorables?"

"*She* did. The way you people go on, you'd think Trump's the only candidate who ever made a gaffe, when the fact is, she's made plenty, and hers . . . well, let's just say they tell you a lot more about her than his do about him. The deplorables thing, for instance—it shows that she's a snob and a hypocrite. All the coastal elites are, the way they're constantly going on about redressing the historical injustices done against blacks, Hispanics, women. And yet when it comes to the injustices that have been done to poor white men—radio silence."

"So you're saying that open carry will help poor white men?"

"Tell me something, Bruce. Do you own a gun?"

"I do not. How about you?"

"Five, actually. Three hunting rifles, a revolver, and a pistol."

"And tonight are you carrying the pistol?"

"No need in this neighborhood. On the other hand, if for some reason I had to go to the South Bronx, I'd definitely carry it."

Bruce laughed. He couldn't help himself.

"What's so funny?"

"I'm not sure . . . I guess it's that what you just said gives me so much better an understanding of why my wife wants to get out of this country. I mean, at least in Italy they have gun control."

"Oh, sure. No guns in the land of the Cosa Nostra. Anyway, what's it like, this apartment?"

"I can't really say. I've only seen pictures."

"Hold on—you mean you're buying it sight unseen?"

"Eva's seen it. I suppose I'll see it when we fly over for the closing."

"But if you haven't seen it, how do you know you want it?"

"Who said anything about wanting it? My wife wants it." Bruce stopped and turned to look Alec in the face. "The thing you've got to understand about Eva and me is that we have a system. She does the wanting, I do the paying. That's how it's always been with us, and if I'm to be honest, until now it's suited me as well as it has her. Maybe better, since it's spared me the burden of having to want things for myself."

"But you must want things. Everyone wants things."

"What about you? What do you want?"

"Oh, Lord, where do I begin? A new set of golf irons, a motorboat, an eighty-six-inch LCD TV, Maria Sharapova on call 24/7 . . . Speaking of which, how are things with your secretary? Have you slept with her yet?"

Bruce frowned.

"Sorry, I meant that as a joke. Not in very good taste, I see now."

"Worthy of your president."

"That's fair. I won't pretend that's not fair . . . All right, let's start again. How's your secretary?"

"All things considered, OK. Of course, the chemo is taking its toll. Luckily it'll be over soon. This round, at least."

"Last time we talked, you said she was having money problems, that you wanted to help her out. Have you?"

"Not yet. I'm trying to figure out the best way."

"There is no best way. Trust me on this. Giving people money is always a mistake. Much wiser to make a donation in her name to the American Cancer Society."

"But it's not the American Cancer Society I want to help. It's this one particular woman. It's Kathy."

"So you *do* want something."

"For her, not me."

"All the more reason why you shouldn't give her money."

"Hold on, isn't part of your president's—"

"Our president's."

"Isn't part of your president's argument against Obamacare that if it's abolished, and all these people lose their health insurance, private charities will step in to make up the difference?"

"Self-sufficiency is the core principle of conservatism. At least my conservatism."

"Survival of the fittest? And yet your people want creationism taught in the schools."

"Look, all I'm saying is that once you switch on the faucet, there's no switching it back off. It's cultivating dependency, like those people who keep bailing out their kids even when they're in their thirties. Or forties. We never did that with our girls. With our girls we laid down the ground rules early on, which were that we'd support them and pay for their education through grad school, but that after that, they wouldn't get anything until Kitty and I were in the cold, cold ground."

"And have you kept to that rule?"

"We haven't had to. They have. Since she moved to Cambodia, Rebecca hasn't asked us for a dime. As for Judy— well, she's a tax lawyer. Her husband's a cardiologist. They've got plenty of money, they don't need ours."

"And do you think they'll raise their children the way you raised them?"

"Probably not. Already Judy's way too indulgent with hers. At least that's my opinion. It was a bone of contention between us when we were still speaking."

"Children never follow the example of their parents," Bruce said, yet even as he was saying it he realized that he was the exception to his own rule. His parents told him as much each time they came to visit, how proud they were of him, and how grateful that he had settled into so much more wholesome a life than that of his unemployed, opioid-addicted brother, at the mere mention of whose name—Kevin—his mother's eyes welled up with tears. "Although at least he's given us five wonderful grandchildren," she invariably added, pulling a Kleenex out of her purse and looking meaningly at Eva.

"So she's still not speaking to you?" he asked Alec.

"Judy? No, but the other day she talked to her mother."

"And how did that go?"

"Not well. What Judy said, in effect, was that the only chance for any sort of rapprochement is if I disavow certain principles I hold dear—as dear as she holds hers. And that I simply refuse to do. Of course, if it was up to Kitty, I'd lie. Lying is Kitty's solution to every problem. But I can't do it. The slope is too slippery. Say that five times fast."

"As I get older, I'm less and less convinced that lying is always a bad thing."

"That doesn't surprise me, since you're lying to your wife."

"You mean about wanting to help Kathy?"

"That, and by not telling her you don't want to buy this apartment in Venice. Correct me if I'm wrong."

"No, you're not wrong. Isabel! Oh, for God's sake, why does she always do this?"

What Isabel had done was stop in her tracks halfway across Madison Avenue, bring her paws together, and shit. "Come on, can't you hurry?" Bruce said to her, watching the walk sign blink and the traffic light shift from green to yellow, but she took her own sweet time.

"She's taking her own sweet time," Alec said.

The light turned red. On Madison the flock of waiting cars, mostly taxis, approached the intersection gingerly, giving the dogs a wide berth.

"And people say New Yorkers aren't nice," Alec said.

15

He decided to give Kathy the check on the day of her last chemo session. This was a Wednesday in late February. On this particular afternoon, he didn't drive her but met her at the outpatient center, where she had gone by taxi after a consultation with her lawyer. To his surprise, Susie was there, as was Michael. It was the first time Bruce had met him. His green hair aside, he seemed a well-mannered boy, slim and neatly dressed, unlike his sister, with her tattoos and leggings and leather jacket. To mark the occasion, Bruce had ordered a bouquet to be delivered from Ode à la Rose, Eva's preferred florist, but it was late arriving. Half an hour before the session was due to wrap up, it still hadn't arrived.

He was about to step into the hall to call the shop and ask what was holding them up when the nurses and nurses' aides gathered round Kathy in a circle. "We got this for you," one of the nurses said, and handed Kathy a card that depicted a smiling stick figure in a pink robe throwing a pink mortarboard into the sky. CONGRATS, CHEMO GRAD! the card read.

"We all signed it," the nurse added.

"Oh, how lovely," Kathy said, tears coming into her eyes.

She was just opening the card and beginning to read the little messages written on it when the flowers were brought in—a Brobdingnagian arrangement of pink and peach roses and white lisianthus. At the mere sight of it, a hush descended. The expression in Kathy's eyes, as she put down the card and looked at the flowers, was that of someone dazzled by a bright light.

"Oh, my God," she said.

Bruce winced. I should have known better, he thought. I should have guessed that a moment this delicate could not withstand such a hammer blow of opulence.

"Never mind those, keep on reading your card," he said, but it was too late; already the nurses were dispersing, already Kathy was drying her eyes. Only Michael seemed to take any real pleasure in the bouquet. "I knew it," he said as he read the note pinned to it. "I knew it was Ode à la Rose. Gorgeous." Cautiously he touched his fingertips to one of the stems, as if he feared damaging it. "The thing you need to understand, Mom, is that this isn't just your typical floral arrangement. This is the haute couture of flower arrangement."

"Is it?"

"I'm sorry," Bruce said.

"Why?" Michael said.

"I couldn't tell from the photo on the website that it was going to be this big."

"Oh, but it's fantastic," Kathy said. "Picture me doing that thing that the Coyote does in the cartoon, where his jaw drops and lands on the ground and he has to pick it up and put it back on."

"I got you something, too," Susie said, rifling through her elephantine handbag. "Hold on, I know it's in here somewhere."

"She'll never find it," Michael said. "That bag is the black hole of Calcutta."

"Shut up."

"It's the Roach Motel. Roaches check in, but they don't check out."

"Fuck off. I know it's here. It's a card I made. A decoupage."

"You must have left it at home. You're always forgetting things."

"No, I know I brought it."

"It doesn't matter," Kathy said. "You can give it to me later."

"But I'm sure I brought it. Well, there's only one way to find out."

With that, Susie dumped the contents of the bag onto the floor.

"I'm not sure you should do that," Bruce said. "I mean, I'm not sure it's hygienic."

"I don't think it's there, sweetheart," Kathy said.

"Will you please be quiet and just let me look?" Susie said.

"God, you are so OCD," Michael said.

"Michael, please," Kathy said.

"You can't stand it when anyone else is the center of attention, can you? Even Mom. Especially Mom. Everything has to be about you."

"Will you please just shut the fuck up?" Susie said. "I'm trying to concentrate here."

"Why are you bothering? I mean, it's a card. It's not like a button or a vape cartridge. Things that big you don't have to hunt for, they're either there or they're not."

"Don't worry, Susie, you can give it to me when we get home."

"But I want to give it to you now," Susie said, "the way the nurses gave you *their* card, and Bruce gave you the flowers."

"As if anything you made could hold a candle to those flowers," Michael said.

"You're one to talk. You didn't bring anything."

"But I don't even want any presents," Kathy said. "I never asked for presents."

"I think you should put all that stuff back in your bag, Susie," Bruce said. "Your mother's right, this isn't the time or the place—"

"What business is it of yours?"

"Susie!"

"OK, fine," Susie said, sweeping the piles of coins and toys and chewing gum into the bag. "I'm going out for a cigarette."

She left. With the help of two of the nurses, Kathy got up out of the recliner.

"I'll bring the car around," Michael said.

"You have a car?" Bruce said.

"Why wouldn't we have a car?"

"It's my car," Kathy said. "Michael doesn't have his own car."

"Of course, I didn't mean to suggest . . . I just assumed you'd be staying at the hotel tonight."

"Well, I would normally, only since the kids brought the car . . ."

"Of course."

"Back in a few," Michael said.

"I'm sorry about all this," Kathy said to Bruce.

"About all what?" Bruce said.

"This," Kathy said. "The kids, the drama about the flowers."

"You don't need to apologize for anything," Bruce said.

Susie returned, carrying a smell of char that made Bruce long for a cigarette, followed shortly by Michael.

"Your carriage awaits," he said, bowing to his mother.

"You know what, honey, would you mind terribly if I stayed in town after all?" Kathy said. "I thought I'd be up for the ride, but now that I'm on my feet, I think I might get carsick."

"We can always stop if you need us to," Susie said.

"What, so she can throw up on the side of the LIE?" Michael said. He touched his mother's shoulder. "Whatever works for you, Mom."

"Do you want me to stay with you?" Susie said.

"What, and leave me to babysit for you?" Michael said.

"That's kind of you, Susie, but there's no need," Kathy said. "I'll be fine after a good night's rest."

Susie looked at her mother, who turned away. Then she looked at Bruce, who didn't turn away.

"Whatever," Michael said.

"When will you be back?" Susie asked.

"Tomorrow, after work. When else?"

"I have no idea. That's why I'm asking."

"I'm sorry to interrupt, but I'm parked in a fifteen-minute spot," Michael said.

He had already kissed his mother goodbye and was about to head out the door when Kathy said, "Wait, honey. Would you mind taking the flowers?"

"I'll take them," Susie said, reaching for the bouquet.

"No!" Michael said. "Not like that! You're crushing them."

"Fuck off."

"Kids—"

"How about if I carry them?" Bruce said.

"I'm not sure they're going to fit in Mom's car," Susie said.

"What kind of car is it?"

"An Outback," Kathy said. "White, like yours."

This took Bruce aback, but only for a moment. "Well, then, there's nothing to worry about," he said. "If they don't fit in the back seat, they will in the wayback."

He was right. "Thank God that's over," Kathy said to him as Michael pulled away from the curb. "I don't want to see those flowers ever again."

"I'm sorry, I should have known better—"

"Oh, it's not the flowers themselves," Kathy said. "The flowers themselves are gorgeous. What I'm saying is that I never want to see anything that reminds me of this place ever again."

But the hotel, when they got there, was full. Bruce was dumbfounded. It had never been full before.

"It seems there's some big thing on at the UN," he told Kathy after a brief argument with the receptionist led nowhere. "Only tonight. They'll have rooms again tomorrow."

"It's no biggie," Kathy said. "When I told Susie and Michael I was feeling sick, I was . . . well, not lying exactly. Let's say exaggerating. The truth is, I didn't want to be stuck in the car for an hour with the two of them bickering. Is that terrible of me? Am I a terrible mother?"

"Of course not. I completely understand."

"In that case, if you don't mind getting me a taxi, I should be able to catch the six o'clock train."

"No need for that. I'll drive you."

"That's kind of you, Bruce, but it doesn't make sense. Penn Station is completely out of your—"

"No, I mean to Syosset. I mean home. What's the matter?"

"I don't know. I think I'm about to faint."

He caught her by the arm before she crumpled. "Careful," he said, easing her onto a sofa.

"I'm sorry," she said. "I'm sorry about that."

"Nothing to apologize for."

"I'm really perfectly OK. I don't need to go to the ER."

"So you weren't lying to your kids. Or rather you were lying to me when you said—"

"I didn't want you to worry. Look, it's nothing out of the ordinary, nothing that requires a visit to the ER or anything like that. My oncologist told me from the start this would happen. 'The sickness that's the price you pay for cure,' she calls it."

"In that case we'll just have to find you another hotel."

This time she didn't argue, but stayed where she was while Bruce strode about the lobby, talking into his phone.

After about ten minutes he hung up. "OK, it's all set," he said. "A hotel I know, a small one, on the Upper East Side. Eva and I stayed there when we were having our plumbing redone. Oh, and I got you a room with a soaking tub."

At the mention of the tub, tears once again breached Kathy's eyes. "I'm sorry I'm so weepy," she said.

"How are you feeling? Can you get up?"

"I think I can. Yes, I can."

Nonetheless, she stayed on the sofa until he brought the car around. The concierge helped him help her out.

Despite whatever was on at the UN, it took them only half an hour to reach the new hotel. The place was so near to Bruce's building that he half expected to see Alec and Sparky or even Eva crossing the street.

"Good evening, Mr. and Mrs. Lindquist, and welcome to the Arbuthnot," the bellman said.

"Thank you, but I won't be staying here," Bruce said. "It's this lady who'll be staying here. And she's not Mrs. Lindquist."

"Good evening, madam, and welcome to the Arbuthnot," the bellman said. "May I take your luggage?"

"I don't have any," Kathy said.

The swiftness with which the bellman calculated and digested the possible implications of this statement was a testament to his training in the art of circumspection. "In any case, your room's ready," he said, leading them into the lobby, where the desk clerk asked Bruce if he'd had a good journey, processed his credit card, and gave him two key cards. Curious—the last time he'd stayed at this hotel, he'd paid no attention to its decor. Now he wondered how the lobby looked to Kathy, with its long sofas upholstered in striped green silk, its mahogany bar, its restaurant, before which a reservation book rested on a brass perch. In the lobby, a roast beef smell lingered. Bad oil paintings, each with its own picture lamp, hung on the paneled walls. And yet here and there touches of the contemporary obtruded. The elevators were swift and required the key card to operate. The room they were taken to, recently renovated, was spare and light, almost Japanese in its minimalism.

"Do you mind that it's on the fourteenth floor?" Bruce asked.

"Why should I?" Kathy said, taking in the king-size bed, the view of the park, the bowl of fruit that sat next to the immense television. "This custom of pretending that buildings don't have a thirteenth floor—I've never seen the point of it. I mean, it's still the thirteenth floor, isn't it, no matter what they call it? And they don't do it with 666—have you noticed that? Plenty of buildings have 666 as their street number and nobody says anything about it." She took off her coat and sat down on a pale lilac armchair positioned to take advantage of the view. "Bruce," she said, "our coming here together, with no luggage—you don't think it raised eyebrows, did it?"

"So what if it did? That's the thing about hotels like this. Their reputation depends on their discretion."

"Are you saying there's a need for discretion?"

"No, I'm just saying that if they . . ." But he couldn't finish the sentence.

Kathy laughed. "You're blushing."

"The point is, they know it's only you who's staying the night. I explained that when I called. What's so funny?"

"Seeing you blush like that. It's that Nordic complexion. Your face will always give you away." She slipped off her shoes and lay down on the bed. "Oh, what a glorious mattress. I'm feeling better, by the way."

"Your color's better."

"It's funny—being here with nothing, nothing at all, is actually kind of liberating. I mean, I don't even have a toothbrush."

"The hotel can give you a toothbrush."

"Or dental floss, or deodorant, or . . . anything."

"Don't worry, I'll get you some dental floss. I'll get you some deodorant."

"No, it's OK, I can get by for one night." But already Bruce had taken his phone from his pocket and was checking Google Maps for nearby drugstores, of which, it turned out, there were no fewer than six within a two-block radius. At some point when he hadn't been looking, Manhattan had turned into an island of drugstores. Like an invasive species of plant, they had killed off everything native. The last time he'd passed it, for instance, the Duane Reade he chose, he could have sworn, had been a musical instruments shop. Nor, in its current incarnation, was it a drugstore in the sense he was used to. Rather, it was a cross between a supermarket and a department store, with miniature grocery carts and the actual pharmacy in the basement. For Bruce, who rarely shopped, the sheer variety of goods on display was a marvel. There were a dozen types of dental floss alone, waxed and unwaxed, satin-textured and extra-wide, mint-flavored and Listerine-flavored and no-flavored. It took him ten minutes to settle on the right one (mint-flavored, in an attractive steel-gray dispenser), after which he bought deodorant, a toothbrush (in case the one the hotel provided wasn't any good), toothpaste, nail clippers, Q-Tips, hand lotion, and body lotion. He bought raisin buns, cinnamon buns, barbecue-flavored potato chips, jelly beans, Evian water, and Diet Coke. He bought Advil, Aleve, Tylenol, a pair of slippers, and an oversize pink T-shirt that he figured could serve in a pinch as a nightgown. He almost bought a three-pack of white panties but at the last minute took them out of the cart and left them in the potato chip aisle.

Kathy had given him one of the key cards so that he could use the elevator. Even so, he knocked on her door before going in. There was no answer. He knocked again—and still there was no answer. "Kathy?" he called. "Kathy!" And then: "I'm coming in."

On tiptoe, he stepped into the room. She was lying on the bed, so deeply asleep that when she opened her eyes and saw him she almost screamed. "Sorry," she said, sitting up. "I'm a little disoriented."

"I brought you some things," he said.

"Thank you," she said, gazing at the array of shopping bags with the same expression of amazement with which, in the chemo suite, she had gazed at the gargantuan arrangement of flowers.

Now it was Bruce who sat in the lilac armchair. "Look, before I lose my nerve, there's something else I want to give you," he said. "I mean, something serious. Not like those flowers. Those flowers were just . . . symbolic. A form. This is different."

"Oh?"

"Am I blushing again?"

"You're pink as a baby. Why are you so nervous?"

From his jacket pocket, Bruce extracted his wallet. From his wallet he extracted a folded check, which he handed to Kathy.

"What's this?" she said.

"Open it," he said.

She opened it.

"Oh my God," she said. "But why on earth . . . Wait . . . Is this for real?"

"It's for real. As for why on earth, I should think the answer's obvious. You have debts to pay."

"But this goes way beyond what I need to pay off my debts."

"I know. I didn't just want to give you enough to get out of the hole, I wanted to give you enough to ensure that you can go on, from now on, without having to worry. Enough so that you can focus on the important thing, which is your health."

Again tears came into Kathy's eyes. "I'm sorry," she said, sitting down on the bed. "I'm just . . . stunned. Also a little bit embarrassed."

"Why?"

"Well, you'd think that after working for you for so long, I'd have learned to handle my own finances better, wouldn't you?"

This gave them both a chance to laugh.

"Bruce, I hope you don't think I've been finagling for this. I haven't. Honestly, if I'd known you might do something like this, I'd never have told you—"

"I just want you to promise me one thing—that you'll spend the money on yourself. On things for yourself."

"What else would I spend it on?"

"Your kids. That's something else I wanted to talk to you about. First Michael. You told me he thinks you and Lou haven't done as much for him as you have for Susie. OK, well, as it happens, our interior decorator, or interior designer, or whatever it is they call themselves these days—he's a friend. Enough of one that I can talk to him and see if he'll give Michael an internship."

"Oh my God, could you? That would mean the world to him."

"Of course, I can't promise it'll pay very well. Or at all."

"It doesn't matter. It's a foot in the door."

"OK, good. I'll get on to Jake first thing in the morning. Which brings us to Susie."

Kathy's smile faded.

"I'm going to be frank with you now, Kathy, even though you might not like what I'm going to say. I don't think you can afford to have Susie and her girls in your house anymore. It's costing you too much, and I don't just mean financially. It's too much stress. Michael's fine, you've said so yourself. And so the question we're faced with is what to do with Susie."

"That's always been the question."

The flatness of Kathy's tone as she said this surprised Bruce. "Well, then, we just have to find the answer."

"And what if there isn't an answer?"

"There's always an answer. For instance, we could find her an apartment."

"But I told you, no one will rent to her."

"Or see if she can get public housing."

"There's a waiting list."

"OK then, what if I find her an apartment and put the lease in my name?"

"No. It won't work. She'll wreck the place. She'll be on the phone to you every five minutes. She'll find killer mold and complain to the landlord and the landlord will complain to you."

"At least she won't be under your feet."

"Of course she will. And under yours too. Don't you get that?"

"Get what?" He stood up from the chair and sat next to Kathy on the bed. "The way I see it, Kathy, the real problem is that you're not used to people wanting to help you. And that's all I want to do. With Susie, I mean. I want to save you from Susie."

"Don't talk about my daughter like that."

"I'm not saying anything you haven't said yourself."

"That's different. I'm her mother. I'm her mother, and she's part of me, and I won't have anyone talking about her like that."

"I'm sorry. I didn't mean—"

"That's my point. You don't *mean*." Kathy was pressing her fingers to her temples. "OK, look, let's start again. Let's reboot. Bruce, much as I appreciate all you're offering, I can't accept it. I wish I could, but I can't."

"Why not?"

"Because I'll owe you too much. I don't want to owe anyone that much ever."

"But you won't. It's a gift. I'm not asking you to pay it back. I'm not asking for anything from you."

"Oh, but you are. You're asking for the satisfaction of seeing everything that's wrong made right. Only it won't be. It'll still be wrong, Susie will still be wrong. She'll just be wrong somewhere else—"

"Exactly."

"—but she'll still be my daughter. You're lucky. You've got money—enough money to rescue, and to choose who you rescue—and you want the satisfaction of exercising that power. And yet there's another side to it. There's my admitting, my having to admit, that if I'd led a better, more orderly life, I wouldn't be in this position, and very possibly neither would Susie."

"You need to stop thinking about the past. That's the point of all this. To give you a fresh start."

"A fresh start . . . I hate that expression."

"Why?"

"Because what good is a fresh start if you're already this close to the end? And I might be. I mean, I could be dead in six months. Or a year. Or six years. I have no idea how to move forward from this, no idea what to do, how to plan."

"You don't have to do anything . . . OK, look, you're right about rebooting. Let's go back to the start. Let's go back to my giving you the check. That's all. The check. Forget the rest. Will you accept the check?"

Suddenly she turned and kissed him. He was startled, and she could tell. He could tell she could tell. The tiniest gesture of resistance on his part—that was all it took before she pulled away. "I'm sorry," she said. "Oh, God—what was I thinking? Excuse me."

She stood and went into the bathroom. She left the door slightly ajar. From where Bruce sat, he could hear water running, the taps of the tub switched on full blast.

He got up from the bed and stepped closer to the door. "Kathy," he said.

"Please go," she said.

"No," he said. "Not until I know you're OK."

"I'm fine. I'll see you tomorrow. We'll talk tomorrow."

"Kathy, please."

This time she didn't answer. The water ran fiercely. Steam billowed through the crack in the door.

The noise he heard—it might have been weeping, or it might have been the water running, or the release of steam.

What should he do now? Force his way in? That's what Alec would have done. Were Alec in his shoes, Bruce felt sure, he'd have considered the half-open door's implications, done a quick risk-benefit analysis, and then gone in or not. Probably gone in. Yet even if the door *was* an invitation, he knew he couldn't bring himself to accept it casually. He could only accept it gravely—or not at all.

It was then that he realized that the obvious next step—the step that everyone, possibly even Kathy herself, seemed to assume he would take—was one he could not bring himself to take.

Was this ungallant of him? Was it ungallant to be willing to console a suffering woman with money but not love? As a boy, whenever he'd had a crush on a girl, he would indulge in a fantasy of coming upon her, weeping, in a wood. Moved by her sorrow, he would take her in his arms and hold her until the embrace verged into a kiss—as if arousal were the inevitable outcome of comfort, or weeping a tactic in a game of seduction. Yet what if weeping was, rather, exactly what it seemed—an expression of brute misery? In that case, to take advantage of the situation would be caddish. Even if Kathy had left the door ajar on purpose, only a cad, someone like Alec, would actually go through it.

He saw now that he had a choice. He could sleep with her or he could give her money. He couldn't do both, since to do both would be to turn a loss into a gain, and in this case, that would be beneath him.

It was not a difficult choice to make. He would do what would help her most.

With great care, as if handling something fragile, he took the things he'd bought at Duane Reade out of their bags and arranged them on the bed. Atop them he laid the check. Then he left the room, stopping to hang the DO NOT DISTURB sign.

It was only when he got to the elevator that he realized he still had the key card. It was in the side pocket of his jacket. As quietly as he could, he retraced the steps to Kathy's room and slipped it under her door.

16

He was late for dinner. The dinner was at a Japanese restaurant in midtown, with Grady, Aaron, Rachel, and Sandra. Although Bruce didn't know it, only a few blocks away, Min and Jake and Pablo were also having dinner, at an Indian restaurant, with Indira Singh.

By the time he arrived, the others had already ordered. They were sitting on silk cushions, around a short-legged table built into a recess in the floor and spread with plates of sushi and sashimi. Bruce hated eating in these—what else to call them?—cavities, just as he hated having to take off his shoes, which looked comically huge, like clown shoes, when lined up alongside Eva's ankle boots, Grady's moccasins, Rachel's Mary Janes, Sandra's Uggs, and Aaron's sneakers, with their dirty white laces and soles. Unsurprisingly, the group was already in the thick of a lively conversation, the subject of which no one bothered to bring him up to speed on; he had to piece it together on his own. It seemed that a young writer, the author of a well-received first novel, was being sued by her ex-boyfriend, also a writer, for plagiarism. According to the ex-boyfriend, she had installed spyware on his computer and used it to steal passages from his work, which she had then incorporated into her own. While she admitted to having installed the software, she insisted she had done so only to find out if the ex-boyfriend was seeing other women. Plagiarism, she insisted, had nothing to do with it.

The scandal fascinated Aaron. "I mean, *spyware*," he said, as Bruce tried to make space for his legs in the narrow fissure Eva had saved for him between her and Sandra. "I'm sorry, but since when is installing spyware on someone else's computer a normal thing to do?"

"Can anyone install spyware?" Grady asked. "Could I?"

"You could if you knew how," Rachel said.

"Really? Where would I go to learn?"

"Google."

"I always thought spyware was the stuff that got onto your computer when you clicked on the links in spam," Sandra said.

"As usual, in his avidity to be the first to share gossip, Aaron's left out the key ingredient to the story," Rachel said, "which is that the computer in question was originally hers—the girl's. She sold it to the boyfriend *after* they broke up."

"That's what I thought I read," Eva said. "That it was because it was her computer that she could still log on to it."

"Yes, by means of the spyware," Aaron said.

"I'm sorry, but who in their right mind would sell their computer to their ex-boyfriend?" Sandra said.

"I don't know, maybe he couldn't afford a new one," Rachel said. "She might have thought she was doing him a favor."

"With the added advantage that she could keep an eye on him," Aaron said.

"The whole thing strikes me as kind of lame," Sandra said.

"Fine, she did something lame," Rachel said. "Haven't we all done lame things with ex-boyfriends? The bottom line is that the plagiarism charge is ludicrous. The guy's just jealous because she's published a successful novel and he hasn't. Men can't stand it when women do better than them. It enrages them. It's like they regard having the greater success as their God-given right."

"Putting aside for the moment the fact that you're indulging in some vast and, I would argue, highly dubious generalizations," Aaron said, "I really don't think any of what you just said excuses the fact that this woman installed software on a computer for the express purpose of having access to everything her ex-boyfriend did without his knowing it. His emails, his texts, whatever he was writing."

"And if she was spying on him, who's to say she wasn't stealing from him?" Grady said.

"Now, if you want to know my theory about that—" Aaron said.

"As if you wouldn't tell us even if we said we didn't," Rachel said.

"Thank you, darling. Anyway, my theory is that when she planted the spyware, she knew perfectly well that he'd find it and make a fuss."

"Do you think she knew he'd sue her?" Sandra asked.

"Not necessarily, but she must have known he'd do something. Consciously or otherwise, she must have wanted him to. She must have wanted the publicity."

"But it's such bad publicity."

"For that generation, there's no such thing as bad publicity."

"I'm sorry, but that's a totally sexist response," Rachel said. "I mean, what if the roles were reversed? What if it was the boyfriend who'd planted the spyware? She'd still be the one who'd be vilified."

"Would she?"

"I think if it were a man, he'd be looked at as some sort of creepy predator," Sandra said.

"It's also worth noting that when she sold him the computer, there were naked pictures of her on it," Aaron said.

"Oh, great, so now we've got another reason to shame her," Rachel said.

"I'm not shaming her."

"Yes, you are. You're implying that because she had naked pictures of herself on her computer, she's a slut."

"Well, do you have naked pictures of yourself on *your* computer?"

"So what if I do? The point is, if it were the man who had planted the spyware, and if the naked pictures were of him, no one would accuse him of being a slut."

"No, just a pervert and an exhibitionist and a stalker. Like Anthony Wiener. *So* much better."

"What I still can't get over is that she actually went through with it," Grady said. "I mean, let's be honest, we've all fantasized about doing things like that, right? But to make the leap from fantasy to action . . . Take Bruce here. Bruce, if you had the opportunity to read Eva's emails without her knowing it, would you take it?"

The way Grady said this, Bruce could tell he was making an effort to bring him into the conversation, to which he had so far contributed nothing.

"No, I wouldn't," he said.

"Oh, come on," Rachel said. "What if, let's just say, you stumbled on a piece of paper on which she'd scribbled her password? Could you really resist?"

"Could you resist if you found mine?" Aaron said.

"Even if he couldn't, I doubt he'd find my emails very interesting," Eva said.

"And what about you, Eva? If you could, would you read Bruce's emails?"

"She'd find them even less interesting," Bruce said.

At this Sandra laughed, a bit more loudly than was merited. The conversation moved on to other subjects. Only Bruce kept thinking about the writer and the boyfriend and the spyware. He hadn't been lying when he said that even if he got hold of Eva's password, which in fact he knew, he wouldn't read her emails. On the other hand, he *had* furtively logged on to Kathy's computer. He had copied her bank and loan statements. And then, when he put her computer back to sleep, what had he thought of? The moment in *How the Grinch Stole Christmas* when Little Cindy-Lou Who stumbles upon the Grinch, in full Santa regalia, shoving the Christmas tree up the chimney and is placated by a glass of water and a lie about a broken bulb. An allegory of innocence and misplaced trust, of giving turned into taking, turned literally upside down. Sitting at that awful table in the Japanese restaurant, drinking sake, his legs cramping, he pondered both the Grinch's story and that of the writer who had planted the spyware, until in his mind the two became hopelessly blurred, until it was Cindy-Lou Who planting the spyware, and the Grinch publishing the novel, and Bruce himself stuffing the Christmas tree up the chimney in the middle of the night.

On the way home from dinner, Eva was unusually quiet. Bruce took the dogs for their walk, expecting to find her in bed when he got back. Instead she was sitting at the kitchen table, typing.

As soon as he walked in, she shut her computer.

"Did everyone do everything?" she asked.

"Everyone did number one. Only Isabel did number two."

"You didn't rush them, did you? You gave them enough time?"

"I gave them the usual time. Do you want me to take them out again?"

"No, no, it's fine." She had her eyes and fingertips on the top of the computer, as if itching to reopen it.

"Is everything OK?" Bruce asked. "You look worried."

"I wouldn't go so far as to say worried. It's just that I just checked my email, and I had a note from Ursula. It seems there's been another hiccup."

"Hiccup? What kind of hiccup?"

"So you know that the palazzo's been in her family for centuries, right? Two centuries at least. And over that time, the various heirs have been sort of, well, carving it up, and selling off bits and pieces of it to each other, so that now no one seems to know who owns what."

"I doubt that. People always know what they own."

"Yes, but they don't always know what they don't own. At least that's the case with Ursula, who apparently thought she owned more than she did."

"You mean the apartment isn't hers?"

"No, nothing like that. All that isn't hers—and she only learned this yesterday—is the foyer."

"Foyer? What do you mean, foyer?"

"What do I mean? I mean the foyer. You know, the one that leads from the stairs and elevator to the front door. Well, as it turns out—and again, she only just found this out—it doesn't belong to her. It belongs to her cousin Enrico in Milan."

"Hold on. How big is this entryway?"

"I don't know. Twelve by twelve?"

"And someone else owns it? I mean, as an independent piece of property?"

She nodded. "From what I gather, this sort of thing happens all the time in these old palazzi. Apartments get reconfigured, split in two or combined into one, and in the process, bits and pieces get forgotten."

"But how could she not know? She must have known."

"I'm only telling you what she told me. Listen." Eva opened the computer. " 'Until this afternoon, I assumed that the foyer was mine. Enrico said nothing about it, and since he almost never comes to Venice, the issue didn't arise until—' "

"So hold on. What she's saying is that this foyer, this hallway we'll have to walk along every time we go in and go out of the apartment—belongs to someone else? That every time we go in and out of our own apartment, we'll be trespassing?"

"I hardly think it counts as trespassing."

"Legally it does. We could be arrested."

"What, do you honestly think the Venice police don't have better things to do than stake out Americans when they come home from shopping?"

"They might if someone gave them a tip. Or a bribe."

Again Eva shut her computer. "I knew you were going to react like this. I could have predicted it."

"Of course you could have, because it's the obvious way to react."

"Bruce, will you please not interrupt? You haven't even let me finish reading you Ursula's email. She's very upset about this. Luckily, though, there's a simple way to resolve the situation, which is that we just go ahead and buy the foyer. As a separate transaction. Ursula's already spoken to her cousin and he's happy to sell it to us."

"I'm sure he is. And I'm sure she is, too, since she's bound to get a cut."

"Bruce!"

"And has he named his price, this cousin?"

"I don't know. How should I know? I only just found out. *She* only just found out."

"Or so she claims . . . Well, one thing's for sure, whatever the price is, it's bound to be extortionate. I mean, by itself, what's a hallway worth? Who buys a hallway? We're the only ones who have any good reason to buy it. He has to know that, this cousin. He has to know he's got us over a barrel—"

"Why is your first impulse to assume that people are venal?"

"Because they usually are."

"I can't believe this. You've never even met Ursula, and yet you're making all sorts of assumptions about her, that she's out to cheat us or gouge us. Why?"

"It's just this habit she has of springing things on us. That business with the kitchen, for instance."

"That wasn't her fault. It was the contractor's fault."

"Eva, I have to be honest. This apartment, this whole thing—the further we go, the less I trust it."

"But why? You know as well as I do, whenever you buy real estate, there are glitches. It was the same with the house in Connecticut, the same with this apartment."

"And yet none of the other people we've bought from kept saying, every time a glitch came up, that they'd only just found out about it, that until that minute they'd had no idea."

"You really have it out for Ursula, don't you? Or is she just the excuse? Who is it you really have it out for? Is it me? Are you angry at me because for once in my life I did something on my own, without asking your permission? Or do you just not take my needs seriously?"

"Eva, I know how much this apartment means to you. It's just . . . Weren't you taken aback when you got Ursula's email? You must have been."

"Of course I was. But then I thought about it, and I saw there was an easy solution to the problem."

"Too easy."

"So what are you suggesting, that we pull out altogether? Is that what you want?"

Although it was, Bruce couldn't find it in himself to say so. "I just think we need maybe to be less . . . conciliatory. To play hardball a little. Maybe tell her that she's the one who ought to buy the hallway from her cousin."

"And what if we do that, and she turns around and sells the apartment to someone else?"

"What, has she told you there are other people interested? A couple from Kansas City, perhaps?"

"No! She hasn't said anything like that. I'm just being realistic. I mean, an apartment like this, such a rarity—it goes without saying other people will be interested, highly interested, and I can guarantee you, none of them are going to be so cheap as to have a fit every time there's a hiccup."

"I'd say this counts as more than a hiccup."

"Why are you doing this? I don't understand. It's like I don't know you anymore."

"I could say the same thing."

"No, you couldn't, because I've been completely forthright. I've made no bones whatsoever about why I want this apartment. And it's not just the hiccups or glitches or whatever you want to call them. You've been resistant from the start. Don't deny it."

"I'm not denying it."

"Yet you won't say why. Or did you think I didn't notice? Ever since I got back from Venice, you've been irritable, glum, constantly losing your temper."

This surprised Bruce. Until that moment, he hadn't realized he had a temper to lose.

After that Eva went to bed. As soon as she'd left the kitchen, Bruce poured himself a glass of whiskey. She was right, of course. There was much to explain his present mood that she didn't know—not the least of it that he had given Kathy, that very afternoon, a substantial check, and left her weeping in a hotel room. Several weeks had passed since the evening he made his raid on her office, and got Sandra's text, and hurried home in a state of near elation. He remembered that evening now, just as he remembered the morning that followed, the phone call from Eva telling him about Ursula's apartment and the impulse that had seized her to buy it.

Was it because of that phone call, he asked himself as he drank down the whiskey, that he had put off carrying through on his plan to help Kathy? What if Eva had called him a day earlier, or not called him at all? Would he have acted differently? Would he have given Kathy the money sooner?

Later? Had second thoughts and given her less money? Or none at all?

Maybe he was confusing effect with cause. Maybe the truth was that he had carried through on his plan not in spite of Eva's decision to buy the apartment, but because of it.

There were no answers to any of these questions. There never are to questions that concern how things might have turned out if something hadn't changed. And something had changed. That much Eva had figured out. She just didn't know what it was.

Did he?

PART V

17

When Min stumbled over her lies, as she did often, her instinct told her to try to repair the damage quickly, before it spread. This was why, after she left the Indian restaurant, the first thing she did was call Jake. Her hope was to smooth over the lie he'd caught her telling before he said anything about it to anyone else, Eva especially. Just how she'd manage this, she wasn't sure. Instinct, as usual, would be her guide. But then Jake hadn't picked up or responded to her texts, and she'd grown anxious. Was he giving her the silent treatment? Maybe. Or maybe he hadn't been paying attention to her at dinner, hadn't even been listening when the conversation turned (when Min turned it) from Venice to Eva and her apartment. In that case, to try to cover up her lie would only be to dig herself in deeper.

The better course of action, she decided, was to say nothing at all to Jake and instead tell Eva about her idea for the article right away rather than wait, as she had originally planned, until Jake made up his mind. Accordingly, a few days after the dinner, she called Eva and asked if she might come by her apartment after work.

"Does it have to be today?" Eva said.

"It's important," Min said.

"OK, but it'll have to be early. How about four thirty?"

"Couldn't it be a bit later than that? Say five thirty?"

"I'm afraid not. We're going out at five thirty."

Min made an Edvard Munch scream face, something she would never have done in front of Eva. Her friend's obliviousness to the fact that she had a job was a long-standing source of irritation to her—an irritation that, as usual, she suppressed.

"OK, then, four thirty," she said.

"See you then," Eva said.

Later that afternoon, as Min was putting on her coat to leave, Indira strolled by her desk.

"Going already?" she asked, glancing at her Apple Watch.

"Oh, yes, didn't I tell you?" Min said. "I have an appointment with this fabulous young architect. A real rising star."

"Terrific. I hope something comes of it."

"Me, too."

"I mean for the magazine."

As if the conversation was over, Indira drifted away, only to stop in her tracks, turn, walk back, and look Min in the eye.

"I don't like having to remind you of this," she said, "but you're really supposed to be at your desk until five. At least."

"I know. I'm sorry. This is an exception."

"I wouldn't be bringing it up if it didn't happen so often— your leaving early, or taking Fridays off, or time off to travel."

"Well, that trip to Venice should certainly pay dividends."

"Technically, I should take that out of your vacation time. I'm not going to. I'm just making a point. Your colleagues, the younger ones especially, they're here every night until eight or nine. Sometimes later. You can imagine how this looks to them. And it's not just you it affects, it's me, since it leaves them with the impression that I'm giving you preferential treatment. Well, see you in the morning."

"Yes, see you tomorrow."

In the taxi uptown, Min did the deep-breathing exercises she had learned, years before, in a yoga class. She was angry, that much she knew. The question was with whom. Was it Eva, for assuming that all she had to do was say jump and Min would jump? Or was it Indira, for behaving like a friend one minute and a boss the next? Or was it herself?

She decided it was herself. It was the least risky course.

Just before four thirty, she rang Eva's bell. "Come in," Eva said, opening the door just enough to let her through. "I'm afraid we're a bit at sixes and sevens at the moment." She mimed wiping sweat from her brow. To Min's surprise, Eva had her hair tied back with a scrunchie and was wearing what passed, in her world, for work clothes: white tennis shoes, pressed jeans, a taupe cotton cardigan over a light blue T-shirt.

"Prepare yourself," she said, and walked Min into the living room, where Amalia was on her knees, wrapping the loveseat in aluminum foil.

"What is this, some sort of conceptual art installation?" Min said.

Though she meant this as a joke, Eva didn't laugh. "Actually, it's an attempt to solve a problem. You see, while we were in Venice—Bruce only told me this after I got back, so as not to worry me, he *says*—Caspar, completely out of the blue, started jumping up on the loveseat and lifting his leg. My first thought was that it was separation anxiety—males mark when they're anxious, you know—but now I've been home a full two weeks and not only is he still doing it, but the others have gotten in on the act. We've been living in a state of constant vigilance, with Amalia and me always at the ready to stop whatever we're doing and come running with the pee-pee cleaner. Isn't that right, Amalia?"

"Yes, Mrs. Lindquist," Amalia said, cutting the foil into sheets.

"We've tried all sorts of things. First we tried bitter apple spray, but it didn't make any difference. Then we tried those dog diapers, and, well, I don't have to tell you what a disaster *that* was. Just trying to get the diapers on—I mean, you *know* what my dogs are like, you *know* what it's like trying to hold down a Bedlington. Well, you might as well be trying to hold down a tornado.

"Anyway, I'd just about reached the end of my rope when Sandra Bleek came by—you remember Sandra, Grady's cousin?—and she told me a friend of hers had the same problem with her dog, and that her groomer suggested she cover the sofa with foil—apparently dogs can't stand the sensation of foil under their paws—so I thought, why not give it a try?"

"And has it helped?"

"Up to a point. The problem now is, every time they jump up on the loveseat, they tear holes in the foil, or try to pull it off with their teeth, and then Amalia has to do the whole thing over again. These days we spend more money on Reynolds Wrap than we do on food, don't we, Amalia?"

"Yes, Mrs. Lindquist," Amalia said.

"I must say, Amalia, you've done a beautiful job," Min said, admiring how neatly Amalia had smoothed the foil sheets and tucked in the corners. "It's like a miniature Christo."

"Let's sit over here," Eva said, leading Min to the dining table. "I've got macarons."

"Oh, how wonderful! I love macarons."

"They're from Ladurée. Personally I prefer the ones from Maison du Chocolat, but you take what you can get. Here, have one."

She held out the box, which Min surveyed before opting, after some internal debate, for lemon.

"Now, if you want to know what I think this business with the loveseat is *really* about," Eva said, "it's the election."

"Really?" Min said, wiping merengue crumbs from her lips. "But wait . . . What could the dogs know about the election?"

"More than you might think. Dogs are incredibly sensitive to these things. For example, Alec Warriner—you know, our neighbor who threw the inauguration party—I don't know if you've seen it, but he has this wheezing, smelly old dachshund that *our* dogs absolutely despise. Anyway, for the last month or so, Bruce and Alec have been walking the dogs together. Ours and his. It started just before we left for Venice. Bruce didn't tell me. I found out from Frank." She leaned across the table as if to deliver a confidence. "My theory is that it's having to share their walks with Alec and that dachshund that's causing the dogs so much stress."

"Have you mentioned this to Bruce?" Min asked, surreptitiously taking another macaron.

"Not yet. What I can't believe is that he's actually spending time with that man. I see it as a betrayal."

"Well, but Eva, it's just dog walking."

"Just dog walking? What do you mean, just dog walking? You've seen the result. You've seen the damage it's doing."

"Yes, because you've pointed it out to me. Bruce probably hasn't noticed."

"That much I'm sure of. He can be so oblivious when he chooses to."

"But he might not be choosing this. For all you know, he might not even *want* to take walks with that man. It might be that whenever he goes out to walk the dogs, that man just tags along, and Bruce is too polite to tell him not to."

"Then why hasn't he said anything about it to me? Why has he kept it a secret?"

"Well, you know Bruce. Probably he doesn't want to upset you."

"More likely he doesn't want to upset Alec. It's always been that way with him. He can't bear to say no to anyone—except me."

"Eva, you know that's not true."

"Do I? I think what bothers me most about this thing is that the dogs have picked up on what Bruce knows perfectly well and chooses to ignore—how deeply I loathe Alec Warriner, how affronted I am by all he represents. They have. They recognize Alec as an enemy, and so the fact that their master is treating him like a friend causes them this incredible stress that they take out on the sofa. It's classic PTSD."

Min helped herself to a third macaron. Although Eva's words were grim, her tone was offhand, almost breezy. She often did this—said dark things in a light way, as if to challenge Min to guess her true mood and see if she responded appropriately.

"Look, why don't you just tell Bruce you'd rather he stop walking with him?" she said.

"And risk his biting my head off? No, thanks."

"Bruce bite your head off? I hardly think—"

"But you've seen it yourself. Remember how impossible he was about that hiccup with the kitchen? Since then it's reached the point where I have to muster all my nerve just to bring up the subject."

"Do you think he's nervous about buying the apartment?"

"I don't know if it's the apartment itself or if he's just grouchy for some other reason and taking it out on the apartment. Whatever the case, he's becoming impossible to talk to."

"Maybe it's the election. It's sure to have upset him too."

"But if it's the election, then why on earth is he going on these walks with Alec Warriner? No, I think what this is really about is how upset *I* am, and that I'm refusing to do what everyone else is doing, which is either lapsing into this state of terrible ennui or putting all their energy into looking the other way. Now, I'm not saying I wouldn't do that if I could, but I can't. My dread is too strong."

Min took a fourth macaron. These days Eva talked about her dread the way other people talked about their arthritis or their colitis.

"The worst part is the complete loss of any basic sense of well-being. It's like the feeling you sometimes get on a plane, when suddenly you know—you just know—that the only thing that will stop the plane from crashing is if you keep saying to yourself, 'The plane won't crash, the plane won't crash.' Over and over, without ever slipping up or letting your mind wander."

"Do you do that?"

"The rest of you, you live as if you're in a bubble, and because you're in the bubble, you're safe from everything outside. For me, though, the bubble isn't there. Instead I'm on the plane. I'm always on the plane."

"But darling, you're not. Plenty of people feel the same way you do."

"You can't know what I feel. No one can know what anyone else feels."

"Well, no, of course not. And yet there is such a thing as empathy. Last night, for instance, I was watching MSNBC—"

"You know I never watch the news anymore. I refuse to watch the news anymore."

"But if you don't watch the news, is it any wonder you feel isolated? Don't get me wrong, I'm not suggesting you watch *him*. I never watch *him*. As a matter of fact, every time he comes on, I mute the volume—it's reached the point where the mute button on my remote control barely works anymore. No, what I do is, I only watch the smart people, the decent people, like Rachel."

"Rachel Weisenstein?"

"Rachel Maddow."

"What, you know her personally?"

"Of course not, I've just . . . come to think of her as Rachel. As a friend, as someone I can rely on to, well, guide me through this morass. There's comfort in that, I find."

"What, in watching a bunch of so-called analysts sitting around a table with empty coffee mugs, congratulating each other on agreeing with each other? The news isn't news anymore, it's just pompous opinionating, the purpose of which is to keep us anxious, because these people, these newspeople, even your beloved Rachel Maddow, they know that as long as they can keep us anxious, as long as they dangle the carrot of consolation in front of us, they've got us hooked. They're no different than the French papers in 1940, just more sophisticated. And more venal."

"Yes, but if you're anxious already, what difference does it make? And anyway, Rachel's not like the others. She's better. So are her guests, like the woman she had on last night."

"You're determined to tell me about it, aren't you? All right, go ahead."

"OK, well, last night Rachel had on this psychiatry professor—from Cornell, I think, or maybe Penn—and she was saying, this psychiatry professor, that Tr—that there's a provision in the Constitution that allows the cabinet or the Congress, I can't remember which, to remove a sitting president from office if it's shown that he's not mentally fit to hold the job. Which, according to her, he isn't. Narcissistic personality disorder was her diagnosis."

"Oh, I can't stand this insistence on medicalizing everything! Why can't people just admit the truth, which is that he's a devil, that there are such things as devils in the world? Here, have another macaron."

"Thanks. But is there really a difference? I mean, whether we call him a devil or say he has narcissistic personality disorder, aren't we talking about the same thing?"

"We most certainly are not. A personality disorder is treatable, with drugs or whatnot, whereas devils simply . . . are. Most of us are alloys of so many things, we can't tolerate the idea of a devil, because it has no complexity—all it is is appetite, for power and for worship and for blood. I think that's what's upsetting the dogs so much. They recognize a devil when they see one."

"I don't know. Maybe it's the old devil-you-know versus the devil-you-don't-know thing."

"No one can know the devil. Not even Rachel Maddow. Are you all right, Amalia?"

"Finished," Amalia said, rising with effort from her knees.

No sooner had she begun to make her way to the kitchen, however, than Ralph jumped up onto the sofa.

"Ralphie, no!" Eva said, leaping up to grab him before he lifted his leg.

The foil was torn. Amalia looked at it in despair. "I can't do no more right now, Mrs. Lindquist," she said. "I'm too tired."

"Of course not, Amalia," Eva said. "Never mind, you go and have a rest in the kitchen."

Murmuring to herself in Spanish, Amalia withdrew. Eva put Ralph down. "Now do you see what I'm living with?" she said to Min. "My only escape valve is Venice. These days all I read are books about Venice, all I look at are pictures of Venice. Oh, sorry, let me see who this is."

Her phone had pinged. She glanced at it, then put it back in her pocket.

"Just Bruce saying he's running late." She resumed her place at the table. "Anyway, what is it you're so eager to talk to me about?"

"What? Oh, yes, of course. I won't beat around the bush. I'll cut right to the chase."

"Isn't the latter an example of the former?"

"Ha! I suppose it is. Well, as I was saying—"

"But you weren't. You haven't."

"OK, well, yesterday afternoon, Indira and I were having a brainstorming session—I'm sure I've told you about Indira, she's our new editor—"

"Yes, quite a number of times."

"Oh, OK, good. So anyway, we were brainstorming, Indira and I, and I happened to mention your apartment in Venice, and her eyes just lit up. She asked if I had any pictures, and I showed her the ones on my phone, and the long and the short of it is, she wants me to do a piece on it for the magazine. Isn't that fantastic?"

"For *Enfilade*?"

"Yes, that is the magazine I work for, last I checked." Again Eva didn't laugh. "But wait, here's the best part. Not only does Indira want to run the piece, she wants to put it on the cover. Well, what do you think?"

"To be honest, I haven't had time to think anything yet."

"Well, no, of course not. It's an important decision. You'll want to take a few days to mull it over. Or more than a few days."

"Have you told Jake about this?"

"I have, as a matter of fact, and he's thrilled. Totally on board."

"But how can he be when he hasn't even made up his mind to do the apartment?"

"Sorry, what I meant was that he says that if he does decide to do the apartment, which we both know perfectly well he will, he's on board with having it published in the magazine— assuming, of course, that you are."

"In other words, his decision is contingent on mine. And mine is contingent on his."

"I suppose you could look at it that way. The way I look at it, though, is that the chance to be on the cover of *Enfilade* may be just what it takes to get Jake off his, excuse me, rear end. He's coming up to the country next weekend, right?"

"On Saturday morning."

"Have Bruce talk to him. Bruce has a way with him. And then he won't have any grounds for objecting to anything about the apartment, because it's slated to be on the cover of a magazine."

"Min, dear, I hope you won't take offense at my saying this, but isn't *Enfilade* a bit—well—lowbrow? I mean for Jake, not me."

"Oh, but that's the old *Enfilade*. It's changed under Indira. You'll see when the next issue comes out. She's done a total overhaul, you won't even recognize it. For example, the March issue has two different covers, different rooms from the same house, in this case this spectacular beach house Alison Pritchard decorated in Puglia."

"Isn't she the one who used to work for Jake and Pablo?"

"For a few years, yes, but then she hung out her own shingle, and now she's huge. Not only is she doing residential projects, she's moved on to hotels, restaurants, the new outpatient center at Sloan Kettering. And then, for the cover of the September issue, we've got Pablo—Clydie Mortimer's apartment on Fifth Avenue. And if *Enfilade* is good enough for Pablo—"

"Clydie Mortimer? Jake never said anything about that."

"He and Pablo are very discreet about these things. Clydie, too. She's not even letting us use her name."

"Come on, have another macaron."

"What about you?"

"I wouldn't care for one."

"All right, then. Let's see . . . this looks like salted caramel. Is it? Yes!" Min chewed. "Oh, there's one more thing. I'll be honest, this part I don't know how you're going to feel about. When I told Indira that you were buying the apartment, naturally she asked me why, so I told her the truth—that it was because of the election—and she was totally fascinated. As a matter of fact, she wants to make that the core of the story."

"Really?"

"I told you she has fresh ideas."

"Yes, you did, and I'm glad she does. The only thing, Min, dear, is that I really have no idea when the apartment will be ready—there are still all the fine points of the contract to work out, you wouldn't believe how complicated these things are in Italy—and then, when you figure in the time for the renovation and the decoration, that brings us to the fall of 2018 or the winter of 2019 at the earliest, and who knows where we'll be then? I mean, for all we know, the press will be under government control and there won't be any *Enfilade*."

"Do you really believe that?"

"What I believe is irrelevant. I'm not a sibyl. I wish I could predict the future, or trust the past to serve as a guide for the future, or feel that the world was moving inexorably toward enlightenment. Once, I might have believed that, but not now. I don't have beliefs anymore. All I have is dread."

"But doesn't dread imply hope—that the things you dread won't actually happen?"

"Obviously, you still regard hope as a good thing. Well, I don't. If anything, I look at hope as dangerous, because in my experience hopes are dashed far more often than they're fulfilled."

"Then you do have a belief. It's a negative belief, but it's a belief still."

Again Eva's phone pinged. "Excuse me," she said. "Oh, thank God, it's from Ursula. I've been waiting for this. Where are my reading glasses?"

"Here, on the table."

"Hand them to me, will you?"

Min obliged. Glasses on, Eva read, moving her lips but making no sound.

After a minute she lifted her head. "What does *usufruct* mean?" she asked.

"Usufruct . . . I used to know. I'm sure I did. Why do you ask?"

"Because Ursula uses it in her text. It's about the garden."

"The garden in Venice?"

Eva nodded. "I didn't want to bring this up until it was a sure thing, but about a week ago we were WhatsApping, Ursula and I—Europeans love WhatsApp, have you noticed? Anyway, I happened to mention how lovely the garden was, and she answered that even though it meant the world to her, she really couldn't afford to keep it up, and yet she couldn't bear to let it go to rack and ruin, either, which naturally I interpreted as a hint that she might want to sell it.

"The next morning I sent her an email. Essentially I told her that if she was serious, we'd consider buying the garden along with the apartment, to which she replied, literally within five minutes, that the thought of selling the garden had never so much as crossed her mind, that she could never bear to part with it, blah blah blah. So then I wrote back that I was sorry, I should never have brought it up and I hoped I hadn't offended her, and she answered that of course I hadn't. And that was that, until yesterday I got another message from her saying that she'd been mulling it over and decided she might be open to selling the garden after all but needed a little more time to think about it. So I told her to take as long as she needed, and now here's what she's written: 'After much soul-searching and more than one sleepless night, I have reached the sorrowful conclusion that, given my dire financial situation, I have no choice but to accept your kind offer to buy my beloved garden—'"

"Oh, Eva! How wonderful!"

"Hold on, I'm not finished. '. . . your kind offer to buy my beloved garden, provided that we can agree on a mutually satisfactory price and on the condition that, for my remaining few years, I am granted usufruct to it.'"

Min was typing on her own phone. "Usufruct," she read aloud. "The legal right of using and enjoying the fruits or profits of something belonging to another." She put the phone down. "Well, that's no problem, is it? That just means she wants to be able to sit in it from time to time. Maybe pick a few roses for her table."

The intercom shrilled. "Amalia, can you see who it is?" Eva called.

"It's Mrs. Bleek," Amalia said from the kitchen.

"Oh, fine, have them send her up."

"Is that Sandra Bleek?" Min asked. "What's she doing in the city? I thought she was staying at Grady's place."

"She is, but she comes into town once a week or so. I told you we had plans tonight, didn't I?"

"You said you and Bruce were going out. Is it with Sandra? Why is she here so early?"

"I asked her to come early. We're having an early dinner, then going to a reading. A literary reading. It's Lydia Davis."

Min, who didn't know who Lydia Davis was, took advantage of the ringing doorbell to look her up on her phone. The photo that appeared on the screen was of a woman more or less her own age, with wide eyes and the uneasy smile of someone who doesn't like having her picture taken. She was holding a cat.

Min put the phone down as soon as she heard Sandra's voice. "Sandra, dear, how lovely to see you," she said.

"Oh, hello," Sandra said, kissing Min on the cheek. "Sorry, I know who you are, but I can't remember your name. I'm terrible with names."

"This is Min Marable," Eva said. "She's the one I went to Venice with. She's just come by to tell me that she wants to put the Venice apartment in *Enfilade*. She works for *Enfilade*."

"Oh, what a great idea." Without being invited, Sandra sat at the table and picked out a macaron.

"That was really lovely of you to bring those the other day," Eva said. "So few people bother anymore with thoughtful little gifts."

"Well, I just happened to be passing Ladurée and I thought, why not? 'Gather ye rosebuds while ye may' and all that. Min, would you care for one?"

"If you insist."

"How many of those have you had?" Eva said.

Min, who was just positioning the macaron between her teeth, took it out of her mouth. "Three, I think."

"Seven."

Smiling, Min put the macaron on a saucer.

"So, any news about the garden?" Sandra asked.

Min gave Eva a look of surprise—had she confided in Sandra about the garden and not her?—that Eva met without hesitation. "Yes, as a matter of fact, I just heard from Ursula, and the news is good. She's ready to sell."

"Hooray!"

"But only on the condition that Eva grant her usufruct to it," Min said.

"Well, that's a twist," Sandra said. "You know, before you sign anything, you probably ought to check with a lawyer on this. The ramifications of usufruct might be different in Italy."

"Have you spent much time in Italy?" Min asked.

"For a few summers, my husband and I—my ex-husband, I should say—rented a place in Todi. Do you know Todi? It's this absolutely lovely Umbrian hill town, only it's crawling with Americans. Not tourists—Americans who live there. Most are artists. Beverly Pepper was the first to stake a claim, so they call it Beverly Hills."

"I know Todi," Min said. "When I was at *Town & Country*—"

"Bruce should be here any minute," Eva said, looking at the ormolu clock on the mantel. "He's leaving work early so we can have time to eat something before the reading. It's in Brooklyn. We'll have to drive, and the traffic might be heavy."

"Will Aaron and Rachel be at dinner?" Sandra asked.

"No, they're meeting us at the bookstore."

Now was the perfect opportunity for Eva to ask Min to join them, but either she chose not to take it or the sound of Bruce's keys in the door distracted her. As was their habit, the dogs scrambled to greet him. "Hello, my lovelies," he said. "Now, Caspar, I hope you've been leaving that sofa alone"—he stepped into the living room—"and I see you haven't. All that effort on Amalia's part! Oh, hello, Sandra," he added, kissing her on both cheeks. "And Min too." He hugged her but gave her only one kiss on one cheek. "Gosh, I feel as if I haven't see you in ages. How are you?"

"Well, I'm fine. Just so excited about Eva's news."

"What news?"

Min looked at Eva, who was frowning. "Sorry, wasn't I supposed . . ."

"Not supposed to what?"

"I was going to tell you later," Eva said to Bruce. "Ursula's just written to say she wants to sell us the garden."

"Garden? What garden?"

"The one in Venice. The one that belongs to the apartment."

"I didn't know that was in the offing."

"It only came up as a possibility the other day. We were exchanging texts, Ursula and I, and she said that she might have to sell the garden, because now, in addition to everything else, the government is after her for back taxes."

"Such a fabulous opportunity!" Min said. "To have the flat *and* the garden! It's the icing on the cake."

"Her only condition is that she wants usufruct to it," Sandra said. "Do you know what *usufruct* means, Bruce?"

"I do, as a matter of fact. It means she'll sell it to us as long as we let her keep it."

"Those are your words, not hers," Eva said.

"Here's an interesting example of the use of *usufruct*," Min said, looking again at her phone. "'The earth belongs in usufruct to the living.' Anyone care to guess who said that?"

No one did.

"OK, well, when I first read it, I assumed it must be someone French—Montaigne, maybe, or Rousseau—but it's not. It's Thomas Jefferson."

"And how much is Signora Foot-and-Mouth asking for this garden she intends to keep?"

"We haven't gotten to that stage."

"If you ask me, it would a lot simpler if she were to give us usufruct to it rather than the other way round."

"A garden in Venice," Sandra said. "It's like something out of a Merchant Ivory movie."

"It's wildly overgrown," Eva said. "Hasn't been cared for properly for years. Still, there are some marvelous roses—really old varieties—as well as a superb magnolia, and a lemon tree, and three or four orange trees. Ornamental orange trees. You can't actually eat the oranges."

"Reading between the lines, I'd say that Ursula wants you to rescue the garden but she's too proud to say so," Min said. "What a pity Jake doesn't do gardens."

"Doesn't he?" Sandra asked.

"No, he says he only understands interiors," Eva said. "For the house in Connecticut, he had to find us a landscape architect."

"Then he can find you one in Venice," Min said.

"So he's agreed to take on the job?" Sandra said.

"Not yet," Bruce said.

"Really. I wonder what's holding him back."

"Jake's at a funny moment in his life," Min said. "Not to put too fine a point on it, he's in his fifties and he's still single. He's approaching his sell-by date and he knows it."

"So are you," Eva said.

"It's different for women. Gay men have a shorter shelf life, I guess you could say."

"That certainly hasn't been Grady's experience," Sandra said. "Quite the contrary, he's, what, sixty-two? And he's having to beat them off with a stick. Boys in their twenties, looking for Daddy."

Min glanced at Eva. Had Sandra touched the third rail? She hoped so.

"All that I mean," Min said, "is that lately Jake seems to have lost his sense of purpose, his sense of . . . well, why he's doing what he's doing. Which is why what we've got to do is persuade him that this project is exactly what he needs in order to reboot. My advice, Eva, is that you put on the thumbscrews. Stop being so patient with him. Remind him, as politely as possible, that there are plenty of other pebbles on the beach."

"What is this, interior decoration tough love?"

"For instance, you could tell him that if he doesn't make up his mind by a certain date, you'll have to ask someone else. Say, Alison Pritchard."

"But I don't want Alison Pritchard. And even if I do, as you say, put on the thumbscrews, who's to say he won't tell me I'm absolutely right, I *should* hire a different decorator, and then where will I be?"

"Forgive me if I'm sticking my nose into things I don't understand," Sandra said, "but would it really be such a mistake to hire Alison Pritchard? From what I gather, she's done a lot of stuff in Italy."

"I don't ever want to work with anyone but Jake. He understands me. It's the sort of relationship that takes years to establish. To have to start that all over again, to have to try to build up a relationship like that all over again, from scratch—it doesn't bear thinking about."

"You sound as if you're describing a marriage."

"It is, in a sense. A sort of marriage. And for me—not for everyone, I realize, but for me—one marriage is enough for a lifetime. If Bruce died, I'd never marry again."

"What do you think of that, Bruce?" Sandra said.

There was no answer.

"Bruce?" Min called.

"Where are the dogs?" Sandra said.

"Oh, I guess he's taken them for a walk," Eva said.

Very briskly she began gathering up the tea things.

18

The bookstore where the reading took place was in Fort Greene. "I'm so excited," Sandra said as she and Bruce and Eva neared the entrance. "Lydia Davis has been such a huge influence on me . . . Oh, but look how crowded it is! Are we late?"

"It's five to seven," Bruce said.

"I had no idea she was such a popular writer," Eva said.

Inside the bookstore, six or seven rows of folding chairs had been set up in front of a podium. All of these were occupied or had coats or bags draped over them, which made them look like improvised scarecrows. The audience consisted mostly of thin, muscular young men in skinny jeans and thin, muscular young women in floral-print dresses. Those who had not found places stood pressed up against the bookshelves that lined the walls.

"I thought Aaron and Rachel were supposed to save us seats," Eva said, scanning the room.

"Aaron just texted me," Sandra said. "He says they're in the back, in the travel section. They can see us, but we can't see them."

"Oh, yes, there they are," Bruce said. "They're waving."

He led Eva and Sandra through the crowd as if clearing a path through jungle. "I'm so sorry about this," Rachel said when they arrived. "We got here half an hour early, but it was already packed."

"Just to reach the travel guides, you need a travel guide," Aaron said.

"No need to apologize," Eva said, gazing at the crowd. "I must say, it does my heart good to see so many young people. I didn't think young people read anymore."

"Oh, they read," Aaron said. "The problem is what they read. Shit like this."

He held up a copy of Lydia Davis's *Collected Stories*.

"Aaron, will you lower your voice?" Rachel said. "We all know you're not Lydia Davis's biggest fan. There's no need to shout it to the rafters."

"You don't like Lydia Davis?" Sandra said.

"I *respect* Lydia Davis," Aaron said. "I just don't understand why people think she's such a big deal. I mean, yes, fine, she was married to Paul Auster, yes, she got a MacArthur and did a not very good translation of *Madame Bovary*. And yet when it comes to her actual writing, to these so-called stories of hers—is there really any there there? Most of them are, like, two sentences long."

"I thought you appreciated concision."

"Concision, yes. But a page that's almost all white space?" Again he held up the *Collected Stories*. "As far as I'm concerned, all this is is a waste of trees."

"Honestly, Aaron, there are times when you can just be so fucking male," Rachel said. "I mean, not just going off on a tirade against Lydia Davis—Lydia Davis, of all people—but starting it off by saying that she used to be married to Paul Auster. As if that has anything to do with anything, as if all that matters for a woman writer is who she's married to."

"Used to be married to," Sandra corrected.

"I agree with you one hundred percent," said one of the thin, muscular young women in floral-print dresses. "Especially when you consider how much, in recent years, she's eclipsed him."

"Susanna's right," said another young woman, this one with flat black hair that fell down her back in the manner of Morticia Addams. "If anything, we should be saying that *he* used to be married to *her*."

"Believe me, I'm not defending Paul Auster," Aaron said. "As a matter of fact, I consider Paul Auster the most overrated American writer in the world, even more overrated than . . . well, Lydia Davis. So far as I'm concerned, everything that's wrong with contemporary French culture can be summed up in Paul Auster."

"Is Paul Auster French?" the black-haired woman asked. "I thought he was from Newark."

"He is from Newark," Rachel said. "What Aaron's alluding to is the fact that he's a god in France."

"In France he sells more books than Zola and Hugo combined," Aaron said.

"So?"

"I'm just stating a fact. Anyway, Rachel, don't you think you should introduce your new find to your old friends?"

"Oh, sorry. Eva, Sandra, Bruce, this is Susanna Varela. She's the marvelous young author I've just signed."

"How exciting," Sandra said, grasping Susanna's hand. "Is this your first book?"

"My first in English."

"Susanna is Brazilian, but now she writes in English," Rachel said.

"And this is my friend Katy," Susanna said.

"I've been meaning to say, I love your dress," Eva said to Katy. "Derek Lam, isn't it?"

"Yes!" Katy said. "I'm so glad, you're the first person who's noticed. I bought it at Beacon's Closet for $29.95."

"Katy's lucky," Susanna said. "She's got a couture body. Ninety percent of what's out there fits her like a glove."

"If only that were true," Katy said.

"Whereas zero percent of what's out there fits me like a glove," Rachel said.

"Are you waiting for someone to disagree?" Aaron said.

Taking Susanna by the arm, Sandra said, "Now tell me about your book. What is it? Is it a novel? What's it about?"

"It's a collection of stories."

"Oh, that's great. What are they like? Can I read some? I'd love to read some."

"She's got two coming out this spring," Rachel said, "one in *Granta* and one in *A Public Space*. Everyone at the office is wildly excited about it. Even the sales reps. Especially the sales reps."

"My stories are about my life," Susanna said to Sandra. "I'm not going to lie and say they're made up, the way so many writers do. They're set mostly in Bahia, in the house I grew up in. The mother is my mother. The brothers are my brothers. The boyfriends were my boyfriends."

"And yet they're written in the most perfectly idiomatic English," Rachel said. "It's like she's channeling Salinger."

"Please, not Salinger."

"Well, who would you rather it be?" Aaron asked.

"Grace Paley. Joy Williams. Mary Robison."

"What I love about Susanna's work is the way she uses this highly American vernacular to describe a completely non-American world," Rachel said. "It creates this extraordinary dissonance, this friction."

"I know you must get sick of this question, but what made you decide to write in English?" Sandra asked.

"I never decided to. Five years ago I married an American and moved to New York. We had a child. I was leading an American life, in American English, so it just made sense to write in English."

"You make it sound so easy. Me, for instance, I *speak* French, but I could never write in French."

"Well, but you aren't married to a Frenchman, are you?" Aaron said. "It's one thing to speak a language, another to share a bed with it."

"And yet you were married to a Spaniard," Eva said to Sandra. "Couldn't you write in Spanish?"

"Rico's Colombian, actually—and he came to the States when he was five. He only speaks Spanish with his mother."

"What about you, Katy?" Bruce said. "Are you a writer, too?"

"Me?" Katy said. "God, no. I work for Speedo."

"As a model?"

"That's flattering, but no, I'm in the marketing department."

"Her job is just how Katy earns her living," Susanna said. "Her real work is painting and collage."

"No, it isn't."

"Yes, it is. She's a phenomenal artist, she just doesn't like to talk about it."

Aaron was about to say more when the lights dimmed. A bookstore employee, a youth with disorderly red hair and the sort of beard that might just have been forgetting to shave, welcomed the audience and introduced the introducer, whose name Bruce didn't catch. From a seat in the front row, a frail woman with white hair took to the podium. She was carrying an enormous handbag through which she rummaged for a full minute before finally extracting a pair of reading glasses and a sheet of densely filled notebook paper from which she began to read aloud in a voice so thin and mumbling it was nearly impossible to make out what she was saying.

"Speak up!" Aaron shouted in his announcer's voice.

Rachel elbowed him. The woman looked flustered. "What?" she said. "What's the matter?"

"We can't hear you!"

A murmur moved through the crowd to the effect that the mic needed adjusting, at which point the youth with the red hair returned and fiddled with the sound equipment.

"Try it now," he said to the woman.

"Hello?" she said into the mic.

"You have to lower it, it's too high," Aaron yelled.

"What?"

"Allow me," the youth said, adjusting the mic so that it was at the level of her mouth.

"Is that OK? OK," she said, and began again to read the introduction. But though her voice was now amplified, it was still so thin that Bruce could hardly make out what she was saying.

Once the white-haired woman had concluded her speech, Lydia Davis took to the podium. She looked a little dazed, as if she were having one of those dreams where you find your-self suddenly and inexplicably on a stage, in costume, and expected to act in a play for which you don't know the lines. That said, her voice was clear and audible, if a little mono-tone. Just as Aaron had said, the stories were short, most of them a paragraph or two, a few consisting of just a single sentence. Although she enunciated every word, Bruce had trouble making sense of them. To him they sounded like the random things you overhear people saying into their cell phones.

When, after about half an hour, Lydia Davis said "Thank you," there was a rush of applause, after which the red-haired clerk escorted her to a desk at the back of the store and instructed the members of the audience who wished to have their books signed to form a line against one of the walls. Although copies of her most recent books were stacked on the desk, hardly anyone bought them. Most of the people in the line, rather, were holding tote bags full of her older books, which, as they arrived at the desk, they handed to her one by one, and which she signed, one by one, without smiling.

"It's like she's in a fugue state," Aaron said.

"I'd like to meet her," Susanna said.

"Me, too," Sandra said. "Should we get in line?"

"No, no," Rachel said. "We'll talk to her after the signing. She might want to go out for a drink with us."

"You mean you know her?"

"Of course I know her."

"You've *met* her," Aaron corrected. "And if you think she'll want to go out for drinks with a bunch of total strangers, you're deluding yourself. She'll have minders, people from her publisher. They'll have made plans for her."

"You don't know that. It's not a launch. The book didn't just come out."

"I'd really love to get my copy of *Break It Down* signed," Sandra said. "That book means so much to me."

"Enough to wait forty-five minutes?" Aaron said. "This thing about having books signed—I don't get it. I mean, a hundred years ago, yes, a signature had some value. But now signed books are a dime a dozen. Have no doubt, once the store's emptied out, they'll have her in the back for twenty minutes signing stock. Which is why my advice is that if you really care about having a signed copy, save time and buy one on eBay."

"But it wouldn't be the same. It wouldn't be *my* copy, the one I've read and reread."

"If Sandra wants to wait and have her book signed, I don't see why she shouldn't," Bruce said.

"Don't worry, I don't expect anyone to wait with me. Or for me."

"I'll wait with you," Susanna said.

"Me, too," Katy said.

"What about Eva?" Rachel said. "Oh, where is Eva?"

"Outside," Bruce said. "You know she can't stand crowds."

"Don't torture yourself, Bruce," Aaron said, patting him on the shoulder. "You head on home. We'll see you this weekend."

"Can we give you a ride?"

"No need. We drove."

"You have a car? I didn't know you had a car."

"Of course we have a car," Rachel said.

"Not as shiny as yours, but it serves in a pinch," Aaron said.

"Where do you park it at night?"

"On the street," Rachel said. "It's ridiculous, a nightmare. Because of alternate-side-of-the-street parking, twice a week Aaron has to get up at the crack of dawn to move it. The rest of the people in our building pay the super to do it, but Aaron's too cheap."

"What can I say?" Aaron said. "I enjoy the challenge. For example, do you have any idea how many holidays alternate side-of-the-street parking is suspended for? Holidays most of us have never heard of. The lunar new year, Purim, Eid al-Fitr, Solemnity of the Ascension, Eid al-Adha, Simchas Torah, Diwali."

"That's a lot of holidays," Bruce said. "Well, I'll be heading off now."

"Oh, but I want to say goodbye to Eva," Sandra said. "I want to, but if I do, I'll lose my place in line."

"Don't worry, I'll tell her for you. And I'll see you this weekend."

"Yes, this weekend," Sandra said, looking toward the front of the line.

Outside the bookstore, Eva was standing on the sidewalk in the posture of someone smoking, though she wasn't smoking.

"Eva, is that you?" a male voice asked.

She turned. It was Matt Pierce.

"I thought so," Matt said. "I just couldn't believe my eyes. Eva Lindquist in Brooklyn!"

He hugged her, a hug she returned sideways, as was her habit, so that her chest didn't touch his.

"I'm not allergic to Brooklyn," she said.

"Well, no, I didn't mean to suggest you were," Matt said. "It's just that I think of you so much as a creature of Manhattan, I have trouble imagining you anywhere else. Anyway, how've you been? I tried to call you a bunch of times, but you never called back."

"I know. I'm sorry. Things have just been so awfully hectic lately, what with the arrangements for Venice, and these problems we've been having with the dogs."

"Oh, no. Are they OK?"

"They're fine, just peeing on the furniture. It's the stress, I think. I'm certainly feeling it. I live these days in a condition of constant dread."

"Don't we all," Matt said. "Even so, this silent treatment, Eva . . . I have to be honest, you hurt my feelings. I mean, the way it seemed from my end, one day we were friends, the next you didn't want to have anything to do me. What happened? Was it the sorrel soup?"

"It wasn't that. It wasn't anything in particular. It was me, not you."

"You know, I'm actually glad we ran into each other, because I don't know if I could have brought myself to tell you this over the phone. Dean broke up with me—in retrospect I suppose it was inevitable—and now I'm, well, a little bit homeless. And before you say it, yes, I know that sounds like being a little bit pregnant, only it's not. The fact is there are levels of homelessness. There's the staying-on-friends'-couches level, which is the one I'm on now, and there's the living-in-a-shelter level, and there's the sleeping-on-the-street level. The bottom line is, I need help. I'm not above asking for help."

It was then that Bruce stepped out of the bookstore. "Oh, hello," he said to Matt, whose name he still couldn't remember.

They shook hands. "Well, it's been lovely seeing you, Matt," Eva said. "I'm afraid we're in a bit of a rush, though. The dogs."

"Yes, of course. It's been good seeing you too. I've missed you. Probably that should have been the first thing I said."

"Goodnight."

"Yes, goodnight," Bruce said.

"And don't forget, the next time you're having a dinner party, I'm here. Also, if you have any friends who might be having dinner parties—"

"Thank you, Matt. Goodnight."

"What was that about?" Bruce asked as they turned onto South Portland Avenue.

"Nothing. He's broke."

"Did he ask you for money?"

"No, he asked me to start having him in again to cook."

"But you had him in two nights ago."

"Are you really that oblivious? That wasn't Matt. Matt hasn't set foot in our kitchen for a month. At least a month. The last time was when we had Jake over."

"Then who was it cooking two nights ago?"

"Ian. Don't you remember? Or did you think they were the same person?"

"How am I supposed to know which one is which when they hardly ever come out of the kitchen?"

"Ian hardly ever comes out of the kitchen. Matt came out of the kitchen all the time. Too much. That was part of the problem. I trust you haven't forgotten the episode with the scones."

"I'll never forget the episode with the scones. Oh, I meant to tell you, Sandra asked me to say goodnight to you for her. She's waiting to get her book signed. After that, Aaron and

Rachel will give her a lift to wherever she's staying. Did you know they had a car?"

"Of course."

"Something else everyone seems to know that I don't. Like who this Lydia Davis is. Or that you had a falling-out with . . . what's his name again?"

"Matt. And it wasn't a falling-out."

"He looked awfully down in the mouth. Couldn't you do something for him, have him do your next dinner instead of . . . who's the other one?"

"Ian. And he's a much better cook than Matt."

"Really? I haven't noticed much of a difference."

"Look, I have my reasons, all right? It's partially the cooking, partially some other things that if you don't mind, I'd rather not go into."

"Still, you can't help feeling sorry for the guy, if he's broke."

"He *says* he's broke."

"What, you don't believe him?"

"I have no idea what his financial situation is. I just don't see why just because he split up with his boyfriend I should be expected to bail him out. I mean, it's not as if he isn't able-bodied. He's got a college degree and most of a PhD. He could get a job if he wanted to."

"Yet you're perfectly willing to bail out Signora Foot-and-Mouth."

"I wish you wouldn't call her that. Her name is Ursula. And it's an entirely different situation."

They had arrived at the Outback. When Bruce aimed his key at it, it squealed. Its lights blinked. Its doors unlocked themselves. Even so, he walked around to open the passenger door for Eva before getting in himself. *Like tucking a child into bed*, he thought.

At first they drove in silence, Eva's gaze focused on the headlights reflected in the window glass, Bruce thinking, as they turned onto the BQE, of Kathy, of the many times she had sat in the seat that now held Eva, pulling it up closer to the glove compartment, since she had shorter legs. To keep Eva from catching on that Kathy had been in the car with him, each time he'd returned from the outpatient center he'd made sure to put the seat back in its original position. And now those days, the days of the outpatient center, were over—unless, when Kathy went in for her next PET scan, something showed up.

"You drink this horrible stuff so that everywhere there's cancer, you sparkle," she'd told him. "The day I was diagnosed, I lit up like a Christmas tree."

"Cindy-Lou Who," he murmured to himself.

"Excuse me?"

"Nothing. What did you think of the reading?"

"It was too crowded."

"Did you like the stories?"

"I suppose they were good. It was hard for me to concentrate."

"You mean because of the crowd?"

She didn't answer. He let a minute pass, then said, "Look, Eva, about this garden—"

"I don't want to hear anything from you right now."

The severity of her tone surprised him. "But I only wanted to explain—"

"There's nothing to explain. The way you behaved today, saying those things in front of Min and Sandra—it was inexcusable."

"I'm not making an excuse."

"And then just disappearing, without a word, leaving me to clean up the mess—"

"All I did was take the dogs for a walk. I needed to clear my head."

"—not that my clean-up efforts made any difference. Min and Sandra have eyes. They have ears. They understood perfectly well what was going on."

"Look, I felt blindsided, OK? Before tonight you hadn't said anything about a garden."

"And that's because every time anything's come up with this apartment, even the most run-of-the-mill thing, you've jumped down my throat."

"Since when is paying cash under the table a run-of-the-mill thing? Since when is paying a bribe—"

"A fine."

"—or buying a hallway? These so-called run-of-the-mill things, Eva—do you realize how much they've cost us so far? Nearly 40K. That's more than we pay Amalia in a year."

"You know perfectly well that what we pay Amalia is way above the going rate, especially when you figure in her Social Security."

"Yes, but Eva, that's all she gets. What we're spending on nothing—literally nothing—it's all she has to support her family on for a year. And now, on top of everything else, there's this garden."

"The garden's not nothing. It'll add to the apartment's value."

"And to its price."

"You know what? Stop. Just stop." Eva drew in her breath. "OK, look, I'm only going to say this once. I'm going to say it once, but first I want you to swear—*swear*—you'll never raise the subject again. Do you swear?"

"How can I when I don't know what I'm swearing to?"

"Tomorrow morning, first thing, I want you to call Rita and tell her it's off. The whole thing. That we won't be buying the apartment."

Bruce kept his mouth shut. It was surprisingly easy. He was used to doing as he was told.

"Of course, we'll lose the money—forty thousand dollars wasted on nothing, as you so kindly pointed out—though for me that's not the worst of it. The worst of it will be telling Ursula. I dread that. Still, I'll do it. I won't lie. I'll tell her the truth."

"That's generally the best policy."

"And then Min. You know why she came over this afternoon? To tell me that her editor wants to put the apartment on the cover of *Enfilade*. Well, we can scratch that now. Jake will be disappointed."

"But he hasn't even agreed—"

"As for Min . . . I shudder to think. She's put her neck out for this. She might lose her job."

"I wouldn't worry about that. Min always lands on her feet."

"Don't be so sure. Magazines are a dying industry."

"She'll cope."

"God, must you be so heartless?"

"What's heartless? You told me to do something and then to swear I'd never bring it up again. I'm just following orders."

"As if it has nothing to do with you. As if from the start, from the very start, you haven't made it eminently clear that as far as you're concerned, this apartment's just a stupid self-indulgence, a whim. Well, you can breathe a sigh of relief now, can't you, because as of this minute, it's over. All you have to do is make the call to Rita and you'll never have to think about it again, you can put your blindfold back on and go back to your safe little routine—your days at the office, and pasta on Mondays, and walks with Alec Warriner."

"Whoa, hold on—what's that got to do with any of this?"

"If you really don't know, why did you keep it a secret?"

"I didn't."

"Yes, you did. I only found out from Frank."

"No, what I mean is, I didn't tell you, but not because I wanted to keep it from you. I just—frankly, it never occurred to me that it was worth telling. It seemed so trivial."

"Trivial! Since when is consorting with the enemy trivial? Since when is upsetting the dogs so much they start peeing on the furniture trivial?"

"What, you think that's because of walking with Alec and Sparky? You're joking, right?"

"I must be if you say so."

"But that's absurd. I mean, all told I've taken maybe three walks with Alec. Four at most. Besides which, even if walking with Alec actually does have something to do with the peeing—I'm not saying it does, but if it does—I still don't see the connection with the apartment."

"That much is obvious. Oh, there's the sign for the LIE. You'd better get in the turn lane."

"I thought I'd take the bridge."

"Better to take the tunnel. There'll be less traffic in the tunnel."

To get into the turn lane, Bruce had to speed up and pass a truck on the right. In response, its driver honked his air horn. Eva covered her ears with her hands.

"Careful! Are you trying to get us killed?"

Again he kept his mouth shut. He understood exactly what his wife was doing—trying to shame him into submission, find his weak spot, then go in for the kill. If he chose, he could have done the same thing to her—God knew she'd given him plenty of ammunition over the years—only he never had. Instead he'd resisted the urge—and not only resisted it, but taken pride in his resistance, which he saw as yet further evidence of his chivalrous spirit. Or was this a lie he was telling himself? Maybe the truth was that he wasn't chivalrous at all, just afraid of fights, so much so that, rather than risk them, he'd always opted to give Eva what she wanted. In which case the hyena, the one that kept tearing his face off and that he kept taking back in, wasn't his wife, but his own cowardice—the peculiar cowardice of the man who dreads the backlash more than he savors the lash.

By now they were merging onto the LIE. The traffic slowed. In his impatience, Bruce nudged his way left, one lane at a time, provoking a taxi driver to roll down his window, stick his head out, and shout, "Go fuck yourself, asshole."

"I think you do," Eva said. "I think you really do want to get us killed."

He laughed. Why hadn't he seen it before? It was so obvious! When you had the bigger engine, you didn't need the louder voice. This was why, when the taxi driver told him to go fuck himself, he hardly felt it. It was just—what was the expression?—water off a duck's back. And if he could do that with the taxi driver—well, why couldn't he do it with Eva? Just stop caring. Keep driving. In which case, so what if she guilt-tripped him, locked him out of the bedroom, stopped speaking to him? All he had to do was decide it made no difference and it would make no difference. It would be water off a duck's back.

"You'd better slow down. We're nearly at the toll plaza."

"Funny that we still call it that, given that there aren't any tollbooths anymore."

"Aren't there?"

"Not since the beginning of the year. It's all E-ZPass now. Remember the days when you used to have to throw coins into a wire basket? How sometimes a nickel would fall onto the ground, and you'd have to get out of the car and get down on your knees and crawl around on the pavement feeling for it? And all the time you knew there were cars behind you, waiting, waiting."

"That's how I feel all the time now."

Water off a duck's back.

"And, look, I was right," Eva said with a touch of triumph. "There's hardly any traffic at all. There would have been more on the bridge."

It was true. There was hardly any traffic at all. They were racing through the tunnel, the lamplight jaundicing the car's interior.

"Eva," Bruce said.

But when he turned to look at her, she wouldn't meet his eye. She remained insistently in profile.

Once out of the tunnel, he felt safer, because now they were in Manhattan, and, aside from Oshkosh, Manhattan was the only place in the world where he knew he would never get lost.

"Funny that even after all these years, Brooklyn should still seem like another planet to me."

Eva didn't answer. Nor did she speak for the rest of the drive, not even when Bruce, having parked the Outback in the garage, opened her door for her. Instead she just got out and walked down the ramp to the street, letting herself stumble forward every few steps to keep from losing her balance.

From his glassed-in cage, Willard Han gazed at Bruce. Bruce gazed back.

The next morning, despite Eva's insistence that he do so, he didn't call Rita. Nor did he call her that afternoon, or the following day.

For the garden, Eva and Ursula settled on a price of $75,000.

PART VI

19

Beyond the Lindquists' country house—beyond the flower and vegetable gardens, the pool, and the ornamental fountain—a large meadow spread out, empty except for a small copse of maples near the perimeter. It was here, on the first Saturday in March, that Min Marable, Sandra Bleek, and Rachel Weisenstein gathered after lunch to share a joint.

"I see you're wearing your pussy hat," Sandra said to Rachel.

"Why not?" Rachel said. "It's cold out."

"Has Eva seen it?"

"I don't know. She might have."

"If she has, I wouldn't worry about it," Min said. "She probably doesn't know what it is."

"I hope not," Rachel said. "She might think it's crude."

"Rachel, you do realize that those flaps are supposed to be cat ears, don't you?" Min said. "I mean, it's not really supposed to look like . . . It's supposed to look like a cat. It's a visual pun."

"Well, yes, of course," Rachel said. "And yet at the same time there is something sort of Georgia O'Keeffe about it. I mean, even you used the word *flaps*."

"Do you know what I read the other day about the pussy hat?" Sandra said. "It seems that since the march, a bunch of women—nonwhite women—have been complaining that it was racist."

"Racist!" Rachel said. "How?"

"Well, isn't it obvious?" Sandra said. "It's the pink. I mean, not every woman's . . . you know . . . is pink. Not even every white woman's."

"Oh, God, I never thought of that!" As if afraid of being attacked, Rachel yanked the hat off her head and stuffed it in her purse. "Oh, but now my head will freeze. My ears will get frostbite. And this is the only hat I brought."

"Then put it back on."

"But Eva might see."

"Then leave it off and go inside."

"And forgo the weed," Min added.

Rachel put the hat back on.

"Aren't you afraid of getting bitten by a deer tick?" Sandra asked, taking a toke.

"In winter?" Rachel said. "I don't think they're a problem in winter. Besides, I've never seen a deer around here."

"You don't have to have deer to have deer ticks," Min said.

"Over the last couple of years, it seems like half the people I know have come down with Lyme disease," Sandra said. "Usually they catch it in time to get it treated, but sometimes there isn't the rash. A friend of my daughter's, for instance, she never had the rash, and she was sick for three years before they diagnosed it."

"It's why Eva doesn't go outside," Rachel said, taking the joint from Sandra.

"That's not true," Min said. "Eva does go outside. In the summer she lies out by the pool."

"Really?" Sandra said. "It's funny, I can't quite imagine Eva in a swimsuit."

"Actually, she looks great in a swimsuit."

"Do you think Eva's ever gotten stoned?" Rachel asked.

"That's privileged information."

"So she has. Come on, give us the details."

"OK," Min said, "but you mustn't ever tell her I told you or she'll kill me. It was just once, years and years ago. We were at a party—I forget whose—and there were these pot brownies, only no one told Eva they had pot in them, and she ate one."

"Oh, God. What happened?"

"She said it tasted funny, and the host, whoever it was, said, 'That's because it's a pot brownie,' and laughed his head off like it was a great practical joke. And she was absolutely furious."

"Probably the pot made it worse."

"I think it made her really paranoid, because suddenly she said, 'What if there's a police raid? We have to get out of here before the police raid.' And I said, 'Eva, the police don't raid parties like this. It's not the fifties anymore.' Come to think of it, it was sort of like what she did that time with Siri, with the iPhone."

"Yes, wasn't that weird?" Sandra said. "What do you think that was about?"

"Isn't it obvious?" Rachel said. "She was testing us, seeing how far we were willing to go."

"Not, as it turns out, very far," Sandra said.

"Later Aaron admitted he would never have really asked Siri that question," Rachel said. "When push comes to shove, he's a wimp. Like most men."

"What you have to understand about Eva," Min said, "is that she's scared in a way we're not. For her it's personal."

"Why?" Sandra said. "She's not black, or Hispanic, or Muslim, God forbid."

"She's Jewish, though," Rachel said.

"So's Trump's lawyer," Min said. "So are half the people who work for him."

"The people who go to his rallies aren't Jews," Sandra said. "They hate Jews."

"Let's not forget she's a woman," Rachel said.

"But not one who'll ever need to have an abortion," Sandra said. "Or a mother of daughters."

At the mention of daughters, Rachel's eyes misted a little. "I wish she'd come to the Women's March," she said. "I think it would have made such a difference to her to have been there. Aaron, too."

"Aaron?" Min said. "Sorry, but would that have been wise?"

"Why not?" Rachel said. "There were plenty of men there."

"No, I know," Min said. "I just mean after what happened. His being fired."

"What's that got to do with the march?"

"Well, someone might have recognized him and . . . not taken kindly to his presence."

"What are you getting at, Min? Is it these accusations Katya's been making? If so, I can assure you, there's nothing to them. They had a heated exchange, it's true, but Aaron never grabbed her arm. He never touched her. Bruises like that—it would have been in the police report."

"There was a police report?" Sandra said.

"And even if it took a few days for the bruises to show up, why didn't she go to a doctor? The fact of the matter is, she's been gunning for Aaron ever since the day she got named editor in chief, and now that she's gotten rid of him, she wants to make sure he'll never work anywhere else. It's so vindictive, especially when you consider the real horrors to which so many women, every day, are subjected."

"Do you know what Eva told me the other day?" Min said. "That since the election, she's felt like she's on a plane, and that unless she keeps saying to herself, over and over, 'The plane won't crash,' it'll crash."

"May I interject a question?" Rachel said. "What is it about Eva? Why are we always talking about her? I mean, God knows, I love her to death, but really, what's so interesting about her? Why do we always come back to her? Just look at us, standing out here freezing our butts off so she won't catch us smoking, and what are we talking about? Her."

"She's like Mary Catherine Gray," Sandra said.

"Who?"

"Mary Catherine Gray. She was this girl I went to school with, and there was absolutely nothing to say about her, nothing at all, and still we couldn't stop talking about her. It was like we were convinced that she couldn't possibly be as nondescript as she seemed, that under her nondescriptness there had to be some enigma, some secret, if only we could get at it."

"And was there?"

"Not that I ever found out. She looked like that girl from the B-52s, the one with the bug eyes."

"Cindy Wilson."

"Unfortunately for her, she had small breasts. If you've got that sort of body, you need big breasts to carry it off."

"Eva has beautiful breasts," Min said. "Of course, if you complimented her on them, she'd pretend to be mortified."

"Do you think she and Bruce have sex?" Sandra said.

"What do you mean?" Rachel said. "Of course they have sex. They're a married couple."

"Excuse me, but what planet are you living on?" Sandra said. "Plenty of married couples don't have sex."

"Especially the gay ones," Min said. "Or if they do, it's with other people. Speaking of which, have any of you noticed how long it's been since we've seen Matt Pierce around here?"

"Was he the one who had to make the scones twice?" Rachel asked.

Min nodded. "What happened was, back in January, Eva had Jake over to dinner, and Matt did the cooking. So afterwards Jake and Bruce were out with the dogs, right, and Eva and I were in the living room, when Matt comes in and starts going on about this new boyfriend of his and how he's pressuring him to have three-ways, and what does Eva think of it, and should he do it. He touched the third rail."

"What's the third rail?"

"Well, that's just it. With Eva you never know what the third rail is until you've touched it, and then it's too late. In this case it was sex. As she put it afterwards, 'Why do people always feel they have to go into the gory details?' End result—there's one more gay boy who'll never bake another scone in this kitchen."

"Poor Matt," Rachel said. "He seemed so nice. And he really must have trusted Eva, otherwise he'd never have asked her advice on such a, well, intimate subject."

"I suppose the lesson here is that we should all watch our step with Eva," Sandra said.

"Yes, you should," Min said.

"Wait a minute," Rachel said, "if Matt's not here, who made lunch today? Was it the shy one? What's his name again?"

"Ian. And no, it wasn't him. At the last minute he couldn't make it, so Eva called Calvin Jessup, who used to cook for her way back in the early aughts. And you can't have mixed Calvin up with Ian *or* Matt, because they're white and he's black. Anyway, he's only filling in."

"You make it sound like it's an official position," Sandra said.

"It is, sort of," Min said. "Something like what used to be called a paid companion—you know, the poor but respectable spinster the rich wife hires to keep her company, lose at cards, and agree with everything she says. Only in Eva's case it has to be a man, a gay man, under forty and preferably good-looking. Oh, and he has to be able to cook, because that's what he gets paid for."

"I wonder where she finds them," Sandra said. "Is there an agency she goes to? Does she put an ad up on Craigslist?"

"Eva? Craigslist? Are you kidding? Oh shit, it's Bruce and Jake. Put it out."

"Where? I can't see them."

"Over there," Min said, pointing to the line of trees that marked where the Lindquists' property ended and Grady's began. "See? Oh, and they've got the dogs with them. Get rid of it."

"Get rid of what?"

"The joint," Min said, pulling it from Rachel's mouth and stubbing it out with her heel. "They can't know we've been smoking. They might tell Eva. Have any of you got anything to cover up the smell? Fanta? Coke?"

"I think I might have a bottle of water," Sandra said, looking in her purse.

"Water won't . . . Oh, hi, Bruce."

"Ladies," Bruce said, his boots crunching the frozen grass as the dogs, off leash, leaped toward the women and sniffed their legs.

"He must smell Mumbles," Rachel said, bending down to stroke Isabel's head and in the same gesture taking off her hat again. "Do you smell Mumbles, boy?"

"Isabel's the bitch," Min said.

"And what brings you out on a day like this?" Bruce asked. "Plotting a palace coup?"

"Just having some girl talk," Min said.

"When it's thirty degrees?" Jake said.

"Well, isn't that the whole point of going to the country in winter?" Min said. "To breathe the clean and frosty air?"

"Speaking for myself, I'd say the point of going to the country in winter is to sit by a toasty fire and drink whiskey," Bruce said.

"In that case, the sooner you finish your walk, the happier you'll be."

"What, you don't want our company for just a few minutes?"

"No. I told you, we're having girl talk, and you're not girls."

"What about Jake?"

"Bruce!" Rachel said.

"He doesn't mind. You don't mind, do you, Jake?"

"At this moment in history, I'd say there are more important things to mind," Jake said.

"OK, if you must know, we've been talking about what's-his-name," Sandra said. "The one who got banished."

"She means Matt," Min said.

"Ah, Matt," Bruce said. "A pity, that. Still, you know the law. Whatever Lola wants—"

"Wait, what happened to Matt?" Jake said.

"He touched the third rail," Rachel said.

"He went into the gory details," Sandra said.

"Don't worry, Jake, you're safe," Min said. "Eva said as much. She said—and I quote—'The thing I appreciate about Jake is that he never insists on going into the gory details.'"

"Jake is indeed a paragon of discretion," Bruce said.

"Or maybe Jake simply doesn't have any gory details to go into," Jake said.

"Oh, come on," Min said. "Everyone does."

"There could be a statute of limitations on gory details. A certain number of years after which your record is wiped clean and you're a virgin again."

"How many years?" Rachel asked.

"That's a point of debate."

"See what I mean?" Min said. "For Jake, evasiveness is an aspect of discretion, which is in turn an aspect of taste. The most crucial aspect, I remember Pablo telling me once. When you're selling taste, he said, you have to demonstrate taste, in your life as much as your work."

"I wonder if that's the case with Eva," Rachel said. "If when people go into the gory details, as she calls them, she regards it as an offense against taste."

"It's not that complex," Bruce said. "Put plainly, my wife is a prude. Always has been."

"Eva? A prude?" Min said. "I protest."

"Protest as you will, have you ever once said 'fuck' in her presence? I'll bet you a hundred bucks you'll find you can't do it."

"That's a matter of etiquette."

"I rest my fucking case."

"Oh, for God's sake."

"If Eva were here, you'd say 'For goodness' sake.'"

"Aaron wouldn't," Rachel said.

"He has a special dispensation."

The Bedlingtons, having concluded their examination of the women's legs, were now exploring the meadow. Isabel was shitting. Caspar was sniffing a twig. Ralph was moving in the direction of the woods.

"Come on, Jake, we'd better get out of here," Bruce said. "Otherwise the dogs might get eaten by panthers."

"Panthers?" Sandra said. "Are you serious?"

All the others looked at her. "You mean you haven't heard of the legendary Connecticut panther?" Bruce said.

"No, but then again I haven't spent that much time in Connecticut."

"An endangered species. Since 2015 only seven have been spotted, all within five miles of this house."

"Hold on, you're joking, right?"

The others burst out laughing. Sandra flushed. "You didn't have to do that," she said. "You know I don't have a sense of humor and you took advantage of it."

"What makes you so sure we're joking?"

Sandra took her phone out of her purse and started typing. "It's a football team," she said after a few seconds. "The

Connecticut Panthers is a football team. Jesus, you nearly scared me to death."

To make Sandra feel better, Jake said, "For a second there he had me fooled, too."

"Shit, he's heading for the woods," Bruce said, hurrying to catch up to Ralph, who was about to cross Grady's property line.

"Do you think we got away with that?" Min asked after the men had left. "I mean, do you think they realized we were smoking?"

"So what if they did?" Rachel said, taking a fresh joint from her pocket and lighting it. "They were probably hoping we'd offer them a hit."

"If Eva found out—"

"Relax, even if they noticed, they're not going to tell her."

"I can't remember what we were talking about," Sandra said.

"Three-ways, and whether Bruce and Eva have them," Rachel said.

"That's not what we were taking about," Min said.

"Call me naive," Rachel said, "but Bruce and Eva having sex with other people—I just can't see it."

"I can't see them having sex with each other," Sandra said.

"Just because you can't see a thing doesn't mean it isn't true," Min said.

"OK, then I'll offer some testimony," Sandra said. "But only if you promise not to make fun of me."

"We promise," Rachel said.

"I don't promise," Min said.

"Then I'll tell you just to prove I'm not as naive as you think I am. Well, it was a few weeks ago, and I'd gone into the city for my meeting with Aaron. As I'm sure I've told you, for the time being, the judge has given my apartment to Rico, which in my view is totally unfair—"

"Yes, you've told us."

"And so whenever I go into the city overnight, I have to find a place to sleep, only I don't want to put too much of a burden on any one of my friends, so I try to—how shall I put it?—spread myself around."

"I'd say that's putting it perfectly."

"Don't worry, your turn will come, Min. Anyway, on this particular occasion I'd made a plan to stay with my friend Susan, only her son—he's a sophomore at Vassar—he's prone to panic attacks, and to make a long story short, he had a doozy of one right in the middle of a biochemistry exam—shortness of breath, the whole nine yards—so he left the exam room, walked straight to the station—he didn't even stop at his dorm—and caught the first train to New York. He didn't call Susan. When she got home from work, she found him hyperventilating in his bed, which was where I was supposed to sleep."

"Oh, dear," Min said. "Don't tell me you had to stay in a hotel."

"No, I called up Eva and asked if I could use her guest room."

"Hold on a sec. You actually called Eva up? You actually called her up and invited yourself to spend the night?"

"Sure, why not?"

"The third rail," Rachel said.

"I wonder why she didn't tell me," Min said. "Anyway, go on."

"Well, I called up, and Bruce answered, and when I explained my predicament, he couldn't have been sweeter. He said that of course I could stay over, I should come by whenever I wanted, come for dinner even, only I couldn't manage dinner because I'd already made plans to have dinner with my daughter. Now, I don't know if any of you have seen it, but their quote-unquote guest room is actually the maid's room. It's off the kitchen and about the size of a closet, with a teeny tiny bathroom, and so as soon as I got into bed I had this terrible claustrophobia attack. I couldn't sleep, and I didn't have any Zolpidem, so I decided to go into the kitchen to do some writing—that afternoon Aaron had lit the flame in me—only I hadn't brought a pen, and I couldn't find one in any of the drawers. I checked the living room too, and then that bedroom they use as a study. I went on tiptoe so as not to wake them, and as I was passing their bedroom, I could hear them . . . not exactly talking. It was more this weird sort of baby talk. I won't try to imitate it."

"Oh, go on," Rachel said.

"Well, I suppose it was like—now, bear in mind, this is just a rough approximation—'Googly-oogly, who's a Munchkin?' And 'What's Lord Ralph up to? What's my little Lady Isabel up to? Lady Isabel is a good girl, isn't she?'"

"Wait a sec. Lady Isabel?"

"That was Bruce. He's the one who said Lady Isabel."

"This is TMI," Rachel said.

"And then the door opened a crack more and one of the dogs came out."

"Oh, God, don't tell me—"

"Exactly. They were talking to the dogs. The dogs were in bed with them."

"Two's company, three's a pack," Min said.

A fit of pot-induced hilarity seized Rachel. She was laughing so hard she was gasping for breath. "Are you OK?" Min said. "Rachel, are you having an asthma attack? Are you dying?"

"It's just . . . it all fits so perfectly," Rachel said. "Sorry." She stood up straight, trying to will herself into dignity. "Actually, when you think about it, it's kind of heartbreaking. Those dogs are their children."

"If you must know, they do," Min said, extinguishing what remained of the joint.

"Do what?" Sandra said.

"Have sex. Fairly often, in fact, and that's all I'm going to say on the subject."

"Then why don't they have kids?"

"It must be by choice," Rachel said. "I've always assumed so."

"I didn't say that," Min said.

"Infertility then?" Sandra said.

"I didn't say that either."

"You did, actually. You said it by saying you didn't say it was by choice."

"What? Can you repeat that?"

"I said you didn't say—OK, let me start again. You said it by saying you didn't say it was by choice."

Min was rubbing her arms, as if she had only now realized how cold it was. "All right, I'll tell you, but only if you promise not to tell anyone else. I mean, this must never get back to Eva. Agreed?

"OK. It's not that either of them is infertile and it's not by choice—not exactly. It's that she has, well, a small vagina—and Bruce has a larger-than-usual penis—and so intercourse doesn't work for them."

"Hold on—what do you mean, a small vagina?"

"According to her, starting in the earliest days of their marriage, she's found intercourse painful. It worried her so much she went to a bunch of doctors—male doctors—and they all told her the problem was psychological, that she just had to learn to quote-unquote relax, but she couldn't relax, because she was always worried that it would hurt. Naturally, Bruce didn't push it—"

Rachel burst into giggles.

"Sorry, poor choice of words. Naturally, Bruce didn't press the issue."

"That isn't all he didn't press."

"Be quiet. So that was that, until about ten years ago, when I was at *Self*, we did this piece where I interviewed a gynecologist—a woman—who'd done a study of vagina size, and what she found was that there's a normal range—we're talking the size of the labia as well as the width and depth of the vault—"

"Vault?"

"That's what they call it on *SVU*," Sandra said.

"So weird," Rachel said. "Like a bank vault."

"Are you done? The point is, there's a normal range that most women fall into. Not all do, though—some really do have extra-small vaginas, and some have extra-big ones. So of course I told Eva this, and she made an appointment to see this doctor I'd interviewed, who measured her, and the upshot—don't even think about it, Rachel—was that she'd been right all along. Her vagina was one of the smallest the doctor had seen, and that's why she finds intercourse painful."

"But wait, didn't you just say they have sex?"

"Intercourse isn't the only way to have sex."

"What do they do then?"

"Let's just say that as in all things, in sex Bruce is the perfect gentleman."

"What, you mean he takes off her coat for her and she comes?" Rachel said. "He pulls out her chair for her and she comes?"

"Use your imagination."

"As Godfrey held the door open for Lucinda, a ripple of pleasure ran through her loins."

"And she reciprocates?" Sandra said.

"As Lucinda prepared to light Godfrey's cigar, a ripple of pleasure ran through his loins."

"That's all I'm going to say," Min said. "From here on my lips are sealed."

"As, apparently, are hers," Rachel said. "No, but in all seriousness, why does Bruce put up with it? *Does* he put up with it? I mean, most men—"

"You shouldn't generalize."

"OK, then I'll stick to what I know. With Aaron, if we couldn't fuck, it would be a deal-breaker."

"Even though he loves you?" Sandra said.

"That's not the point. I mean, it's a moot point, because it's never been a problem for us, thank God."

Suddenly she had tears in her eyes.

"Are you OK?" Min said.

"I don't know. It's probably the pot. I wish you hadn't asked me that question, Sandra."

"Believe me, I wasn't thinking of you when I asked it. I was thinking of Rico."

"Oh, God, but what if I'm wrong? What if, if for some reason I couldn't—we couldn't—would he leave me?"

"Of course not. He loves you."

"But what does that even mean, to say you love someone? Even with people who love each other, things can happen—things that make it impossible for them to stay married."

"Oh, but Rachel, honey, they won't happen to you. Really. Just because they happened to me." Sandra tried to put her arm around Rachel's shoulder, but Rachel flinched away. "And like you just said, in your case it's not an issue, so why fret?"

Rachel was weeping loudly now.

"Don't worry, she always does this when she gets high," Min said. "She'll be over it in a second."

"I shouldn't have said what I did."

"Are you sleeping with Aaron?"

"What?"

"Are you sleeping with my husband? That is, when you have your so-called meetings to go over your so-called work?"

"What? No, of course not. Jesus. It never even crossed—I mean, my relationship with Aaron is totally professional. I pay him four hundred dollars an hour, for Christ's sake."

"How much?"

"Plus we have our meetings in your apartment. Sometimes your kids are there."

"But I'm not. I'm slaving away in my fucking office, and he's at home, and you're paying him four hundred dollars an hour, which he never told me, and which is a hell of a lot more than I make."

"I can't believe he charges you four hundred dollars an hour," Min said.

"It's the going rate," Sandra said.

"Maybe I should get in on this racket."

"Will you please lay off? It's not a racket, and I'm not sleeping with him."

Now it was Min who was laughing.

"Oh, I see, so all this is just another joke?" Sandra said. "Why does everyone tease me? It's been true my whole life."

"It's sort of hard to resist."

"But isn't that a reason to resist it? As a measure of respect or affection? Or don't you like me? Why not? Do I threaten you? Are you afraid I'm going to horn in on your territory, try to take your place with Eva?"

"No one could ever take my place with Eva."

"Who says? What makes you think you're so special? You act as if you're the only one who understands her, the only one she could ever possibly confide in. Yet I notice she never told you she invited me to stay over that time."

"You said it was Bruce who invited you."

"Is there a difference? According to you, Bruce never does anything without her permission."

"Oh, just fuck off, will you?"

"OK, what do you and Aaron do during your quote-unquote meetings?" said Rachel, whose attention had not progressed beyond this point in the conversation.

"Well, each week he gives me a prompt, I write something, then I read it aloud to him. Only if I come to a sentence he doesn't like, he makes me stop."

"But that's not even original," Min said. "That's how what's-his-name taught. You know, Captain Fiction or whatever."

"Aaron's a hard sell. It was four weeks before he let me read past the first sentence. I burst into tears, I was so happy."

"Four meetings a month, at four hundred a pop, that makes sixteen hundred dollars."

"What was the sentence?" Min asked.

"I'm not ashamed to tell you. I worked so hard on it, I've got it memorized." Sandra cleared her throat. "'For most of her life, she had devoted her life to making sure she would never be left, and then one morning she woke to find she was living a life she could never leave.'"

"That's actually quite good," Rachel said.

"Thank you," Sandra said.

"There's just one thing I don't get," Min said. "You did leave Rico."

"You're assuming the character's me. It's not."

"Then who is it?"

"Who do you think?"

The women were silent for a moment. Then Min said, "It isn't Eva, is it?"

"Why should it be?" Rachel said. "She isn't the only woman in the world, last time I checked."

"Well, I suppose it's the idea of devoting your life to making sure you'll never be left," Min said. "Only that implies she's come to feel trapped, which I don't think she has."

"So why is she buying an apartment in Venice?"

"Hold on, are you suggesting she's buying the apartment to get away from Bruce? If so, you're completely off base. It has nothing to do with Bruce."

"Are you sure?"

"Of course I'm sure. For God's sake, we've just been talking about it."

"And yet it's not as if Bruce can just up and go to Venice whenever he feels like it," Rachel said. "There's his job, there are the dogs. No matter which way you frame it, if she buys this apartment she'll be spending a lot of time away from him."

"So what? Plenty of couples have long-distance marriages and are perfectly happy."

"Eva and Bruce? A long-distance marriage? When they've spent practically every night together since they met?"

"I'm sorry to interrupt," Sandra said, "but why are you both so sure the protagonist is Eva?"

"Who else could it be?"

"Well, it could be a man. I could have changed the gender to disguise his identity. It could be Bruce. Of course, I'm the last person to ask. I'm only the author."

Off in the distance, the dogs were yelping. Min looked at the joint, now only a stub, then passed it to Rachel, who dropped it to the ground. "I can't see how it could be Bruce," she said. "I mean, he's the one who earns the money. Of course, he loves her desperately."

"Hasn't it occurred to either of you that she may not be the one who feels trapped? That it might be him?"

"That's ridiculous," Min said. "You speak like you know them, yet you hardly know them. I'm the one who knows them."

"You may know them too well. So well you can't see them clearly anymore."

Suddenly Rachel started laughing again. "God, will you just listen to us?" she said. "I mean, we've been out here—how long, an hour?—and what are we talking about? Eva. Still. And when you think of all the other things there are to talk about!"

"I'm not the one who keeps bringing her up," Min said.

"Hold still, there's something on your face," Sandra said.

"What? Oh, God . . ."

"Stay still, I'll get it," Sandra said, reaching her fingers toward Min's cheek and pinching it so hard that Min cried out. "No, it's OK. It's just a bit of ash."

"Are you sure?"

"It probably blew over from Grady's. His gardener's always burning leaves."

"It's getting colder," Rachel said. "How long have we been out here? It feels like hours."

"I think about half an hour," Min said. "Time always seems to move more slowly when you're stoned."

"Or maybe this is the way time really moves," Sandra said, "and when you're *not* stoned, it feels speeded up."

"Wait, what are you saying?" Min said. "That time itself changes, or just our perception of time?"

"Is there a difference?"

"Of course there's a difference. It's like—you know, when there's a countdown to something and you're watching the clock, three minutes is an eternity. But then when you're not paying attention, three minutes goes by like three seconds. And yet no matter how those three minutes feel, they're always three minutes."

"Are they?"

"Of course. Because if they weren't—if time was always compressing and expanding—the earth's orbit would always be changing. One day the sun would set at four and the next at ten."

"Stop it, Sandra."

"Stop what? I'm just asking questions."

"No, you're not. You're trying to confuse us."

"Whatever time it is, we probably ought to be getting back inside," Rachel said.

"You're right," Min said. "Otherwise they might think we've been eaten by panthers."

20

Your mission, should you choose to accept it," Bruce said. He and Jake were walking on the fringe of the woods, letting the Bedlingtons lead them.

"I suppose you're wondering why I called you here today," Bruce said.

Jake bent down and worked a burr out of Ralph's paw.

"These dogs are ambulatory Swiffers," he said.

"You're not answering my question."

"How can I when you haven't asked it?"

"It's not a question I want to ask. It's a question I've been asked to ask."

"I think I know what it is. What I don't get is why she's so insistent it should be me. If it were my apartment, I'd want an Italian, someone like Roberto Peregalli."

"You know as well as I do Eva would never have anyone but you. She's afraid of what she isn't used to. It's why she's gone to such great lengths to circumscribe her life—and mine. Not that she's entirely to blame for that. It's served me too."

Jake picked up a branch and threw it, but the dogs were too captivated by some fugitive smell—the feces of a rodent or a raccoon, he guessed—to pay it any heed.

It was cold, and getting colder. "So am I to gather that we won't be allowed back in the house until I've given you an answer?" he said.

"I wouldn't put it that way exactly," Bruce said. "Anyway, let me ask you another question—or maybe it's the same question put a different way. What's stopping you from saying yes?"

"The same thing that's stopping me from saying no. Fear."

"Of what? Eva? Venice?"

"More Venice."

"You lived there once, didn't you?"

"Years ago, when I was in my twenties. And so naturally I have certain feelings about the place."

"It seems that everyone has feelings about the place except me. Then again, we've only been twice. Aside from the canals and there being no cars, it didn't seem very different from any other European city—expensive restaurants, cheesy gift shops, badly lit museums."

"For me it isn't Venice itself. It was that some things happened to me there. Bad things. Of course, they didn't have to happen there. They just happened to happen there."

"And you haven't been back since?"

He shook his head. "I'm sorry if I'm coming across as evasive. I'm not in the habit of saying how I feel about things. I'm told Eva appreciates that about me. And now I have a question for you."

"Shoot."

"You want me to say it's a sure thing, my decorating the apartment. Well, is it a sure thing you're buying it?"

"The question that underlies all other questions. At this point, I'd say chances are the answer will be yes. Mind you, if you'd asked me earlier in the week, I'd have said chances were the answer would be no. For instance, I trust you've heard about the garden?"

"Min mentioned it."

"You don't do gardens, do you?"

"No, I'm strictly an interiors guy."

"A pity. Anyway, this garden . . . for a while there, it looked like it might be a deal-breaker. And not just the fact of the garden, or the cost of the garden, but the way Eva told me about it. Or didn't tell me. Instead she told Min and Min blurted it out."

"No surprise there."

"Only this time it really brought us to the brink. At least that's how it felt to me. Like a reckoning. Now I think, I really think, that if I hadn't pulled us back, she'd have let us go over the cliff. She'd have let us crash."

"What do you want me to say to her? I mean, which answer would make your life easier?"

"One answer would make it easier in one way. The other would make it easier in another way."

Almost without realizing it, they had circled back to the house. "It's the dogs," Bruce said. "Something I appreciate about the dogs—they have their own priorities. Right now they're hungry."

"And we're cold," Jake said.

"Then let appetite be our guide."

So then he said, 'The way I see it, the only moral justification for eating meat is if you kill the animal yourself.' To which Denise replied, 'Honey, find me the perfect leopard skin and I'll eat the leopard.'"

Calvin waited for Eva to laugh. He was standing in front of her behemoth six-burner stove, stirring flour into the white sauce for the macaroni and cheese with lobster he was making for dinner. The Connecticut kitchen was a good five times the size of the Park Avenue kitchen, with room for a Tuscan refectory table, an early American hutch, and a sofa, slipcovered in a blue cotton check, on which Eva was at present lounging, looking through the March issue of *Enfilade*.

"Of course, I can't vouch for the truth of that story," Calvin said. "It was one of the cater waiters who told me. I was in the kitchen at the time."

"I didn't know you knew Clydie and Denise," Eva said.

"I didn't know you did."

"Well, I don't—I mean, I never met Denise, and Clydie I only know because her country place is just a few miles down the road. Min knows her better."

"She must be very old. At least as old as Denise was when she uttered that famous line about the leopard skin."

"Does the house feel strange to you today?" Eva asked, glancing at the French doors and noting that Beatie had neglected to wipe away the nose marks that the dogs had left on the glass.

"Only because it's empty," Calvin said. "Everyone's out except Aaron, who's fallen asleep in front of the fire. Listen, you can hear him snoring."

"That snore. I wonder how Rachel stands it."

"Dieter was an incredibly loud snorer. When he left me, I told myself not having to listen to him snore anymore was the silver lining, but then I found that I missed his snoring. I couldn't sleep without his snoring. In the end I had to buy a white noise machine."

"I've never thought of snoring as white noise. It's more gray noise. Or smog-colored noise."

Calvin considered asking Eva why she didn't just say "black noise," then, thinking the better of it, whisked sherry into his white sauce as Eva got up and pressed her own nose against the glass. Where had they all gone? she wondered. What were they doing? As a rule, she imposed no restrictions on her weekend guests other than that they show up for meals. And yet for so many of them to be away at once, and on such a cold afternoon, seemed pointed, as if she were being deliberately left out of something.

"It gets dark so early these days," she said. "Funny to think that if this were July, we'd be out by the pool."

"Speaking for myself, I can't stand the sun," Calvin said. "If it were up to me, from Memorial Day to Labor Day I'd never leave my apartment. My air conditioner's a Maserati. Of course, since Dieter moved out, it's been harder. I get lonely. I eat too much."

This came as no surprise to Eva. Even when Calvin was younger, and a regular fixture in her kitchen, he had been on the heavy side. Now he was forty, and must have weighed 250 pounds. Although she would never have been so gauche as to say so, his weight gain had been the main reason why, though far more gradually and kindly than was the case with Matt, she had eased him out of the central role he had once played in her life. Obesity repulsed her—and not just morbid obesity. Even from the sight of Bruce's widening stomach, when he took his shirt off, even from her own naked body, when she caught a glimpse of it in the bathroom mirror, she had to avert her eyes. Which was to say nothing of Min's recent ballooning.

Ashamed by the unkindness of her thoughts, she got up, strode over to Calvin, and put her hands on his shoulders. "Dearest Cal, you're so good to do this," she said. "And on such short notice."

"It was serendipity. Literally five minutes before you called, I had a cancellation—a fiftieth wedding anniversary."

"What happened?"

"The wife had a stroke."

"To think that you've come so far since I met you, that you're so in demand!"

"Well, there are trade-offs. For instance, I don't get to work for private clients as much as I used to. Now it's mostly corporate stuff—fundraisers, retirement banquets."

"I'm glad it's you tonight. With Clydie, you have to be so careful. It might have been too much for someone with less experience."

"You mean Matt?"

"You know Matt? How?"

"How does anyone know anyone? New York is a village."

Eva let out a theatrical sigh, returned to the sofa, and pulled her legs up to her chest. "Oh, Cal, I'm such a coward. Of course I should have said something to him, made a clean break, but you see, I just couldn't, because . . . Oh, but I'd rather not go into it. Let's just say there are things I can tolerate and things I can't, and one of the things I can't is want of tact."

"So it wasn't his cooking?"

"Well, there was that too. Once he forgot to put baking powder in a batch of scones. Oh, and another time he made some sorrel soup that was inedible."

"Sorrel soup is always inedible. It's one of those things everyone pretends to like and no one does."

With a creak of hinges, the door from the dining room swung open and Aaron stumbled in. "What time is it?" he asked, yawning.

"That door," Eva said.

"Three twenty," Calvin said.

"Wow. I fell asleep without realizing it. Oh, I meant to ask—why are all the curtains pinned up?"

"To keep the dogs from attacking them. Whenever they hear another dog barking, they run to the window and have a go at the curtains. In the end we decided it was easier to pin them up than to have to keep darning the tears."

"Is it also for the dogs that you've got that bedsheet laid over the rug in the upstairs hall?" Calvin asked.

"What? I told Beatie to take that up before the weekend. Anyway, yes, you see, Ralph has a tendency—there's no polite way to say this—to scooch his rear end on that rug, and it's such a nightmare getting the stains out."

"With all the provisions you have to take, the question that naturally comes to mind is why you have dogs in the first place," Aaron said.

"Some things matter more than decor," Eva said.

"I suppose I understand that," Aaron said. "I mean, it's not as if Mumbles hasn't wreaked havoc in his time. Especially before we had him neutered. The last straw was when he sprayed the bed. We had to throw out the mattress."

"Cal was just saying that no one likes sorrel soup," Eva said, in the tone of one eager to change the subject. "That people only pretend to like sorrel soup. What's your view on sorrel soup, Aaron?"

"Having never tasted it, I can't offer one, though I will note that among people who identify themselves as liberals, it's common to pretend to like things they don't because they think they're supposed to."

"The first time I took Dieter to Memphis, we went to this ribs place," Calvin said. "He wasn't sure whether to have the beef ribs or the pork ribs, so he asked the waitress which she recommended. 'Let me put it this way,' she said. 'The beef ribs are good for you, but the pork ribs are *good*.'"

Aaron let out a laugh like a car backfiring. "Oh, that's great! Can I steal that line? It sums it up so perfectly."

"What?"

"Well, the fundamental difference—between *plaisir* and *jouissance*, the fraudulently beneficent and the authentically

SHELTER IN PLACE 299

disturbing, Barbara Kingsolver and—I don't know—Beckett, or Proust."

"What's wrong with Barbara Kingsolver?" Eva asked.

"She is the embodiment of liberal piety at its most middlebrow and tendentious. Her novels are the beef ribs of fiction."

"Just to be clear, I don't actually have anything against beef ribs," Calvin said. "As a matter of fact, I love beef ribs."

"OK, then, they're the sorrel soup of fiction."

"I don't think that's fair," Eva said.

"To Barbara Kingsolver or to sorrel soup?"

"To either."

"Now, come on, Eva, tell us the truth. Have you actually ever read Barbara Kingsolver?"

"Have you?"

"I've dipped in. To paraphrase Wilde, you don't have to drink the whole cask to know the vintage."

"Then you're in no more of a position to dismiss her than I am."

"OK, fine, choose someone else. There are plenty who fit the bill. The point is, having some warm and fuzzy impulse to make the world a better place isn't enough. It doesn't make you an artist. What's been lost is any appreciation of virtuosity, of flair. You don't find it so much in the visual arts or the performing arts, because there you actually have to learn how to do something in order to do it. Whereas with writing, there's this notion that anyone can do it, that if you can write a tweet, you can write a novel."

"So you're saying that all novels that aspire to do good are by definition bad?"

"I suppose I am saying that, yes. To my mind, the two ambitions are antithetical."

Eva laughed. "I can't believe I'm hearing this. I mean, here we are, in a moment of national crisis, global crisis, with democracy about to fly off its hinges, and you're badmouthing a writer for having a conscience? No, don't interrupt me. I'm going to have my say. I'm sick of this line you literary people take that writers who care about social justice are by definition boring do-gooders, and the only ones who count are the ones who write whole books without ever using the letter *e*, or where the main character's grandmother is a zombie, or someone's going up an escalator for a thousand pages. You mentioned Proust. Well, what about Zola? Today everyone pooh-poohs Zola, but he published *J'Accuse*, for God's sake. In the middle of the Dreyfus Affair, he put his life on the line, went on trial, had to go into exile."

"Excuse me, but Zola was no Proust. And Kingsolver is no Zola."

"Let's not forget she endowed that prize."

"Yes, for quote-unquote socially engaged fiction."

"What's wrong with that?"

"Can you name me a single book that's won it? And in the meantime she's living on a farm raising Icelandic sheep."

"You certainly know a lot about her, considering how much you claim to despise her."

"And you know nothing about her, and yet you're defending her."

"I wonder why *Icelandic* sheep," Calvin said.

"What's this about sheep?" Bruce asked, walking through the French doors with Jake and the dogs, who immediately started barking.

"Sheep," Bruce repeated.

Their barking intensified.

"Wow, they know the word *sheep*?" Calvin asked.

"It's one of their sixty words. They've learned it from the drive up here, which takes us right past a sheep farm."

"What other words do they know?"

"Oh, let's see. I'd better spell them out instead of saying them, otherwise we'll have a riot. Well. D-I-N-N—"

"Why are you wearing that silly hat?" Eva said.

"E-R. This? I found it in the field while we were walking the dogs and I just . . . put it on. What do you think? Does it suit me?"

"It's you," Aaron said.

"You might have told me you were taking the dogs out."

"I did. T-R-E-A—"

"No, you didn't. Again."

"T-S-I-E."

"Sound carries strangely in old houses," Calvin said. "Someone says something from the next room and you don't hear it. And yet you can hear perfectly what someone else is saying on the third floor."

"Well, now that you're back, maybe you can tell me what's happened to the girls."

"Oh, they're outside, in that copse of maples," Jake said.

"What are they doing there?"

"Double, double, toil and trouble," Bruce said, cackling and putting his hands on his wife's shoulders. Then, when she didn't laugh: "No, in all seriousness, they're just standing in a huddle, gossiping."

"But they could have done that in the house. Why did they go outside?"

"Min said something about wanting to breathe the clean and frosty air," Jake said.

"She must be a fresh-air enthusiast," Bruce said. "Remember, darling, when you had to fill out that roommate form at Smith? Wasn't that one of the categories?"

"A pity you and I weren't asked to fill out that form before we got married," Eva said.

"My wife is referring to one of our few points of conjugal disharmony," Bruce said. "Whereas I'll put up with noise for the sake of a breeze, Eva will put up with stuffiness for the sake of silence."

"Is it so strange that horns honking and trucks rattling keep me awake?"

"And yet it was the same in our last apartment, where the bedroom faced the back. It's the same here."

"Only people who haven't lived in the country think it's quiet. There are all sorts of noises in the country. Animals, birds. Insects."

"You should get a white noise machine," Calvin said.

"I've always meant to ask, who was your roommate at Smith?" Jake said.

"What, you mean Eva's never told you about Melody Joy Greenblatt?" Bruce said. "And yes, that really was her name."

"That wasn't her fault."

"I agree. It's the parents I blame. When you call your child Melody Joy, you're asking for trouble."

"Especially if your last name is Greenblatt," Aaron said.

"I never understood what you had against her," Eva said. "She was very smart."

"Smart, yes. Game, no. The thing you have to understand"— Bruce turned to Jake and Aaron—"is that in those days, the

Smith campus was like Fort Knox. Sneaking onto it at night was like crossing the Berlin Wall. Many was the time I took my life into my hands to get into Eva's dorm room. And then when I got there, Melody Joy wouldn't play ball. She wouldn't leave."

"It was her room, too."

"Still, she could have gone downstairs for an hour or so. She never would, not even when I bribed her with chocolate."

"You took the wrong approach. You should have sweet-talked her. She had a crush on you."

"Are you kidding? It was you she had the crush on."

"Don't be silly."

"As you have doubtless noticed, my wife is congenitally oblivious to the concupiscence of others. Especially when she's the object of it."

"I'd hardly call Melody Joy concupiscent. She was too cerebral to be concupiscent."

"Any idea what became of her?"

"I wish I knew. Every issue, I check the class notes in the alumnae magazine, but she's never there. She doesn't go to the reunions either."

"Maybe she changed her name," Bruce said. "Didn't she use to talk about changing her name?"

"She joked about it. It was after we read that Flannery O'Connor story where the girl with the wooden leg changes her name from Joy to Hulga."

"She was going to change her name to Hulga?" Calvin said.

"Of course not. It was a joke."

"Still, I'll bet it happened in those years," Bruce said. "I'll bet more than a few girls changed their name to Hulga."

"Look, I just found her," Aaron said, holding up his phone. "Dr. Melody Joy Greenblatt, professor of art history at

Michigan State. Specializes in conceptual art. Oh, and here's a coincidence. She'll be in Venice this summer—something to do with the Biennale. Mundo piccolo."

"*Mondo* piccolo. Clearly you never studied Italian."

"Or Spanish," Calvin said.

The door opened again and Sandra peered in. "I hope I'm not interrupting," she said.

"That door," Eva said. "For weeks I've been asking Beatie to put some WD-40 on the hinges."

"Beatie has a lot on her plate right now," Bruce said. "Her son just got out of prison."

"She hasn't cleaned the windows, either. Or taken up the sheet over that rug."

"Where's your social justice agenda now?" Aaron said. "Oh, and while we're on the subject, Sandra, which do you prefer, beef ribs or pork ribs?"

"What?"

"And please bear in mind that your entire future as a writer depends on the answer."

"Really? Well, I haven't really thought about it. The fact is, I don't eat that much red meat."

Aaron let out another torrential laugh, at which Sandra blushed. "Oh, so this is another joke at my expense? It seems to be the theme of the day."

"What can I say? You're an easy target."

"And Bruce wearing that hat. Is that a different joke or part of the same one?"

"Why is everyone so worked up about my wearing this hat?"

"Tell me, Sandra, are you by any chance a youngest child?" Jake asked.

"In my case that's a complicated question," Sandra said. "By my mother, yes. But then, after she died, my father married again and had three more kids. I was ten at the time. I always felt like the hinge between the two families."

"That could be a title," Aaron said. "*The Hinge*."

"Where are Rachel and Min?" Eva asked.

"They've gone up to their rooms to rest. We came in through the back porch, and now I'm heading back to Grady's to change for dinner. In fact, that's why I popped in—to tell you I just got a text from him. He and Cody are on their way home from the airport—he's been off on one of his South Pacific cruises—so I asked them to join us for dinner. I hope that's OK."

"Who's Cody?"

"Grady's new boyfriend. They met on the cruise."

"Well, I'm not sure," Eva said. "I mean, Calvin's only making enough food for the nine of us."

"Don't worry, I always plan for such contingencies," Calvin said.

"In that case, fine," Eva said, not bothering to hide her annoyance, which Sandra either failed to pick up on or chose to ignore.

After she left, Eva got up and paced. "Of all the nerve," she said. "I mean, whose house does she think this is? You don't invite people to other people's dinner parties. You just don't."

"But darling, it's only Grady," Bruce said.

"That's beside the point."

"How? He's our neighbor and our old friend, on top of which Sandra's his cousin and houseguest."

"At this point I'd hardly call her his houseguest, considering she's been living there for months and months."

"That's my point. If it wasn't for Grady, we'd never have met her. Plus he'll have just gotten off a long flight."

"Then he'll be too tired to come to dinner."

"Maybe. Or maybe he'll be starving. And it's not as if he hasn't been to dinner here a hundred times before. It's the neighborly thing to do."

"I know that. Of course I know that, and of course I would have said yes if she'd asked me. But she didn't ask me. She told me. And then there's this new boyfriend, about whom we know nothing. Zero. Do you know him, Calvin?"

"Afraid not."

"I thought you knew everybody."

"He must be from a different part of the village."

Min was the next to come in. "What's all the shouting?" she said. "I could hear it all the way from the third floor."

"Oh, that door hinge!" Eva said. "It's driving me nuts. And with Clydie coming . . ."

"Relax, I'll put some WD-40 on it myself," Bruce said.

"I thought you were resting," Eva said to Min.

"I was," Min said, "only I heard shouting and wanted to make sure everything was all right."

"See what I mean about how sound travels in these houses?" Calvin said.

"Everything's fine," Bruce said from the pantry. "Eva's just a little upset because Sandra invited Grady and his boyfriend to dinner without asking her."

"What? How dare she!"

"It's not that I mind their coming. It's that she took me off guard. I don't like being taken off guard."

"Of course you don't," Min said, sitting next to Eva on the sofa and putting an arm around her. "Now, darling, I'm going to speak frankly. Of course, we all like Sandra—that goes without saying—but if we're to be honest, shouldn't we also admit that she can sometimes be a teeny bit presumptuous? A teeny bit, well, grand?"

"She can't help that. It's how she was raised."

"Trust me, I know how she was raised, and her grandmother definitely did not raise her to invite strangers to other people's dinner parties, much less to call up her acquaintances out of the blue and invite herself to stay the night."

"That was my fault," Bruce said. "I'm the one who took the call."

"And how did you feel about that, Eva? Be honest."

"Well, I certainly would have appreciated a little more warning. Which isn't to say I'm inhospitable."

"I can't imagine anyone accusing you, of all people, of being inhospitable."

"Is it possible we don't have any WD-40?" Bruce asked.

"If you don't mind, I think I'll have a rest before dinner," Jake said.

"Oh, Jake, before you go, have you seen this?" Eva said, holding up the copy of *Enfilade*. "It's the new issue. The room on the cover, it's by Alison Pritchard. Didn't she use to work for you and Pablo?"

"She did, yes. And no, I haven't seen it."

Eva handed him the magazine, the cover of which showed an expensively austere dining room furnished with a chunky table in anigre, Saarinen chairs with shiny pink leather cushions, and an Alvar Aalto ceiling lamp. On the Josef Frank sideboard, roses were arranged in an Edmund de Waal vase. One side of the room was glass, with a view of green-blue water, while the other was papered in a pale orange silk and hung with two Color Field paintings—Barnett Newman, Jake was pretty sure.

FEMINI-MINIMALISM, the headline read. ALISON PRITCHARD REBOOTS THE TWENTY-FIRST CENTURY.

"Well, what do you think?" Eva asked.

"I like it," Jake said. "It's fresh."

"There's that famous discretion again," Min said.

Turning the heat off under his sauce, Calvin came over to have a look. "Oh, I know that house," he said. "It's in the Salento. Some friends of mine rented it last summer."

"But I thought you never left your apartment in the summer."

"In this case I made an exception, because they've got fantastic air-conditioning. Funny, I don't remember those paintings being there."

"Maybe they were borrowed for the shoot," Aaron said.

"They absolutely were not borrowed for the shoot," Min said. "We *never* do that. The owners must have put them up after Cal left."

"What surprises me is that it's so unlike the sort of thing you and Pablo do," Eva said.

"It's true that Alison's aesthetic is more minimalist," Jake said.

"Is that why she left?" Min said. "Or was she fired?"

"Open to interpretation. The official line was that she and Pablo had quote-unquote creative differences."

"But we don't want the official line. We want the truth."

"Sometimes the official line *is* the truth."

"I notice Jake still hasn't told us what he thinks of the room," Bruce said, still from the pantry.

"You're right," Jake said. "I was hoping to take advantage of the fact that the conversation was moving in other directions to avoid answering that question."

"A skill well worth cultivating," Calvin said.

"Although this time we're not letting you get away with it," Min said. "Well, come on."

Jake gave the cover a second look. "How best to put it?" he said. "There's nothing wrong with it, but there's nothing right with it."

"Another great line!" Aaron said. "May I steal it?"

"It's already stolen. I stole it from Pablo, who no doubt stole it from someone else."

"Min, you're the editor," Eva said. "In your professional opinion, how much of a difference does the cover of a magazine like *Enfilade* make to a decorator's career?"

"Oh, huge. It puts them on the map. Or keeps them on the map. I hope you're listening to this, Jake."

"I'm hearing it."

"That's not the same thing."

"You know, the more I think about it, the more I realize I never felt comfortable in that house," Calvin said. "There was something sort of inhuman about it. Or anti-human. As if the rooms didn't want people in them."

"In other words, the sort of place where you'd eat sorrel soup," Aaron said.

"It's true that it's not what you'd call a homey home," Min said. "Or maybe that's just me. Home is such a relative concept."

"Speaking for myself, home is where you sleep best," Calvin said. "Me, I never sleep better than when I'm in my own bed."

"Really?" Aaron said. "That's funny, because I never sleep worse than when I'm in my own bed, maybe because when I'm in my own bed, I'm always worrying about whether it's time to change the sheets, or change the cat's litter, or why aren't the kids home yet, and that keeps me awake. Whereas here at Eva's—I mean, the cat could be dead, the kids could be out all night, and I'd never know, so I sleep like a rock."

"And the sheets are always clean," Min said.

"And yet it's not home," Calvin said. "I mean, it's not *your* home."

"I had hoped that after all these years you'd have come to think of this as your home away from home," Eva said.

"Oh, but we do," Min said. "Of course we do."

"What does *home* even mean?" Jake said.

The others looked at him. "I'd have thought you, of all of us, would be the best equipped to answer that question," Eva said.

"But that's assuming that the people who are best at doing something are also the best at talking about it," Aaron said.

"Decorating I understand," Jake said. "Curtains, fabrics, colors I understand. What I don't understand is what people mean when they talk about home. I'm not sure I've ever understood that."

"Well, isn't it obvious?" Min said, picking up the magazine and holding it before him, as if it embodied some idea she herself could not put into words. "Home is where you feel . . . at home."

"House and home," Aaron said, taking the magazine from her. "A pet peeve of mine is the way people treat these words as synonyms."

"Aren't they?" Bruce said.

"No, they are not. A house is a physical thing. Home is a concept."

"Not always. On your way into the village, you may have noticed a billboard advertising Gene, Ray, Jim, and Pete's Homes. And on it there's a picture of an old lady, and above her head is a speech bubble that says, 'Gene, Ray, Jim, and Pete got me a great deal on my home.'"

"What is it, a real estate agency?"

"No, they sell mobile homes. Trailers."

"Beatie lives in a trailer," Eva said.

"Which she almost certainly bought from Gene, Ray, Jim, and Pete. And which she almost certainly calls her home."

"Let's not forget the old folks' home," Calvin said. "As in 'It was a sad day when we had to put Grandma in the home.'"

"I think these days people are more likely to say 'retirement community.'"

"Not where I grew up."

"Where did you grow up?" Jake asked.

"In Byhalia, Mississippi, just across the state line from Memphis. We did have a house, at least. My sister lives in it now. It's the tradition in our family that when one generation gets too old for the house, they move into a trailer on the property and the house is passed on to the next generation."

"I'm glad you said *trailer*," Eva said.

"When you think about it, does any other language have a word that's quite the same as our *home*?" Min said. "The closest I can think of is French—*chez moi, chez toi*."

"As in 'Chez moi is where the heart is'?" Aaron said.

"Click your heels three times and say 'There's no place like chez moi,'" Calvin said.

"Une chambre n'est past une maison," Min sang. "Et une maison n'est pas un chez soi. Quand il n'y a personne . . ."

"Why does this entire conversation seem to me so dire?" Aaron said.

"Because none of us has answered Jake's question," Eva said. "None of us has said what we mean when we say we feel at home somewhere."

"It's all right. I didn't really expect an answer."

"Well, how about where you grew up?" Min said. "For instance, it's been years since I lived in Quincy, and still, every time I go back, this feeling comes over me. A feeling of homecoming."

"It's one thing if you felt you belonged where you grew up when you were growing up there," Calvin said. "But what if you didn't? What if, as a kid, all you did was count the days until you could get the hell out?"

"Or you ended up where you did totally by chance?" Aaron said.

"You can still come to feel you belong there," Min said. "It may take time, but you can come to feel that way."

"I give up," Bruce said, coming out of the pantry. "Clearly we don't have any WD-40."

"Well," Rachel said, stepping through the squeaky door, "and what are we . . . Oh my God, Bruce. Why are you wearing that?"

"I found it outside, in the snow. Whose is it?"

"It's hers," Aaron said.

"Give it back," Rachel said. "It looks ridiculous on you."

"I bow to your higher sense of fashion," Bruce said, then took off the hat and returned it to Rachel, who stuffed it into her purse.

"Thanks. Well, so what are we talking about?"

"House and home," Aaron said. "And being eaten out of them."

"Don't listen to him, he's just trying to be clever," Min said. "We're talking about what home means."

"What would you do," Eva said, "if someone you knew—someone you trusted—told you they were planning to leave, to move to another country, because of the election?"

For a moment no one spoke.

"I mean, if it actually happened," Eva said, "if Grady, for instance, really were to sell his house and move to Uruguay, would you think he was overreacting? Or would you think that maybe you should leave, too?"

"Well, I'm not sure," Min said.

"If it were Grady, I suppose the first thing I'd think was that he'd found an Uruguayan boyfriend," Aaron said.

"Aaron, please," Rachel said, and turned to look Eva in the eye. "OK, here's my answer. If that happened, if it happened today, right now, I wouldn't do anything. I'd take a wait-and-see approach. I'm sorry if that's not what you want to hear, Eva, but I have to be honest. Even with the election, I don't feel my personal freedom has been compromised. I just don't."

"Don't you mean you don't feel your personal *safety* has been compromised?" Jake said.

"That's what I said."

"No, you didn't. You said you didn't feel your personal *freedom* had been compromised."

"I don't see a problem with that equivalency," Min said. "The way I see it, to feel free, you have to feel safe."

"But how can you?" Jake said. "I mean, freedom and safety—how can you ever have both?"

"How can you not?"

"Well, because to be safe, really safe, you have to have money, and money, by necessity, ties you into certain . . . well, economic structures. And then you have to rely on those structures if your money is to have any value beyond the paper it's printed on. And those structures can collapse. Or turn against you."

"He's right," Aaron said. "Look at Madoff. Look at the stock market crash. When the market crashed and all those banks started failing, the first thing that went through my mind was that I should close our IRA and get the cash and hide it, like those old women in Italy you're always hearing about who, when they die, their children find they've got forty million euros stuffed into the mattress."

"It was that sort of thinking that brought on the crash," Bruce said. "It's an ouroboros."

"There are different kinds of freedom," Min said. "We're not just talking about money."

"No matter how you define freedom, to be truly free is not to be dependent," Jake said. "And that means giving up the pretense that you're safe."

"But it's not true," Eva said, raking her hair with her fingers. "The night of the inauguration, when we were in Venice, Min and I went out for dinner. We had those marvelous spiny crabs, and rice with shrimp and arugula, and then afterwards we took a walk. One of the strangest things about Venice is how silent it is at night. At night it's not like any other city. You feel as if you're the only person there. And so we walked, and all we could hear was the water splashing, and our heels clicking, and the cats howling, and everything that terrified me at home seemed so far away, as if it could never touch me—the inauguration, the Warriners' party, it was as if all of it was happening on another planet, or wasn't happening at all, because how can such things happen when the world contains such an extraordinary silence—and yes, maybe it was because I have money, because I could afford to escape, but I did feel safe, and I did feel free."

Suddenly Calvin threw the dishcloth he was holding on the floor. "You think just because you can afford to speculate about this, everyone can," he said, "when the truth is, most people can't. Most people on this planet, we never feel safe and we never feel free. All we feel is scared."

"You're right, you're right," Eva said, covering her eyes with her hands.

"Venice was a Fascist stronghold under Mussolini," Bruce said. "In '43 the city willingly handed over its Jews to the Germans."

Eva turned to him. "What do you mean by that? Why did you say that?"

"I'm just agreeing with you that we shouldn't pretend we can count on anything. Houses are Jake's business, money is mine. If I didn't believe I could protect wealth, I'd be out of a job. And I can do that. I can protect wealth. But I can't protect people. Not even wealthy people."

"You don't understand what Eva's saying," Min said. "In Venice you're immersed in the past, so the present recedes. Now, I'm not saying the history of Venice isn't bad—a lot of it is horrible—and yet when you're in such an old place, you don't feel the pull of the immediate so much, or you feel it differently, maybe because you experience the past, even the violent past, as art, and that gives you a clearer perspective."

"Sex and art are what have always drawn foreigners to Italy," Aaron said. "The Brits who settled in Florence, for instance, they went because they thought that with all that sex and art they'd be freer than at home. And they *were* freer, until the Fascists came in, and even after that, some of them stayed. Berenson stayed. But it was dangerous."

"Do you think I don't know all this?" Eva said. "Do you think I don't think about this every hour of every day? Having money didn't save anyone from the gas chambers. The ones who escaped were the ones who saw the writing on the wall."

"No, they had to have money, too," Calvin said. "It wasn't enough to see the writing on the wall. Escaping isn't an option in ghettos. It wasn't then for Jews and it isn't now for blacks."

"That's comparing apples and oranges," Aaron said.

"How? You don't know what it's like being a black man today. Every time I go out, every time I see a cop, I worry about getting shot."

"This conversation isn't getting us anywhere," Min said.

"On the contrary, it's getting us somewhere," Jake said. "Just not somewhere any of us wants to go."

22

Rachel thinks I'm having an affair with Aaron," Sandra said.

"She told you that?" Bruce said.

"She told all of us when we were outside smoking pot," Sandra said. "You did realize we were smoking pot, didn't you?"

"It would have been hard not to. Why didn't you just go over to Grady's?"

"He claims he's allergic to smoke." Sandra brushed back her hair so that it wouldn't fall into Bruce's mouth. It was five in the afternoon and they were lying, entangled and fully clothed, on one of the twin beds in Grady's guest room. An hour earlier, Bruce had told Eva he was going out to get some WD-40. He hadn't specified *where* he was planning to get the WD-40, or even that he was planning to buy a new can as opposed to borrowing the old one that Sandra had texted him to say she'd found in Grady's garage. Though the WD-40 might be a ruse, it wasn't a lie, a distinction Bruce still considered essential to the maintenance of his honor.

"Can you hoist yourself off me for a sec?" Sandra said. "My spine is going numb."

He rolled to the left. "How's that?"

"Oh, thank God. I can breathe again."

He laughed. "Tell me honestly, do you think we're too old to be doing this?"

"On a bed this narrow, yes."

"Do you want to get up?"

"No. Do you?"

"No."

"Good."

She kissed the veined top of his hand. He kissed each of her knuckles, then the tips of her fingers, then the phone she was clutching in anticipation of the text Grady had promised to send when his car was twenty minutes from the house. "It's strange, I remember this feeling so vividly from when I was a teenager," she said. "My grandmother would be out, and I'd have a boy over, and as the hour of her return approached—my grandmother was famously terrifying—the boy would start to get fidgety and want to leave, only I wouldn't let him. I'd make him stay."

"That's where I'm different. I want to stay."

"How does it feel, wanting that?"

Bruce considered the question. "Well, there's a rush, certainly. The element of risk. Gets the adrenaline going. Not to mention the fact that I never get enough time with you, and so I'm always thinking I should savor every second, only how can you savor every second when every second you're worrying about savoring every second?"

"It's the being-in-love paradox."

"Will it pass? Is it just a function of the newness of the thing, or that it's . . . I can't think of the right word."

"Transgressive? Perilous?"

"Something like that."

"I wish I could tell you. I only had two affairs while I was married to Rico, and they weren't like this. They were crimes of opportunity."

"What about Aaron?"

"He was never an opportunity. That's why I was so blown away when Rachel said what she did. I mean, in retrospect I can see why she thought so, given that I spend so much time alone with him. And yet when she actually came out with it . . . I don't know, maybe it was because I was stoned, but I was just floored. Now I wonder if my reaction was *too* authentic, if I should have taken advantage of the situation and pretended she'd hit a nerve."

"Why?"

"Because it's to our benefit. Remember, Min heard the whole thing, and you can bet she'll report it all to Eva. It will put her off the scent."

"You're assuming she's on the scent. She's not. It would never occur to her that I could have an affair. That's my doing as much as hers, by the way."

"So are you saying that since you got married, you've never—"

"Not until now."

"Not even with Min?"

"Min! What on earth would make you think that?"

"Just something she said that suggested she knew certain . . . details."

"Anything Min knows, she knows from Eva."

"Are you sure? You can trust me. I hope you trust me."

"Hold on, what exactly are we talking about?"

"OK, I'll tell, but you have to promise not to look at me while I'm saying it, otherwise I might burst out laughing. When I get embarrassed, I laugh. I can't help it."

"I'll close my eyes. There, they're closed."

"OK, deep breath. According to Min, you and Eva don't have intercourse. And the reason you don't have intercourse is that she has a small vagina, and you have a larger-than-average penis, and so intercourse isn't—well—on the menu."

Bruce opened his eyes. "Oh, my," he said. "So it's true that women will talk about anything."

Sandra was laughing now. "I'm sorry," she said. "The point is, I wouldn't have paid any attention if I hadn't had firsthand experience of your—well—person."

"My person?"

"People say that. My grandmother did."

"It's true what Min said about Eva's . . . person. For a long time it was a great worry to her. Now she doesn't seem to be as bothered by it."

"So with me, this is the first time . . . in all these years . . ."

He nodded.

She put her hands on his cheeks. "Oh, Bruce! Oh, I'm touched. Flattered. Probably I shouldn't be. Oh, but you poor baby. How does it feel?"

"I think I've been fairly vocal about how it feels."

"No, what I mean is, now that you've rediscovered it, how does it feel to look back on all those years you went without?"

"You mean do I regret them? I'm not sure. Sometimes I think I don't understand regret, maybe because my career has taught me to buy when everyone else is selling."

"In other words, when you finally get something you've never had, you value it more than if you'd had it all along."

"I don't know. Having not had it all along, I don't know what having it all along feels like."

"You know, in a funny way we owe all this to Eva. I mean, if she hadn't gone to Venice, you wouldn't have gone that night to Aaron and Rachel's for dinner. And if you hadn't gone that night to Aaron and Rachel's for dinner—"

"We wouldn't be here now."

"It does seem like serendipity, doesn't it?"

"Probability theory suggests the opposite—that what looks like a plan is really just coincidence. Like all the numerological stuff people were spouting after 9/11, as if the numbers themselves were significant, when in fact you could do the same thing with any two numbers. It's cooking the books."

"I wonder what a cooked book would taste like. Probably it would depend on the book."

"You could write a story about it for Aaron."

"With whom, by the way, I'm not sleeping. With whom I've never slept. In case you were wondering."

"I wasn't. And even if you were, it wouldn't be any of my business."

"Yes, it would."

"No, it wouldn't. You're a free agent now. You can do what you want."

"I am doing what I want. And I think we've moved past the point where you can say I'm a free agent."

A ping sounded, startling Sandra into dropping her phone, which fell to the carpeted floor. "Oh, but it's not mine," she said after she picked it up. "It must be yours."

Bruce pulled his phone from his pocket and read the text. "It's Eva. She's asking where I've got to."

"In that case you'd better scoot. I wonder why Grady hasn't texted. He must be caught in traffic. Either that or he's forgotten. Under the best of circumstances he's forgetful, and then when you factor in the jet lag—"

"Oh, that reminds me—that's something I need to warn you about. When you invited Grady and his friend to dinner tonight, Eva wasn't exactly pleased about it."

"Why not? I thought she thought of Grady as family."

"She does. That's not the issue. The issue is that you didn't ask her first."

"Didn't I?"

"So it seems. I'm not as sensitive to these niceties as she is."

"Oh, dear. I'm sorry. Should I apologize? No, I'd better not, otherwise she might suspect you told me. And yet, now that I think about, she's right, I should have asked her, just as I shouldn't have asked if I could stay the night that night."

"Funnily enough, that came up in the conversation, too. Min brought it up. Don't worry, I took the rap. I said it was my doing, which it was. I wanted you there. I suppose Eva must have told Min."

"No, she didn't. I did. It was when we were out having our breath of . . . fresh air. Of course, when I mentioned it, I assumed she already knew, and so when she let slip that she didn't, I guess I took advantage of the situation. I went on a fishing expedition, as they say, in the course of which I learned that she's jealous of me, that she thinks I'm out to steal Eva away from her."

"Good. Let her think that."

"But Bruce, she's right. What I mean is, I'm not just pretending with Eva. I really have been courting her—and not just as a strategy, but because I feel a real connection with her. Is that terribly hypocritical of me?"

"There's no law that says you're not allowed to like Eva. And besides, it's not like you're lying to anyone. You're just . . . not stopping Min from barking up a certain tree."

"Even though we may not be lying, we're being deceitful. There's no getting around that."

"Deception is often practiced for the purpose of protection."

"But for how long? How long can you keep that up?"

Two pings sounded at once. They looked at their phones.

"It's Grady."

"It's Eva again."

"You'd better go."

"I'd better go."

"Where have you been? What kept you?"

"I told you, I was getting some WD-40."

"You didn't answer my texts and your phone kept going to voicemail. For all I knew you could have been in a car accident."

"You're overreacting. I was only gone forty-five minutes."

"You were gone an hour and seventeen minutes. And in the meantime they've arrived. Early."

"Who's arrived?"

"Clydie—and she's brought along two houseguests. Naturally, she didn't let me know in advance. What is this— why does everyone seem to think they can bring people to my dinners without asking me?"

"Have you told Calvin?"

"Of course I have, and he's not pleased. I mean, two extra guests he can handle. But four!"

A screeching sounded. "God, that door," Eva said. "Look, you'd better go and change. Give me the WD-40, I'll have Jake spray it on."

"Oh, but I couldn't find any WD-40. That's why I was gone so long. I tried three different places. Obviously there's been a rush on it."

Eva's phone vibrated. "It's Sandra. Grady's just back, but he wants to take a shower first. They'll be another half hour. That's lucky, it'll buy Calvin some time. Oh, and we have to reset the table. Jake, thank God!"

"What is it?"

"I'm sorry to ask you to do this, but I've got Clydie in the living room, and Pablo and Min's boss—I can't remember her name. Which means we have to add two more places to the table, which means changing the china. I used the Royal Copenhagen and I've only got ten settings of that, so it'll have to be the stuff from Pottery Barn. Could you do it for me, Jake?"

"Hold on, what are Pablo and Indira doing here?"

"Clydie brought them. What's her name again?"

"Indira."

"Indira. Actually, since you know her, why don't you go in? Bruce has to shower. He was gone an hour and a half looking for WD-40 and not finding it."

"What about the table?"

"I'll take care of the table. Oh, this is madness!"

"It's your own fault," Bruce said. "You know what Clydie's like."

"Yes, everything's my fault, including your ridiculous last-minute wild goose chase after WD-40."

"Only because you wouldn't shut up about the door hinge."

"What's going on? What's the matter?" Min asked from the stairs.

"Go into the living room with Jake. Your boss is here, with Pablo and Clydie."

"Indira? Why?"

"She and Pablo are staying the weekend with Clydie. I'm getting very tired of explaining this over and over, so please, just go in and keep them amused while Bruce showers and I reset the table."

Eva and Bruce left, one through the door to the kitchen, the other up the stairs. "Indira *and* Pablo?" Min said.

"So it seems," Jake said. "After you."

They put on smiles only once they were in the living room. From the sofa on which she was sitting with Indira, Clydie peered up at them through her huge glasses. Rachel and Aaron sat opposite them, on armchairs. Pablo was inspecting things.

"Have I met you?" Clydie said to Min.

"Yes, you have," Min said brightly. "I'm Min Marable. I was with Indira the day we came by to see your apartment."

"Oh, of course. With Pablo. The night of the long Canalettos."

"Min, this is a surprise," Indira said. "No one told me you'd be here."

"I'm often here," Min said. "Eva is my best friend."

"I must say, Jake, this is an original look," Pablo said, examining the pinned-up curtains.

"Oh, that's not a look," Rachel said. "Eva just keeps them like that so the dogs can't get at them. When they hear other dogs barking, they lunge at the windows and try to tear through the curtains. If you look closely, you can see the teeth marks."

"What kind of dogs are they?" Indira asked.

"Bedlington terriers," Min said. "They're in the kitchen."

"Aren't they the ones that look like barracudas?" Clydie asked.

"More often they're said to look like lambs," Aaron said.

"They're barracudas," Clydie said firmly.

"I wonder if there's an article in this," Min said. "Decorating that's pet safe."

Clydie said, "I remember when we visited Nancy Lancaster once—I can't remember which of her houses it was, she had so many—Ditchley, I think—and of course, you know, she had all those dogs. And there was dog hair everywhere, and they'd pissed on all the furniture. She'd had John Fowler make up these amazing little dog beds for them, with canopies, only they wouldn't go near them. The dogs wouldn't. They were always on the sofas, pissing."

"She was famous for those dog beds," Pablo said.

"Speaking of Nancy, I've been meaning to ask how Rose is doing. I haven't seen her in ages."

"I'm afraid she's dead, Clydie. She died ten years ago."

"Did she? Oh, well, that explains it. I ought to be dead myself."

"Heaven forbid," Aaron said.

"I mean it. I have no right to be as old as I am. I really have no idea why I'm still alive. I'm sure there are others more deserving of such longevity."

"There's an old Italian saying," Jake said. "People who break your balls never die."

"And who are you? I'm sure I know you."

"I'm Pablo's business partner. I was also at your apartment on the night of the long Canalettos."

"Yes, I thought it was from Venice that I knew you. Back when Denise still had the palazzo. You were a lot younger, of course."

"It was thirty years ago," Pablo said. "Jake had taken a gap year of sorts. He was renting a room from Ursula."

"Oh, of course! Now I know how I know you."

"Excuse me, but do you mean Ursula Brandolin-Foote?" Eva said, coming in from the dining room. "If so, that's an amazing coincidence, because I'm buying her apartment."

"Ursula's apartment? Why?"

"Just—to have a place there. In Venice. We're all hoping Jake will decorate it. He decorates all my homes. He hasn't agreed to yet, even though Indira's promised to put it on the cover of *Enfilade* if he does."

"I have?" Indira said.

"Indira thinks the article should be about *why* Eva bought the apartment," Min said quickly. "Tell Clydie why you're buying it, Eva."

"Well, there are a lot of reasons—"

"It was because of the election," Min said.

"Oh, don't talk to me about the election," Clydie said. "A friend of mine, a dear old friend in his nineties—he voted for Sanders in the primary, and afterwards he sent me a little poem. 'Roses are reds, violets are blue, I just voted for a Socialist Jew.'" She laughed to show her teeth. "Lucky for him, he died late in October."

"It's true that it was the election that spurred me to buy the apartment," Eva said. "So that we'd have someplace to escape to."

"Yes, but why Venice, of all places?" Indira asked, leaning forward and propping her arms on her knees to suggest keen interest. "I've been so curious about that."

"Well, because it's Venice. It's so beautiful."

"Also Eva's writing a biography of Isabella Stewart Gardner," Min said.

"No, I'm not," Eva said.

"Do you think Venice is beautiful?" Clydie said. "Speaking for myself, I've always found it rather dreary. So did Denise. She had her worst depressions there. Tried to do herself in twice. For me, Venice is a city for suicides." She adjusted her glasses and peered at Jake. "But of course, that's how I know you. It was your friend who jumped into the canal."

"What's this, Jake?" Eva said.

"A long time ago, a friend of Jake's jumped off a bridge in Venice," Pablo said.

"What was his name again?" Clydie said. "Victor?"

"Vincent."

"Oh, Jake, I'm so sorry," Rachel said, reaching an arm in his direction. "Oh, but you've never said anything about it. Why haven't you ever said anything about it?"

"I've never been one to go into the gory details," Jake said. "I'm told people appreciate that about me."

"Vincent Bulmer, yes," Clydie said. "Charming lad. He had the AIDS, didn't he? Was that why he jumped?"

"We *believe* that's why," Pablo said. "We don't know for sure."

"Well, if it was, I consider it brave of him."

"How is suicide brave?" Indira asked. "Suicide is selfish."

"Of course it's selfish," Clydie said. "It's claiming authority over your own life."

"And in the process causing great pain to the people who love you."

"As if dying of the AIDS doesn't?" Clydie shook her head decisively. "Take the word of a decrepit old woman, he was brave to do it. I often wish I was that brave. If I were, I'd hang myself tonight."

"But Clydie, what about Jimmy?" Min asked.

"Any sorrow Jimmy will feel at my passing, his inheritance will more than compensate for."

"I wish Sandra and Grady would hurry up," Eva said. "We should really eat. It's macaroni and cheese with lobster, Clydie. I remember you like that."

"All this has me wondering about Ursula," Clydie said. "Haven't seen her in years. How is she doing?"

"Oh, she's marvelous," Min said. "When Eva and I were in Venice, she had us over for tea. That's how the whole thing started."

"Was it Ursula who introduced you to Jake?" Clydie asked Eva.

"No, I've known Jake forever," Eva said.

"Eva doesn't know I have a history with Ursula," Jake said. "Or rather she didn't until now."

"Actually, in this case I was the one who did the match-making," Aaron said.

"Really? Why didn't you tell me?" Eva said.

"She asked me not to. She's funny that way. I'm not sure why, because the truth is, I don't really know her very well. Back in the nineties, she did a few translations for me, and then later—I mean after I left New Directions but before I broke free from the shackles of publishing altogether—I sometimes hired her to do reader reports. She can read six languages, including Serbo-Croatian."

"It seems everyone knows Ursula better than I do," Eva said, sitting on the arm of the sofa.

"Isn't that great?" Min said. "It's as if she's been part of the family all along."

Right then Bruce bounded in, his hair flinging droplets of water and his face red from scrubbing. Hearing him, the dogs trotted in from the kitchen.

"Clydie, how nice to see you," he said, shaking her hand. "Can I offer you a drink?"

"Thanks, I've already had two. Ah, and these must be your barracudas."

"My what?"

"Come here, killers," Clydie said, holding out her hand, which the dogs approached meekly, their tails low, as if in deference to an authority they recognized by instinct. Only when the doorbell rang did they start barking.

"I'll get that," Jake said.

He left to answer. A few seconds passed, and Sandra tiptoed in, in a red satin dress and with her hair, which she usually wore loose, in a chignon. "Sorry we're late," she said. "It's started snowing again, you know."

"And here's Grady, back from the tropics!" Bruce said, patting Grady on the back.

"Yes, and in a grumpy mood after a very long flight, followed by a very long wait for the luggage, followed by a very long drive through very cold weather," Grady said. "Oh, but I haven't introduced Cody. This is Cody. We met on the cruise. He was giving tango lessons."

A rather unprepossessing young man, his scarf wound over his mouth in the manner of an Edward Gorey protagonist, nodded in greeting.

"Well, now that we're all assembled, shall we go in?" Eva said, motioning toward the pass-through to the dining room. "Bruce, why don't you help Clydie up?"

"Thanks, but I can get up on my own," Clydie said. "I do it at least twice a day."

The group processed into the dining room, where Calvin waited. "Hello, Clydie," he said, holding out his hand. "Calvin Jessup. So nice to see you again."

"Do I know you?" Clydie said. "If I do, I can't remember you, which is odd. Usually I remember black men."

"Shall we sit?" Eva said. "Clydie, why don't you sit here, next to Bruce? And Rachel on the other side, then Grady, then Sandra—"

"Wait!" Clydie said. "Don't sit! Don't anyone sit!"

"Why not?"

"There are thirteen places. Don't you know that when there are thirteen at table, the first person to sit down will die?"

"Are you sure?" Sandra said. "I thought it was the last person to sit down who died."

"Actually, it's the first person to get up who dies," Rachel said. "It was in a novel I published, and there the characters came up with an easy solution. When the meal was over, everyone got up at the same time."

"What if one of us has to go to the bathroom?" Min said.

"Hush, Min," Eva said.

"Hold on," Aaron said, waving his phone, "I've been looking this up, and from what I'm seeing, when there are thirteen at table, it's the youngest who dies. It doesn't have anything to do with who gets up first or who sits down first. The tradition seems to derive from the Last Supper, where Christ was the thirteenth and the youngest."

"Well, who's the youngest here?" Rachel said.

"I suppose it must be Cody," Grady said. "Cody's . . . Sorry, how old are you, Cody?"

"Twenty-three," Cody said.

"Drat, beaten by a hair," Calvin said.

"Oh, but I don't even care," Cody said. "I'm not even a Christian. I was raised Zen Buddhist."

"No, I forbid it," Clydie said. "The last thing I need is another death on my conscience. There's only one solution, and that's to round up a fourteenth guest."

"Well, what if we put one of the dogs in a chair?" Aaron said.

"Then the dog will be the one to die," Eva said. "The dogs are only seven."

"That's in human years," Bruce said. "In dog years they're forty-nine."

"No, they're forty-three," Aaron said. "Seven dog years for each human year is an old wives' tale. If you want to calculate a dog's age properly, you count the first year as one human year and each of the rest as seven."

"But that's neglecting the fact that small dogs live so much longer than big dogs," Sandra said.

"Bedlingtons are especially long-lived," Eva said. "Millie was nearly eighteen when she died."

"Who's Millie?" Aaron asked.

"The grandmother of these three," Bruce said.

"Hold on, if the dog's supposed to be the fourteenth guest, we won't be thirteen anymore, so why are we even talking about this?" Rachel asked.

"Folks, please, there's a simpler way to handle the situation," Calvin said. "I'll eat in the kitchen and you'll be twelve."

"But Calvin, you're as much a guest as any of us," Eva said.

"No, I'm not, I'm the cook," Calvin said. "And I shall eat in the kitchen, as befits my lowly status."

"In that case I'll join you," Clydie said. "I want you to tell me how we know each other. I find black men so very fascinating."

"Eva, may I have a word with you?" Grady said. "I'm sorry I didn't mention this before—blame the jet lag—but Cody's vegan. That means he doesn't eat meat, dairy, or eggs."

"I know what vegan means."

"I hope it's not a problem. What's for dinner, by the way?"

"Macaroni with cheese and lobster."

"Do you think Calvin could take the cheese and lobster out of one of the portions?"

"Calvin, could you take the cheese and lobster out of one of the portions?"

"No."

"It's all right," Cody said. "I'm not all that hungry."

"I think there's a salad," Eva said. "And bread, of course."

"That's fine."

"No, it isn't," Grady said. "You need a proper meal."

"Don't worry, I'll rustle something up for you," Calvin said, putting his arm around Cody's shoulders and leading him into the kitchen.

"Jesus," Grady said.

"Well, I suppose we can sit now, given that instead of thirteen we're now"—Eva counted on her fingers—"ten." She scanned the number of empty seats. "Wait, we're only nine. Who's missing?"

"Whoever isn't here, raise your hand," Aaron said.

"Don't be helpful," Rachel said. "Hold on, let me see . . . It's Jake. Jake's the one who's missing."

"I wonder where he's got to," Min said.

"Jake!" Eva called into the echoing house.

There was no answer.

"Maybe he's in his room," Min said. "I'll go and check."

On the stairs, though, she doubled over and nearly fainted. All evening, ever since Eva brought up the magazine cover in front of Indira, she'd been having stomach cramps.

After a few seconds she felt steady enough to finish her climb to the third floor, where she knocked on the door of Jake's room.

"Jake?" she called. "Jake?"

Still no answer.

"He's not there," she said when she got back downstairs.

"And the dogs are gone," Eva said. "He must have gone out with the dogs."

"But why?"

"How am I supposed to know?"

"It's Clydie's fault," Pablo said. "She should never have mentioned Vincent."

"Who's Vincent?" Grady asked.

"A friend of Jake's who died."

"Oh no. Recently?"

"No, it was ages ago."

"I'll see if I can find him," Bruce said, pulling his parka from the coatrack in the front hall.

When he went into the kitchen, the door hinge squeaked. Min made to follow him but was stopped by a hand on her shoulder.

She turned. It was Indira.

"Min, might I have a word?" Indira said.

23

Simon: r u there

Simon: jake

Simon: why don't u answer me did i do something wrong

Simon: say something wrong

Simon: i've been thinking about what u said about venice

Simon: i'll come if u want me to

Simon: your worried i'll be disappointed but i'm worried u will be

Simon: or maybe neither of us will be 😴

Sim: i hope ur ok

Simon: i'm watching my phone

Simon: i love u my prince

Simon: goodnight

24

From the kitchen, Bruce stepped through the French doors into the cold and welcoming night. Since he'd got back from Grady's—it seemed years ago—the temperature had dropped ten degrees; the snow was falling harder and had started to stick. Through the double-paned windows he could still hear voices, but they were soft and unintelligible, like the voices on a television in a distant room. "Jake!" he called, waving his flashlight in an arc that took in slices of the patio, the broken fountain, the pool, the firepit, the yard with its edging of woods. And when he got no reply: "Ralph! Caspar! Izzy!"

Distant barking, then—the barking of his own dogs, higher in timbre than that of his neighbors' dogs, the ones whose nocturnal revels regularly drove the Bedlingtons to such frenzies of curtain tearing. "Guys, over here, pronto!" he called, clapping his hands, and was relieved when Caspar came shambling toward him out of the dark, his eyes lambent in the flashlight's beam.

"Jake? Are you there, Jake?"

"Over here."

Bruce followed the voice to the copse of trees where earlier in the day they had bumped into Min, Rachel, and Sandra.

"Are you OK?"

"I'm OK." Jake was wiping steam from his glasses with his shirttail.

"I'm glad. When we couldn't find you, we were worried."

"Sorry about that. I tried to make as discreet an exit as I could."

"But you took the dogs."

"Yes, that was supposed to be part of the discretion. I figured if you noticed I was gone, and then that the dogs were gone, you'd just assume I'd taken them for a walk and forget about it. Just go on with your dinner."

"When you'd vanished into thin air? How could we?"

"I didn't think my absence would be that noticeable. Stupid of me, I see now. A sort of inverted narcissism . . . It's funny, for most of my life the only thing I've been sure of is how to behave, how I'm supposed to behave. But now it seems I can't even do that anymore."

"You must understand, no one's angry at you," Bruce said. "Just concerned. I mean, walking out like that—it's not like you. It may be like me, but it's not like you."

"You're right," Jake said, "but then again, how often do I find myself caught in the headlights of someone else's memory? And things were crazy enough already, weren't they, what with Pablo and Indira showing up unannounced, so that when Clydie suddenly chiming in about Venice and Vincent and Ursula—and in front of Eva, no less—Eva, to whom I really should have explained all this myself, weeks ago—I just . . . lost it."

"Is that why you left? Because of Eva?"

"Partly. Mostly, though, I so very much didn't want to hear Clydie talk about Venice, and Ursula, and Vincent . . . You know what's the strangest part of all this? In New York, Clydie and I have known each other, what, two decades? And yet, until tonight, neither of us ever put it together that we'd met in Venice. Or maybe that's not so strange, when you consider how long ago it was, and that Ursula introduced me to hundreds of people over there, mostly women, and mostly so much older than me that they just sort of . . . blurred together. If I'd been in the trade longer, I might have known to listen for Clydie's name, but I hadn't. I'd only just finished Parsons. I was twenty-two."

"I'm sorry if I missed something," Bruce said, "but what exactly did Clydie say to you? What was it you should have explained to Eva?"

"That I know Ursula. That I've known her since I was . . . God, twenty-two. The first time Eva mentioned her name, that night when you had me over for dinner to tell me about the apartment, I should have fessed up. But you see, I've spent so much of my life trying to steer clear of Ursula, and Venice, and anyone who might have known me in Venice, much less anyone who might have known Vincent, that I guess it's become second nature."

"Hold on, who is this Vincent?"

"Who *was* this Vincent. He was my lover. Well, that was the word we used in those days. And now he's been dead . . . what, thirty years?"

"And all this came up tonight?"

"Clydie brought it up, but she doesn't know the real story. She's got a confused version of it."

"What's the real story?"

"You sure you want to hear it? There are some gory details."

"Go on."

"OK, but remember, you asked. Well, after I finished up at Parsons, Aunt Rose—I'm sure I've told you about her, she brought me into the business—she arranged for me to spend three months in Venice. It was a graduation present of sorts. The idea was that I'd take a decorative painting course at the Accademia di Belle Arti—a friend of Pablo's was teaching it—and go to see some Palladian villas, and just generally soak in the atmosphere. At that point Pablo had been working for Rose, what, five years? Already she looked at him as her heir apparent, and, well, I was in love with him. Totally, passionately, unrequitedly in love with him, which he knew, and said he found touching, which I think he really did, because he treated me like an adored younger brother, in a way that was kind but also sort of sadistic, since that wasn't how I wanted to be treated. How I wanted to be treated wasn't in the cards.

"Anyway, in Venice I needed somewhere to live, obviously, so Pablo arranged for me to rent a room from Ursula, with whom he was having an affair. Or had been having an affair. Maybe by then it was over, it's hard to remember. I'm not even sure Ursula was divorced yet.

"So then I get there, to Ursula's, and the room, it turned out, wasn't even a room, really, it was this sort of alcove off the kitchen, with a curtain instead of a door, and just enough space for a very narrow bed. Later I learned it was where Ursula's maid usually slept, that she'd kicked the maid out for the duration and the maid was having to sleep on a settee in her dressing room. She'd pretty much lied about the whole thing, I guess because she needed the money—she always needed money—and also maybe she figured if I was there, Pablo would come to Venice more often.

"Anyway, in those days, in addition to the one she lived in, Ursula owned three or four other apartments that she rented to visiting academics, and it was in one of these, directly upstairs from hers, that Vincent was living. He taught art history at Bard, and that year he had a fellowship to do research in Venice—his specialty was Carpaccio—and one afternoon when he came down to pay his rent—we all paid Ursula in dollars, under to the table—she introduced him to me and offered him some tea, and we just sort of . . . fell madly in love, or convinced ourselves that we had. Which wasn't anything new for Vincent—he'd had a bunch of relationships by then, including one that had lasted for six years—but for me it was just amazing, because nothing like it had happened to me before. My whole experience of love until that point had consisted of crushes on my teachers, Pablo mostly, plus the occasional one-night stand with a classmate, or someone I picked up on the street, that inevitably left me with that Peggy Lee is-that-all-there-is feeling. And now here was Vincent, who could have been one of my teachers, because he was a lot older than me. Well, fourteen years older, which felt like a lot at the time. The age difference scared me but it also thrilled me, because in so many ways he reminded me of Pablo, only, unlike Pablo, he wasn't straight and seemed to be as enamored of me as I was of him. And so I started spending every night with him, in his apartment, even though I was still paying Ursula for the so-called room."

"What did Ursula think?"

"She thought it was great, as did her maid, who got her alcove back.

"It's funny, only recently have I started to realize what a big role Venice played in the whole thing. Earlier, when I said it could have happened anywhere, I was lying, I see now. I mean, sure, it could have, but it wouldn't have been the same story, or have had the same ending. Because Venice, its foundation—the city's literal foundation—is an illusion. Illusions sustain it, and of all the illusions, the most potent may be the assumption that the city will actually last, that it won't sink into itself, or be submerged by a flood. And so when you're there, in this place that honestly shouldn't exist, that goes against nature, you can imagine something similar for yourself—that you won't sink into the mud or get swept away by a tidal wave. Which is why it seems especially . . . dare I say appropriate . . . that when Vincent got sick—Vincent, whose name is an anagram of Venice with a *t* stuck on the end, did you pick up on that?— that it should have been there."

"It was AIDS, I assume?"

"What else would it have been?"

"And did you know that when you got together—that he had AIDS?"

"I guess that depends on how you define *know*. If you're asking if he told me outright, the answer is no, he didn't. As for whether *he* knew . . . I've thought about that a lot over the years. It's possible he knew but didn't say anything out of fear that I'd leave him, which I might have, or that he knew but couldn't bring himself to admit it to himself, much less to me, or that he knew but believed himself to be immune somehow, to have some sort of special dispensation. I mean, you must understand, at this point nothing bad had ever happened to him in his life. Nothing. All the schools he'd ever applied to had accepted him, all the prizes he'd competed for he'd won, all the reviews he'd ever gotten—he'd written two books—had been raves. Plus everyone loved him—his family, his students, his teachers, his friends, of whom he had dozens, hundreds, it seemed, men, women, couples, so many of them there wasn't a single point, I don't think, when someone wasn't visiting, staying at the Gritti, or at a pensione near the station, or with him—with us—in the apartment upstairs from Ursula's, though usually the only ones he asked to stay were the good-looking men, older than me but younger than him, with whom we'd invariably end up having three-ways. And then his former boyfriends—I don't know why this amazed me so much, but not once in his life had he ever been broken up with. In every case he was the one who'd done the breaking up. Mind you, he wasn't happy about this, he took no pleasure in it, he just saw it as something that went with the territory of being who he was. And then it all changed."

"What happened?"

"Maybe a month after we met, he had to go to Munich for a conference, and when he got back he came down with this terrible cough, and started running a fever, which he attributed to the fact that his flight back to Venice was full of children with runny noses. In other words, just a cold, which would pass. Only it didn't pass. Every morning he'd wake up saying he felt a million times better and head off to work, only to come back at lunch exhausted. Soon it got so bad he started having to cancel on his friends who'd come to Venice to visit him. I think the truth was that he was afraid of what he'd see in their eyes when they looked at him."

"Was that when you realized what was going on?"

"I'm not sure *realize* is the right word. I mean, yes, the possibility crossed my mind. How couldn't it? That was just how it was in those days—if a gay man got sick, the first thing you thought was AIDS, though you never said so. Later things changed a bit, people started to feel they could speak openly about it without suffering terrible repercussions, but in those days—bear in mind this was still fairly early, '87 or '88—in those days if you were in my position, if you were twenty-two and worried your older lover might have AIDS and was trying to keep it from you . . . well, what were you supposed to do? Where were you supposed to go? Especially in Italy? There wasn't any ACT UP then. I don't think Rock Hudson had died yet. The test, I'm pretty sure, you could get, but the results took weeks to come through, and if you tested positive, the word on the street was that the government might make your doctor give them your name and then they'd round you up and put you in a camp, which was what was happening in Cuba, or tattoo a scarlet A on your behind, which was what William F. Buckley proposed. All of which provided a really great excuse not to have the test, which at this point was basically the devil you knew versus the devil you didn't know, and given that choice—and how often I've been given it—I've always gone with the devil I don't know, only in this case I really saw him as a devil, one of the ones from Signorelli's painting of Hell, because the fact of the matter was that since we'd met, Vincent and I had had a lot of sex, most of which wasn't of the variety that the authorities of the period would have deemed *safe*, or, as they later put it, *safer*, which was really just dotting the *i* on the fact that no one really knew what was safe and what wasn't. Are these details too gory for you?"

"No. Go on."

"So things went on like that through November, and then Vincent got *really* sick—tired all the time, a hacking cough that wouldn't quit, fevers that spiked to 103 or 104. I kept trying to get him to see a doctor, but he wouldn't. He just refused. And then Pablo showed up. I forget what his reason was, some project or other—really it was just an excuse to check on me and to see Ursula, whom he still must have been having an affair with, and who must have clued him in on what was going on, because no sooner had he arrived than he went straight upstairs, took one look at Vincent, and called a doctor. She was the one who said he had to go into hospital, that if he didn't go into the hospital subito, she couldn't guarantee he'd last the night. And so Ursula called an ambulance, and of course, this being Venice, it was a boat ambulance, on which we rode along the Grand Canal, past the back gardens of the palaces, and the docks decorated with flags and red carpets. It was dusk, and the sky had a spectral quality that made the ambulance seem like one of those funeral gondolas for which Venice is famous, and the canal itself one of the rivers in Hell—the Lethe or the Styx. And then we got to the hospital itself and there was this phalanx of doctors and nurses waiting for us, and here's the thing: They were all wearing gloves and gowns and masks and paper caps. Now, let me make one thing perfectly clear—this was still fairly early in the game, there were still a lot of unknowns about how the virus was spread. Why, for all I know, Vincent might have been the first AIDS patient they'd ever had at that hospital. And yet it's one thing to act out of an excess of caution, and another to make a patient feel like a leper, which was, I'm sorry to say, what they did, with the result that as soon as Vincent saw them—and, really, they might have been Galactic Stormtroopers, the way they were dressed—he just went off the deep end. He said he wanted to go home, that there was no way he was staying, that we couldn't make him say.

"It was a terrible scene. I remember some nuns hurrying by, fiddling with their beads, and Pablo running back and forth between Vincent and the doctors, and Ursula demanding to see the hospital director, who was some sort of cousin of hers, though in the end that didn't prove necessary, because suddenly Vincent stopped yelling and sort of went limp, and they took him off to the isolation unit and put him on oxygen and an IV drip. And for the next few days, that was how it was. Just to go in and see him, you had to put on gloves and a mask and a gown, the same as the staff. And so when the doctor broke the news to him—that he had pneumonia—*that* pneumonia—he couldn't see my face or the doctor's face, though I could see his. At first I looked away, but then I looked at him square on, because frankly I wanted to see what it looked like, what someone who had just gotten the news looked like, maybe so that I'd know what to expect when it happened to me."

"What did you see?"

"Do you know those early Renaissance portraits of the Annunciation to Saint Anne? Not the Annunciation of the Virgin, but Saint Anne, her mother, when the angel comes down to tell her that the child she's carrying will be the mother of the son of God. The look on Anne's face in those paintings . . . that was what I saw. Wonder and horror together—which they never should be. Which I hope I'll never see together again.

"Now, when I remember all this, I don't feel guilty anymore. Or afraid. Just sad, because for years, my excuse—the excuse I gave myself—was that I was young, too young to be expected to cope with what was happening. And I *was* young. I mean, at that point in my life, the only death I'd known was my mother's, and when my mother was dying, I was still a child, and people treated me as a child. No one expected anything of me. Not even my mother expected anything of me. Instead everyone worried about me—in some ways more than they did about her. And so when I got the news about Vincent, on the one hand I just accepted that, having made whatever avowals I'd made, it was now my duty to take care of him until he died. And yet on the other hand, I was desperate to escape, and that was also because—I'm sorry to keep repeating this—I was twenty-two. And if, as I say that, you're thinking that by putting all this emphasis on my youth, I'm trying to let myself off the hook a little, that I'm pleading extenuating circumstances, you're right. I am."

"What happened next?"

"Well, the crisis passed. He got better—well enough to move back into the apartment. Everyone was telling him he should go home, go back to the States, but he wouldn't. He had a year in Venice, and by God he was going to stay in Venice. Only suddenly he required all this nursing—not just pills, but injections and inhalations, some of which he had to take every six hours, round the clock. And I just . . . screwed up royally on that front, not only because I had no experience of it, but because Vincent was so desperately needy. Our roles had reversed. Now he was the child, and I was the adult, and I was supposed to be there all the time, and never leave him alone. He couldn't bear to be alone—and I couldn't bear to be with him. I was always looking for excuses to get away, if just for an hour or two—and then when I got back, almost inevitably he'd say something bitter and recriminatory. We'd fight.

I hit him once. In the face. I'm ashamed to admit it, but it's true. Another time I left the apartment without telling him, left for an entire day, which I spent wandering the city, eventually ending up at the train station, where I picked up a Belgian backpacker and went with him to his hotel.

"That was the day he jumped off the bridge. That's the part that Clydie got wrong, by the way. He didn't die from jumping off the bridge. Of course, it makes a better story to say that he did—you assume it was one of the really big bridges, the ones that cross the Grand Canal—when in fact it was just this tiny little bridge near Ursula's place—I don't think it even has a name—very low, and crossing a very narrow, very shallow canal, with maybe three feet of water and then a bed of silt and mud. Luckily, some gondoliers were having their lunch nearby. They were the ones who hauled him out and held him until the carabinieri came and arrested him. They were waiting for me at Ursula's when I got back. I remember she went with me to the *questura*, where they questioned me for two hours, maybe three. They were very kind. They didn't hold me in the least responsible. They only held him responsible, because in Catholic countries, attempting suicide really is looked on as a crime.

"Anyway, as soon as the interview was over, I went back to Vincent's apartment, packed my things, and—this is the part I'm most ashamed of—went off to find the Belgian backpacker. And I did find him, and spent the night with him, and then the next morning I took the train to Milan, where I called my father, who was frantic, because Pablo had called him and Ursula had called him and no one could find me. It was my father who bought me the ticket to New York. I flew back the next day.

"The rest of the story I only know by hearsay. It seems that by this point word had gotten out to all of Vincent's friends, who took collective action, staying with him in shifts and making sure he ate healthy foods and took his meds until he was well enough to go back to the States. As I said, some of them were really rich, and they must really have loved him, because they tried everything there was to try, taking him to Mexico to get a drug the FDA was dragging its heels on, and to France to get a drug the FDA had refused to approve, and finally to Switzerland for this insane treatment where they pumped all the blood out of your body, fed it through a machine that supposedly cleansed it, and then pumped it back in, but it didn't do any good. None of it did any good. The day after his thirty-seventh birthday, he died.

"So that was that. Only here's the thing. At the time, I thought of him as being so much older than me—whereas now I realize how young he was. I mean, thirty-six—do you realize that in six years that will be as many years as I've been alive since he died? Do you realize how young that is?"

"Was there a funeral?"

"There was. I didn't go. Or to the memorial. No one wrote to me, none of his friends tried to contact me. Maybe they didn't realize the role I'd played, or maybe I exaggerated my own importance. I don't know. All I know is since then, there have been no more love stories for Jake. Don't think I haven't tried. I have. I've just never been able to make it work, even with one fellow who, if things had been different, if I hadn't felt so much guilt and terror, maybe I could have."

"Did it get easier after you got tested?"

"Oh, but I never did get tested. To this day, I've never been tested. All this time it's been the devil I don't know, and you know what? I've gotten to know him anyway, because basically for the last thirty years we've been in a holding pattern together. And yet, is that really the worst thing in the world, to live in a holding pattern? I mean, sure, it's frustrating, but you get used to it after a while. The waiting, it becomes the thing you're waiting for . . . and then one night, entirely out of the blue, an old woman remembers your name.

"I'm sorry. I've talked too much."

"No, you haven't," Bruce said, and almost added: "Look, I'm the one person here who can understand this. Because I'm doing the wrong thing myself, even though I know it's wrong. Because I'm in the throes of an elation that I have the audacity to think will last, even though I know it won't. Because I came to care so much about a woman to whom I owe nothing that I gave her two hundred thousand dollars, and now that I've given it to her, we can barely say a word to each other. Because I've become a secret-keeper. Because I've become a liar."

In the distance, a window opened. "Bruce?" Eva called. "Bruce, are you all right?"

"I'm fine," Bruce answered. "We're fine." Then, to Jake: "It's cold. We should go back in. Oh, and if it puts your mind at ease, you don't have to tell Eva. I'll tell Eva."

"Tell her what?"

"That you've made up your mind about the apartment. That your answer is no."

"But it's not no. It's yes. If she'll have me."

"Oh, she'll have you. That much I can guarantee. She'll have you."

25

Again Bruce was sitting on a bed with a silent woman, methodically outlining a plan of rescue. That the bed was in a hotel on West Forty-third Street, and the silent woman not Kathy, but Sandra, made surprisingly little difference to the import of his monologue.

Sandra listened patiently. She did not fidget or crack her knuckles or tear apart a Kleenex. Her grandmother had raised her to respect her elders and to keep her back straight in company.

When Bruce was done speaking, he took a long gulp from the tiny bottle of Evian he'd gotten out of the minibar fridge. He rubbed his eyes. He wiped his nose.

"Well, what do you think?" he said.

"What do I think?" she said. "That you're a good man. Too good for your own good."

"Of course, when I came up with the idea, I had no clue that Eva was going to find this apartment. In fact, it was the next day that she told me."

"If you'd known, would you have done anything differently?"

"I've thought about that. I don't think I would have. I think I still would have given Kathy the money. What I wouldn't have done was let the business with the apartment get so out of hand."

"Do you want to stop it?"

"In some ways, yes. I mean, let's say you were one of my clients and you were asking me, from an investment standpoint, if I thought buying an apartment in Venice was a good idea. What would I tell you? I'd tell you that from an investment standpoint, you'd do better to buy real estate in Florida or Hawaii or New Mexico—anywhere in the States, really— since buying abroad invariably entangles you in a whole separate tax system, legal system, economic system. I'd tell you that, then I'd tell you to do what you want."

"But I'm not one of your clients. Neither is Eva."

"My policy is that what people want is none of my business. My business is what they can afford."

"Even your wife? Even yourself?"

"Oh, what *I* want . . . That's a question I've only just found an answer for." He smiled as he said this. "As for Eva, I can only take her at her word. I suppose what rankles me is that there are so many people at so much more risk than she is. And yet the only person she's out to save is herself."

"Whereas you're out to save Kathy."

"At least that's altruistic. It's not just self-preservation."

"And yet self-preservation has one virtue, which is that it doesn't pretend to be anything other than what it is. With altruism, there's almost always a hidden motive. The benefactor wants to be lionized or, worse, have the person he's helping at his mercy. Otherwise why would people who give money to universities want buildings named after them?"

"Neither is the case here. No one knows what I'm doing for Kathy except Kathy. And her kids. And you."

"So what happens next? What happens, for instance, when Eva finds out about the check?"

"She won't. I've made sure of that. I wrote it from an account she doesn't know about."

"And yet she knows something's up."

"Something, but not what."

"You could just tell her."

"Why should I? What business is it of hers?"

"Married people's lives are always each other's business. Even after they get divorced, that's true. In addition to which—and please forgive me if I'm stepping out of bounds here—there's the issue of the money. Of course, I don't know exactly how much this apartment is likely to cost you, but I can make a rough estimate. I mean, am I right that we're talking about a pretty substantial outlay of cash here?"

"Yes."

"To which you have to add the money you gave Kathy."

"Yes."

"Which, if Eva learned about it, she'd probably find . . . concerning, right? I mean, to the point that it might make her think twice about the expense—"

"I shudder to imagine what she'd think."

"She's not stupid, Bruce. She knows what you can afford and what you can't."

"*Afford*—it's amazing how that word keeps coming up. And yet what does it mean, really? I mean, when I think of my clients, if they were to decide to just stuff all their money into a safe behind a painting, or have some huge cellar full of gold coins into which they could dive headlong like that duck, Uncle what's-his-name—"

"—they'd have broken bones."

"—they'd only get poorer."

"My own ideas of finance, I'll admit, are crude. Basically they're derived from nineteenth-century novels. You know, 'Miss Bleek had five hundred a year.' Things seem less clear-cut now."

"I doubt they were so clear-cut then."

"You still haven't answered my question, you know. You still haven't told me if you can—this time I won't say *afford*—if you can manage it. Not to put too fine a point on it, I have no idea how rich you are. I mean, I know you're rich. I just don't know how rich."

"Rich enough that I can't really say how rich I am."

"But how can that be? Everyone has a net worth."

"Once you pass a certain point, your net worth ceases to correspond to anything real. It's less a matter of what you have than what you can get hold of."

"In that case, I want you to consider something. I want you to consider the possibility that buying the apartment might actually be a good idea. Not as an investment, and not for Eva, but for you." Sandra was silent for a moment, letting the remark sink in. "I didn't think about saying that before I said it. If I had, I'd never have had the courage to get it out, because of course I know it's way too soon to be talking about these things. I know there's a gun I'm jumping, but sometimes you have to. You have to. Even if there's every chance the thing— affair, relationship, whatever you want to call it—will peter out. And if it does, so much the better, because it will make life that much easier for all of us. But what if it doesn't? I guess what it comes down to is that if Eva buys the apartment, she'll start spending a lot of time in Venice, and there'll be that much more time that you and I will have here. By ourselves. It's a chance to try it out, to give ourselves a trial run, and if we can have that chance and we don't take it . . . well, I'll regret that. Maybe you won't, but I will. Because there have been other times—I'm full of clichés today—when the iron was hot and I didn't strike. And I regret them."

"Is the iron hot now?"

"For me, yes. Is it for you?"

"Isn't the answer obvious?"

"Last Saturday, when we were at Grady's, you talked about the rush. I like the rush, too. I like a little danger. And yet, given the choice, I'd rather have time with you, alone, in a bed big enough that we can both sleep in it without doing permanent injury to our spines, than a few minutes in a narrow bed waiting for Grady to get home, or in a hotel room where God knows who else has been in the bed. And we won't get that, Bruce, we won't get what we want—at least what I want— unless Eva gets what she wants, which is the apartment. And if she doesn't get it . . . I don't know Eva that well, I won't pretend I do, but I know this about her—that her longings are as fragile as they are ardent. When the iron cools, so does she. I mean that if this chance falls through, she might not look for another. And we'll have lost ours."

For a few seconds Bruce was silent. Then he said, "This is all so new to me. Not just you, or this, but this whole way of thinking."

"Then let me say one more thing. You've told me about your money situation. Well, let me tell you about mine. When my grandmother died, she left me five million dollars, more or less. That's *my* money. It's not community property. Rico can't touch it."

"Good. It means you don't have to worry."

"Oh, but that's not why I'm telling you. The reason I'm telling you is . . . well, I have wealth, and you're—what is it you are? A wealth management consultant?"

"Wealth management adviser."

"Whatever. Here's what I'm proposing—that I give you my wealth and you manage it."

"That wouldn't be ethical. If you want an adviser, I can recommend someone else."

"Believe me, I understand why you might think it's a conflict of interest. And it would be if you'd suggested it, but you didn't. I'm the one who's suggesting it. And the reason I'm suggesting it is that if you have access to my money, and at some point find yourself short of cash, you could use it—"

"Sandra—"

"Of course, we'd have a signed agreement. It would be understood that any money of mine that you used, you'd have to get my permission first, and that you'd reimburse me. With interest if you like." She put her hands on his neck. "I'm not trying to buy you. I just want to do for you what you're doing for Kathy. Make things easier. Give you a backup plan, in case the economy goes south, or haywire, or Trump changes the tax code, or the plumbing in the new apartment turns out to be a thousand years old."

"But why?"

"So that we can have our chance."

"I don't know what to say. I don't even know what to think. All my life, I was sure my course was mapped out for me."

"It was. But now you've crossed a boundary."

"But how did it happen? That's what I can't fathom."

"You did it yourself," Sandra said. "You did it the day you decided to help Kathy."

26

"Time present and time past," Aaron said.

It was five in the afternoon, the first Saturday of spring, and they were sitting—Aaron, Rachel, Jake, Sandra, and Matt Pierce—on Eva's back porch, watching Bruce trying to get the fountain on the patio to start. Eva herself was gone, as was Min. That afternoon they had left for Venice, where in a few days Bruce would meet them for the closing.

Aaron had on the pussy hat. "Time present and time past," he repeated, pulling the flaps down toward his ears. "Why did Eliot go out of fashion, do you think? Was it because he was an anti-Semite?"

"His fall from fashion preceded his fall from grace," Matt said. "Not the usual sequence."

"T. S. Eliot—he was the one who wrote *Cats*, right?" Sandra said.

"Don't overplay the ignorance card," Aaron said. "It's only charming up to a point."

"And in Eliot's case I'm not sure it's even accurate to say that he's fallen from grace," Matt said.

"Forgive me if this is a gauche question, but what are you doing here?" Aaron said. "I thought you'd been banished."

"I had, but then Bruce called and asked me to come up for the weekend. It's because Eva's away, I suppose."

"Do you know, this is the first time I've been here without Eva," Rachel said. "It makes me feel self-conscious. As if I'm breaking some rule."

"I wonder if she knows we're here," Jake said.

"Why should it matter?" Sandra said. "Why should she mind if Bruce has you up for the weekend?"

"She wouldn't mind Bruce having us up," Matt said, "she'd mind his not telling her. Except for me—she'd mind his having me up."

"I'll be the first to admit it, I miss her," Jake said. "There's an emptiness without her. For better or worse, she's the sun around which we orbit."

"In that regard, I don't see that her absence makes any difference," Sandra said, "since you're orbiting around her regardless."

"And you?"

"Me? I don't count. I'm the outsider."

"Funny, it doesn't feel like that," Rachel said. "It feels like you've been part of this house as long as we have."

"Look at Bruce," Aaron said, standing and walking to the windows. "Look at that concentration. It isn't patience. It's nothing like patience. And yet until he gets that fountain working, he won't quit. He'll stay there all night if he has to."

"Instead of disquisiting on his determination, have you thought about offering to help him?" Rachel said.

"I don't think he wants any help," Sandra said. "I think he wants to do it himself."

"Time present and time past are both perhaps present in time future . . . That *perhaps* in the second line—do you think it's a failure of nerve, Sandra?"

"Perhaps."

"Perhaps *perhaps* is always a failure of nerve," Matt said.

"Is that a joke?" Sandra said.

"You know, I don't actually think it was the anti-Semitism that cost Eliot his place in the stratosphere," Rachel said. "I think it was Harold Bloom, in the eighties, when he got the Yale English department to change the title of the prerequisite course for the major from 'Major English Poets, Chaucer to Eliot' to 'Major English Poets, Chaucer to Stevens.'"

"Rachel will take any opportunity to remind us that she went to Yale," Aaron said.

"You know perfectly well that's not why I brought it up," Rachel said. "I brought it up to make a point, which is that the turn against Eliot happened a good two decades before critics started calling him on the anti-Semitic stuff."

"For years I've been ashamed to admit how much I love Eliot," Aaron said. "It was only after I lost my job that I decided to come out of the closet. Because really, you shouldn't be ashamed of the things you love, the things that made you who you are, and that was what *The Waste Land* was for me. When I was in high school I must have read it a thousand times. Ten thousand times."

"I never said it wasn't a great poem."

"Oh, but you believe it isn't. It's all right. Yale indoctrinated you, as it probably would have me—if I'd gotten in."

"Must you keep bringing that up? More than a quarter of a century on and he's still bitter that he didn't get into Yale."

"Not half as bitter as I am that you did."

"If the strength of our feelings was in proportion to the events that provoke them, the world would not be the place it is," Jake said.

"Look, now the dogs are getting in on the act," Sandra said. "They're trying to distract him, to get him to play with them. Good luck. They never will."

"I've never known dogs to eat so fast as these do," Matt said. "This afternoon I gave Isabel a piece of cheese and she wolfed it down. I doubt she even tasted it."

"Sometimes having a thing matters most," Sandra said.

"And then she wanted another piece, and another."

"That's why it's better not to want things," Jake said.

"But if we never wanted things, we'd never go anywhere," Rachel said.

"Exactly," Jake said.

"Humankind cannot stand very much reality," Aaron said.

At last the fountain started. At its first tentative spurt, the observers on the porch applauded. The dogs barked. Bruce bowed.

"Congratulations," Jake said, coming outside with Sandra.

"Fall seven times and stand up eight," Bruce said, wiping water from his face.

He went inside to dry off and the dogs followed him, leaving Jake and Sandra to gaze at the fountain in the dusk light. "Spring always gets a jump on me," Jake said. "Look, the daffodils are done. The crocuses are nearly done. The tulips will be done before I'm back."

"So you've decided to go?"

"Yes, I'm going. It's funny, from the beginning Min treated it as a fait accompli, as if it was really just a matter of admitting that I had no choice. Well, she was right."

"When do you leave?"

"After Eva gets back. I want a week or so alone there, to look the place over. Then she'll fly over and join me."

"Will Bruce come with her?"

"I doubt it. Min might. You know that *Enfilade* is shutting down, right?"

"Really? Why?"

"The same reason as with so many other magazines. Not enough readers, not enough ads."

"Poor Indira. To have left one magazine for another and then to have it shuttered—"

"Don't worry about Indira, she's already got herself another job. It's a new magazine called *mood board*, all lowercase. A quarterly, very chic, bound like a book. Jimmy Mortimer, Clydie's son, is putting up the money."

"In other words, Clydie is."

"So now the question is whether Indira will take Min with her. And if she doesn't, what Min will do next."

"She'll have to find another job."

"Or maybe she's finally ready to wind up her magazine career and try something else."

"Such as?"

"Well, Eva's going to need someone to keep her company in Venice, right? I mean, when Bruce isn't there. And that'll be a full-time job, for which Min is eminently qualified."

A breeze came up. "So lovely, these first warm days," Sandra said, staring gravely at the fountain. "All we have to do now is wait for the blizzard."

"What blizzard?"

"The one that always shows up just as spring is taking hold, killing everything that's just come into bloom."

"But you don't know there'll be a blizzard."

"It's what I fear, which for me is as good as knowing."

"Were we always like this, do you think? Governed by fear?"

"Once bitten, forever shy. I suppose the way I see it is that if I accept the blizzard as inevitable, at least I won't be blind-sided by it."

"And then if it doesn't come, its not coming will seem like a kindness."

"Well, we have to find good news somewhere, don't we? Even if it's just in the worst-case scenario not happening."

"And what are you two talking about?" Rachel asked, emerging so suddenly it was as if a piece of shadow had broken off from the dusk.

"The seasons," Jake said.

"I remember reading an interview with Teresa Stratas," Sandra said. "She was talking about sitting with Lotte Lenya when she was dying. And she asked her which was her favorite season, and Lenya said, 'I love them all.'"

"I wish I could be so generous, but I have very strong feelings about the seasons," Rachel said. "My favorite, unques-tionably, is spring, followed by fall, followed by winter, followed by summer."

"I'd put winter second," Jake said.

"I'd put it first," Sandra said. "It's so nice to be in bed with someone else on a cold night."

"Do you think it's strange for Bruce, sleeping alone?" Rachel said. "I mean, has he ever actually spent a night in this bed without Eva?"

"I have, actually," Bruce said, coming out of the house in dry clothes. "As a matter of fact, I was up here the weekend after the inauguration, just before Eva and Min came back from Venice. Sandra was, too. She'd texted me to say Grady was out of town and she was alone, so I drove up on the spur of the moment."

"We kept each other company," Sandra said.

"Oh, I see," Rachel said.

"I wonder what Matt's planning for dinner," Jake said.

"He's not. Aaron's doing the cooking. He's insisted."

"Oh, God, not another whole fish," Bruce said.

"What's wrong with his whole fish?"

"Nothing, it's just that this time I'd prefer not to have the head."

"Whoever I decide is the guest of honor will get the head," said Aaron, who had stepped outside with Matt to join the others. "Maybe it'll be you, Matt."

"I wouldn't mind. They say the best meat on a fish is the cheeks."

"Why are you wearing that hat, Aaron?" Bruce asked.

"Oh, I don't know. I suppose on the off chance that some paparazzo shows up, snaps my picture, and tweets it. And you know what? Even if it goes viral, even if I get death threats, I won't care, because hey, as of last week I'm officially unemployable. I can do whatever I want."

"You're not unemployable," Rachel said. "It was one job interview."

"I am persona non grata."

"But I thought you were glad to be out of the industry," Sandra said.

"It's one thing to refuse an invitation," Aaron said, "another to be told you'll never get one."

"Aaron, please, it was one interview," Rachel said. "There'll be others."

"And in every one of them, Katya's name will come up."

Tears welled in Rachel's eyes. "Oh, that woman," she said. "I could kill her, I really could. I mean, OK, you may have lost your temper—and yet to claim you got physical—he'd never do that to a woman. Ask Sandra. Ask any woman who's ever worked with him."

"It's true he's never grabbed me by the arm so hard it bruised," Sandra said.

"Let's face it, she says I grabbed her, so I grabbed her." With surprising pique, Aaron yanked off the pussy hat and threw it on the ground. "Fate has simply decreed that from here on my life will take a different path than I'd anticipated. That, rather than serve literature by publishing books, I shall serve as a different sort of midwife, working closely with writers like Sandra, in the faint hope that when she wins the National Book Award, in the audience a few mutterings may sound to the effect that if her novel is as good as it is, a certain Aaron Weisenstein deserves some credit for the minuscule role he played in its creation. Not that I want you to include my name in the acknowledgments, Sandra. Quite the opposite, I want you to promise me *not* to include my name in the acknowledgments. Or, better yet, not to have any acknowledgments at all. I mean, what's the point? No one needs to know what an invaluable contribution your cat made—"

"I don't have a cat."

"Or that if it hadn't been for the encouragement of Mrs. Colleen Oscopy, your fourth-grade teacher, you could never have reached the pinnacle you occupy today."

"Stop it, just stop it," Rachel said. "Six months from now, when Aaron's working again—"

"Or when he's been offered the job of his dreams and turned it down—"

"—when Aaron's working again, we won't even remember we had this conversation."

Leaving the pussy hat on the ground, Aaron and Matt went back inside. From the kitchen door the dogs bounded out again, ran past the group gathered on the patio, and began barking at the fountain's spray.

Bruce laughed. "Come on, let's rile them up," he said, taking Sandra's hand and leading her in a gallop toward where the dogs were gathered.

Rachel stole closer to Jake. "What do you think that means?" she asked. "His coming up that weekend to keep her company—and now this? Look at them."

Jake looked. No sooner had Sandra reached the fountain than Bruce put his arms around her waist. He was so much taller than her that when they kissed, he had to bend his back and she had to stretch her neck.

For a few seconds Jake and Rachel were struck dumb, not just by the unexpectedness of the moment but by its beauty. For as Bruce and Sandra kissed, it was clear that the couple—and there was no doubt in Jake's mind that this was what they were—were either too lost in each other to realize they could be seen, or realized they could be seen and were indifferent to their audience: unspectacular, neither ashamed nor proud, neither trying to be discreet nor showing off. The kiss was simply what it was—a kiss—made lovelier by the setting sun, and the capering dogs, and the fountain casting its jets into the sky. And the onlookers regarded it as such, and did not judge.

After a minute or so it ended. Holding hands, laughing a little, the pair wandered off into the gloaming. The dogs followed them for a few feet, then turned back toward the house.

It was their dinnertime.